D0422068

# Deliverance

**A vivid description of the Divine Purpose particularly outlining God's progressive steps against wickedness and showing the final overthrow of the Devil and all of his wicked institutions; the deliverance of the people; and the establishment of the righteous government on earth.**

BY J. F. RUTHERFORD

Author of

*The Harp of God Creation Life*
*Reconciliation Government*
*Prophecy Light*
*and other*
*books*

3,380,500 Edition

*Publishers*

INTERNATIONAL BIBLE STUDENTS ASSOCIATION
WATCH TOWER BIBLE & TRACT SOCIETY
Brooklyn, New York, U. S. A.
*Also:* London, Toronto, Strathfield, Cape Town, Berne, Magdeburg.
*MADE IN U. S. A.*

AS A TESTIMONY TO THE NAME OF

**THE ALMIGHTY GOD**

THE CREATOR OF THE HEAVENS AND THE EARTH

**THIS BOOK IS DEDICATED**

*"Ye are my witnesses . . . that I am God."—Isa. 43: 12.*

# PREFACE

THIS book contains a message of good news. It enables the people to have before them the positive evidence from which they may determine who is their worst enemy and who is their greatest friend. It shows why the people have been subjected to so much affliction and suffering and how they may and will be delivered from all their foes.

The names of the three great persons herein made conspicuous are: Jehovah the Father, and the Logos and Lucifer his sons. The son Lucifer organizes and carries on a wicked rebellion which Jehovah does not hinder until his own due time, when he intervenes and puts down the rebellion and the rebels. By and through his loyal Son, the Logos, he completely delivers the people and then showers upon them his gracious blessings.

This book contains a statement of the outworking of the divine purpose. It establishes faith, creates hope, and makes glad the soul. In due time all the peoples of earth must have an opportunity to know the message this book contains. The time is now due when they must begin to hear it. Let every one who reads tell it to his neighbor. The day of deliverance is at hand!

THE PUBLISHERS

# INTRODUCTION

DELIVERANCE! It is a welcome word. Its need for man has become crucial. Peoples of earth find themselves weary and burdened of soul. The disabilities of body and mind are galling. Every man has his burden, and he would gladly welcome deliverance from that burden. With some the burden is financial, with others mental, with others physical; and nearly all suffer from discontent and disappointment. The vanity of the schemes of men is apparent to all. Many such have been tried, and all have proven failures. Is there no way out of the difficulties and burdens that hang over the peoples of earth? There is!

He who created the heavens and the earth, made also the man from whom sprang all the race. The name of that great Creator is Jehovah God. He knew the end from the beginning and made ample provision for every contingency. Concerning him this great truth long ago was written: "Known unto God are all his works, from the beginning of the world." (Acts 15:18) That he willed man should some day know about his purposes is also certain. It is written in his Word that in due time every man shall know the Lord, and that the knowledge of him and his way for man's deliverance shall fill the whole earth as the waters fill the deep. The physical facts all about, which are now daily observed by men, prove that the time is at hand when the obtaining of that great knowledge is beginning. Millions of people are beginning to see the way of deliverance and are taking courage. You should walk with that great army, learn and grow happy. This book shows you how to learn.

No; this is not another scheme of man. This book is devoted exclusively to pointing out God's way of deliverance. It entirely excludes all human creeds and all theories of church systems. Its message is taken from the Word of God, now due to be understood. You will be able to prove to yourself whether or not the divine arrangement herein disclosed is true. It is worth your time and effort.

Deliverance from the burdens of sickness, suffering, sorrow, disappointment and death is man's great desire. The plain way that leads to endless life in happiness he would gladly welcome. It is the will of God, the great Creator, that all men should come to a knowledge of the truth; and in due time that opportunity shall be granted to all. The way is now opening. "And this is life eternal, that they might know thee the only true God, and Jesus Christ, whom thou hast sent." (John 17:3) It is therefore fitting and essential for you to read that which explains the great divine way that leads to endless life and happiness. This book was written for that very purpose.

Good news brings peace of mind and gladness of heart. To know that humankind will be relieved of all burdens is not only good news, but is thrilling. The good news of man's deliverance by Jehovah will bring light into your life and fill your very being with peace and joy.

# Deliverance

## Chapter I

### *Creator and Creatures*

WHY is there so much distress and perplexity in the world? Why are the nations so desperately preparing for war? Why is there so much selfishness among men? Why do men manipulate the prices of the food and raiment of the people and profiteer therein? Why do the politicians and the clergy deceive and mislead the people and lend their support to the selfish interests? Why are the people so much oppressed? Why are the people afflicted with famine, pestilence and disease? Why are they the victims of sickness, sorrow, suffering and death? Why is man in bondage to so many evil things? Who is responsible for all this unhappy condition? May we hope that the people will ever be delivered from this sad state and enter into the joys of peace, prosperity, health, life, liberty and happiness? Why am I? Whence did I come, and what can I do to help my fellow man?

These and many like questions crowded into the mind of the young man who desired to better the conditions for himself and his fellow man. He set out to find, if possible, the satisfactory answers to his questions. He visited and made inquiry of philosophers, doctors, clergymen, savants and other professedly wise men. The answer of each one, based upon human opinion, was entirely unsatisfactory.

What value is to be found in the unsupported opinion of imperfect men? Are not all of these men a part of the great multitude that travel the same unpleasant road? There must be some evidence that will speak with authority upon which a reasonable mind can rely. Thus soliloquized the youthful inquirer. Then he came upon a man of mature years. His head was clothed with silver locks. He had a kind face, and pleasant speech. When the questions were propounded to him this man did not venture his own opinion. In substance he replied:

"You are right in concluding that the unsupported opinion of man is of little or no value. There is one Eternal God, from whom proceeds everything that is good. There is a great wicked one who is the enemy of God and the oppressor of man. That enemy has long had the power of death. The righteous God has not interfered with this wicked one in carrying on his wicked work, but has used what has transpired for the testing of his creatures. Wickedness will not always prevail. In due time the wicked one and his wicked influence will be destroyed. Deliverance of the people is certain.

"These great truths of which I speak are set forth in that wonderful book we call the Bible. It does not contain the opinions of imperfect men; it is the Word of Almighty God, the Maker of heaven and earth. It was written by holy men of old as their minds were directed by the power of the great Jehovah. I mean that it was written under divine inspiration. It discloses the origin of man, why man has suffered, and how and when mankind will be delivered from all enemies and from all oppression. These great truths are so stated in the Bible that for many centuries they have been a secret and could not be understood until God's due time. It is now due time to understand them.

"We are now well on in the twentieth century. There is a great increase in knowledge and much running to and fro in this day; and God said that these things would mark the time when his Book, containing his secret, could be understood. Of course the all-wise One would have a purpose from the beginning which must work out according to his own will. The time is come for man to understand how this divine purpose has been operating. I bid you to carefully examine God's great treasure-house of knowledge. Therein you will find the full and satisfactory answer to all the questions you have propounded."

Thus advised the searcher for truth sought and obtained the book, the Bible, and read therein: "The [reverence] of the Lord is the beginning of wisdom" (Ps. 111:10); and, 'The secret of the Lord is with them that reverence him; and to them will he show his purpose.' (Ps. 25:14) With reverential mind and honest purpose the answers to the foregoing questions were sought in that great treasure-house of knowledge, and what follows in these pages is what was therein disclosed.

### THE CREATOR

Jehovah is the name of the great Creator. That name signifies his purpose concerning his creatures. "Thou, whose name alone is Jehovah." (Ps. 83:18) "Immortal" means not subject to death but possessing life inherent. It is written concerning the great

Jehovah God: "Who only hath immortality, dwelling in the light which no man can approach unto; whom no man hath seen, nor can see: to whom be honour and power everlasting." (1 Tim. 6:16) He first revealed his name to Moses. (Ex. 6:2) He is the great Creator of heaven and earth. (Isa. 40:28; 42:5) Every good and perfect gift proceedeth from him. (Jas. 1:17) He is the rewarder of them that diligently seek him. (Heb. 11:6) He is from everlasting to everlasting. (Ps. 90:2; 93:2) "In the Lord Jehovah is everlasting strength."—Isa. 26:4.

### THE LOGOS

Of necessity there must have been a time when Jehovah God was alone. That time was before the beginning of the creation. His Word discloses the beginning of creation. The mind of John was moved upon by the invisible power of God, and under inspiration he wrote: 'Originally was the Logos, and the Logos was with God; and the Logos was a god. The same was originally with God. All things through him came into existence; in him was life, and the life was the light of men.'—John 1:1-4.

The term Logos is one of the titles applied to the first or beginning of God's creation. (Rev. 3:14) Concerning him it is written: "Who is the image of the invisible God, the firstborn of every creature. For by him were all things created, that are in heaven, and that are in earth, visible and invisible, whether they be thrones, or dominions, or principalities, or powers; all things were created by him, and for him: and he is before all things, and by him all things consist."—Col. 1:15-17.

By these scriptures we are advised that the Logos was the only direct creation of Jehovah God, and that thereafter the Logos was Jehovah's active agent in the creation of everything that came into existence.

Solomon makes record concerning the Logos and represents him speaking of himself in these words: "The Lord possessed me in the beginning of his way, before his works of old. I was set up from everlasting, from the beginning, or ever the earth was. When there were no depths, I was brought forth; when there were no fountains abounding with water. Before the mountains were settled, before the hills was I brought forth: while as yet he had not made the earth, nor the fields, nor the highest part of the dust of the world. When he prepared the heavens, I was there: when he set a compass upon the face of the depth; when he established the clouds above; when he strengthened the fountains of the deep; when he gave to the sea his decree, that the waters should not pass his commandment; when he appointed the foundations of the earth: then I was by him, as one brought up with him, and I was daily his delight, rejoicing always before him."—Prov. 8:22-30.

It seems to be clearly settled by the Scriptures that the Logos (which means one who speaks for another) was the honored messenger of Jehovah God from time to time. He was sent on missions as the special ambassador of Jehovah. (Ex. 3:2, 15; Gen. 18:1; Ex. 23:20; Josh. 5:14) Being the beginning of God's creation and his special messenger, as his name implies, the Logos would of necessity occupy a confidential relationship to Jehovah. It would therefore be reasonable that Jehovah would speak with him and consult with him about creation.

The Scriptures do not indicate the order of the creation of those angels that belong to the invisible realm of God; but it is disclosed that such include cherubim, seraphim, angels and others, all of whom are designated "sons of God".

Cherubim are spirit creatures who evidently occupy a position of importance in the execution of the purposes of God.—Gen. 3:24; Ezek. 10:14-16.

Seraphim, the Scriptures indicate, also are heavenly creatures serving in positions of importance relative to the execution of the divine purpose.–Isa. 6:2-6.

Angels are messengers or ambassadors who are entrusted with the transmission of messages and execution of orders from the courts of heaven.—Gen. 19:1,15; 28:12; Ps. 91:11.

All the creatures of God, who therefore receive their life from him, are properly designated his sons. In the course of events concerning his realm these sons, at stated times, present themselves before Jehovah.—Job 1:6; 2:1.

### LUCIFER

Amongst the mighty creatures of Jehovah God is the one first called Lucifer. His name means light-bearer or "morning star". God's prophet speaks of him as the "son of the morning". It would be difficult to find words more descriptive of beauty. He belonged to the heavenly realm and was therefore in the holy kingdom of God, and the description of him shows that he was shining forth amongst the others of that glorious place. This description indicates that he was more showy than the other creatures of heaven. Of him it is written that "every precious stone was thy covering, the sardius, topaz, and the diamond, the beryl, the onyx, and the jasper, the sapphire, the emerald, and the carbuncle, and gold: the workmanship of thy tabrets and of thy pipes was prepared in thee in the day that thou wast created. Thou art the anointed cherub that covereth; and I have set thee so; thou wast upon the holy mountain of God; thou hast walked up and down in the midst of the stones of fire. Thou wast perfect in thy ways from the day that thou wast created, till iniquity was found in thee".—Ezek. 28:13-15.

The Logos, the active agent of Jehovah God in the creation of all things, of course, created Lucifer. These two, Lucifer and the Logos, are designated in the Scriptures as "the morning stars". The Logos was always the delight of the great Eternal One because of his faithfulness. Since the Scriptures declare that all the creation of God is perfect (Deut. 32:4), the presumption must be indulged that all these creatures in heaven were beautiful and glorious, dwelling together in peace and in harmony, and all giving glory and praise to Jehovah God.

In the course of time it pleased the Almighty Eternal One to prepare a place for the habitation of man, whom he then purposed to create. The record is: "In the beginning God created the heaven and the earth," and he "made the cloud the garment thereof, and thick darkness a swaddlingband for it". In heaven these creatures no doubt were informed that the planet earth was being prepared as a place for the habitation of the creature man whom God would create in his own image, and this knowledge must have greatly delighted God's heavenly creatures. It is recorded that when God laid the foundation of the earth for man's habitation "the morning stars sang together, and all the sons of God shouted for joy". —Job 38:4-9.

The Scriptures clearly teach that there were two mighty creatures designated "morning stars", to wit, The Logos and Lucifer. There must have been a great convocation of the glorious creatures of heaven at the beginning of the creation of earth, and it was at this convocation that the creatures were advised by the Creator of his purpose to prepare a habitation for man and to create man; and there these two mighty ones, "the morning stars," sang together a song of praise to the Eternal One, and every one of the sons of God was so thrilled by the song that they shouted together for joy. So far as men know there is no other planet that is inhabited. The creation of the earth for man would be of most profound interest to the creatures of the heavenly realm.

### CREATION OF MAN

The earth was created; and upon it were placed the plants and the herbs, the beast and the fowl, the fruits and the flowers. But there was no man to till the ground nor to enjoy the produce thereof. God must have spoken to some one of his purpose to create man, and it is reasonable that the Logos would have been the one to whom he spoke. It is recorded: "And God said, Let us make man in our image, after our likeness; and let them have dominion over the fish of the sea, and over the fowl of the air, and over the cattle, and over all the earth, and over every creeping thing that creepeth upon the earth. So God created man in his own image, in the image of God created he him; male and female created he them. And God blessed them, and God said unto them, Be fruitful, and multiply, and replenish the earth, and subdue it; and have dominion over the fish of the sea, and over the fowl of the air, and over every living thing that moveth upon the earth.''—Gen. 1:26-28.

It seems quite clear that the ''image'' and ''likeness'' here do not mean form or organism. The four divine primary attributes possessed by Jehovah forever are wisdom, justice, love and power. The perfect man, the intelligent creature, must have been endowed with these attributes; and as God has dominion over the universe, so man was given dominion over the creatures of the earth and was clothed with power to produce his species, fill the earth and subdue the planet.

God did not create man and then give him an immortal soul, as many have been induced to believe. The words ''soul'', ''creature'' and ''man'' mean the same thing. Every man is a soul, but no man can possess a soul. The statement or method of creation is plainly set forth in the Scriptures: ''And the Lord God formed man of the dust of the ground, and breathed into his nostrils the breath of life; and man became a living soul.''—Gen. 2:7.

Then God caused all the beasts and the fowl to pass before Adam, and he gave each one its name. Each beast and each fowl found its mate or kind. ''But for Adam there was not found an help meet for him.'' ''And the Lord God said, It is not good that the man should be alone, I will make him an help meet for him." (Gen. 2:18-20) Then the woman was made and brought unto the man.

That part of the earth where man first saw the light must have been surpassingly beautiful. "Eden" means a paradise. It was on the eastern side of Eden that God planted a garden, and there he put man, whom he had formed, to dress and to keep it. This was the home of Adam and his wife.

Taking as a basis this brief record, which we know is true because made under divine supervision, we may draw upon the imagination for a moment. In heaven there was a great and happy multitude of angels, strong, vigorous, and beautiful. There were the cherubim and seraphim, holding responsible positions of trust and confidence. There was Lucifer, the bright shining one, who surpassed the others in show and beauty. And there was the Logos, the great and mighty right arm of Jehovah God, by whom all things were created that were made. All these creatures were the delight of the Mighty Creator, and especially was that true of the Logos. Up to that time all were loyal and true to God.

On the earth now was the perfect man, strong, vigorous and handsome; with eyes so keen that they knew no dimness, and with the agility and swiftness of the hind. And with him was his wife, possessing grace and surpassing beauty such as no man now on this earth has ever beheld, for she was perfect. Without doubt there was some means of communication established between those of heaven and the perfect creatures of earth.

The man and the woman were endowed with power and authority to bring forth children and to fill the earth with their descendants, and the heavenly creatures must have observed this with the keenest interest and joy. There is no evidence that any of the heavenly creatures were endowed with power to produce any offspring. The propagation of the race on earth was then new and novel, and all the heavenly hosts must have waited and watched with deepest concern for the time to come when man would fill the earth with a joyful race of people, all of whom would worship and praise the great Jehovah God. Happiness reigned in heaven and happiness reigned on earth. The environment was beautiful, pleasing to the eye, a joy to the heart, and all to the praise of the Eternal God, the Creator.

## Chapter II

# *The Rebellion*

EVERY perfect creature must be a free moral agent. The creature must have the liberty to exercise his power for good or evil as he may choose. In no other way could he be tested and proven. God could have made all of his creatures so that they could not do evil, but had he done so that would have prevented them from exercising freely their attributes and God would thereby preclude himself from testing and proving his creatures.

The heart is the seat of affection or motive. It is that faculty of the creature which induces action. If impurity enters the heart, impurity of action is almost certain to follow. Hence it is written: "Keep thy heart with all diligence; for out of it are the issues of life."—Prov. 4:23.

Love is one of the divine attributes. Love is the perfect expression of unselfishness. Selfishness, the very antithesis of love, begins in the secret intent of the heart. Selfishness expels love. With love gone the heart becomes malicious. The creature possessing a malicious heart is one who is extremely selfish, having no regard for duty or obligation to others and fatally bent on accomplishing his purposes regardless of great wrong that may result to others.

The glory and beauty of the heavenly creatures, the perfection of the human pair in their Eden home, and the power and authority of man to fill the earth with his kind, furnished the opportunity for exercising either selfishness or love. The test came, and some of the mighty creatures of heaven fell under the test. The joy of heaven and earth was turned into great woe.

The tragedy of Eden has never known a parallel. In fact all other crimes and tragedies may be traced to the one there committed. Its enormity is enhanced by reason of the intelligence and greatness of the perpetrator of the crime and of his confidential relationship to the Eternal Creator. That terrible crime blighted the hopes of men and angels, filled the earth with woe and caused the very heavens to weep. It started the wheels of wickedness and has caused them to roll on down through the corridors of the ages, spreading war, murder, disease, pestilence and famine, thus crushing out the life-blood of countless millions.

So powerful, deceptive and cunning has been that arch criminal that the sensibilities of mankind have been stunned and benumbed, and the people for centuries have been kept in ignorance of the cause and its far-reaching effects. But now it seems certain that the time has come for God to pull back the curtain and let man have a better view and understanding of the terrible criminal and of his crime, that men may flee from the influence of the wicked one and find refuge in the arms of the Savior of the world.

Jehovah was man's benefactor and friend. He had created Adam, given him a wife, provided him with a beautiful home, made him prince of all he surveyed, clothed him with power to fill the earth with a perfect race of people, to subdue the earth, and rule it. Naturally Adam would love God. In addition to that he was so created that he would instinctively worship the One who was his friend and provider.

The will of God is his law. When that will is expressed toward man it is the law of God by which man is to be governed. A refusal to obey God's law makes the creature a disloyal subject. Without law there could be no way of testing man's loyalty. There must be a rule of action commanding that which is right and prohibiting that which is wrong. God provided a law for man. It was in connection with the food of Adam that God expressed his will or commandment. No evil effects would of course result merely from the food, because all the food was perfect; but the evil result would be from the act of disobedience of God's law. The loss of life to man meant the loss of everything. God could not permit an unlawful creature to possess eternal life. He provided man's food, and in connection therewith said: "And the Lord God commanded the man, saying, Of every tree of the garden thou mayest freely eat; but of the tree of the knowledge of good and evil, thou shalt not eat of it: for in the day that thou eatest thereof thou shalt surely die."—Gen. 2:16, 17.

It was in keeping with God's loving provision for man to appoint an overseer or helper or protector who would aid man in avoiding the doing of that which was wrong and would bring upon him the penalty for the violation of God's law. It was the bright shining one, Lucifer, whom God selected and placed in Eden as overlord or protector of man. Concerning him and his appointment to this responsible office God said: "Thou art the anointed cherub that covereth; and I have set thee so." (Ezek. 28:14) "Anointed" means that Lucifer, the cherub, was clothed with power and authority in the name of God to do certain things; and in this instance he was clothed with power and authority as overlord in the "garden of God" to look after the interests of man and to keep him in the right way. "Cherub" means an officer or deputy to whom are delegated certain heavenly powers and duties. The word "covereth" means to screen, to shield, to protect. It therefore follows that Lucifer was clothed with power and authority to act as an overseer for man; to screen, to shield and protect him from taking a wrongful course by violating God's law. It was his solemn duty, both to man and to God, to direct and influence humanity to go in the right way, that man might thereby honor God and prolong his life on the earth.

God had also clothed Lucifer with the power of death. (Heb. 2:14) It was therefore a part of the official duty of Lucifer to put the man to death if he did violate God's law. For this reason Lucifer occupied a confidential or fiduciary relationship toward God and man. There was committed into his hands a sacred trust of keeping God's newly-begun government on earth in a pure and proper condition. To betray that trust in order that he might overturn God's appointed means of government in Eden would be an act of treason. The perpetration of the crime of treason under such conditions would cover the perpetrator with perfidy and make him a nefarious, despicable creature and the blackest of all criminals. He being clothed with the most honorable position in the universe aside from that of the Logos, even different from the Logos because placed as overlord and protector of a domain, the betrayal of that trust is so terrible that it could not be properly stated in human phrase. The beauty, the purity and innocence of the perfect man and perfect woman, in an environment far more beautiful than any human eye has ever seen since, makes more pronounced the depravity of the heart that could commit the terrible crime hereinafter described.

Being one of the "morning stars" who witnessed the creation of man and of his perfect home, and being appointed to the position of trust and confidence as man's overlord, Lucifer of course knew that God had empowered man to produce his own species and that in due time the earth would be filled with a perfect race of people. He knew that man was so created that he must worship his benefactor. He knew that he must destroy in the mind of man the thought that God is his benefactor. Lucifer became ambitious to control the human race and to receive the worship to which God was justly entitled.

Lucifer was impressed with his own beauty and importance and power, and forgot that he owed an obligation to his Creator. Selfishness entered his heart. His motive was wrong and his heart became malignant. He was moved to take action concerning Adam, and his motive was wicked. Concerning this purpose the prophet records of Lucifer: "For thou hast said in thine heart, I will ascend into heaven, I will exalt my throne above the stars of God: I will sit also upon the mount of the congregation, in the sides of the north: I will ascend above the heights of the clouds; I will be like the Most High." (Isa. 14:13, 14) The

Scriptures clearly show that Lucifer's process of reasoning was like this:

'I am overlord of man in Eden. I have the power to put man to death, but even though man violates God's law I will not exercise that power. I will induce man to believe that God is not his friend and benefactor but in truth and in fact is deceiving man. Besides this, God will not be able to put man to death and at the same time maintain his own consistency; because he has declared that that tree in the midst of Eden is the tree of life, and to eat of that tree means that one will live forever. I will therefore take man to that tree and direct him to eat, and then he will not die, but will live forever.

'But before I do that I will first induce Adam to believe that God is keeping him in ignorance and withholding from him the things that he is justly entitled to receive. Adam loves his wife. I will first induce Eve to do my bidding, and then through her I shall be able to control Adam. I will so throw the circumstances around Adam that he too will be induced to eat of the forbidden tree of knowledge, and then I will refuse to put either of them to death. Then I will immediately take them to the tree of life and have them eat of that fruit. Then they will live forever, and not die. By this means I will win them over to me and I will keep them alive forever. I will defy God; and while he has a realm of angels and other creatures of heaven that worship him, I shall be like the Most High and shall be worshiped even as God is worshiped.'

The Scriptures show that thus did Lucifer plan a rebellion. It was a cunning scheme that Lucifer thus devised; he thought it was a wise scheme. Evidently God knew about it from its inception, but he did not interfere until Lucifer had gone to the point of committing the overt act by overreaching man and inducing him to sin. Concerning this, God said: "Thine heart was lifted up because of thy beauty; thou hast corrupted thy wisdom by reason of thy brightness." (Ezek. 28:17) This selfish meditation in the heart of Lucifer was the beginning of iniquity in him. Up to that time he had been perfect. Of him God says: "Thou wast perfect in thy ways from the day that thou wast created, till iniquity was found in thee." (Ezek. 28:15) The imperfection of Lucifer dates from that moment. That was the beginning of rebellion. That selfish meditation in his heart led to the terrible crime of treason and all the baneful effects that have followed since.

### THE CRIME

Lucifer, having carefully planned his crime, now proceeds to carry it out. To do so he resorts to fraud, deception and lying. When the Logos was on the earth he stated that Lucifer "is a liar, and the father of it" (John 8:44), thereby showing that Lucifer gave utterance to the first lie that was ever told. That lie was, "There is no death"; and the emissaries of the wicked one have been telling that lie to the people ever since.

Lucifer employed the serpent to carry out his scheme, because the serpent was more subtle than any other beast of the field which the Lord God had made. Lucifer therefore spoke through the serpent and said: "Yea, hath God said, Ye shall not eat of every tree of the garden? And the woman said unto the serpent,

LUCIFER EMPLOYS THE SERPENT

Page 26

We may eat of the fruit of the trees of the garden: but of the fruit of the tree which is in the midst of the garden, God hath said, Ye shall not eat of it, neither shall ye touch it, lest ye die. And the serpent said unto the woman, Ye shall not surely die: for God doth know that in the day ye eat thereof, then your eyes shall be opened; and ye shall be as gods, knowing good and evil. And when the woman saw that the tree was good for food, and that it was pleasant to the eyes, and a tree to be desired to make one wise, she took of the fruit thereof, and did eat; and gave also unto her husband with her, and he did eat."
—Gen. 3:1-6.

God had given his word that this tree produced a fruit that would increase the knowledge of those that ate it. The result was that when Adam and Eve did eat this forbidden fruit their knowledge was increased in harmony with God's announced law. They were now conscious of the fact that they had done wrong, because they hid themselves amongst the trees in the garden from the presence of the Lord. He brought them before him. They entered a plea of guilty, confessing that they had done wrong, and thereupon God entered against them the following judgment, to wit:

"Unto the woman he said, I will greatly multiply thy sorrow, and thy conception: in sorrow thou shalt bring forth children; and thy desire shall be to thy husband, and he shall rule over thee. And unto Adam he said, Because thou hast hearkened unto the voice of thy wife, and hast eaten of the tree of which I commanded thee, saying, Thou shalt not eat of it: cursed is the ground for thy sake; in sorrow shalt thou eat of it all the days of thy life: thorns also and thistles shall it bring forth to thee; and thou shalt eat the herb of the field: in the sweat of thy face shalt thou eat bread, till thou return unto the ground; for out of it wast thou taken: for dust thou art, and unto dust shalt thou return."—Gen. 3:16-19.

The Scriptures mention three classes of fruit-bearing trees in the garden of Eden, to wit: (a) every tree that is pleasant to the sight and good for food; (b) the tree of life in the midst of the garden; and (c) the tree of knowledge of good and evil. (Gen. 2:9) God told Adam that he might eat of all the trees that were good for him. "And the Lord God took the man, and put him into the garden of Eden, to dress it and to keep it. And the Lord God commanded the man, saying, Of every tree of the garden thou mayest freely eat; but of the tree of the knowledge of good and evil, thou shalt not eat of it: for in the day that thou eatest thereof thou shalt surely die."—Gen. 2:15-17.

There is no evidence that Adam knew anything about the tree of life that was in the midst of Eden. On the contrary, he must have been ignorant of it, because there was no specific command given to him concerning it. Lucifer, as the officer in charge, being clothed with the power of death and entrusted with the high office of overlord of man, would, of course, know all about the tree of life. The fact that God gave Adam command about other trees in the garden and said nothing about the tree of life is evidence that man knew nothing about this tree. The eating of the tree of knowledge of good and evil doubtless would open the way so that Adam would shortly know about the tree of life. But now comes the proof showing conclusively that Adam had had no opportunity to eat of the tree of life and that therefore he must have been in ignorance of it until immediately before his expulsion from Eden.

God summoned the guilty parties before him and, upon a full hearing of the facts, pronounced judgment against the woman and against the man and against the serpent which Satan had employed to deceive Eve. The final judgment against Lucifer or Satan is set forth in the prophecy of Ezekiel, and it provides that in due time he is to be destroyed and never shall be again. Immediately following the pronouncement of the judgment against man God addressed some one, then and there present, and it seems almost certain that he was speaking to the Logos, his true and trusted Son. We read: "And the Lord God said, Behold, the man is become as one of us, to know good and evil: and now, lest he put forth his hand, and *take also of the tree of life, and eat, and live for ever.*" (Gen. 3: 22) Mark the words of Jehovah here recorded: "Man is become as one of us, *to know* good and evil."

Knowing the situation was critical God seemingly acted immediately, before man had an opportunity to get to the tree of life and eat of it, and even before Lucifer had time to inform man of the location of the tree. The words addressed to the Logos were cut short; the sentence seemingly stops in the middle, without being finished, to wit: "And now, lest he put forth his hand, and take also of the tree of life, and eat, and live for ever:—" Note the record. God did not speak another word, but acted immediately; and his action is recorded in the next verse, which reads:

"Therefore the Lord God sent him forth from the garden of Eden to till the ground from whence he was taken. So he drove out the man: and he placed at the east of the garden of Eden, cherubims, and a flaming sword which turned every way, to keep the way of the tree of life."—Gen. 3:23, 24.

It was doubtless God's purpose at some time to permit man to partake of the tree of life and live forever, and, had he proven faithful under the test, that would have been his reward. Lucifer therefore caused him to fail in the test, caused him to fail to retain life, and caused him to bring upon himself and all his progeny the great sorrow and distress that have afflicted humankind down through the centuries.

Lucifer had manifested his unfaithfulness and treachery and doubtless intended to act as quickly as possible and lead man to the tree of life and let him eat of that fruit. He knew that God had given his word that the fruit of that tree was a fruit of life, and that if man should eat of it he would live and not die. Lucifer therefore reasoned that he would be able to prove to Adam and Eve that God was purposely deceiving them and keeping them in ignorance and keeping them away from the opportunity for life; and that he, Lucifer, was telling them the truth and was bringing them a great blessing, and that hence he was entitled to be worshiped by them and by all their offspring.

Had Adam eaten of that fruit of the tree of life immediately he could not have been put to death by Jehovah himself, because God cannot be inconsistent. God had given his word that this was a tree of life; and for him to permit man to eat of it and then put him to death would make void his word, which is impossible for God to do. (Ps. 138:2; Isa. 46:11; 55:11) Therefore, in order that God might keep his word inviolate and enforce his judgment against Adam he immediately expelled him from Eden and set a powerful officer on guard with a flaming sword turning in every direction, to keep man out of Eden and away from the tree of life.

In due time every intelligent creature of God will have an opportunity under full and fair conditions to follow the course of Lucifer and take the consequences, or to follow the righteous commands of God and receive the reward of being permitted to partake of the tree of life and live forever.

Why did not God kill man forthwith? Other scriptures show that at that time man had not exercised his powers to beget children. No children were born. Hence God permitted Adam to continue on earth 930 years, during which time he begat and brought forth his children. Now he has permitted a sufficient length of time to elapse for the birth of a sufficient number of Adam's posterity to populate the earth. All of these have suffered from the baneful effects of sin, eventuating in death; but in due time they shall come forth and be brought to a knowledge of the truth, that they may know the reason why they have suffered. Then they shall have an opportunity to abide in sin and suffer eternal destruction or to follow the righteous commands of God and live for ever.

Adam was sentenced to death. This sentence was enforced against him by compelling him to eat of the fruits of the unfinished part of the earth, which gradually resulted in his death. Within that period of 930 years his children were brought forth. While these were not formally sentenced to death, they were all born sinners. The imperfect Adam, undergoing the death sentence, could not beget perfect children. Hence it is written by the psalmist: "Behold, I was shapen in iniquity; and in sin did my mother conceive me." (Ps. 51:5) To the same effect is the apostle's statement in Romans 5:12: "Wherefore, as by one man sin entered into the world, and death by sin; and so death passed upon all men, for that all have sinned." Thus is seen the terrible and far-reaching effects of this rebellion. It has brought all the suffering and sorrow, sickness and death, wars, famines and pestilences to which humankind have been heir during the past six thousand years. The very first son that Adam had was a murderer, and Lucifer the Devil induced him to commit the murder; therefore Lucifer was a party to the crime. Lucifer is guilty of every murder that has ever been committed on this earth.

No longer did God permit his creature Lucifer to go by the name which signified 'a bright shining one'. His name was changed from Lucifer, and he was thereafter known by the four names, to wit: Satan, which means adversary or opponent; Devil, which means slanderer; Serpent, which means deceiver; and Dragon, which means devourer. He has been defiant and arrogant, and has opposed God ever since the time of Eden. He has slandered God's holy name and brought reproach upon him and upon everyone who has sought to do the Lord's will. He has used every possible means to deceive the people and turn their minds away from God. He has sought to devour or destroy everyone that has faithfully tried to obey God's holy will.

This archenemy has had many emissaries on earth who have paraded themselves in the name and as the representatives of the Lord. Amongst these were the clergy of Jesus' time, and to them and of them he said: "Ye are of your father the devil, and the lusts of your father ye will do. He was a murderer from the beginning, and abode not in the truth, because there is no truth in him. When he speaketh a lie, he speaketh of his own: for he is a liar, and the father of it."—John 8:44.

The rebellion did not stop with that of Lucifer and man. In heaven there was a host of angels, many of whom afterwards rebelled. The children of Adam increased. The women were beautiful in form and fair to look upon. The angels saw that men and women cohabited and children resulted. It was the will of God that the angels should remain on the spirit plane and that they should not leave their estate or life on the spirit plane and mingle with human creatures and cohabit with women. But many of these angels, misled and seduced by Satan the Devil, joined in the rebellion against God, as it is written: "And it came to pass . . . that the sons of God saw the daughters of men that they were fair; and they took them wives of all which they chose. There were giants in the earth in those days; and also after that, when the sons of God came in unto the daughters of men, and they bare children to them, the same became mighty men, which were of old, men of renown. And God saw that the wickedness of man was great in the earth, and that every imagination of the thoughts of his heart was only evil continually.''—Gen. 6:1, 2, 4, 5.

In due time these rebellious ones who kept not their first estate were imprisoned. (Jude 6; 2 Pet. 2:4) Many other angels of heaven joined Satan in his rebellion, and for centuries these have been serving with him and following his wicked course of reproaching God and oppressing men. (Dan. 10:13; Eph. 6:12; 1 Ki. 22:22) The Scriptures declare that in God's due time all these wicked angels who joined the rebellion with Satan shall be destroyed.

What terrible havoc this rebellion wrought! The great, beautiful and wonderful Lucifer, now degraded and covered with perfidy, becomes the very embodiment of wickedness. Many of the pure and holy angels of heaven, once enjoying the smile of the great Jehovah God and the fellowship of the faithful Logos, turned to wickedness, and in due time are to be destroyed. Adam, once pure, holy, perfect, strong and vigorous, was driven from the perfect Eden into the unfinished earth. His offspring have ever since been compelled to earn their bread in the sweat of their face and to suffer disease and sickness; and eventually in sorrow they go down to the grave. Above all, man was deprived of sweet communion with the mighty eternal God. All these centuries man has been in bondage to sin and death, groaning and travailing under his burdens, desiring, begging and praying that sometime and in some way he might be delivered.

God early began the operation of his marvelous arrangement for the deliverance of man and for his restoration. Exercising his power in exact harmony with justice, wisdom and love, God has been working out his great purpose to this end. Now the time has come for the peoples of the earth to begin to get a clearer vision of God's great purpose of salvation and to learn how and when he will bring about man's complete deliverance.

## Chapter III

# *Hypocrisy and Faithfulness*

MUCH of the Bible is written in symbolic language and could not be understood until God's purpose had progressed in course of fulfilment, and then not until God's "due time".

The serpent is used as a symbol of Satan the enemy, and those who yield willingly to the influence of the Devil and support his cause are called 'the seed of the serpent'. Woman is used as a symbol of the righteous organization of Jehovah God; and those who love righteousness and hate iniquity and who strive to follow in the righteous way are spoken of as 'the seed of the woman'. When God pronounced judgment at the time of the rebellion he said to the Serpent, the Devil: "I will put enmity between thee and the woman, and between thy seed and her seed; it shall bruise thy head, and thou shalt bruise his heel." (Gen. 3:15) From that very day forward Satan the Devil has opposed God and fought against every one who has diligently tried to serve Jehovah. By resorting to ridicule and mockery Satan has delighted to reproach God in every possible way. Of course God could have imprisoned or destroyed the Devil; but his Word discloses that it has been the purpose of Jehovah to let this wicked one come to the full in wrongdoing, before he executes his final judgment against the Devil.

About 250 years after the expulsion of Adam from Eden, Enos the grandson of Adam was born. By that time, so far as the Bible discloses, every one of the human race followed the course of wickedness. The Bible record does not indicate that between Abel and Enoch there was even one good man who loved God and righteousness. This warrants the conclusion that all were under the control of Satan the wicked one. That being true, Satan must have thought that he had succeeded in having all men to worship him, in turning away all men from God; and that therefore by mockery and hypocrisy he would reproach God forever. It was in the days of Enos that hypocrisy began to be manifest for the first time, and that was in connection with religious worship. It is written: "Then began men to call themselves by the name of the Lord." (See margin, Genesis 4:26.) It seems quite clear that this was a scheme of Satan to have men call themselves by the name of the Lord and yet pursue a course in opposition to God, thereby to ridicule God and hold his name up to scorn. These men were tools of Satan the Devil and were therefore hypocrites.

This discloses a scheme of Satan which he has ever followed since; namely, *to have in his system of government an organized religion by which means he could deceive the people and ridicule Jehovah God.* This is mentioned here because it discloses the fixed policy on the part of the Devil to use religion as a part of his deceptive and fraudulent schemes. Evidently he does this because he knows men are so constituted that they will worship something; and if he is unable to induce them to worship himself directly he will cause them to worship something else or to ridicule God at any cost. It is observed that he has many such schemes in vogue now on the earth, causing the people to worship anything except the true and living God.

A few generations later Enoch was born. He was the seventh generation from Adam. Of course Adam was wicked, because he had violated God's law and continued in the evil course. Aside from Abel every one from Adam to Enoch was evidently unrighteous. The human race was going the road of corruption and wickedness. Enoch was the exception. He believed in Jehovah God. He believed that some day God would reward all those who would obey him. Satan the Devil had been so active that the peoples of earth by that time even doubted the existence of Jehovah God. It was necessary for Enoch to exercise faith that God actually exists. This was necessary in order for him to please God. "Without faith it is impossible to please him [God]; for he that cometh to God must believe that he is, and that he is a rewarder of them that diligently seek him." (Heb. 11:6) That he pleased God is shown by the following statement: "And Enoch walked with God: and he was not, for God took him." (Gen. 5:24) To the same effect Paul testifies: "By faith Enoch was translated that he should not see death; and was not found, because God had translated him; for before his translation he had this testimony, that he pleased God."—Heb. 11:5.

Enoch, because of his faith in God, was an outstanding figure amongst all the men of earth. He was a witness on the earth for God. Surely he was known amongst the other men and known by the fact that he believed on God and served him while all others were against the Lord. Such faith under such adverse conditions was pleasing to God, and God rewarded that faith by translating Enoch. In those days it was usual for men to live upwards of eight hundred years. Enoch lived 365 years and then God took him away. No one saw him go, no one buried him, and no one knew where he went. Satan the Devil had the power of death, and without doubt would have killed Enoch had not God prevented him from so doing. God has the power of death, of course; but he did not put Enoch to death for any wrongful act on Enoch's part. Nor did Enoch die because of sickness, the result of the inheritance from Adam, his grandfather. The Devil had nothing to do with putting Enoch to death. He was a young man, compared with other men of his day. While in the vigor of youth, and while he walked with God and joyfully conformed himself to God's righteous law, the Lord manifested his pleasure in the faith of Enoch by taking him suddenly away from earth's wicked scenes, putting him peacefully to sleep without his having to pass through the bitter waters of a violent or agonizing death.

It seems reasonable that Enoch never saw anyone die; because Paul testifies that Enoch did not see death. The apostle, after enumerating a number of faithful ones, including Enoch, says, "These all died in faith." (Heb. 11:13) It follows, of course, that Enoch was not taken away to live on some other planet, but that God took him quietly and suddenly, putting him to sleep without pain or anguish and without fear of the terrible monster death. Here God began to indicate that at some time he would destroy death and deliver all those who have faith in him from all their enemies, including the enemy death. —1 Cor. 15:25, 26.

It is recorded that Enoch prophesied that in some future time the Lord would come with a mighty host of angels and execute judgment upon the ungodly. (Jude 14, 15) Of course he would give utterance to this prophecy in the presence of other men, and they in turn would mock and jeer and taunt him, and the Devil would use every power at his command to destroy Enoch. But the Lord Jehovah held his hand over Enoch. From this scripture it seems quite evident that God had told Enoch, or by some means put it into Enoch's mind, that sometime in the future he was going to send his mighty Representative to execute judgment upon all the enemies of God and to deliver the people from bondage. The spirit of the Lord moved upon the mind of Enoch and caused him thus to prophesy, because his heart was right toward God. This was the first prophecy of a coming Deliverer.

Thus by these two men, Enos and Enoch, are made manifest hypocrisy, a detestable thing in the sight of God, and true faith, which is pleasing to God. Hypocrisy, the fruit of wickedness, is from the Devil; faith is a gift from God. Thus God early made manifest his rule, from which he will never deviate, that those who have faith in him and walk with him in the way of righteousness and in obedience to his command shall be rewarded by deliverance from the enemy and be given the blessings of life. The goodness and mercy of the Lord endure forever. His loving-kindness is marked by his every act.

GIANTS IN THE EARTH Page 45

## Chapter IV

# *World Destroyed*

WITHIN the meaning of the Scriptures the word "world" signifies the peoples of earth organized into tribes or forms of government, under the supervision of an overlord or superhuman power. The superior power is invisible and is spoken of under the term "heaven"; while the organization on earth is visible and is spoken of as "earth".

Sixteen hundred years after the tragedy of Eden found the human race in a deplorable condition. The peoples of earth dwelt together in families or tribes; and the superior power that controlled them was Satan and a host of his evil angels, operating in conjunction with and under his direction. This was the invisible part of that "world". Having the power to materialize in human form, some of these angels did that very thing and then cohabited with the women of the human race. The result was a race of giants. "The sons of God came in unto the daughters of men, and they bare children to them; . . . The earth also was corrupt before God, and the earth was filled with violence. And God looked upon the earth, and, behold, it was corrupt; for all flesh had corrupted his way upon the earth."—Gen. 6:4, 11, 12.

The people who walked about the earth in human form constituted the visible part of the world. This part of that world was exceedingly corrupt, and the invisible part of it was the chief cause for the corruption. Satan, the great adversary of God, was the real responsible one. Still impressed with his own greatness, egotistically believing that he could defeat God in his purposes, he devised various schemes to that end. He saw the human race dying, and doubtless reasoned that if the angels should materialize and cohabit with women they would produce a superior race, and that this would make his kingdom more powerful. For this reason Satan was the inducing cause for the debauchery of angels and women.

So strong was the enemy's influence that all the people came under his control except Noah and the members of his household. It is written concerning Noah that he was perfect in his generation. This was not perfection of physical organism but the perfection resulting from complete devotion to Jehovah. "But Noah found grace in the eyes of the Lord. These are the generations of Noah: Noah was a just man, and perfect in his generations, and Noah walked with God."—Gen. 6: 8, 9.

God told Noah of his purpose to bring a great flood of waters upon the earth and thereby destroy both man and beast. "And God said unto Noah, The end of all flesh is come before me; for the earth is filled with violence through them; and, behold, I will destroy them with the earth."—Gen. 6: 13.

By this we are not to understand that God would destroy the mundane sphere, the planet earth, but that he would destroy the visible part of the world, the organization of the adversary. "And, behold, I, even I, do bring a flood of waters upon the earth, to destroy all flesh, wherein is the breath of life, from under heaven; and every thing that is in the earth shall die. But with thee will I establish my covenant: and thou shalt come into the ark; thou, and thy sons, and thy wife, and thy sons' wives, with thee."—Gen. 6:17, 18.

Noah believed God. He was obedient to him, and his faith was pleasing to the Lord. "By faith Noah, being warned of God of things not seen as yet, moved with fear, prepared an ark to the saving of his house; by the which he condemned the world, and became heir of the righteousness which is by faith."—Heb. 11:7.

The righteous course of Noah testified against the Devil's organization, both visible and invisible, and marked it with God's condemnation. Noah was a witness for God, and for this reason Satan the Devil had turned all others against Noah and against God. Of course the Devil would do everything within his power to destroy Noah, but was unable to do so because Noah had the protection of Jehovah. The mixed breed of human and angelic creatures had resulted in a race of giants that were wicked beyond description. Seemingly God was forced to take action to destroy this mongrel race from the face of the earth. At the death of Noah and his family there would be no one on earth as a witness for the Lord. Hence God must clear out this wicked progeny, carry Noah and his family over in the flood, and then start the race anew. And this he did.

### THE DELUGE

Noah warned the people of the impending judgment of the Lord against the wickedness prevailing in the earth. They gave no heed to his warning. No rain had ever fallen upon the earth (Gen. 2:5, 6), and it was not a difficult matter for Satan to induce the people to believe that none ever would fall. No one gave serious heed to the warning of Noah, but, on the contrary, they scoffed at him and made all manner of sport of his prophesying before them. In obedience to God Noah built the ark, which was completed after a long period of time; and during its construction he continued to preach to the people.

At the appointed time Noah and his family, and the beasts of various kinds, went into the ark. Then the Lord opened the windows of the heavens, and a great deluge of water swept from one end of the earth to the other and destroyed every living creature upon the face of the earth. This of course included the progeny of the angels and women; but the wicked angels themselves, who had left their first estate, will be finally disposed of at the great judgment day.—Jude 6; 2 Pet. 2:4, 5.

But why should God bring the flood upon the earth? Was it merely to destroy wicked creatures? Other scriptures indicate that such was not the sole nor even the most important reason. The issue in the minds of the people was then, and is now: *Who is the mighty God?* Satan, unhindered, had induced almost all men, and a host of angels, to believe that he, Satan, was superior to Jehovah. He became arrogant in the extreme, boasting of his greatness and power; and doubtless he exhibited it in a marked degree. God would teach all his creatures that every good and perfect thing proceeds from himself, and that to follow the enemy Satan would result in disaster. He would teach all intelligent creatures that he is the great eternal One and that from him alone proceed the blessings of life, liberty and eternal happiness. The principle was later stated by the Lord Jesus in these words: "This is life eternal, that they might know thee the only true God, and Jesus Christ, whom thou hast sent."—John 17: 3.

The flood was so terrible that its marks are still upon the earth; and all peoples, regardless of whether they believe in God or not, have been taught by tradition that at some time in the past there was a great deluge upon the earth. In due time they will learn the real reason why the flood was sent. The goodness and mercy of God were again manifested in this lesson that he gave to men and angels.

It is important to notice what occurred in the days of Noah, and particularly the event which marked the end of that antediluvian "world". The flood was typical of a greater and more terrible trouble coming upon this world, in which Jehovah God will demonstrate to all his creatures that he is the Almighty, the Most High. The spirit of the Lord had moved upon the mind of Noah to teach him of the approaching flood, but it is manifest from the words of Paul that the deluge foreshadowed something even greater to come at the end of this age.—Heb. 11: 7.

Long centuries after the flood Jesus said: "As the days of Noe were, so shall also the coming of the Son of man be." (Matt. 24: 37) All the people, aside from his family, mocked Noah because he preached of the coming disaster upon the then evil world. Then all, aside from Noah and his family, formed a portion of the Devil's own religious system and worshiped the

Devil or some of his creatures. Now at this present time the religious systems make sport of the preaching of the gospel concerning the impending fall of Satan's organization and the establishment of God's kingdom of righteousness. In Noah's day only a few were witnesses for God. Now only those who love and serve the Lord Jehovah with pure hearts are really on the side of the Lord. It is to the faithful class that Jehovah now says: "Ye are my witness, that I am God."

As the issue in Noah's day was, "Who is God?" even so now the issue is, "Who is God?" That evil world, of which Satan was the ruler, Jehovah destroyed with the flood as an expression of indignation against wickedness and against the wicked one; and for the purpose of teaching all his intelligent creatures that in Jehovah resides all power, which operates in complete harmony with wisdom, justice and love, and that the oppressed creatures of the human race will find complete deliverance only by taking heed to the mighty provision which God has graciously made for the deliverance and eternal blessing of his obedient creatures.

## Chapter V

# *Enemy Organizes*

ONLY eight persons survived the flood. These were carried over from the old world which had perished. This foreshadowed that the world then beginning is also to pass away, and that from this world shall many people be carried over to the new world, which shall then be established with the great Deliverer in charge; and these shall learn of him the way to eternal life. Noah and his family were living examples of God's power to save those who trust in him. Noah loved God and was faithful to him; and by the experience of the flood God was teaching his intelligent creatures that the wicked shall not flourish forever, but that they shall perish in his own due time, and that only the *faithful* will be blessed with life everlasting. This rule is stated by the prophet thus: "The Lord preserveth all them that love him: but all the wicked will he destroy." —Ps. 145:20.

After the flood God began anew the work of populating the earth which he had created for man. "And God blessed Noah and his sons, and said unto them, Be fruitful, and multiply, and replenish the earth. And you, be ye fruitful, and multiply; bring forth abundantly in the earth, and multiply therein."—Gen. 9:1,7.

For 350 years after the flood Noah lived on the earth, and his children and grandchildren increased. Because Noah loved and served God he would of course teach his children to love and serve the Lord as the only true and living God. Satan was responsible for the deflection of the sons of God who had left their first estate, violating the law of the Lord, and brought his indignation down upon them. Now he saw and realized what his wicked course had brought forth. After Satan had seen all the wicked ones of earth destroyed, and all of the angels who had left their first estate placed in prison, this should have been sufficient to teach him that he could not successfully fight against God. But he did not learn his lesson. Egotistical and arrogant, he pursued his wicked course. While Noah was on the earth, teaching his children and grandchildren to love and serve God, Satan made but little progress in seducing mankind.

Then Nimrod came upon the scene and became a mighty hunter of wild beasts. And now the Devil influenced the people to worship Nimrod. With Satan it was anything to turn the minds of the people away from the Lord Jehovah. Being a powerful spirit creature Satan exercised his power by influencing the thoughts of men, by injecting into their minds wicked thoughts. And this he did that he might again get complete control of the human race and turn them away from God.

It appears from the record that Satan's next attempt was to organize the people into one compact body or government, that he might with greater ease control and direct all the people according to his own selfish ways. The Scriptural record upon this point reads: "And the whole earth was of one language, and of one speech. And it came to pass, as they journeyed from the east, that they found a plain in the land of Shinar; and they dwelt there. And they said one to another, Go to, let us make brick, and burn them thoroughly. And they had brick for stone, and slime had they for mortar. And they said, Go to, let us build us a city and a tower, whose top may reach unto heaven; and let us make us a name, lest we be scattered abroad upon the face of the whole earth."—Gen. 11:1-4.

This was the first attempt after the flood on the part of the Devil to organize the people into a government or world power. "A city" is a symbolic expression referring to a government; and on the occasion above mentioned Satan induced the people to conclude that now they must build a city and a tower. They proceeded to do so. The Tower of Babel, builded by the people at the instance of Satan, was the Devil's defiance of Almighty God. Clearly this was his method of planting in the minds of the people the thought that they did not need God but that by their own efforts they could provide for their own kind of worship and their own uplift, and could save themselves when it was necessary, which was another wily scheme to turn them away from the true God. The Devil has not changed his methods even to the present time.

The building of the Tower of Babel by the people finds a parallel in the course pursued by the Evolutionists and Modernists. They say: 'We do not need God, nor do we need a Savior. We do not need the Bible. Our wisdom exceeds the wisdom of all men of the past. We worship power and our own ability to accomplish our uplift.' Thus the Devil, using the savants and self-constituted wise men, turns multitudes of people away from the true and living God.

From that time until now Satan has pursued a similar policy of organizing the peoples of earth into world powers and through the instrumentality of a few men controlling the masses. He has succeeded in steeping them in ignorance of God's great provision for salvation and turning them away from the path that leads to life. He has implanted greed and selfishness in the minds of the governing factors of the world powers, and by the use of a false religious system, enforced by the strong arm of the military, has frightened the people into yielding to the wicked influence of the governing factors.

God permitted the people of the plains of Shinar to go to the full limit of their folly. They were building this tower that they might make for themselves a name, which the Devil had induced them to believe would safeguard them from being scattered abroad upon the face of the whole earth. Of course he would expect to hold them in the vicinity of the tower and the city, and to cause it to be a mecca or place of worship to which all the peoples of earth would look for instruction; and thus he would control them. He had almost succeeded now in turning the minds of the people away from God that they would no longer trust him. Satan no doubt thought that again he had won the victory over God and that now he would hold the people in subjection to himself and have their worship.

Then the Lord Jehovah took action for the benefit of mankind. Seeing Satan again turning the minds of the people away from him the Lord knew that they would fall completely under the hands of the adversary; and now he would give them a lesson to teach them that Satan was not the true God but that the

Lord alone could help them. Here the record is that God came down to see their organization and their power; and then, for the people's good, he changed their language. It will be noticed in the Hebrew (Gen. 11:1) that the people were all of one lip. Their lip must have been shaped in the same general manner and they all spoke one kind of words.

The Lord, by the action which he now took, demonstrated his own supremacy. "And the Lord came down to see the city and the tower, which the children of men builded. And the Lord said, Behold, the people is one, and they have all one language; and this they begin to do: and now nothing will be restrained from them, which they have imagined to do. Go to, let us go down, and there confound their language, that they may not understand one another's speech. So the Lord scattered them abroad from thence upon the face of all the earth; and they left off to build the city. Therefore is the name of it called Babel; because the Lord did there confound the language of all the earth: and from thence did the Lord scatter them abroad upon the face of all the earth."—Gen. 11:5-9.

By this experience some of the people might have begun to think that there is a great God who is above all and who is all-powerful. But would the people ever learn that they could not trust the Devil? Would they ever learn that the great Jehovah God alone can give everlasting blessings? Let us follow the history of the race and see.

## Chapter VI

# *First World Power*

AFTER the fall of the Tower of Babel and the scattering of the people throughout the earth they gathered in tribes in various parts of the earth. Many of these found an abiding place in Egypt, and there Satan erected his first great world power on earth. According to history Menes was the first ruler. Without hindrance from God, and therefore by his permission, men there built a great world power. It proved to be a mighty military system and a great oppressor of the people. It was an empire of riches, learning and religion; and these three elements combined to rule the people and make their burdens grievous to be borne.

In the meantime God was dealing with Abraham, Isaac and Jacob, and working out his great purpose which he had made from the beginning. In due time Joseph, the beloved son of Jacob, was sold by his brethren to a band of wandering tradesmen; and by them he was carried away to the land of Egypt. Both Joseph and his father served Jehovah God, and Jehovah overruled for good this experience of Joseph's being carried away. After a time Joseph, on a false charge, was wrongfully confined to prison, where he lingered indefinitely. Then the king of Egypt had a dream which he could not understand and none could interpret for him. He called the magicians, the Devil's representatives on earth, to interpret his dream; and they could not. He was told of Joseph in prison, and the king sent and had Joseph brought before him. Here again the Lord Jehovah rewarded his faithful servant. By the grace of the Lord God Joseph interpreted the dream of the king, foretelling that there were to come upon the land of Egypt seven years of plenty and seven years of famine; and he advised the king to cause to be laid up great quantities of food during the seven years of plenty to be used during the famine. Joseph was here a faithful and true witness to the only true God, and for his faithfulness God rewarded him. *God never fails to reward faithfulness to him.*

The king then made Joseph the first man of the land under the king, and Joseph thereafter became the active ruler of the land of Egypt: "And Pharaoh said unto his servants, Can we find such a one as this is, a man in whom the spirit of God is? And Pharaoh said unto Joseph, Forasmuch as God hath shewed thee all this, there is none so discreet and wise as thou art: thou shalt be over my house, and according unto thy word shall all my people be ruled: only in the throne will I be greater than thou."—Gen. 41:38-40.

Joseph was a great and good witness to the people of Egypt. He showed the people an outline of the Lord Jehovah's great purpose to redeem them and deliver them and to bless them. Of course they did not understand it then, but it was written more particularly for the benefit of the people now who are being permitted to understand the divine purpose.

During the seven years of plenty Joseph, with absolute power, had caused great stores of grain to be laid up. When the famine was sore upon the land the people were in need. Joseph bought all their corn for the king. The next year the people came back and said to Joseph: 'We have no corn for sale.' Joseph then said to them: 'Sell me your cattle.' And he bought all the cattle from the people for the king. The next year the famine continued and the people came to him and said: 'We have no corn and no cattle'; and then Joseph said: 'Sell me your land.' And he bought all the land for the king. The famine continued upon the people, and the next year they came back and said to Joseph: 'We have neither corn, nor cattle, nor land, but we will voluntarily sell ourselves and become the servants of Pharaoh the king.' (Gen. 47:14-23) Thus the people gave up everything that they might get bread from the hands of Joseph.

This pictured how in due time the people will become the voluntary servants of the antitypical Joseph, the Lord of righteousness, that they may get the bread of life and live. Joseph readjusted the affairs of Egypt, and the people were content. Thus God showed the people how goodness and faith bring the reward of peace and blessing. Joseph was therefore a mighty witness for the Lord in the land of Egypt.

After the death of Joseph there came to the throne a new king in Egypt who fell an easy victim to the wiles of Satan the Devil. "Now there arose up a new king over Egypt, which knew not Joseph." (Ex. 1:8) Under the reign of this arrogant tool of Satan the people soon forgot the goodness that they had received from Jehovah through the hands of his faithful servant Joseph. Egypt then grew to be a great and wealthy world power, the like of which the earth had never known. The Devil now overreached the people;

they forgot God and worshiped four-footed beasts and creeping things instead. They fell easy victims to his scheme of government.

The ultrarich were sponsors for the military, the learned became the political schemers, and the priests of the devil religion led the people into a senseless worship of the Devil and things which he created for them to worship. These three elements, the commercial, political, and ecclesiastical factors which Satan organized, operating together formed the world power by which he controlled the people. Such a world power is properly symbolized by a beast. The government, and by that is meant the ruling factors, became arrogant and rebellious against God and great oppressors of the people. Images of the Pharaohs are preserved to this day, and upon the face of them will be seen the expression of arrogance, disdain and contempt. Satan established amongst the people various images and false gods which he induced them to worship; thus following his usual practice of placing before mankind anything that would turn them away from the true and living God, that they might not learn about the divine purpose.

All this time God was not without some witness in the land. Joseph had brought his father and his brethren into Egypt. Their offspring had greatly multiplied, and now there was a host of Israelites in the land of Egypt. These were the people of God who worshiped the true and living God, and from the death of Jacob they were recognized by Jehovah as his chosen people on the earth. For this reason the Devil saw to it that they were greatly oppressed. He would have caused their complete destruction except for the protection of the Lord. Without doubt the Lord permitted his people to abide for a time in Egypt in order that he might teach his intelligent creatures certain lessons which they needed, and which in due time they would begin to understand.

When Jacob was on his deathbed he prophesied that there should come from the tribe of Judah a mighty One who would be the great Deliverer of the people, and that unto him should the gathering of the people be. (Gen. 49:10) The Devil knew about this prophecy, of course. He set about to devise schemes for the destruction of this promised One. The children of Israel continued to reside in Egypt, and their offspring had multiplied at a greater rate than the Egyptians'. Therefore the king gave instructions that the midwives should take notice at the time the Hebrew women gave birth to children and that if a son was born it should be killed, but if the child was a daughter it should be permitted to live. Clearly this was a scheme of the Devil; he would have all the males killed in order that he might be certain to get the One that was promised to come through the tribe of Judah. The Devil was taking no chance of this mighty One's being born and being permitted to live. But of course he had not the power to thwart God's purposes, even though he egotistically thought he had.

God helped the Israelitish women, and the birth of Hebrew children continued. Finally Moses was born, and by a miracle of God he was saved from being destroyed. He was taken into the home of the royal family, or rather into the royal house, and there received all its privileges. (Ex. 2:1-10) The Lord saw to it that Moses was preserved, because of and through

Moses he would now make a type of the mighty Deliverer who was to come; and we shall hereafter see how the Devil employed the same kind of scheme to destroy the Savior of the world that he employed to destroy Moses.

Moses had faith in God. (Heb. 11:24, 25) Moses would rather take his chances with his own people and serve the true and living God than to have all the comforts and ease and honor that the Devil and his world power could confer upon him. God continued to overrule and shape the conditions of his chosen people, that in his own due time he could give a testimony to man of his goodness and loving-kindness.

Conditions arose that made it necessary for Moses to go to live in another land. Oppressive measures employed by Pharaoh the king of Egypt against Israel grew worse and worse. Their cries came up to Almighty God. "And the Lord said, I have surely seen the affliction of my people which are in Egypt, and have heard their cry by reason of their taskmasters; for I know their sorrows; and I am come down to deliver them out of the hand of the Egyptians, and to bring them up out of that land unto a good land and a large, unto a land flowing with milk and honey; unto the place of the Canaanites, and the Hittites, and the Amorites, and the Perizzites, and the Hivites, and the Jebusites. Now therefore, behold, the cry of the children of Israel is come unto me: and I have also seen the oppression wherewith the Egyptians oppress them. Come now, therefore, and I will send thee unto Pharaoh, that thou mayest bring forth my people, the children of Israel, out of Egypt."—Ex. 3:7-10.

Moses went at the direction of Jehovah to act for the people of Israel, and Aaron was sent by the Lord to assist Moses. Obedient to the command of the Lord Moses and Aaron appeared before Pharaoh and said: "Thus saith the Lord God of Israel, Let my people go, that they may hold a feast unto me in the wilderness." A mighty world power now was Egypt, and the Devil was its invisible ruler. Egotistical and wicked beyond description of human words Satan caused his visible representative, the king of Egypt, to manifest the greatest degree of arrogance and defiance to the Almighty God. To the request made by Moses to the ruler of Egypt, the Devil's representative said: *"Who is the Lord, that I should obey his voice to let Israel go? I know not the Lord, neither will I let Israel go."*—Ex. 5:2.

The oppressive burdens of the Israelites were then greatly increased. God said to Moses in substance: 'I will show Pharaoh who I am. Now you shall see what I will do to Pharaoh.' (Ex. 6:1) The oppression and injustice heaped upon the people of Israel in the land of Egypt furnished God an opportunity to make a demonstration of his power, and to testify again to man that the Lord is the almighty and eternal God and that he is the God of justice, wisdom, love and power. The people had forgotten God, and now the time had come for God to go down into Egypt and through his visible representatives *to make for himself a name.* Afterwards the prophet, referring to this event in Egypt, wrote: "And what one nation in the earth is like thy people, even like Israel, whom

God went to redeem for a people to himself, and to make him a name, and to do for you great things and terrible, for thy land, before thy people, which thou redeemedst to thee from Egypt, from the nations and their gods?" (2 Sam. 7:23) Then God said to Moses: "And the Egyptians shall know that I am the Lord, when I stretch forth mine hand upon Egypt, and bring out the children of Israel from among them." —Ex. 7:5.

In carrying out his purposes God again sent Moses and Aaron in before the king of Egypt and requested that the people might be permitted to leave Egypt. This was refused. Then God sent plagues upon Egypt. The river was turned into blood. There came a plague of frogs, lice and flies. Pharaoh would repent and promise to let the children of Israel leave Egypt, only again to become arrogant and refuse to let them go.

Then God said to Moses: "Yet will I bring one plague more upon Pharaoh, and upon Egypt; afterwards he will let you go hence: when he shall let you go, he shall surely thrust you out hence altogether." (Ex. 11:1) The Lord now began to make preparation for a great demonstration by which he would teach the people and all others of his intelligent creatures that he is the great Jehovah God. He directed Moses to call together the leaders of Israel and instruct them that each family should on the tenth day of Nisan, the first month, take up from the flock a lamb without blemish, a male of the first year, that they should keep this lamb up until the fourteenth day of that month, and then it should be killed and the blood sprinkled upon the doorposts and over the door. This was arranged as a protection to the Israelites who would observe this law. "For I will pass through the land of Egypt this night, and will smite all the firstborn in the land of Egypt, both man and beast; and against all the gods of Egypt I will execute judgment: I am the Lord. And the blood shall be to you for a token upon the houses where ye are: and when I see the blood, I will pass over you, and the plague shall not be upon you to destroy you, when I smite the land of Egypt."—Ex. 12:12, 13.

Moses caused the Israelites to carry out the instructions, and everything was made in readiness for the night. Each family that had taken up the lamb and had sprinkled the blood on the doorposts went inside and waited. On that eventful night, when the arrogant king and the other Egyptian subjects of the Devil who trusted in the wicked gods for protection were sleeping, apparently in security and peace, the great God of the universe caused his angel to pass over the land and cast down their false gods and smite with death every one of the firstborn of Egypt. None were spared except those of the Israelites who had obeyed the Lord by sprinkling the blood over the doorposts. The smiting included both man-child and beast, even from the son of the king to the humblest in the land. At midnight the king arose and found his firstborn silent in death. The alarm was given and a great cry and wail went up from all the people all over the land, because there was not one house of all the Egyptians where there was not one dead.

The king called for Moses and Aaron and commanded that they and all their children leave the land immediately. "Also take your flocks and your herds, as ye have said, and be gone; and bless me also. And the Egyptians were urgent upon the people, that they might send them out of the land in haste; for they said, We be all dead men." (Ex. 12:32,33) Thus God, true to his word, gave Pharaoh the king ample reason to know who is God, in answer to his arrogant and disdainful question. (Ex. 5:2) The Lord had smitten and destroyed all the Egyptians' images and false gods throughout the land, and had filled the land of Egypt with grief and woe. It is recorded: "For the Egyptians buried all their firstborn, which the Lord had smitten among them: upon their gods also the Lord executed judgments."—Num. 33:4.

Seemingly this terrible disaster which befell all the firstborn of Egypt, and which threw down and destroyed all their false gods, would have been a sufficient lesson to Pharaoh, and even to his superlord the Devil, that it is useless to fight against God. But the egotism and arrogance of the wicked one seemingly know no limitation. God knew what would be in the heart of Pharaoh, and what Satan would induce him to do. He purposed now to further teach them a lesson: "That the Egyptians may know that I am the Lord."—Ex. 14:4.

A great multitude of Israelites, the men alone totaling 600,000, camped on the shores of the Red Sea. After the king of Egypt had mourned a time for his dead son, and awakened to the fact that the Israelites had fled, he ordered his army of chariots and men to follow the Israelites and destroy them. The Egyptians came upon the Israelites encamped. The Israelites were greatly afraid, and cried unto the Lord and reproached Moses for having brought them there to be slain by the Egyptians. "And Moses said unto the people, Fear ye not, stand still, and see the salvation of the Lord, which he will shew to you to day: for the Egyptians whom ye have seen to day, ye shall see them again no more for ever. The Lord shall fight for you, and ye shall hold your peace."—Ex. 14:13, 14.

And now behold the mighty power of God. He caused his angel to go before the camp of Israel and to cause the pillar of cloud to stand between the Israelites and the Egyptians, but he gave light to the Israelites. Then Moses, at the command of the Lord, "stretched out his hand over the sea; and the Lord caused the sea to go back by a strong east wind all that night, and made the sea dry land, and the waters were divided".—Ex. 14:21-31.

Having been safely delivered on the eastern shores of the Red Sea, saved from the hordes of the Egyptians, the children of Israel sang a song of deliverance. "Then sang Moses and the children of Israel this song unto the Lord, and spake, saying, I will sing unto the Lord, for he hath triumphed gloriously: the horse and his rider hath he thrown into the sea. The Lord is my strength and song, and he is become my salvation: he is my God, and I will prepare him an habitation; my father's God, and I will exalt him. The Lord is a man of war: the Lord is his name." —Ex. 15:1-3.

Thus ended the Devil's first world power. Like a mighty millstone it was cast into the sea. Thus God executed his judgment against the false gods and magnified his own name. (Ex. 12:12) The Lord purposed that the people should ever remember that day for their good. To this end he caused his prophets to make record of that great event for his own good purposes:

"And Jethro said, Blessed be the Lord, who hath delivered you out of the hand of the Egyptians, and out of the hand of Pharaoh, who hath delivered the people from under the hand of the Egyptians. Now I know that the Lord is greater than all gods: for in the thing wherein they dealt proudly he was above them."—Ex. 18:10, 11.

"Thou, even thou, art Lord alone: thou hast made heaven, the heaven of heavens, with all their host, the earth, and all things that are therein, the seas, and all that is therein, and thou preservest them all; and the host of heaven worshippeth thee. And didst see the affliction of our fathers in Egypt; and heardest their cry by the Red sea; and shewedst signs and wonders upon Pharaoh, and on all his servants, and on all the people of his land; for thou knewest that they dealt proudly against them. So didst thou get thee a name, as it is this day."—Neh. 9:6, 9, 10.

"Nevertheless, *he saved them for his name's sake, that he might make his mighty power to be known.*" —Ps. 106:8.

Jehovah was good to the nation and people of Egypt through the ministration of his faithful servant Joseph. The Egyptians failed to appreciate that goodness and refused to take heed to God, but followed after the Devil and his representatives. God expressed his indignation against Satan and the world power he had builded, and at the same time made a picture of greater things to come.

Egypt was typical of the end of the world, and pictured the present organization of world powers which shall go down in a terrible time of trouble. (Rev. 18:21-24) God's goodness has been wonderfully made manifest to the peoples of this world. His goodness has been spurned, and this has been done at the instance of Satan the enemy. What befell Egypt shall be repeated, only on a far greater scale.—Matt. 24:21, 22.

But why should God kill the firstborn of Egypt and then overwhelm the entire army in the sea? Was that done merely to express the vengeance of God, and was it done for a selfish reason? There was no selfishness on God's part whatsoever. Life is a gift from God. (Rom. 6:23) All the human race, because of Adam's sin, live only by the grace of God and without any right to live. The firstborns of Egypt, of course, came within this rule. God's purpose provided that in the future he would awaken these out of death and give them individually an opportunity for life under favorable conditions. The heart of each one of the governing factors of Egypt was closely attached to his firstborn. The death of the firstborn, as a punishment for their defiance of God, would show these governing factors of Egypt that their gods were false gods and had no power to give them life, and no power or ability to stand before the great Jehovah God.

These scriptures above quoted declare that this great demonstration of power was that God might get for himself a name. In whose mind did God desire to magnify himself and make for himself a name? Not in the mind of the Devil, because the Devil had gone on in the way of wickedness in utter defiance of God and was then under the sentence of death. It was in the minds of the people of Israel that God desired to establish a name for himself. He had selected that people as his own and would now use them for his own purposes. It was therefore for their benefit, and for the benefit of all the peoples of God who should come after, that God performed this marvelous act.

Let the people take notice that Jehovah is the Almighty God and that the destruction of Egypt was but one of the steps in the outworking of his great purpose. As the peoples of earth learn that the power of Almighty God operates always in exact harmony with love, and for the benefit of mankind, then they will learn to love and obey and serve him and will receive from the Eternal One the blessings which he has provided for all those that do manifest their love and obedience for him.

God had saved the firstborn of each household of the Israelites because of the faith and obedience of their fathers. This should serve as a lesson to them that ever thereafter they should render obedience to the true and loving God. Would they do it?

Chapter VII

# *The Typical Organization*

AN ORGANIZATION is a systematic arrangement to carry into operation a fixed purpose. "Known unto God are all his works, from the beginning of the world." (Acts 15:18) Having a fixed purpose from the beginning God would of course have a systematic arrangement of his creatures for the carrying of that purpose into operation. (1 Cor. 14:40) The very creation of God testifies that he does everything in order and with proper organization. "The heavens declare the glory of God: and the firmament sheweth his handywork. Day unto day uttereth speech, and night unto night sheweth knowledge. There is no speech nor language, where their voice is not heard. Their line is gone out through all the earth, and their words to the end of the world. In them hath he set a tabernacle for the sun."—Ps. 19:1-4.

Order is one of the hardest lessons for creatures to learn. A deflection from God's way is displeasing to him. Deflections of the human race are usually caused by weakness and by being overreached by others. A wilful and deliberate going contrary to the Lord's appointed way is treason.

Humility means to be submissive to God and to follow his appointed ways. Humility is the very opposite of pride. "Pride goeth before destruction, and an haughty spirit before a fall." (Prov. 16:18) God pushes the proud away from him, and shows his favor only to the humble-minded. (1 Pet. 5:5) He who joyfully conforms himself to the way of God proves his love for God. (1 John 5:3) We may be absolutely certain that the all-wise God has one way for carrying his purpose into action. It would be inconsistent for him to have divers ways. It has ever been the policy of the Devil to induce men to believe that they have a sufficient amount of initiative and wisdom to make their own arrangement, and to carry it out without reference to the Word of God. Those who follow such a course come to grief. "Great peace have they which love thy [God's] law: and nothing shall offend them." (Ps. 119:165) Nor shall they be turned away from God's organization and purpose. If they love the Lord's way and joyfully seek to do it they will trust him implicitly, and thus doing will enjoy the peace of God that passeth the understanding of men. The evidence is overwhelming and absolutely conclusive that God has a purpose. Man must learn God's systematic method of organization for carrying his purpose into operation. This is what we are here studying. Man should not spend all his time in trying to learn if God has a purpose. That should be easily understood. Man should devote himself to ascertaining how God is carrying out his purpose, and then get himself in exact harmony with God's way and joyfully follow therein.

From the time of Eden until the overthrow of Egypt the great lesson God was impressing upon the minds of his willing and obedient ones was that the Lord is the Almighty God, in whom are vested wisdom, justice, love and power, in equal and exact balance. He selected the descendants of Jacob, otherwise called Israel, and organized that people into a nation in furtherance of his own fixed purpose. The first lesson that he taught the Israelites was that the Lord is God. For their benefit he got himself a name when he overcame the Egyptians and overthrew their false gods. The lessons given Israel were for their benefit and for those who should follow thereafter.

A shadow is a reflected image, as from a mirror or from the clear surface of still water. It is the representation of something real. The word "type" is sometimes used in a similar sense. It is a figure or representation of something to come. God's dealing with the nation of Israel, and particularly in the law which he gave to that people, was to foreshadow better things coming later. As Paul puts it: "Which are a shadow of things to come," (Col. 2:17) and, "For the law, having a shadow of good things to come." (Heb. 10:1) Referring then to the experiences of Israel the record is: "Now all these things happened unto them for ensamples: and they are written for our admonition, upon whom the ends of the world are come." (1 Cor. 10:11) Based upon these and corroborative scriptures the conclusion is reached that the nation of Israel, organized by the Lord, was his typical organization and foreshadowed something better to follow in God's due time. For this reason the Lord's dealings with Israel hold the greatest interest to all who desire life and who would know God's way of leading men to life and happiness.

The beginning of God's typical organization was Abraham, who was first called Abram. He was the grandfather of Jacob, afterwards called Israel. He is known as the father of the faithful. He was counted a righteous man and the friend of God. As a man he was imperfect, of course, being one of the descendants of Adam; but his heart was right and he believed on and served God, and therefore his faith was counted for righteousness.—Rom. 4:9, 24.

Abram resided with his father Terah in Ur of the Chaldees. Only two generations had passed since Adam's death, and by tradition Abram would learn of Adam's wrongful course. He would learn about Abel, and also how God rewarded the faith of Enoch. He would learn, too, that it was the faith of Noah that caused God to save him from the flood and to use him to again begin to people the earth. The young man Abram chose the way of faith and trust in the Lord God. (Gen. 12:1-3) In obedience to God's command Abram left the land of his nativity and journeyed to the strange land then occupied by the Canaanites and hence known as the land of Canaan. (Gen. 12:5) Then Abram journeyed on to the south part of the country. There was a famine in that land, and Abram went down into Egypt.

To Abram God had made the promise that he should have a seed, and that through him and his seed the blessings of all the families of the earth should come. The Devil hated that seed. (Gen. 3:15) Doubtless he knew of the promise made to Abram. He therefore began to devise a scheme to have the wife of Abram debauched by Pharaoh, one of Satan's own servants, and thus compel God to either accept this unholy offspring as the seed or else repudiate his own word. Satan so arranged it that the princes of Pharaoh would see the beautiful wife of Abram, and then go to Pharaoh and commend her to the king who, to gratify his lust, would be an easy tool to carry out the Devil's scheme. (Gen. 12:15-17) Accordingly Pharaoh had Sarah, the beautiful wife of Abram, brought into his palace, intending to gratify himself. But the Lord God protected Abram and Sarah by bringing great plagues upon the house of Pharaoh; and the king, becoming alarmed, sent Sarah away undefiled. Thus failed another wicked scheme of Satan.

Abram then returned to the land of Canaan, and God again made promise to him that he should have that land for himself and for his seed after him. (Gen. 13:15) When Abram was ninety-nine years old God appeared unto him and said: "I am the Almighty God: walk before me, and be thou perfect. Neither shall thy name any more be called Abram, but thy name shall be Abraham; for a father of many nations have I made thee. And I will make thee exceeding fruitful, and I will make nations of thee, and kings shall come out of thee. And I will establish my covenant between me and thee, and thy seed after thee, in their generations, for an everlasting covenant, to be a God unto thee, and to thy seed after thee. And I will give unto thee and to thy seed after thee, the land wherein thou art a stranger, all the land of Canaan, for an everlasting possession; and I will be their God."—Gen. 17:1, 5-8.

Ever on the alert to thwart the purposes of the Lord, again Satan made an attempt to have Sarah, the wife of Abraham, debauched that the promised seed might be defiled. Again God thwarted the wicked one's purpose.—Gen. 20:1-7.

When Sarah had passed the time according to women, and Abraham was one hundred years old, God overruled these seemingly unfavorable conditions and caused Sarah to conceive and bear a son; and he was named Isaac. The Lord made the promise then to Abraham: "In Isaac shall thy seed be called." (Gen. 21:1, 12) That Isaac foreshadowed 'the seed of promise' through whom the blessings must come to mankind is clearly stated by the divine record. See Galatians 3:8, 16; 4:22-28.

At this point God made a living picture which foreshadowed the unfolding of a part of his purpose. In this picture Abraham was used to represent God, while Isaac was used to represent the only begotten and beloved Son of God, who was afterwards called by the name Jesus. Abraham's offering of Isaac upon the altar foreshadowed that the Son of God would be offered as a great sacrifice to provide a sin-offering for the benefit of the world, to the end that in God's due time the peoples of the earth might be delivered from the enemy, from his wicked influence and from his wrongful acts which had brought death upon the human race. Abraham did not understand what the picture meant. With him it was purely a matter of faith. God commanded him what to do, and that he did. It was a test of Abraham's faith, but he bravely met the test and God rewarded his faith.

In making this picture the Lord God directed Abraham to take Isaac, his only son, whom he loved dearly and in whom he had all his hopes centered, and to go to Mount Moriah and there offer up his son as a burnt offering. Because God had told Abraham that "in Isaac shall thy seed be called" and that the blessings shall come through him, this was a crucial test to offer up as a sacrifice this only son. In obedience to the Lord's command Abraham provided wood for the altar, fire, and a knife; and with this provision he and his son journeyed to Mount Moriah. Abraham built the altar, laid the wood in order, bound his son Isaac and laid him on the altar upon the wood, and then stretched forth his hand and took the knife to slay his son. In another instant the knife would fall and his son would be dead. God's purpose here was to test and prove Abraham's faith. Abraham having met the test, the Lord God arrested the hand that would have slain the son. The record reads:

"And the angel of the Lord called unto him out of heaven, and said, Abraham, Abraham: and he said, Here am I. And he said, Lay not thine hand upon the lad, neither do thou any thing unto him: for now I know that thou fearest God, seeing thou hast not withheld thy son, thine only son, from me. And Abraham lifted up his eyes, and looked, and, behold, behind him a ram caught in a thicket by his horns; and Abraham went and took the ram, and offered him up for a burnt offering in the stead of his son. And Abraham called the name of that place Jehovah-jireh: as it is said to this day, In the mount of the Lord it shall be seen. And the angel of the Lord called unto Abraham out of heaven the second time, and said, By myself have I sworn, saith the Lord; for because thou hast done this thing, and hast not withheld thy son, thine only son; that in blessing I will bless thee, and in multiplying I will multiply thy seed as the stars of the heaven, and as the sand which is upon the sea shore; and thy seed shall possess the gate of his enemies: and in thy seed shall all the nations of the earth be blessed: because thou hast obeyed my voice." (Gen. 22:11-18) The shadow made by this picture was afterwards carried out in every particular.—John 3:16, 17.

Afterwards Rebecca became the wife of Isaac, and Rebecca was barren. Then Isaac entreated the Lord for his wife, and Rebecca conceived. Twin sons were born and were named Esau and Jacob. God made it clear that Jacob should succeed to the promise, and that through him should the seed for the blessing of mankind come. Satan, alert to acts of wickedness and following his usual course, devised a scheme to have Esau kill his brother Jacob. (Gen. 27:42, 43) Jacob fled into the land of Haran. On the way he slept on a hill, afterwards called Bethel. For a pillow he used a stone, for a mattress the bare ground, and for a covering the canopy of heaven above. While he slept the Lord appeared unto him in a dream and said to him: "I am the Lord God of Abraham thy father, and the God of Isaac: the land whereon thou liest, to thee will I give it, and to thy seed; and thy seed shall be as the dust of the earth; and thou shalt spread abroad to the west, and to the east, and to the north, and to the south: and in thee and in thy seed shall all the families of the earth be blessed. And, behold, I am with thee, and will keep thee in all places whither thou goest, and will bring thee again into this land; for I will not leave thee, until I have done that which I have spoken to thee of."—Gen. 28:13-15.

It was this same Jacob whose son Joseph was sold into Egypt and later became the ruler of that land, and gave a witness in the name of the Lord God.

It was this same Jacob who was the father of the great multitude of Israelites whom God miraculously delivered from Egypt. From that day to this God caused a chain of events to picture and foreshadow the gradual unfolding of his great purpose, pointing to the Savior of the world who shall deliver from the enemy and from his wicked influence every one of the human race who will show faithfulness unto God.

Jacob had twelve sons, and they became the heads of the twelve tribes or divisions of the nation of Israel. Jacob grew old, and the time came for him to die. He called before him his sons and, his mind being moved upon by the invisible power of God, he uttered this great prophecy: "The sceptre shall not depart from Judah, nor a lawgiver from between his feet, until Shiloh come; and unto him shall the gathering of the people be."—Gen. 49: 10.

"Scepter" means the right to rule. "Lawgiver" means one who shall guide the people in the way that they shall go, who shall shield and protect them and teach them the way to life. "Shiloh" means the Messiah, or great Deliverer. "Unto him shall the gathering of the people be." Thus the Lord God caused a prophecy to be uttered by Jacob, foretelling the coming of him who would undo the wicked work of the Devil and who would do also that which Lucifer should have done when he was perfect, before iniquity was found in him.

### LAW COVENANT

We left the children of Israel standing safe on the eastern shores of the Red Sea, singing a song of deliverance from Egypt. (Ex. 15: 1-21) Three months later they were in the desert land of Sinai. Moses, whom God had used as their deliverer from Egypt, went up into the mountain; and there the Lord God said unto him: "Thus shalt thou say to the house of Jacob, and tell the children of Israel: Ye have seen what I did unto the Egyptians, and how I bare you on eagles' wings, and brought you unto myself. Now therefore, if ye will obey my voice indeed, and keep my covenant, then ye shall be a peculiar treasure unto me above all people: for all the earth is mine. And ye shall be unto me a kingdom of priests, and an holy nation. These are the words which thou shalt speak unto the children of Israel. And Moses came and called for the elders of the people, and laid before their faces all these words which the Lord commanded him. And all the people answered together, and said, All that the Lord hath spoken we will do. And Moses returned the words of the people unto the Lord."—Ex. 19:3-8.

On the third day thereafter God confirmed the law covenant which he had made with Israel in Egypt at the time of the passover; and now he gave to them specific laws which should be their guide, amongst which is the following: "And God spake all these words, saying, I am the Lord thy God, which have brought thee out of the land of Egypt, out of the house of bondage. *Thou shalt have no other gods before me.* Thou shalt not make unto thee any graven image, or any likeness of any thing that is in heaven above, or that is in the earth beneath, or that is in the water under the earth: thou shalt not bow down thyself to them, nor serve them: for I the Lord thy God am a jealous God, visiting the iniquity of the fathers upon the children unto the third and fourth generation of them that hate me; and shewing mercy unto thousands of them that love me, and keep my commandments. Thou shalt not take the name of the Lord thy God in vain; for the Lord will not hold him guiltless that taketh his name in vain."—Ex. 20:1-7.

Emphasis is here laid upon the point that God provided by this covenant, and the law thereof, that the people should have no other gods besides him; that they should make no graven images, and should not bow down to them nor serve them. What was the moving cause for this law? Was it because Jehovah feared that his adversary, his disloyal son the Devil, would get the worship to which he, the Lord, was entitled? Was it selfishness on the part of God that moved him thus to provide by the law that there should be no other gods? No! None of these reasons is correct. The Devil has made many men believe that it was selfishness that induced Jehovah to act, but this is not true. God had already demonstrated his unlimited power and his ability to destroy the creatures of heaven and earth, including Satan the Devil, whensoever he might desire. It is impossible for God to fear. Then why did he make this provision in the law? The Lord God knew that the insatiable desire of Satan was, and is, that he might have the worship of other creatures. He knew that if the people followed after Satan they would be led into wickedness and must die. Surely the great flood and the destruction of the Egyptians were sufficient to prove this to all reasonable creatures. "As I live, saith the Lord God, I have no pleasure in the death of the wicked."—Ezek. 33:11.

The delight of the Lord was not in the destruction of the wicked ones. He would teach an all-important lesson to his intelligent creatures. He would have the people believe and understand that the one way that leads to life and happiness is by doing good, and that none can do good who are out of harmony with the great Eternal Good One. The love of God for mankind provided the law covenant, and particularly the command that the Israelites should have no other gods besides him.

God has now used the Israelites to make shadows or pictures of his great purpose of salvation. His purpose provides for a mighty Deliverer, and he had given his word that this mighty One would come through the seed of Israel. Without some protection thrown about the people of Israel, Satan would overreach them, turn them away from God, and that people would lose the blessings which God had provided for them; namely, an opportunity of being the line through which the great Deliverer should come. God therefore made his law to shield and protect the Israelites, and to serve as their teacher; to lead them in the right way until the coming of the great and mighty One who should deliver the peoples from the oppressor. The promised blessings could not come through the law covenant, but the law was necessary to hold the Jews in line and keep them in a right attitude of mind and heart to accept the Heir through whom the blessings must come. In discussing this point Paul says:

"For if the inheritance be of the law, it is no more of promise: but God gave it to Abraham by promise. Wherefore then serveth the law? It was added because of transgressions, till the seed should come to whom the promise was made; and it was ordained by angels in the hand of a mediator."—Gal. 3:18, 19.

SHADOWS

The law that God gave to Israel had its beginning in Egypt at the time of the passover. That law directed that a lamb should be taken for the purpose of sacrifice, and that the lamb should be one without blemish. At a specific time it was to be slain, and its blood sprinkled upon the doorpost and over the door, and this blood was to serve as a protection to the first-born of that household during the night of the passover, and would also furnish a basis for the deliverance of the people from the Egyptians on the day following.

This foreshadowed something better to come. The lamb foreshadowed the One who should become the great Redeemer of mankind, to take away the sin of the world. When Jesus came he was the antitypical Lamb. The prophet John the Baptist said of him at the beginning of the Master's ministry: "Behold the Lamb of God, which taketh away the sin of the world." (John 1:29) The law which provided for the passover therefore pointed to Christ. The passover must be observed once each year. When Christ Jesus died upon the cross he was the great antitypical passover lamb who died once for all, thereby providing the great redemptive price for all mankind.—Heb. 10:10; 2:9.

The law required the Israelites once each year to perform their atonement day sacrifice service, and this was a shadow of better things to come. For this purpose the law directed Moses to have built in the wilderness a tabernacle. It consisted of a tent lined with boards, and built in two compartments designated the "holy" and the "most holy". It was surrounded by a wall of curtains, the enclosure of which was known as the "court". On the atonement day the high priest was required to slay a bullock in the court and to take the blood of that bullock in a vessel, with incense and a censer of fire, and go into the most holy and there sprinkle the incense upon the fire before the mercy seat, and then to sprinkle the blood upon the mercy seat and before the mercy seat seven times.

The account of the atonement day sacrifice is set forth in the sixteenth chapter of Leviticus. The blood of the bullock thus offered was for a sin-offering, as it is written: "And Aaron shall offer his bullock of the sin offering, which is for himself, and make an atonement for himself, and for his house." (Lev. 16:6) Then the priest was required to take a goat, known as the Lord's goat, and kill it and use its blood as a sin-offering, taking it into the most holy the same as was done with the blood of the bullock; and that constituted the sin-offering for the people. This sacrificing ceremony was performed once each year. It foreshadowed the great sin-offering that would be made in the future on behalf of the people. The tabernacle was merely a pattern or figure, foreshadowing a better thing.—Heb. 9:1-24.

Paul, in his epistle to the Hebrews, particularly in the ninth chapter, tells us that the tabernacle was a pattern of heaven itself; also that the sacrifices of the animals represent the blood of Christ Jesus, who offered himself without spot to God for the great redemptive price of mankind. It is not the purpose to here discuss in full the meaning and significance of the atonement day sacrifices. A discussion of this can be found at length in *Creation,* a book published by the publishers of this volume. The purpose now and here is to show that the atonement day sacrifices required by the law were merely shadows of better things to come, proving that Israel was a typical people and that they, being organized by God, constituted God's typical organization.

Moses was the mediator of that law covenant. That Moses was a type or shadow of a greater One to come he himself testifies when he states: "The Lord thy God will raise up unto thee a Prophet from the midst of thee, of thy brethren, like unto me; unto him ye shall hearken. I will raise them up a Prophet from among their brethren, like unto thee, and will put my words in his mouth; and he shall speak unto them all that I shall command him."—Deut. 18:15, 18.

This law covenant foreshadowed that God will make a new covenant and that the Lord Jesus Christ will be the Mediator of that covenant, and through him the blessings of the people shall come.—Hebrews, chapters eight and nine.

God's purpose in using the Israelites was that he might through them make types foreshadowing the outworking of his great arrangement for the redemption and deliverance of the human family. All other nations of the earth were under the control of Satan, worshiping the Devil or some of the Devil's workmanship. Without a shield or protection, and without a teacher to keep them in the right way, Satan would overreach the Israelites; and the whole world would again be turned to wickedness. Unless the Israelites had faith in God and worshiped him alone they would have no protection, and no teacher to guide them. Hence God gave to that people his law and commanded that they should have no other gods besides him. With them the Lord God established the true religion, and that for their own good. God had made his purpose and given his word that it should be performed. He must keep his word inviolate and carry out that purpose as made.—Isa. 55:11; 46:11.

God's dignity would preclude him from commanding any creature to worship him for his own good. He owed the human race nothing. Strictly adhering to justice God would have wiped the human race completely out of existence, but his love for man led him to make provision for man's deliverance; and having made it, he will carry it out. The reason for the law covenant with Israel may therefore be summed up as follows: (a) It was made for the good of the people, and as a schoolmaster to lead them in the right way until the coming of the Redeemer; (b) to prove to the people and to all mankind that no one can get the blessings of life by his own efforts; and (c) to prove the necessity of a great Redeemer, Mediator and Deliverer.

For forty years God led the children of Israel through the wilderness before they were permitted to enter into the land of Canaan. During that period they had opportunities to learn many lessons. Their experience in the wilderness, under the leadership of Moses, was typical; foreshadowing the experiences of Christians who follow in the footsteps of Christ Jesus during the wilderness period of the Christian era, during which time the Gentiles have been in power, ruling under the supervision of the god of this world, to wit, Satan the Devil. (2 Cor. 4:3, 4) At the end of that period of forty years the Israelites entered into Canaan, now Palestine, and there the Lord continued to deal with them and use them to make shadows of better things to come pertaining to his kingdom and his manner of bringing deliverance and blessings to the people.

In due course God permitted the Israelites to have a king. Saul was anointed as the first king of that people. After a brief reign he was commanded by the Lord to go and destroy the Amalekites, one of the representative tribes of the Devil's arrangement. The Amalekites had opposed God's chosen people when they were marching to Canaan. The Devil had induced them to do so and used them for that purpose. Their wickedness had now come to the full.

Saul failed and refused to carry out the instructions of the Lord, although he pretended to do so. Because of his disobedience he was rejected from being king. Samuel, the prophet, speaking as the mouthpiece of the Lord, said unto Saul: "Hath the Lord as great delight in burnt offerings and sacrifices, as in obeying the voice of the Lord? Behold, to obey is better than sacrifice, and to hearken than the fat of rams. For rebellion is as the sin of witchcraft, and stubbornness is as iniquity and idolatry. Because thou hast rejected the word of the Lord, he hath also rejected thee from being king."—1 Sam. 15:22, 23.

Being rejected of the Lord, Saul thereafter sought solace and comfort at the hands of the Devil by communing with the Devil's colleagues, the wicked spirits. (1 Sam. 28:6-11) Saul's experience represents and foreshadows that of the nominal, or so-called "Christian", churches. As declared by the Prophet Jeremiah, God planted the church a noble vine and today we see it degenerated into a strange vine of the earth. (Jer. 2:21-23) The so-called "Christian" churches, the systems, have forsaken the Lord and have joined hands with the Devil; and now they seek solace at his hand by communing with the wicked spirits. These systems are confusing to the people, as their name Babylon indicates. They have mixed with all the nations and rulers of the earth and have made them confused with their false doctrines. Concerning them it is written: "I will shew unto thee the judgment of the great whore that sitteth upon many waters: with whom the kings of the earth have committed fornication, and the inhabitants of the earth have been made drunk with the wine of her fornication." —Rev. 17:1, 2.

These wicked systems, like their prototype, parade before the people in the name of the Lord to mislead the people. But God has rejected them even as he rejected Saul.

David succeeded Saul as king. "David" means beloved, and foreshadows those who love the Lord and who are faithful to him. The Devil sought in every way possible to kill David because he was faithful to God. David was not a perfect man, yet it is written that God called him "a man after mine own heart". (Acts 13:22) This was because of David's faithfulness to the Lord. Whenever he, because of weakness, had committed a wrong he was quick to confess it to God and to ask for forgiveness; and under all circumstances he faithfully represented the Lord. He foreshadowed the true Christians, fighting the good fight of faith and refusing to compromise in any manner with the Devil or any part of the Devil's organization. After David came the peaceable and glorious reign of Solomon, which foreshadowed the peaceful and glorious reign of the great Prince of Peace, the Christ in glory.

God's dealing with Israel over a long period of time was also to use that people as witnesses for him. Many times Israel was unfaithful to the Lord and turned away from him, and many times they cried unto him and he heard the cry and delivered them out of the hands of their enemies. These experiences foreshadow how the Lord, in the exercise of his loving-kindness, will in due time deliver all the human race that call upon his name and serve him.

Zion is the name of God's universal organization. Any part of that organization is properly called Zion. When Israel was in harmony with God, and when they were the people of God, that nation was a part of God's organization, and therefore called Zion. When Israel was carried away captive to Babylon and her people were asked to sing a song of Zion, they wept when they remembered Zion and recalled how blessed were that people when they were a part of God's organization and obeyed him.—Ps. 137:1-3.

The people of Israel, organized into a nation and entered into a covenant with God, were typical of the true Zion which God has chosen as his dwelling place and out of which he shines. (Ps. 132:13; 50:2) Of course the enemy Satan has always opposed Zion. He corrupted the chosen people of God from time to time by inducing them to worship devils and to turn away from the true God. Being in a covenant with God and departing therefrom to worship idols was an illicit relationship with the wicked ones. This the Lord denounced as harlotry with other gods, and for this he punished them. But when Israel repented and returned, and asked for forgiveness, the Lord restored that people to his favor. (Jer. 3: 1-12) God knew that Satan induced them to turn away from him, and he showed his loving mercy toward them. Time and time again when the Israelites had been overreached by the Devil and were hard pressed by the enemy, they cried unto the Lord; and he heard and delivered them out of the hands of their enemies. See Judges, chapters six and seven.

While the greater number of the Israelites were unfaithful to the Lord, there never was a time from the day that Israel was delivered out of Egypt until the coming of Christ Jesus that the Lord God was without some faithful witness in the earth. Some of that typical people remained true to the Lord until the coming of the mighty One of whom Moses was a type.

## Chapter VIII

# *Arrogance Rebuked*

THE manifest purpose of Satan at all times has been to reproach Jehovah. God has permitted him to go so far and then no further. In his own good time the Lord God has rebuked the Devil, not for the benefit of that wicked one, but for the benefit of the people, that they might not all entirely forget that there exists the Almighty, the Creator of heaven and earth.

At stated times Satan has organized world powers, and the predominant features of these disclose his method of organization against God. Egypt excelled in wealth and military power. Her rulers at times were exceedingly presumptuous. God administered severe rebuke to her presumptuous ruler, as hereinbefore stated. Assyria, another great nation, worshiped the devil gods and reproached Jehovah, and was a mighty political power. Babylon the Great, as the Scriptures seem to clearly point out, particularly magnifies the ecclesiastical element of the Devil's organization. It will be observed that in all these world powers the ruling factors consisted of three elements; to wit, commercial, political and ecclesiastical. In each of these world powers the commercial, the political or the ecclesiastical element was made specially prominent, and each one opposed Jehovah. With Egypt the commercial power was the greatest; with Assyria the political power excelled; with Babylon the ecclesiastical element was to the fore.

God's prophet Daniel likens world powers to wild beasts, and by the same symbol the powers are known or designated in Revelation. There could be no more fitting symbol than "beast" for a world power, because the history of each shows that it has been beastly, cruel and oppressive; and each one has been used by the Devil to reproach Jehovah God. Of course all these world powers have had visible rulers, but their real ruler or god has been Satan the Devil. There has been but one nation on earth that could not properly be included in this category of beastly powers; to wit, the nation of Israel. It was organized by Jehovah for the benefit of the people to illustrate God's purpose concerning all the peoples of the earth. Israel failed because of unfaithfulness to God, and then Satan became the god of the entire world. All these world powers or governments have been instruments in the hands of the wicked one and in some form have opposed the development of God's purpose of salvation.

At times it might have seemed that the powers of wickedness had completely overwhelmed and defeated the God of righteousness. But not so. The Almighty has permitted Satan and his angels to pursue a course of wickedness without let or hindrance until such time as he sees it is good, and therefore necessary, to interfere and manifest his power, that the people might not entirely forget his name. In all these world powers the three elements mentioned, to wit, commercial, political and ecclesiastical, have appeared prominently. In these latter times the three elements, under the supervision of the Devil, have united in forming the most subtle and wicked world power of all time. They operate under the title of "Christendom", which is a fraudulent and blasphemous assumption that they constitute Christ's kingdom on earth.

Hypocrisy first made its appearance in the time of Enos, when the people first called themselves by the name of the Lord; but it remained for the latter days, where we now are, to witness the greatest demonstration of hypocrisy that has ever been on earth. This parades under the title of "Christendom", and by it Satan has deceived millions of people to believe that this fraudulent organization is the political expression of God's kingdom on earth.

Egypt, Assyria and Babylon, each in turn, had their rebuke from Jehovah God. The Scriptures clearly indicate that Christendom, the most powerful and subtle of the Devil's organization, is destined to receive the most complete rebuke that has ever been administered to any power; and with its complete fall Satan shall be bound that he may deceive the nations no more. At different times throughout the ages God has administered rebukes to Satan's institutions; but these have merely foreshadowed the great, tremendous and overwhelming rebuke that shall shortly end Satan's rule on earth.

In this chapter the purpose is to call attention to the presumption and arrogance of one of Satan's representatives and visible rulers, an ancient Assyrian king, and to the terrible rebuke which the Lord administered to him. This circumstance marks a progressive step in the unfolding of the divine purpose and enables the student to have a better appreciation of what to expect to take place in the great and terrible day of God Almighty which is impending and immediately about to fall. That we may have some intimation of God's expressed indignation against arrogance and presumptuousness, attention is here called to the rebuke that he administered to Sennacherib, the Assyrian king.

Hezekiah was then king of Israel, the chosen people of God. Prior to his reign the king of Assyria had besieged and taken Samaria, and had laid hold on and carried away many Israelites as captives. God permitted this to happen to the Israelites because they had forgotten him and gone a whoring after the Devil and his gods. Hezekiah "did that which was right in the sight of the Lord, according to all that David his father did. He removed the high places, and brake the images, and cut down the groves, and brake in pieces the brazen serpent that Moses had made: for unto those days the children of Israel did burn incense to it: and he called it Nehushtan. He trusted in the Lord God of Israel; so that after him was none like him among all the kings of Judah, nor any that were before him. For he clave to the Lord, and departed not from following him, but kept his commandments, which the Lord commanded Moses. And the Lord was with him; and he prospered whithersoever he went forth: and he rebelled against the king of Assyria, and served him not. Now, in the fourteenth year of king Hezekiah did Sennacherib king of Assyria come up against all the fenced cities of Judah, and took them".—2 Ki. 18:3-7, 13.

The name Sennacherib means "moon-god", and is a symbol of Satan. This king first directed his efforts to the crushing of the enemies of Assyria; later to Hezekiah king of Judah. Sennacherib attacked the fenced cities of Judah and took them. Then Hezekiah removed the silver and gold from the temple and from the king's house and gave them to Sennacherib, evidently for the purpose of appeasing his wrath and stopping his march on Jerusalem. Surely in this he showed lack of faith in God; but thereafter the Lord forgave him. Sennacherib determined to take Jerusalem; but before beginning the assault he sent messengers up to Jerusalem to deliver a message to King Hezekiah, for the evident purpose of destroying Hezekiah's confidence in God. He believed that he could break down Hezekiah's faith and confidence in Jehovah and that he would cease his rebellion and give his allegiance to the king of Assyria, and then Assyria would control all Palestine.

The messengers of Sennacherib appeared before the walls of Jerusalem and boasted of the great power of their king, and reproached the Almighty God. When Hezekiah heard the insolent message from the Assyrian king he was greatly troubled. He rent his clothes and covered himself with sackcloth, and then he went into the house of the Lord. He called a messenger and sent him to Isaiah the prophet of God with a message that "this day is a day of trouble, and of rebuke, and blasphemy: for the children are come to the birth, and there is not strength to bring forth. It may be the Lord thy God will hear all the words of Rabshakeh, whom the king of Assyria his master hath sent to reproach the living God; and will reprove the words which the Lord thy God hath heard: wherefore lift up thy prayer for the remnant that are left". —2 Ki. 19:3, 4.

The Prophet Isaiah had confidence in God. He trusted him implicitly, and the Lord directed him what to do. And then he sent King Hezekiah this message: "Thus shall ye say to your master, Thus saith the Lord, Be not afraid of the words which thou hast heard, with which the servants of the king of Assyria have blasphemed me. Behold, I will send a blast upon him, and he shall hear a rumour, and shall return to his own land; and I will cause him to fall by the sword in his own land."—2 Ki. 19: 6, 7.

King Hezekiah, being strengthened in faith because of the message received from God's prophet, sent away the messengers of Sennacherib. Then Sennacherib wrote an insolent letter to King Hezekiah and sent his messengers with it to the king of Judah. In this letter he said: "Let not thy God in whom thou trustest deceive thee, saying, Jerusalem shall not be delivered into the hand of the king of Assyria. Behold, thou hast heard what the kings of Assyria have done to all lands, by destroying them utterly; and shalt thou be delivered? Have the gods of the nations delivered them which my fathers have destroyed: as Gozan, and Haran, and Rezeph, and the children of Eden which were in Thelasar?"—2 Ki. 19: 10-12.

Hezekiah received the letter and read it, and then he went up into the house of the Lord and spread the letter before the Lord. In his extremity he laid the whole burden before the Lord and called upon him for needed help. No one has ever thus called upon the Lord without receiving some reward for his faith. "And Hezekiah prayed before the Lord, and said, O Lord God of Israel, which dwellest between the cherubims, thou art the God, even thou alone, of all the kingdoms of the earth; thou hast made heaven and earth. Lord, bow down thine ear, and hear: open,

Lord, thine eyes, and see; and hear the words of Sennacherib, which hath sent him to reproach the living God. Of a truth, Lord, the kings of Assyria have destroyed the nations and their lands, and have cast their gods into the fire: for they were no gods, but the work of men's hands, wood and stone; therefore they have destroyed them. Now therefore, O Lord our God, I beseech thee, save thou us out of his hand, that all the kingdoms of the earth may know that thou art the Lord God, even thou only."—2 Ki. 19:15-19.

Only the Devil could prompt such a contemptuous and insolent letter as that sent by the Assyrian king to Hezekiah. Up to that time there had never been such expressed insolence against Jehovah God. The Devil is the author of all such presumptuousness, arrogance and insolence. The time had come for the Lord Jehovah to rebuke this arrogance, in order that the people might know and keep in mind that he is the great Jehovah. The Lord there directed Isaiah to prophesy against Sennacherib thus:

"Whom hast thou reproached and blasphemed? and against whom hast thou exalted thy voice, and lifted up thine eyes on high? even against the Holy One of Israel. By thy messengers thou hast reproached the Lord, and hast said, With the multitude of my chariots I am come up to the height of the mountains, to the sides of Lebanon, and will cut down the tall cedar trees thereof, and the choice fir trees thereof: and I will enter into the lodgings of his borders, and into the forest of his Carmel. But I know thy abode, and thy going out, and thy coming in, and thy rage against me. Because thy rage against me and thy tumult is come up into mine ears, therefore I will put my hook in thy nose, and my bridle in thy lips, and I will turn thee back by the way by which thou camest. Therefore thus saith the Lord concerning the king of Assyria, He shall not come into this city, nor shoot an arrow there, nor come before it with shield, nor cast a bank against it. By the way that he came, by the same shall he return, and shall not come into this city, saith the Lord. For I will defend this city to save it, for mine own sake, and for my servant David's sake."—2 Ki. 19: 22, 23, 27, 28, 32-34.

Now, because of the faith of Hezekiah in Jehovah God, and because of his refusal to render obedience to the Devil and his representatives, the Lord God gave him assurance that this cruel and presumptuous invader should not prevail; and Hezekiah relied upon the Lord.

There must have been much suppressed excitement in the holy city that night. Before its walls was now encamped a mighty army of warriors under the leadership of a general who had never before known defeat. Inside of the walls the old men of Israel would be looking as best they could to the protection of their wives and little ones; while the younger and more vigorous ones would keep watch on the walls, armed and ready for an attack. With trembling and fear the inhabitants of the city would wait for what might come before the dawn of another day. It was a night of great suspense. Some would have faith in Hezekiah and God's prophet Isaiah, and would believe that the Lord would hear their prayers and would speak to the people through the prophets, and would protect them; while many others would be without faith.

The Lord God pulled the curtains of night about the walls of the holy city, and it lay wrapped in darkness. No one would dare go outside of the walls of the city that night. In the morning, with the first grey streaks of light coming over the eastern horizon, the watchmen on the walls and in the towers would be straining their eyes, expecting with the coming of another day to see the enemy in battle array moving against the city. But to their great amazement and surprise, as they looked they saw no one stirring. There seemed to be no life in the camp of the enemy. With the light of day fully come the sentinels discovered what had come to pass. While the Israelites had waited breathlessly for the assault of the enemy the Lord had stretched out his right hand against the enemy, and now there lay prone in the dust the lifeless bodies of 185,000 of Sennacherib's bravest warriors.

The brief record of the Lord concerning what happened that night is stated in the Scriptures thus: "And it came to pass that night, that the angel of the Lord went out, and smote in the camp of the Assyrians an hundred fourscore and five thousand: and when they arose early in the morning, behold, they were all dead corpses. So Sennacherib king of Assyria departed, and went and returned, and dwelt at Nineveh. And it came to pass, as he was worshipping in the house of Nisroch his god, that Adrammelech and Sharezer his sons smote him with the sword: and they escaped into the land of Armenia. And Esarhaddon his son reigned in his stead."—2 Ki. 19:35-37.

Thus the Lord had expressed his indignation against this great presumption and arrogance, and had given the people another reason to believe that Jehovah is God and that there is none besides him.

For many centuries the Almighty God tenderly led the children of Israel. All the way Satan the enemy tried to interrupt them and turn them away from God. At times Israel would fall away to the Devil and bow to the devil religion and his representatives. The Lord would withdraw his favor from them and permit them to be punished by their enemies. But when they were sorely distressed, and when they repented and cried unto the Lord God for help, he manifested his mercy and loving-kindness toward them and brought them back unto himself. Many times the Lord sent his holy prophets to warn the Israelites of the disaster that would follow their going away after the Devil and his representatives. To offset these warnings, and to deceive the people and oppose God, the Devil would send false prophets who would hypocritically appear before the people in the name of the Lord, claiming to represent Jehovah God and prophesying lies to the people. (Jer. 27:14) Thus is disclosed the policy of Satan, which we can easily trace down to the present time, namely, to have his representatives assume to be the representatives of Jehovah. The Israelites repeatedly refused to obey God. Because of the gross wickedness of that people, God determined to remove his protection from that nation. Before doing so, however, he sent Jeremiah his prophet to warn them against the impending disaster, that they might repent and turn again to him. Satan the enemy at the same time sent amongst the people false prophets, who prophesied contrary to Jeremiah. Then again the Lord God, that his power might be demonstrated to the end that the people might remember and continue to know that he is the only true and living God, thus expressed his disapproval of this wicked prophet: "Then said the prophet Jeremiah unto Hananiah the prophet, Hear now, Hananiah, The Lord hath not sent thee; but thou makest this people to trust in a lie. Therefore thus saith the Lord, Behold, I will cast thee from off the face of the earth: this year thou shalt die, because thou hast taught rebellion against the Lord. So Hananiah the prophet died the same year."—Jer. 28:15-17.

But Satan continued to send his false prophets in the name of the Lord to mislead the people. Even so it is at this very day. Many preachers who claim to be preaching in the name of the Lord try to keep the people in ignorance of the true God and the unfolding of his great purpose of salvation.

Zedekiah was the last king of Israel. He did much wickedness in the sight of the Lord. Satan used him to reproach Jehovah God. He became disobedient and arrogant and presumptuous before the Lord. Then the Lord God, for the good of the people and that they might remember him as their true friend and benefactor, uttered this decree against Zedekiah: "Therefore thus saith the Lord God, Because ye have made your iniquity to be remembered, in that your transgressions are discovered, so that in all your doings your sins do appear; because, I say, that ye are come to remembrance, ye shall be taken with the hand. And thou, profane wicked prince of Israel, whose day is come, when iniquity shall have an end, thus saith the Lord God, Remove the diadem, and take off the crown; this shall not be the same: exalt him that is low, and abase him that is high. I will overturn, overturn, overturn it; and it shall be no more, until he come whose right it is, and I will give it him.''—Ezek. 21: 24-27.

It was in the year 606 B.C. that this decree was enforced and that the people of Israel fell to their enemies and were carried away as captives to Babylon, where they were required to serve that nation for seventy years. Even though afterwards a remnant of Israel was brought back into their own land, never again did that people have a king. In the above prophecy God again made promise of the coming of him whose right it is to be the ruler of the peoples of earth and who must of necessity, in God's due time, be the deliverer and the instrument in the hands of Jehovah for the blessing of the peoples of the earth.

Satan knew that with many of the Jews their religion was the chief thing with them. He knew therefore that in order to deceive them he must send men amongst them who claimed to represent God. When it is so clearly shown by the Scriptures that Satan fraudulently did this thing to the Jews, may we not with stronger reasoning expect just such a fraudulent scheme to be practiced upon the peoples of the earth during the Christian era by Satan's sending amongst them men who claim to represent the Lord and to preach in his name but who, in truth and in fact, are the representatives of the Devil? This is exactly what subsequent facts herein set forth prove. As the Lord promised the Jews at the time of their overthrow that a deliverer shall come, this promise likewise applies to Christians and to all who shall ultimately turn to the Lord.

## Chapter IX

# *The Deliverer*

PAUL was one of the inspired witnesses of God who wrote a portion of the Lord's Word. At the time Paul wrote, more than four thousand years had passed since the tragedy of Eden. During that period the peoples had suffered, and since then continue to suffer, bodily pain and mental anguish, sorrow, sickness and death, being in bondage to the great oppressor. Knowing of this, and having likewise experienced much of it, Paul wrote: "For we know that the whole creation groaneth and travaileth in pain together until now." (Rom. 8:22) At the same time, quoting from the Prophet Isaiah, he said: "There shall come out of Sion the Deliverer."—Rom. 11:26.

Zion is the name applied to God's organization. It is plainly written that out from God's organization, Zion, shall come the Deliverer of the human race. If a man really believes that Jehovah God exists and that he is the Almighty God, the Most High, the Creator of heaven and earth, that he is all-powerful and is the very expression of love, and that he has promised deliverance to the human race, then why should man look to any other source for deliverance? It is clearly manifest that Satan the enemy, for a selfish purpose, has deceived mankind, and that in selfishness and wickedness he has strenuously opposed every effort looking to man's relief. It must appeal to every reasonable mind that none other, aside from

Almighty God, through his organization, can provide deliverance of man from his enemies.

Evolutionists teach that the remedy for man's uplift is by his own efforts, and that he needs no Savior or Deliverer. Such teaching not only is unreasonable, but upon the face of it shows that it emanates from the Devil, and that he puts forth such a theory for the very purpose of deceiving the people and turning them away from God and away from his provision for man's deliverance. Every sane man knows, from experience as well as from observation, that he and all other men are imperfect. Not only that, but every one must know that he is sinful. How can man be relieved from these imperfections? God answers: "Come now, and let us reason together, saith the Lord: Though your sins be as scarlet, they shall be as white as snow; though they be red like crimson, they shall be as wool."—Isa. 1:18.

The fact that God has asked man to reason with him shows that he is not going to arbitrarily deliver man and give to him blessings without man's consent. If the destiny of man were fixed, without regard to whether he accepts or rejects the provision made for him, then there would be no occasion for him to reason with the Lord. This for ever puts to silence the theory of predestination of every creature.

Furthermore, the fact that God invites man to reason upon the question of his salvation is conclusive proof that God's provision for man's salvation is reasonable, not a foolish one as some would make it appear. Again, the Devil deceives many who say: 'No matter what a man believes, just so long as he is honest in his belief, that is sufficient. The belief of one is as good as that of another.' One man says: 'My parents were good Catholics, and their religion is good enough for me.' Another says: 'My mother was a Methodist, and her religion is good enough for me.' The parents of both the Catholic and the Methodist may have been equally honest; but it is absolutely certain that not both could have been right, because their theories of salvation are very different. How then should we determine what to do? The Lord answers: 'Come, reason with me in the light of my Word, and I will show you the way to life.' Jesus adds: "This is life eternal, that they might know thee the only true God, and Jesus Christ, whom thou hast sent."—John 17: 3.

To reason means to arrive at a just conclusion, by starting at a premise or fixed basis and step by step applying the known facts according to fixed principles or rules of action. A principle is a rule of action.

The question at issue is the salvation of man. The premise is: Man is imperfect, in a dying condition, suffering in his present condition and desiring deliverance therefrom. That is conceded by all. The conclusion is: God's purpose provides for complete relief, by arranging for deliverance of man from all these disabilities and for his complete restoration to life and happiness. The facts upon which this conclusion is reached are set forth in the Word of God, the Bible, which is true because it is the Word of the infinite and eternal One. These facts are supplemented by things that each intelligent person sees and experiences.

The primary attributes that are inherent in Jehovah are wisdom, justice, love and power, working always harmoniously.

Man was created in the image and likeness of God, in that God endowed him with these attributes of wisdom, justice, love and power. While it is true that man failed and is greatly degenerated, yet every sane, intelligent man in some degree retains the image of God and possesses in a small degree some justice, some wisdom, some love and some power. These attributes he must learn to exercise harmoniously. He cannot exercise them perfectly, but he can exercise them to some extent, nevertheless.

That which goes to make up every man is mind, will, heart and organism. The mind is that faculty of the person by which man searches out facts, weighs and considers those facts, and reaches a conclusion.

Will is that faculty by which man determines to do or not to do certain things. It is the faculty of determination, a determination after the mind has considered the facts and reached a conclusion.

Heart, as used herein, does not mean the organ which propels the blood through the arteries; but the word is used symbolically, and denotes that faculty of the man which induces action. It is the seat of motive. It is the seat of affection and love. Man is said to have a bad heart when it appears that his motive in acting is deliberately wrong. He is said to have a good heart when it appears that his motive in acting is good.

No creature can exist without an organism. A human body of flesh is the organism of man, and the breath of life in that organism animates the organism and causes all the faculties to function. Hence we read that God formed man of the dust of the ground and breathed into him the breath of lives, and man became a living soul. (Gen. 2:7) Every man *is* a soul. It has been the fraudulent teachings of Satan and his agencies that have induced men to believe that man *possesses* a soul, and that the soul is the "immortal" part of him.

Wisdom, justice, love and power are attributes of the creature. They are faculties of the mind. In these attributes man is like unto God. Every man is a character. No man possesses a character, even as he does not possess a soul. When a man is good or bad it is said of him that he is a good character or that he is a bad character, because he is either a good or a bad man. A perfect character is a person possessing all these four attributes in equal and exact balance. God is the perfect character. The primary attributes are equally balanced in him, and they always work in exact harmony.

God created man with the purpose of giving him everlasting life on earth. Wisdom provided that man must first be put to the test before being granted the prize of life everlasting. The test was: Would man be true and faithful to God? Adam was put to the test and failed.

Justice demanded that Adam forfeit his life because he had violated the law of God, and justice must see to it that the law is enforced. Man could not be excused for his wilful wrongdoing without violating justice. Justice alone operating would destroy man for ever. Love, which is the perfect expression of unselfishness, provided for man's redemption and deliverance and that all the obedient ones, under the test, would be given the blessings of restitution to human perfection and be granted life everlasting. Thus it is seen that wisdom, justice and love were acting in exact harmony.

Power carries into operation the purpose of God. The four attributes of Jehovah therefore work always in harmony and always in equal and exact balance.

It must be conceded that the all-wise Creator had a purpose from the beginning. Satan being the one who for selfish reasons induced man to violate God's law, it would follow that he would oppose every step in the execution of the Lord's purpose which looks to the redemption and deliverance of man. Furthermore it would follow that *every suggested plan for man's deliverance that is contrary to God's purpose is from the Devil,* and is advanced by him for the very purpose of turning away the minds of men from the provision of God. God's provision is right and reasonable. None other is reasonable. It is therefore easily seen that all the remedies suggested by men not only are unreasonable but have proceeded from the Devil, and are injected into the minds of men in order to keep men from considering God's purpose.

There would be no necessity for more than one line of action for man's blessing. It is conceded that there are thousands of man-made plans held before the people. The reasonable mind must at once conclude that none of these are right, because they are unreasonable and because they are all different; and when he sees the real reason for them he sees they are all suggested by the wicked one. This should cause the intelligent man to more carefully seek to understand the divine purpose and its outworkings. Therefore God invites man to come and reason with him. He says: If you do this it matters not how wicked you have been, I will show you the right way; and if you follow my way I will make you as white as the bleached wool and as pure as the snow from heaven.

Now let us reason upon God's purpose as set forth in the Bible. Man finds himself in an unhappy condition, sick, suffering and dying. What is the reason? God answers: 'Adam sinned and was justly sentenced to death. This took place before any of his children were born. All of his offspring were born imperfect and inherited imperfection from Adam, therefore all came under condemnation.' Condemnation means disapproval. "Wherefore, as by one man sin entered into the world, and death by sin; and so death passed upon all men, for that all have sinned." (Rom. 5:12) "I was shapen in iniquity, and in sin did my mother conceive me."—Ps. 51:5.

Why would God permit all to be born in sin? This is answered by the scripture: "But the scripture has shut up together all under sin, in order that the promise by faith of Jesus Christ might be given to the believers." (Gal. 3:22, *Diag.*) Of course an imperfect child would spring from an imperfect father. In wisdom and in love God provided for redemption of man, and the redemption price is valuable for the entire human race. Paul thus puts it: "Therefore, as by the offence of one judgment came upon all men to condemnation; even so by the righteousness of one the free gift came upon all men unto justification of life."—Rom. 5:18, 19.

Justification to life is a gift from God. The first

thing essential to a gift is knowledge. No man could accept a gift without knowing that the thing was offered to him. God has provided that his intelligent creatures shall have knowledge. He presents this knowledge to man in at least two ways: (1) By precept, which means the commandments or the authoritative rule of action, or his expressed will as set forth in his Word, the Bible; (2) by example, which means that which corresponds with or resembles something else which is to be followed; a pattern or picture, such as shadows and types as hereinbefore defined, and including the use of men for the purpose of teaching lessons to other men.

The Lord has spread this course of learning over a wide range; and now at the end of the age, where we now are, God has shed greater light upon his Word and upon the transpiring incidents, that those who desire to know may have a knowledge of the outworking of his purpose. (1 Cor. 10:11) For this reason it is now possible to understand much about the Scriptures that heretofore was not understandable by men. The student therefore has the keenest interest in watching the majestic steps of the Almighty God, as he unfolds his great purpose leading up to the selection of him who shall deliver the human race. Also, it is of interest to mark Satan's attempt to interfere with God's purpose.

The first clear proof that God was beginning to work out his purpose for man's cleansing and deliverance is found in the promise made to Abraham, in which the Lord said to Abraham: "In thy seed shall all the nations of the earth be blessed." This promise must mean that God purposes to arrange for the removal of man's disabilities; and then to restore him, if obedient, to the conditions enjoyed before the tragedy of Eden. This promised blessing must come through the seed. The seed must be developed and made manifest before the blessing could begin. Who then is the seed? Paul answers the question: "Now to Abraham and his seed were the promises made. He said not, And to seeds, as of many; but as of one, And to thy seed, which is Christ."—Gal. 3:16.

"Christ" means anointed one. "The anointed one" means him who is clothed with authority to do certain things. We must then understand that God would clothe some one with authority to bring to mankind the blessings which he has promised. "Messiah" means the same as "Christ". The Jews have long looked for their Messiah to come, and through him the bringing to them of the promised blessings. The typical people of God, when in Egyptian bondage, represented all the human family in bondage to the Devil and to his organization. Moses delivered the people from the hands of the wicked Pharaoh, and in thus doing he pictured Christ or the Messiah who shall deliver all mankind from Satan and the evil resulting from his influence. Moses said that he was a type of the great Messiah or Deliverer. He said that such a one, when he should come, would be clothed with authority to speak in the name of God; and that the people must obey him in order to have the promised blessings. Moses told the people that God had said to him:

"I will raise them up a Prophet from among their brethren, like unto thee, and will put my words in his mouth; and he shall speak unto them all that I shall command him. And it shall come to pass, that whosoever will not hearken unto my words which he shall speak in my name, I will require it of him.''—Deut. 18:18, 19.

When Jacob was on his deathbed he uttered a prophecy showing that the Deliverer must come through the house of Judah. (Gen. 49:10) David was a descendant of the tribe of Judah. He was anointed to be king over Israel. His name means beloved. He was a type of the mighty One who would deliver the human race. It is written of David that he was a man after God's own heart. (Acts 13:22; 1 Sam. 13:14) Why was David a man after God's own heart, seeing that David was guilty of the crime against Uriah? For that crime God punished him. But the reason he was a man after God's own heart was that he never for one moment turned away from the true God to serve any other gods. The Devil was never able to seduce David to worship idols. David was always faithful and true to Jehovah. He did not at any time compromise the Lord's righteous cause with that of the unrighteousness of Satan's organization. Be it noted here that David also pictures that class of creatures who will be found approved by the Lord. No one will ever have God's approval and be accepted as a member of his kingdom who turns away from worshiping, either directly or indirectly, the true God; or who lends aid, counsel, comfort or support to any part of the Devil's organization. He who has the approval of the Lord God must be absolutely faithful to the Lord.

Satan used every means at his command to destroy David, but God prevented him from so doing. ''But when the Philistines heard that they had anointed

David king over Israel, all the Philistines came up to seek David; and David heard of it, and went down to the hold. The Philistines also came, and spread themselves in the valley of Rephaim. And David inquired of the Lord, saying, Shall I go up to the Philistines? wilt thou deliver them into mine hand? And the Lord said unto David, Go up; for I will doubtless deliver the Philistines into thine hand. And David came to Baal-perazim, and David smote them there, and said, The Lord hath broken forth upon mine enemies before me, as the breach of waters. Therefore he called the name of that place Baal-perazim."—2 Sam. 5: 17-20.

God gave David the victory over the nations who were enemies to Israel, and over them who were his personal enemies. "And David spake unto the Lord the words of this song, in the day that the Lord had delivered him out of the hand of all his enemies, . . . In my distress I called upon the Lord, and cried to my God; and he did hear my voice out of his temple, and my cry did enter into his ears. He delivered me from my strong enemy, and from them that hated me: for they were too strong for me. They prevented me in the day of my calamity: but the Lord was my stay. He brought me forth also into a large place; he delivered me, because he delighted in me. The Lord rewarded me according to my righteousness: according to the cleanness of my hands hath he recompensed me. For I have kept the ways of the Lord, and have not wickedly departed from my God. For all his judgments were before me: and as for his statutes, I did not depart from them. I was also upright before him, and have kept myself from mine iniquity. Therefore the Lord hath recompensed me according to my righteousness; according to my cleanness in his eyesight.

"With the merciful thou wilt shew thyself merciful, and with the upright man thou wilt shew thyself upright. With the pure thou wilt shew thyself pure; and with the froward thou wilt shew thyself unsavoury. And the afflicted people thou wilt save: but thine eyes are upon the haughty, that thou mayest bring them down. For thou art my lamp, O Lord; and the Lord will lighten my darkness. For by thee I have run through a troop: by my God have I leaped over a wall. As for God, his way is perfect; the word of the Lord is tried; he is a buckler to all them that trust in him. For who is God, save the Lord? and who is a rock, save our God? God is my strength and power: and he maketh my way perfect. He maketh my feet like hinds' feet, and setteth me upon my high places. He teacheth my hands to war; so that a bow of steel is broken by mine arms. Thou hast also given me the shield of thy salvation: and thy gentleness hath made me great. Thou hast enlarged my steps under me; so that my feet did not slip."—2 Sam. 22:1, 7, 18-37.

Jehovah limited the promise of the coming Deliverer to the house of David, and therefore we must expect to find in the sacred record that he who is to be the Deliverer is of the house of David. "The Lord hath sworn in truth unto David, he will not turn from it; Of the fruit of thy body will I set upon thy throne. If thy children will keep my covenant, and my testimony that I shall teach them, their children shall also sit upon thy throne for evermore."—Ps. 132: 11, 12.

The Lord God did not permit David to build the temple, because he was a man of war and had shed blood. But David was always faithful to God, and because of that faithfulness God subsequently favored one of David's descendants, as it is written: "Because David did that which was right in the eyes of the Lord, and turned not aside from any thing that he commanded him all the days of his life, save only in the matter of Uriah the Hittite."—1 Ki. 15: 5.

David assembled the people of his realm to tell them about the house of the Lord, or the temple, which he had intended to build. "Then David the king stood up upon his feet, and said, Hear me, my brethren, and my people: As for me, I had in mine heart to build an house of rest for the ark of the covenant of the Lord, and for the footstool of our God, and had made ready for the building: but God said unto me, Thou shalt not build an house for my name, because thou hast been a man of war, and hast shed blood. Howbeit the Lord God of Israel chose me before all the house of my father to be king over Israel for ever: for he hath chosen Judah to be the ruler; and of the house of Judah, the house of my father; and among the sons of my father he liked me, to make me king over all Israel: and of all my sons (for the Lord hath given me many sons) he hath chosen Solomon my son to sit upon the throne of the kingdom of the Lord over Israel. And he said unto me, Solomon thy son, he shall build my house and my courts: for I have chosen him to be my son, and I will be his father. Moreover, I will establish his kingdom for ever, if he be constant to do my commandments and my judgments, as at this day."—1 Chron. 28:2-7.

Then David, as the anointed of the Lord, therefore as the mouthpiece of the Lord, said unto Solomon his son, who had been selected to rule over Israel: "And thou, Solomon my son, know thou the God of thy father, and serve him with a perfect heart, and with a willing mind: for the Lord searcheth all hearts, and understandeth all the imaginations of the thoughts: if thou seek him, he will be found of thee; but if thou forsake him, he will cast thee off for ever."—1 Chron. 28:9.

The reign of Solomon was marked with peace. His wisdom and riches exceeded those of any other man of his time. Other nations came and paid him homage and tribute. But the wily enemy Satan was not idle. He found a way to overreach the wise ruler. It seems quite evident that woman is an easy instrument in the hands of the Devil. He used Eve to cause trouble in Eden. Ascertaining the peculiar weakness of Solomon, the enemy Satan surrounded him with a company of attractive women. The daughter of Pharaoh, one of the Devil's representatives, became Solomon's wife. Besides this woman he had other heathen wives, to the number of seven hundred. These women, who were devil worshipers, were used by the Devil to turn Solomon's mind away from the great Jehovah God. Solomon became an idolater and worshiped the Devil and lost the great opportunity that was set before him.

Concerning the deflection of King Solomon, and the withdrawal from him of the right to the promise of God, it is written: "But king Solomon loved many strange women, (together with the daughter of Pharaoh,) women of the Moabites, Ammonites, Edomites, Zidonians, and Hittites; of the nations concerning which the Lord said unto the children of Israel, Ye shall not go in to them, neither shall they come in unto you: for surely they will turn away your heart after their gods. Solomon clave unto these in love. And he had seven hundred wives, princesses, and three hundred concubines: and his wives turned away his heart. For it came to pass, when Solomon was old, that his wives turned away his heart after other gods: and his heart was not perfect with the Lord his God, as was the heart of David his father. For Solomon went after Ashtoreth the goddess of the Zidonians, and after Milcom the abomination of the Ammonites.

"And Solomon did evil in the sight of the Lord, and went not fully after the Lord, as did David his father. Then did Solomon build an high place for Chemosh, the abomination of Moab, in the hill that is before Jerusalem; and for Molech, the abomination of the children of Ammon. And likewise did he for all his strange wives, which burnt incense, and sacrificed unto their gods. And the Lord was angry with Solomon, because his heart was turned from the Lord God of Israel, which had appeared unto him twice, and had commanded him concerning this thing, that he should not go after other gods: but he kept not that which the Lord commanded. Wherefore the Lord said unto Solomon, Forasmuch as this is done of thee, and thou hast not kept my covenant and my statutes, which I have commanded thee, I will surely rend the kingdom from thee, and will give it to thy servant. Notwithstanding, in thy days I will not do it, for David thy father's sake: but I will rend it out of the hand of thy son. Howbeit I will not rend away all the kingdom; but will give one tribe to thy son for David my servant's sake, and for Jerusalem's sake, which I have chosen."—1 Ki. 11:1-13.

Probably Satan thought he had won the victory by overreaching this wise ruler of Israel to whom the promise of God had been made. But not so. Jehovah cannot be defeated. He held the tribe of Judah in his hand to use according to his purpose. It is written concerning David and his sons: "And these be the names of those that were born unto him in Jerusalem; Shammuah, and Shobab, and Nathan, and Solomon." (2 Sam. 5:14) His son Nathan therefore became the line through which the promised seed came.

A barren woman amongst the Jews was a reproach, because the Jews were in expectancy of the birth of a son who would be the king of their nation and who would drive out their enemies and deliver them into full freedom. Prophetically Isaiah had written of such a king and his power: "For unto us a child is born, unto us a son is given, and the government shall be upon his shoulder; and his name shall be called Wonderful Counsellor, The mighty God, The everlasting Father, The Prince of Peace."—Isa. 9:6.

In the city of Nazareth in the land of Galilee there dwelt a virgin named Mary. She was a direct descendant of Nathan, one of the sons of David, therefore of the house of David and of the tribe of Judah. At the time she was espoused to Joseph, who was also of the tribe of Judah, of the house of David, and a descendant of Solomon. Unto this humble Hebrew woman the Lord God sent his angel Gabriel: "And the angel came in unto her, and said, Hail, thou that art highly favoured, the Lord is with thee: blessed art thou among women. And when she saw him, she was troubled at his saying, and cast in her mind what manner of salutation this should be. And the angel said unto her, Fear not, Mary: for thou hast found favour with God. And, behold, thou shalt conceive in thy womb, and bring forth a son, and shalt call his name Jesus. He shall be great, and shall be called the Son of the Highest: and the Lord God shall give unto him the throne of his father David: and he shall reign over the house of Jacob for ever; and of his kingdom there shall be no end. Then said Mary unto the angel, How shall this be, seeing I know not a man? And the angel answered and said unto her, The holy [spirit] shall come upon thee, and the power of the Highest shall overshadow thee; therefore also that holy thing which shall be born of thee shall be called the Son of God."—Luke 1:28-35.

Satan, having access to heaven, and watching the movements of the righteous messengers of God, would be on the alert to learn anything concerning the 'seed of promise'. He must have known of this mighty angel's coming from the courts of heaven to visit the virgin of Galilee. He must have heard the announcement to her that she was to conceive and give birth to a son and that this son would be the 'seed of promise' which in due time would destroy the Devil and his works. In keeping with his wickedness Satan began to lay his plans to have the babe destroyed. Mark the subtle and wicked way that he went about it.

Under the law a woman guilty of adultery was subject to be stoned to death. (Lev. 20:10) Being espoused to Joseph, Mary was, under the Jewish arrangement, then to all intents and purposes his wife and subject to the law. Satan sought to have Joseph make a public exhibition of her, which would have meant that she would have been publicly executed; and were this done, the unborn child would have been killed. But the Lord God thwarted Satan's purposes. Joseph, being a just man, had no desire to make a public example of Mary by having her brought before the executioners and stoned to death, but had determined in his own mind to privately rid himself of her. "Now the birth of Jesus Christ was on this wise: When as his mother Mary was espoused to Joseph, before they came together, she was found with child of the holy [spirit]. Then Joseph her husband, being a just man, and not willing to make her a public example, was minded to put her away privily. But while he thought on these things, behold, the angel of the Lord appeared unto him in a dream, saying, Joseph, thou son of David, fear not to take unto thee Mary thy wife: for that which is conceived in her is of the holy [spirit]. And she shall bring forth a son, and thou shalt call his name JESUS: for he shall save his people from their sins."—Matt. 1:18-21.

### THE BIRTH OF JESUS

This is a day of great inventions; because it is the day the Lord foretold by his prophet. The radio and airships are amongst the marvels of the age. Imagine the curtains of night having been drawn and silence brooding like a silent spirit over the earth. In the quietness of his bedchamber a man rests, but sleep is gone from his eyes. Stretching out his arm he touches the dial of his receiving set and turns it. There come to him from some unseen place the strains of sweet music, telling of the glory of God and the marvelous provision made by him for the blessing of mankind. His heart responds in gladness. Then suddenly through the thick darkness there also bursts a flood of light, and he beholds in the canopy above him a great fleet of airships illuminated with myriads of lights and carrying a multitude of sweet singers. The music and the lights thrill his soul and he instinctively cries out: "How wonderful! How marvelous!" But this illustration is inadequate. It pales into insignificance when compared with what took place on the night of the birth of Jesus.

Four thousand years had sped by since the tragedy in Eden. Two thousand years had gone since God had called to Abraham and said: 'I will multiply thy seed as the stars in heaven and as the sands upon the sea shore; in thy seed shall all the nations of the earth be blessed.' During all that period of time the peoples of earth had groaned in pain and travailed in suffering, waiting for the time of deliverance. Throughout that period the angels of heaven in harmony with God had been watching for the birth of him who would be the Savior of the world. The time drew on when this great event was to take place.

The earthly preparation was simple and is told in a few words. No amount of preparation that man could have made would have added any dignity or honor to that occasion. The Lord God saw to it that not one of the Devil's earthly representatives was permitted to witness the birth of his beloved One. The Pharisees and other ecclesiastics of that day posed before the people as the representatives of God, even as the clergy do now; but not one of these was called to witness the birth of the Redeemer of man. On the contrary, God selected a few plain and honest watchmen of sheep to be the witnesses to this unparalleled event.

In heaven the preparation was on a more elaborate scale. To Gabriel had been assigned the honorable duty of journeying from the courts of Jehovah as bearer of the message to the virgin Mary that she should bear a son who would deliver the peoples from their enemies and restore the obedient ones to full fellowship with God. Nine months had elapsed since the delivery of that all-important message. In the meantime Gabriel had returned to heaven and doubtless communed with many others of the holy angels of heaven, advising them of his mission to earth. There are millions of such glorious creatures before the throne of God. (Dan. 7:10) The great Jehovah would issue the order for the organization of a multitude of the heavenly host to act as a guard of honor to accompany the special messenger to earth, there to testify to the birth of his beloved Son. There must have been tremendous rejoicing in heaven and songs of boundless praise to God when this mighty throng began its journey to earth. Probably some few days would be required to make the journey from heaven to the earth; and while the heavenly messengers proceeded on their way the stage on earth was being set.

Joseph and Mary, responding to the decree of Cæsar to report for the purpose of being taxed, were on their way to Bethlehem. Joseph was a man of small means, but honest; and above all, he served Jehovah God. He would not have a great retinue of servants with him, nor would the populace hail him by the way and bow before him or kiss his toe. How unlike men of the present time who think they are charged with some exalted duty and privilege! With his virgin wife seated upon an ass, and with staff in hand, he trudged by her side over the hills and through the valleys, unaccompanied by visible attendants. Satan knew where this blessed man and woman were going, and the reason why; and without a doubt he would have slain them by the way had not God prevented him. It is equally certain that some of the holy angels of heaven were delegated to walk by the side of Joseph and his bride, and when they stopped to rest these messengers would encamp about them and guard them from the assaults of the enemy and save them from all harm.—Ps. 34: 7.

After a few days of hard journeying they arrived at Bethlehem, late in the evening, and found all the available space in the lodging houses occupied. From place to place they went and applied, and each time being turned away they finally found a place to rest where the cattle were usually housed. What a fit place for the Savior of the world to be born!

It was nighttime. The shepherds had gathered their flocks into the corral and were keeping watch lest the wild beasts should carry some away. These were plain, humble but kindly men; otherwise the Lord would not have used them. They were familiar with the promises God had made to their forefathers. It is not unreasonable to think that even at that very

BIRTH OF THE BABE JESUS Page 122

time they were recounting to each other these promises and discussing the future, that some day the Lord would send to them a King who would deliver them from the Roman yoke. They would be familiar with the prophecies concerning the coming of the King and Deliverer; and with no light by which they might read, and while they must be awake and watching, they would sit and talk about the things dear to their hearts.

The hour had now come. The heavenly throng was due. God does everything on time. In the van of this marching heavenly host was one mighty angel of God, to whom had been delegated the authority to announce the birth of the beloved Son. Probably this angel was Gabriel; because he had been sent on the previous mission to Mary. As they came near to Bethlehem, doubtless the multitude halted while the leader of that heavenly company advanced and made announcement to the humble men who were to be the witnesses of the birth of Jesus. The shepherds watched their flocks, waiting for the dawn of day. "And, lo, the angel of the Lord came upon them, and the glory of the Lord shone round about them: and they were sore afraid. And the angel said unto them, Fear not: for, behold, I bring you good tidings of great joy, which shall be to all people. For unto you is born this day, in the city of David, a Saviour, which is Christ the Lord."—Luke 2: 9-11.

The glory of the Lord shone round about these shepherds; and that glory must have been a great light in the heavens, because usually the glory of the Lord appeared unto witnesses in this manner. (Acts 9: 3) That was a far more wonderful and beautiful light than all the illuminated fleets of air-planes that could fly over cities in modern times. Then there fell upon the ears of that shepherd company sweet strains of music such as no mortal ear had ever heard. It was a song of the mighty host of angels that had accompanied this special one from heaven. This chief messenger who had made the announcement was now joined by a multitude of the heavenly host singing praises to God; and this is what the shepherds heard: "Glory to God in the highest, and on earth peace, good will toward men." —Luke 2:14.

Not only was that a sweet and melodious song, but it was a prophecy that he who was born at that hour in the city of David would in God's due time vindicate the name of his Father, bring peace on earth and establish good will between and toward all men. This song of the multitude of angels must have been wafted back to heaven and there joined in by all the holy ones before the throne of the Almighty God. As the sweet anthem thundered on through space the very stars and planets would dance for joy and join in the song of praise. We are told that they did this very thing when God laid the foundation of the earth as a place for the habitation of perfect man. (Job 38:7) How much more must they have sung the songs of praise when he was born who would save mankind and make earth a fit place in which to live!

Who was this One now born in the manger at Bethlehem, and whence had he come? The record of God is that in the beginning he was the Logos. He was the first and only direct creation of God. Thereafter he was the active agent of Jehovah in creating all things that were created. In obedience to the will of Almighty God his life was now transferred from the spirit to the human plane. The Logos was 'made flesh and dwelt amongst men', that he might take away the sin of the world.—John 1:1-29.

God had foretold through his prophet that the mighty ruler and deliverer should be born in the city of Bethlehem. (Mic. 5:2) In due time and at the proper place this prophecy had been fulfilled, and nothing Satan could do could in any wise interfere with the progression of the divine purpose. Of course Satan would know about the birth and about the announcement of the birth made by the holy angels of heaven. We may even be sure that another company of mighty angels of God would keep Satan and his wicked angels back from interfering with the birth of the Savior. This wonderful event and this marvelous manifestation of the power of God should have served to convince all those angels who had fallen away with Satan that Jehovah God is all-powerful, that nothing can prevent him from carrying out his purpose, and that their hope of eternal life and blessing would be for ever blasted by their continuing to follow Satan. It should have been sufficient to induce even Satan to cease his wrongful course. But Satan, totally depraved and fatally bent on continuing in wickedness, still pursued his nefarious course and drew along with him a host of wicked ones as his assistants.

### CONSPIRACY

Satan the enemy began to devise ways and means for the destruction of the babe Jesus. The Romans were in control of Palestine; and Herod acted as a petty ruler and king under the supervision and control of the Romans. He was a very wicked man and a willing instrument in the Devil's hands. He would not hesitate to destroy anyone who he thought might interfere with his occupancy of the office of king. He was one of those conscienceless and wicked politicians who would resort to any mean and wrongful act, and stop at nothing to accomplish his purposes. Yielding to the influence of Satan he had put himself in this position.

At the same time there dwelt in Persia savants or "wise men", so called. They were sorcerers and magicians who worshiped the stars and other objects, which is proof conclusive that they were idolaters and worshiped the Devil. (1 Cor. 10:20) Magicians or men of this kind were employed by the various rulers of the Devil's organization, as advisers. These "wise men" were mediums, through whom the adversary operated. Satan used such as his visible instruments at various times. (Ex. 7:11) Many of them may have been sincere men, but they had been overreached by the Devil and had turned away from the true and living God to worship anything except the Lord Jehovah. Being tools in the hands of the enemy Satan, he could use them to carry out his wicked schemes, the details of which they would not even understand.

These so-called 'wise men of the east' were astrologers who believed that a star is assigned for each creature when born into the world, according to his relative importance. There are many incidents showing that Satan and his wicked angels have power to produce lights and to cause them to move through space and to make them appear like stars. We know, however, that stars do not move in this way. To these astrologers Satan caused a light to appear which had the appearance of a star; and he induced them to believe that this was the star of the child born to be king of the Jews.

The enemy's scheme was to bring these "wise men" to Herod and have them inquire of the king, 'Where is the one born to be king of the Jews?' That information would immediately start the thought of murder in the heart of Herod, and he would search out the babe and have it murdered lest it should interfere with his kingdom. The Lord God let the enemy Satan carry out his scheme until the danger point, then held him back. Subsequent facts show that it must have been between one and two years after the birth of Jesus that the Devil attempted to carry out this conspiracy.

Joseph and Mary were then living in a house at Bethlehem. These astrologers or "wise men" appeared before Herod and said: "Where is he that is born King of the Jews? for we have seen his star in the east, and are come to worship him." (Matt. 2:2) The information which they brought Herod upon this occasion troubled him and his official family. The first thing he thought of was his clergy allies, the priests and Pharisees. He sent messengers and gathered them in before him.

Without a doubt the Devil was invisibly present, directing each move of Herod; in fact, moving all parties to the conspiracy like as a player moves his pawns upon a chessboard. When the clergy appeared before the king he demanded of them to tell him where Christ should be born. (Matt. 2:4-6) Then Herod, directed by his superlord the Devil, next arranged a private audience with the "wise men" and got all the information possible from them concerning the "star" that they had seen. Without doubt Satan engineered this in such a way that Herod would think that *he* was carrying out the scheme.

Then Herod gave the order that these men should be sent to Bethlehem. (Matt. 2:8) Here is another glaring case of hypocrisy. We recall how hypocrisy had its first appearance. The Devil sees to it that it crops out always at the proper time for his purposes. Little would Herod worship the Lord God or his beloved Son when he was found. He had no thought of so doing. His purpose was to locate the babe that he might murder him. The astrologers started on their way to Bethlehem; and the Devil saw to it that the light, supposed to be a star, went before them. Let it here be noted that stars do not move first from east to west and then from south to north, nor in any other direction at the suggestion or whims of men, nor for the purpose of guiding men. This of itself is proof that the light was not a star, even though these men doubtless thought it was a star. It was a light produced by the Devil, as one of the means for carrying out his wicked conspiracy.

The several astrologers arrived at Bethlehem. "And when they were come into the house, they saw the young child with Mary his mother, and fell down, and worshipped him: and when they had opened their treasures, they presented unto him gifts; gold, and frankincense, and myrrh." (Matt. 2:11) The babe was now located, and Satan thought he was about at the point where he would soon have the child destroyed. But God interfered:

"And being warned of God in a dream that they should not return to Herod, they departed into their own country another way. And when they were departed, behold, the angel of the Lord appeareth to Joseph in a dream, saying, Arise, and take the young child and his mother, and flee into Egypt, and be thou there until I bring thee word: for Herod will seek the young child, to destroy him. When he arose, he took the young child and his mother by night, and departed into Egypt: and was there until the death of Herod, that it might be fulfilled which was spoken of the Lord by the prophet, saying, Out of Egypt have I called my son. Then Herod, when he saw that he was mocked of the wise men, was exceeding wroth, and sent forth, and slew all the children that were in Bethlehem, and in all the coasts thereof, from two years old and under, according to the time which he had diligently inquired of the wise men."—Matt. 2:12-16.

The fact that Herod caused all the children of two years and under to be slain is proof that it was more than a year after the birth of Jesus that this conspiracy was carried out. To thwart the wicked designs of the enemy and to preserve his beloved Son, God moved him into Egypt and there kept him until Herod's death. (Matt. 2:19-21) Later, Joseph and Mary returned to the city of Nazareth, and there the lad was subject to Joseph and his mother until he attained the age of his majority.

MINISTRY OF JESUS

Jesus came into the world that he might bear witness to the truth of God's kingdom. (John 18:37) When he reached his legal majority at thirty years of age he began his ministry, that the purposes of God might be accomplished. His first act was to report to John at the Jordan, asking to be baptized. He was a perfect man. Why should he be baptized? Baptism or water immersion is a symbol of being buried or put to death. The baptism of Jesus was a symbolic representation of the fact that Jesus, at a great sacrifice to himself, had yielded unto his Father to do his Father's will, no matter what that will might be, even unto death. (Matt. 3:15-17) John, in putting Jesus under the water and raising him up out of the water, represented Jehovah; and symbolically this act declared: Jesus is in the hands of his Father to do his Father's will, to accomplish his Father's purposes, and this will lead to his death; but the Father will raise him up out of death. Here at the Jordan he fulfilled what the prophet had before said for him: "Lo, I come: . . . to do thy will, O my God: yea, thy law is within my heart."—Ps. 40:7, 8.

At the time of Jesus' baptism in the Jordan, it is written concerning him, "the heavens were opened unto him, and he saw the spirit of God descending like a dove, and lighting upon him: and, lo, a voice from heaven, saying, This is my beloved son, in whom I am well pleased"; thus giving an outward demonstration to John, as a witness that this was God's beloved Son, born to be the Deliverer of mankind.

Satan the enemy did not miss so important an occasion as this. No doubt he heard these words of approval spoken concerning Jesus. He immediately began to devise ways and means for the destruction of Jesus. He knew that the life of Jesus depended upon his being loyal and faithful unto God his Father. Satan was egotistical enough to believe that he could induce Jesus to be unfaithful to Jehovah and thereby bring about self-destruction. Jesus had been forty days and nights in the barren mountain without food and, of course, would be hungry at the end of that long fast. Satan seized the opportunity to present to him a temptation, appealing to his fleshly wants and needs, which temptation, on the face of it, seemed innocent; and yet Satan knew that it, if yielded to, would lead to the death of Jesus. He said to Jesus: "If thou be the Son of God, command that these stones be made bread." (Matt. 4: 3) He thought, of course, that Jesus would say: I will make myself some bread and satisfy my hunger.

To be loyal means to be obedient to the letter and spirit of the divine law. The law of God is his expressed will, particularly that which is written in the Scriptures. To be faithful means to be uncompromisingly devoted to the Lord at all times, and never at any time to render allegiance to another or to even sympathize with a course contrary to that of Jehovah.

Doubtless Jesus possessed the power to change the stones into bread and by that means to satisfy his hunger. The argument might be presented: What harm will result to anyone from making bread of these stones? The answer is, God had not commanded him to do so. It was the will of God that Jesus should be governed by God's expressed will, and to await the Father's due time to direct him in what course he should take. Being faithful to the Father he refused to yield to this temptation, and responded to Satan: "It is written, Man shall not live by bread alone, but by every word that proceedeth out of the mouth of God." (Matt. 4:4) Otherwise stated, bread may be needed for the natural requirements of the body, but such will not sustain life except temporarily. Life is a gift from God, and he who possesses life must abide by the word that proceeds from the mouth of God.

Then the Devil tried another method. He knew that Jesus was born to be king of the Jews. "If thou be the Son of God, cast thyself down: for it is written, He shall give his angels charge concerning thee: and in their hands they shall bear thee up, lest at any time thou dash thy foot against a stone." (Matt. 4:6) Paraphrasing Satan's words, he said to Jesus something like this:

'You have come for the purpose of setting up a kingdom, to be king of the Jews. You are going about it in a poor way. Your conduct is that of one meek and lowly of heart. By pursuing this course you will have great difficulty in convincing the people that you are king. There is a lot of rich men in this country, and there are associated with them scheming politicians; and of course the priests are with them, likewise the scribes and Pharisees. They are men of great influence, to whom the people look for advice. Before you can accomplish anything you will have to do something to overshadow their greatness and thereby convince the people that you are sent from heaven. Why not demonstrate to them that you are sent of God? No man has ever gone upon that temple spire and jumped off. You now go up to the top of the temple and jump down into the valley below. You being the Son of God, your Father will see to it that you are not injured; and then the people will say, Surely you are sent from God and are not a man; and they will make you king immediately. In proof of what I say, that God will not let you be injured, it is written that he shall give his angels charge concerning you and in their hands they shall bear you up lest at any time you dash your foot against a stone.'—Ps. 91:11.

This was a subtle and wily temptation, but it did not induce the Lord Jesus to be disloyal to God. For the Lord Jesus to yield to this would be to tempt his Father. Even though he might know that his Father would not permit him to be injured under such circumstances, yet it would be wrong for him to put the Father to this test. Therefore Jesus replied to Satan: "It is written again, Thou shalt not tempt the Lord thy God." (Matt. 4:7) Again the Devil had failed.

And now Satan must try one more scheme to see if he could not accomplish his purposes. God made Lucifer overlord of the world, and when he became Satan this commission was not taken away from him. He was at that time the god of the whole world. Paul so states in 2 Corinthians 4:3, 4. Jesus always recognized Satan as the "prince of this world", and did not deny his title. (John 12:31) And now Satan laid before Jesus a subtle temptation. To paraphrase his language, he said: 'All the kingdoms of this world are mine, and all the glory of them. You recognize that I am the prince and ruler of this world. You have come for the purpose of being king. In order for you to be king of the world you will have to oust me. But I will surrender to you now. I will give you all the kingdoms of this world; and I will ask but one thing of you, and that is, That you fall down and worship me.'—Matt. 4: 8, 9.

Satan at that time again manifested his insatiable desire to be worshiped. He knew, also, that if the Lord Jesus should worship him for one minute then Jehovah God would take away from Jesus all his rights and privileges. Yet Satan was egotistical enough and presumptuous enough to believe that he could induce Jesus to take that course. He was maliciously bent on Jesus' destruction. The reply of Jesus showed his utter contempt of the tempter and the temptation. He said: "Get thee hence, Satan: for it is written, Thou shalt worship the Lord thy God, and him only shalt thou serve." (Matt. 4: 10) Here was positive testimony that every creature in the universe must, at some time, choose between the worship of God and the worship of wickedness, and that in God's due time sufficient knowledge will be brought to every man that he will have an opportunity thus to choose. Satan had failed in this temptation. The Lord Jesus had won the victory, and it is written: "Then the devil leaveth him."

### PERSECUTION

Jesus began his ministry by preaching, "The kingdom of heaven is at hand." (Matt. 4: 17) Seeing that nearly 1900 years have passed since he uttered those words and that there is wickedness yet on the earth, what could Jesus have meant by those words? "Kingdom" primarily means the governing factors authorized to rule. When God overthrew Zedekiah, the last king of Israel, he said: "I will . . . overturn it . . . until he come whose right it is; and I will give it him." (Ezek. 21:27) Now with the anointing of Jesus he received the right to rule. Therefore he had come whose right it is. There was delegated to him the authority to be King; hence he could say with authority: "The kingdom of heaven is at hand." The royal One, the King, who in due time should exercise his legal authority, was present. It was not necessary for him to begin his reign at that time in order to make the statement above quoted true. It was the will of God that he should possess this right for a long period before he should actually begin to exercise his authority as king. This right, as the Scriptures show, he began to exercise nearly 1900 years later.

At his first coming Jesus began to instruct the people in the way of righteousness and to teach them to worship Jehovah as the true and living God; to heal the sick and open the eyes of the blind, and to cast out demons. Gracious words fell from his lips, and "the common people heard him gladly". (Mark 12:37) The many miracles that Jesus performed drew the attention of the people to him, and great multitudes came to hear him. He fed them upon bread and fish for their bodies, and he also provided food for their minds. The common people were anxious to know about Jehovah God and his ways, and how he would bring about their relief and blessing. At that time the clergy had long had the rule over the people. These were made up of Pharisees, scribes and priests. It was their duty to teach the people the Word of God, but this they failed to do. Like their counterparts of the present time, they fed themselves and let the flock of the Lord seek pastures anywhere they could, or else starve. Being austere and assuming great piety, these had repelled the people and caused them to stand in awe of them.

It was so different with Jesus. He came and walked amongst the common people and talked with them. He took the mothers' babes from their arms, caressed their cheeks and spoke words of kindness to them. His words cheered everyone with whom he came in contact. The multitudes were so moved by his words of kindness and loving ministration, and by the miracles he did, that they would have taken him by force and made him king. (John 6:15) But it was not God's due time for him to begin his reign. The purpose of God must be carried out as it was thought, and Jesus was more than willing to perform his part.

The nation of Israel was a typical nation, to whom God had given the law, which performed the function of a schoolmaster to lead that people unto Christ. (Gal. 3:24) The word here rendered "schoolmaster" is from the same word as that from which our English word "pedagogue" comes, and originally meant one who would lead the children to school and care for them. The law performed this function toward Israel. Christ had now come. The Jews as a nation had been shielded by the Lord until Zedekiah's time, and even since then all those who returned to Jerusalem from captivity and showed faith in God had likewise been shielded. Had the nation accepted the Lord as their king they would have been transferred from their covenant with Moses as mediator, to Christ the greater than Moses; and all the royal family of the new kingdom would have been selected from amongst the Jews. The Jews were therefore looking for the time to set up a kingdom, and those who really believed in Jesus were anxious to take him and make him king.

Satan the enemy was ever on the alert to find some means whereby he might put Jesus to death. He soon found some ready tools to be used for his wicked purpose. The religious leaders of Israel, made up of the scribes, Pharisees and priests, doctors of the law, etc., were these ready instruments. They were anxious to hold the common people subject to them. They were extremely selfish, even as their counterparts today are extremely selfish. Satan knew that it would be an easy matter to array these religious leaders against Jesus. With malicious hatred deeply rooted in their hearts he knew that he would find a way for them to bring Jesus before the financial and political factors of the government, charge him with disloyalty or treason, and thereby succeed in having him put to death, and that in an apparently legal manner. He set about to carry this scheme into operation. He injected into the minds of the Pharisees wicked thoughts against Jesus.

Early in the ministry of Jesus the Pharisees and other members of the clergy began to take issue with him. They diligently sought to find some way to accuse him and his disciples of a breach of the law. These Pharisees were sticklers for the letter of the law, but the spirit of it they ignored. Even so it is today among the clergymen. For instance, they insist upon having a Prohibition law upon the statute books, yet they avail themselves of the opportunity to take a drink when the occasion affords; and some of them find a way to stock their cellars with the forbidden stuff. The purpose of calling attention to this here is to show that Satan has ever made inconsistent all those whom he can control. Deception is one of the Devil's chief methods of operation. He makes one thing appear to be accomplished, while he is really doing the very opposite.

When the Pharisees saw the disciples of Jesus plucking corn on the sabbath day that they might eat, the pious souls who stood for the letter of the law vigorously protested that the acts of the disciples were in violation of the law. Jesus at the time tried to teach them the spirit of the law; that the sabbath was made for man and not man for the sabbath. But they were not willing to hear. When Jesus healed a sick man on the sabbath day the pious Pharisees were greatly angered. They immediately took counsel together as to how they might put Jesus to death. (Matt. 12:14) Malicious murder had been planted in their hearts by the Devil, and now they were willing to carry it into operation.

On another occasion Jesus spoke a parable in the presence of the scribes and Pharisees, to this effect: "There was a certain householder, which planted a vineyard, and hedged it round about, and digged a winepress in it, and built a tower, and let it out to husbandmen, and went into a far country: and when the time of the fruit drew near, he sent his servants to the husbandmen, that they might receive the fruits of it. And the husbandmen took his servants, and beat one, and killed another, and stoned another. Again, he sent other servants more than the first: and they did unto them likewise. But, last of all, he sent unto them his son, saying, They will reverence my son. But when the husbandmen saw the son, they said among themselves, This is the heir: come, let us kill him, and let us seize on his inheritance. And they caught him, and cast him out of the vineyard, and slew him. And when the chief priests and Pharisees had heard his parables, they perceived that he spake of them. But when they sought to lay hands on him, they feared the multitude, because they took him for a prophet."—Matt. 21:33-39, 45, 46.

Satan was really the one who desired to kill Jesus. He knew that Jesus was the heir of the promise that God had made to Abraham. He was using his invisible power to cause the Pharisees to bring about Jesus' death. He was now making some progress. But it was not yet God's due time to permit this to happen. Jesus knew what was in their minds, and that is why he spoke the parable to them.

On another occasion Jesus referred to himself as the Son of God. Satan's emissaries the clergy, on the pretext that this was blasphemy, again sought Jesus' life for this 'offense'. We read: "For he whom God hath sent speaketh the words of God: for God giveth not the spirit by measure unto him. The Father loveth the Son, and hath given all things into his hand. He that believeth on the Son hath everlasting life: and he that believeth not the Son shall not see life; but the wrath of God abideth on him." "But Jesus answered them, My Father worketh hitherto, and I work. Therefore the Jews sought the more to kill him, because he not only had broken the sabbath, but said also that God was his Father, making himself equal with God."—John 3:34-36; 5:17, 18.

There was really no excuse for the Pharisees to permit the Devil to overreach them. They knew that God had by precept and by pictures foreshadowed the coming of the Messiah. They knew that the time was due for him to come. In fact, they knew that Jesus was the One. But because of selfishness in their own hearts, and with a desire to hold power over the people, they were ready tools of the Devil; and he took advantage of them. Of course Jesus knew that Satan was back of it all, and knew that these men were seeking his life. They did not deceive him for a moment.

On another occasion he said to them: "I know that ye are Abraham's seed: but ye seek to kill me, because my word hath no place in you. I speak that which I have seen with my Father: and ye do that which ye have seen with your father. They answered and said unto him, Abraham is our father. Jesus saith unto them, If ye were Abraham's children, ye would do the works of Abraham. But now ye seek to kill me, a man that hath told you the truth, which I have heard of God: this did not Abraham. Ye do the deeds of your father.

"Then said they to him, We be not born of fornication; we have one Father, even God. Jesus said unto them, If God were your Father, ye would love me: for I proceeded forth and came from God; neither came I of myself, but he sent me. Why do ye not understand my speech? even because ye cannot hear my word. Ye are of your father the devil, and the lusts of your father ye will do. He was a murderer from the beginning, and abode not in the truth, because there is no truth in him. When he speaketh a

CHILDREN OF THE DEVIL Page 142

lie, he speaketh of his own: for he is a liar, and the father of it. And because I tell you the truth, ye believe me not. Which of you convinceth me of sin? And if I say the truth, why do ye not believe me? He that is of God heareth God's words; ye therefore hear them not, because ye are not of God."—John 8:37-47.

On this occasion Jesus plainly told these men that the Devil was their father, that he was back of them, that they were carrying out Satan's purposes, and that they were seeking the life of the Son of God because they were from the Devil.

That Satan the Devil was the real one who was arranging to bring about the death of Jesus there cannot be any doubt. Jesus knew that; he knew that the Devil was using the clergy and that through them he was preparing Judas to carry out his purpose. Speaking in the synagogue, in the presence of his disciples and others, Jesus said: "As the living Father hath sent me, and I live by the Father: so he that eateth me, even he shall live by me. This is that bread which came down from heaven: not as your fathers did eat manna, and are dead: he that eateth of this bread shall live for ever."—John 6:57,58.

Many who had followed Jesus up to that time turned aside and followed him no more. "Then said Jesus unto the twelve, Will ye also go away? Then Simon Peter answered him, Lord, to whom shall we go? thou hast the words of eternal life. And we believe and are sure that thou art that Christ, the Son of the living God. Jesus answered them, Have not I chosen you twelve, and one of you is a devil? He spake of Judas Iscariot the son of Simon: for he it was that should betray him, being one of the twelve."—John 6:67-71.

Jesus was not at all being deceived. He knew that he was carrying out his Father's purposes, and he knew what would be the result. Straight forward and onward he went with his work. He continued to minister unto the needs of the poor, healing the sick, opening the eyes of the blind, making the lame walk and raising the dead. The exercise of Jesus' great power in the raising of Lazarus from the dead furnished the Devil with an opportunity to again stir up the clergy. They were now to the point of frenzy and were anxious to act. Now was the opportune time for the clergy to draw into the conspiracy their allies, the financial and political factors of the government. This they proceeded to do, under the supervision of their overlord Satan.

They now determined to go to the ruling factors and show them that their country was in danger (?) because of this man Jesus, and that unless something be done they would lose their property and their right to hold office. Where selfishness is the moving cause others of like selfish interests are easily drawn into a compact. Satan was the god of the world. The financial, political and ecclesiastical factors were his. Now he needed but to hold before their eyes the danger of losing the things that they cherished, in order to induce them to act.

"Then gathered the chief priests and the Pharisees a council, and said, What do we? for this man doeth many miracles. If we let him thus alone, all men will believe on him: and the Romans shall come and take away both our place and nation. And one of them, named Caiaphas, being the high priest that same year, said unto them, Ye know nothing at all, nor consider that it is expedient for us, that one man should die for the people, and that the whole nation perish not. And this spake he not of himself: but being high priest that year, he prophesied that Jesus should die for that nation; and not for that nation only, but that also he should gather together in one the children of God that were scattered abroad. Then from that day forth they took counsel together for to put him to death."—John 11:47-53.

The passover season drew nigh and everybody expected Jesus to come up and observe the passover, because he kept the law in spirit and in letter. Knowing this the clergy, under the supervision of Satan, began to prepare to take Jesus: "Now both the chief priests and the Pharisees had given a commandment, that, if any man knew where he were, he should shew it, that they might take him."—John 11:57.

But some may here ask: Why recount all these terrible things that the clergy of that time did, and liken them unto the clergy of the present time? What good can be accomplished by that? The answer is that the purpose in so doing is not to injure any man. It is not the purpose to hold men up to ridicule. No real good can come from resorting to such a course. The real purpose is to prove to the reasonable mind that the enemy of God and of Christ, and of the people who desire righteousness and truth, is Satan the Devil; that he is the one who has arranged the wicked schemes and conspired to hold the people in subjection to him through selfish and wicked men; that he is the one who has planted selfishness in the hearts of human creatures; and that to accomplish his purposes he has united the commercial, political and ecclesiastical elements in a compact of self-interest that he may carry on a government of the people contrary to God's way. All the remedies offered by men have failed because they have all been interfered with by Satan, either directly or indirectly.

Furthermore, it is the purpose here to show that the remedy that will bring about relief to the people is the remedy of God, and none other; and that in due time God's remedy applied for the benefit of the people will bring complete deliverance and the blessings which the people so much need and desire. When the people see that the clergy are the tools of the Devil, even as the Pharisees were when Jesus was on earth, the power of the clergy to deceive the people will be broken, and having the eyes of their understanding opened the people will be able to see God's remedy and to put themselves in a proper attitude of mind and heart to receive the blessings when they are ministered unto them.

The purpose therefore in stating these things, and in showing the operation of God's purpose and the opposition by the Devil, is for the benefit of mankind; that the people may see who is their real enemy and who is their real friend. A real friend is one who loves you all the time (Prov. 17:17), and it will be found by studying the operation of Jehovah's purpose that in everything God has manifested his love for the people and upon every occasion. The time has come for God to establish his name in the minds of the people, not for his benefit, but for their benefit.

But why should God permit the Devil to persecute his beloved Son and use the religious teachers of that time to aid him in that wicked persecution? The answer to that is: God knew that Satan would kill Jesus at the very first opportunity unless he should prevent it. He knew that the hypocritical religious leaders of that day, who had already proven unfaithful to him and unfaithful to their trust, would be the willing tools of the Devil to accomplish his wicked ends. It was a test that God permitted to come to them. Jesus had plainly told them that the Devil was their father. He was not trying to keep them in the dark. He was trying to help them. They claimed to be the representatives of God. Jesus was telling them: 'If you were of God my Father, then you would do his works; but since you do the works of the wicked one you prove that you are from him.' God was permitting the religious leaders to have a great test, and under this test they failed. In other words, they failed and refused to follow and obey Jehovah God, but followed and obeyed the Devil.

God could have prevented the persecution of his beloved Son, but his wisdom dictated otherwise. It was necessary for Jesus to learn obedience by the things that he suffered under adverse conditions. He also must have a test, and when the test was laid upon him he met it in every way.—Heb. 5:8, 9; Phil. 2:5-11.

God arranged to put a test upon Adam as a perfect man before he could grant him everlasting life. Adam failed under that test. God had permitted a test to come to the religious leaders of Jesus' time, and they failed. Jesus was now a man, and before him was set the greatest prize in the universe. It was the purpose of God that his Son should also be tested before being granted this great prize. Jesus met the test and won.

Now it is due time for the people to see and to understand the truth; and particularly to see that all the warfare amongst themselves, the conflicts between religious systems, and the crimes and wickedness that stalk about in the earth, all these unrighteous things originated with Satan, who has used these agencies to turn the minds of the people away from God. The time is here for the people to see that God is their friend and benefactor. Let each one put out of his mind for all time that there is here any attempt or desire to array one class against another. But the truth must be set forth in contrast with the wicked one and his wicked course, in order that the people may know that Jehovah is God, that his beloved Son Jesus is the Christ, and that the Lord has outlined a way to life and that there is none other.

The time came when Jesus must offer himself formally to the Jews as their king. This must be done on the tenth day of Nisan, just preceding the passover, because it was the purpose of God that it should be done. In fulfilment of the prophecy of Zechariah (9:9, 12) Jesus, seated upon an ass, rode into the city of Jerusalem. It was the custom of kings to ride on an ass when coming to be crowned as king. The fame of Jesus had now spread throughout Palestine. Many people believed on him. Great multitudes gathered by the way and laid down their garments in the road, cut down boughs from the trees and put them in the way for Jesus to pass over, thus representing their acceptance of him; and the people cried out unto him: "Hosanna to the son of David! Blessed is he that cometh in the name of the Lord: Hosanna in the highest!"—Matt. 21:1-9; John 12:13.

This great outburst of spontaneous applause from the common people made the blood of the Pharisees boil, and the Devil saw to it that fuel was added to the flame of anger. Now the Pharisees quickly called a council of blood. "The Pharisees therefore said among themselves, Perceive ye how ye prevail nothing? behold, the world is gone after him."—John 12:19.

A few days later was the passover. As one who kept the law perfectly, Jesus celebrated this passover. While eating it with his disciples great sorrow came upon him, and he said to them: "One of you shall betray me." In an undertone Jesus, speaking to the beloved disciple John, said to him in substance: Watch the one to whom I hand the sop when I dip it in the dish; he is the one that will betray me. Then Jesus handed the bread to Judas: "And after the sop Satan entered into him. Then said Jesus unto him, That thou doest, do quickly."—John 13:27.

What could be meant here by the expression: "After the sop Satan entered into him"? Surely it meant that from that moment Satan had full possession of the mind of Judas, and now Judas was bent on carrying out his wicked purpose. This is positive proof that the Devil was really the one seeking the death of Jesus, because he knew Jesus was the Son of God and he desired to get rid of him in order that he might keep control of the world.

Then Judas hurried away to meet his coconspirators, into whose hands he had agreed to betray Christ

Jesus for the paltry sum of thirty pieces of silver. (Matt. 26:15,16) Of course Judas also knew that Jesus was the Son of God; but he had permitted bitterness to spring up in his heart, and now he was anxious to carry the conspiracy out and anxious to have some selfish profit. He got his money and then joined the mob and led them to Jesus. With that hypocrisy which had its conception and birth with the Devil, and its manifestation on a former occasion, Judas now approached the Lord Jesus and kissed him and by this sign indicated to the mob that he was the one to be taken. Jesus did not resist the mob, but, yielding to them, was led away.

The supreme court was already convened, knowing beforehand that the arrest would be made. It was contrary to the law for that court to meet at night; but the priests and Pharisees and the doctors of the law, the rich men and the politicians composing that court, were now ready to ignore the law. The chief priests and the leaders, yea all the religious leaders of the Jews, were there to aid and to abet the arch-conspirator. So maliciously bent were they upon the destruction of Jesus that the clergy and their allies sought false witnesses against Jesus in order that they might put him to death. (Matt. 26:59) Members of that court, which court was supposed to be an august and righteous body, had now gone mad; because into their hearts the wicked one had planted wicked murder of the innocent. Being unable to find witnesses who were willing to testify to any wrongful act against Jesus, members of that devilish court, in utter violation of their own law and the rules of the court itself, compelled the defendant Jesus himself to give testimony. The high priest then made himself prosecutor and vehemently propounded this question: "Tell us whether thou be the Christ, the Son of God." (Matt. 26:63) Jesus answered him: "Thou hast said." Upon this testimony he was adjudged guilty of blasphemy, and the verdict of the court was: "He is guilty of death."—Matt. 26:63-66.

When will the people learn the statement, long ago made by the inspired witness of God, that Satan is the god of this world and has blinded the minds of men? (2 Cor. 4:3, 4) Is it not easy to be seen that when Satan desires even the courts of the land to wickedly do his bidding he can have it done? The Lord God will shortly permit the people to see that Jehovah is God and that his righteous way will completely deliver them. Let us proceed with the examination of the outworking of God's purpose, that we may have cause to rejoice.

The defenseless, harmless, righteous One stood before this court and was adjudged guilty of death; and that without a cause. Now he was led before the high political ruler for a confirmation of the sentence; and although that august ruler and ally of the profiteers and clergy found no wrong in Jesus, yet he had not the moral courage to turn him loose. Conditions are no different now.

It was the supreme hour for the Devil to act, and he held a tight hand over all his servants who were then engaged in this wicked work. Yielding to the importunities of the clergy, the political chief formally consented to the sentence of death; and then, that he might free himself from the responsibility thereof, Pilate took water and in the presence of the people washed his hands and exclaimed: "I am innocent of the blood of this just person." The Jews willingly took the blame upon themselves, and then Jesus was led away to be executed.—Matt. 27: 24, 25.

Hypocrisy and mockery proceed from the Devil. No one having the spirit of the Lord would resort to such methods. Jesus had said: "I am the Son of God." The enemy Satan, thinking he had Jesus now within his power, purposed to make the name of the Son of God despicable, and to have the mob mock him as such. The Devil knew that Jesus was the Son of God, and now to have him mocked would be a reproach to the Father. The enemy therefore induced his earthly representatives to go through many mocking ceremonies. They first put on Jesus a scarlet robe, which is a symbol of royalty; then they made him a crown of thorns and put that on his head as a symbol of authority; then they put a reed into his hand, a symbol of right to rule, and then they hypocritically bowed before him in worshipful attitude, and mockingly said: "Hail, King of the Jews!" Truly here were fulfilled the words of the prophet: "The reproaches of them that reproached thee are fallen upon me." (Ps. 69: 9) The Devil was here reproaching Jehovah. He had been reproaching him all along, and now these reproaches had reached a climax and they were heaped upon his beloved Son Jesus.

Not content with this, but with a further exhibition of malicious hatred on the part of Satan the enemy, his emissaries were induced to spit upon the Lord Jesus and to take the reed out of his hand and strike him with it. After going through these many ceremonies of mockery Jesus was again dressed in his own clothing and prepared by them to be crucified. As a further indignity upon his head vinegar was provided, mixed with gall, and given to him to drink. Then he was cruelly nailed to the tree and thus subjected to the most ignominious death known to man. While he was hanging upon the tree, the chief priests and other members of the clergy further showed their malicious hatred by leading the mob and deriding and mocking the Lord Jesus. We see that God permitted Satan and his emissaries to go to the fullest extent of wickedness, and that then God made it known that he was taking cognizance of what was transpiring and that with him resides all power.

For three hours gross darkness covered the land. Thus the Lord Jehovah pictured that with the taking away of his beloved Son darkness would settle down over the world. At the end of that period of darkness Jesus cried with a loud voice and died. At the moment of Jesus' death Jehovah caused the earth to quake. The mountains shook and the rocks were torn away. In the temple there was a great curtain thirty feet long by thirty feet wide and four inches thick which, at the moment of Jesus' death, was rent in twain from top to bottom. (Matt. 27:51) Great fear and terror came upon those who were assigned to witness the crucifixion, when they saw this manifestation of Jehovah's power. They said concerning Jesus: "Truly this was the Son of God." Never before and never since was the death of a man marked by such a manifestation of power from Jehovah God. Again God was giving the people the lesson that Jehovah is God, and in due time some will benefit therefrom.

The body of Jesus was prepared for burial and laid in the newly prepared tomb of Joseph of Arimathæa. The heir to the throne of the kingdom of God was dead. With malicious glee the enemy Satan considered that he had won the long fight, and that now he was even greater than God. Thus ended the earthly ministry of the only true and good man that was ever on earth. He was without fault, without spot or blemish. He was holy, harmless, undefiled and separate from sinners. He was the Son of God, and to this time he had faithfully performed his part in the divine purposes.

In God's due time a test must come to every man as to whether he loves righteousness and will obey God, or prefers wickedness and will follow a wicked course. Every intelligent human creature must have an opportunity to exercise such free moral agency. The opportunity came to the scribes, Pharisees and others at the crucifixion of Jesus. Some of the Jews who participated in the death of Jesus were ignorant of the fact that he was the Son of God. Some of the rulers also were ignorant. (Acts 3:17) But the scribes, Pharisees and priests were not ignorant. Judas was not ignorant, and of course the Devil was not ignorant. The ignorant ones who sinned against the Lord God and against Christ Jesus will be forgiven. But those who knew that he was Christ sinned against the holy spirit. "And whosoever speaketh a word against the Son of man, it shall be forgiven him: but whosoever speaketh against the holy [spirit], it shall not be forgiven him, neither in this world, neither in the world to come."—Matt. 12:32.

There are those at this very day who know that

Jesus Christ is the King of kings and Lord of lords, and who know that there are a few humble ones who are giving testimony of these facts to the common people. And yet these self-constituted wise men assume a sanctimonious air, parade in the name of the Lord Jesus and claim to represent him, but wilfully sin against the light they have and persecute those who are calmly telling of God's great purpose of salvation. The Lord Jesus referred to this self-same class in the parable of the sheep and the goats.—Matt. 25:31-46.

To sin against the holy spirit does not mean to sin against a creature or person, but means to deliberately go contrary to the light of truth. The holy spirit is the invisible power of God that illuminates the minds of men. Therefore to sin against the holy spirit means a wilful and deliberate course, contrary to one's knowledge of what is right and wrong. One who sins against the holy spirit is possessed of a malicious heart; which means that such a one has no regard for the law of God, and no consideration for the rights of others, but is fatally bent on doing wickedness in order to accomplish a selfish purpose, and doing it knowingly.

### WHY SHOULD JESUS DIE?

Could not God have prevented the death of his beloved Son? Seeing that God is all-powerful it follows that he could have prevented the death of his beloved Son. If Jesus was holy and without sin, then why should he die? When he left the courts of heaven to come to earth and become a man it was the will of God that he should die as a man in order to provide the great redemptive price for man. It was necessary for the perfect man to die in order that the human race might have an opportunity for life. That being true, is Satan any the less reprehensible because he conspired to put Jesus to death and because he incited his emissaries to kill Jesus? No. God had not delegated the authority to Satan to put Jesus to death. Neither had he authorized anyone else to conspire to destroy Jesus. Satan maliciously sought his death because he knew that Jesus was the Son of God and because he expected and feared that Jesus would be King over the people and would take away the rulership from him.

The scribes, Pharisees and others who knowingly participated in putting Jesus to death did so selfishly and wickedly, according to their own words, for fear that they would be deprived of their position as office-holders amongst the people. (John 11:47, 48) In fact, Satan had no power to take the life of Jesus had Jesus even called upon his Father to exercise his unlimited power in his behalf. When Peter smote off the ear of the high priest's servant, we read, "then said Jesus unto him, Put up again thy sword into his place: for all they that take the sword, shall perish with the sword. Thinkest thou that I cannot now pray to my Father, and he shall presently give me more than twelve legions of angels? But how then shall the scriptures be fulfilled, that thus it must be?"—Matt. 26:52-54.

Jesus was so completely devoted to his Father that he would not do anything contrary to his Father's will. He said: "For I came down from heaven, not to do mine own will, but the will of him that sent me." (John 6:38) "I am the good shepherd: the good shepherd giveth his life for the sheep. As the Father knoweth me, even so know I the Father: and I lay down my life for the sheep. And other sheep I have, which are not of this fold: them also I must bring, and they shall hear my voice; and there shall be one fold, and one shepherd. Therefore doth my Father love me, because I lay down my life, that I might take it again. No man taketh it from me, but I lay it down of myself. I have power to lay it down, and I have power to take it again. This commandment have I received of my Father."—John 10:11, 15-18.

Knowing it to be the will of his Father that he should die, Jesus willingly went to death and would not even ask for power to intervene to prevent it. Certain ones of the Jews crucified the Lord. (Acts 2:36; 7:52) The moving cause for them to do so, however, was the influence of Satan the enemy. God permitted the death of his Son in this manner in this, that he did not prevent it; and he did not prevent it because it was his will that Jesus should die that his purpose might be carried out. He could have arranged for his Son's death in some other manner; but, since Satan was maliciously bent on killing Jesus, God permitted the Devil to show his utter depravity, and at the same time he put the test upon those who would follow Satan, knowing that thereafter he would raise Jesus out of death.

It is of the greatest importance that man understand the reason why Jesus had to die, because by so understanding man is enabled to see the great love of God that has been and is exhibited toward man.

### REDEMPTION FIRST

As we progress with the examination of the divine purpose as revealed and unfolded through the Word of God it is observed that Jehovah wills to deliver the human race from sin and death and from all the powers of the wicked one. Who will deliver man from this bondage? What are the legal requirements? When will it be done? and how? These are questions of vital importance, and the death of Jesus is directly related to the proper answer to each of them. Deliverance could not take place until after redemption. Otherwise stated, the rights of man must first be purchased and then mankind may be delivered. Therefore this is the proper place to examine the question of redemption, and in its examination will appear the reason why the perfect man Jesus must die.

Adam was a perfect man when in Eden. Because of sin he was sentenced to death. God's announced law required that the violator thereof should die. Justice therefore required the enforcement of the law, which meant the death of Adam. When the judgment of an earthly court of final jurisdiction is entered there is no power that can reverse that judgment. With stronger reasoning can that rule be applied to Jehovah's court. When he sentenced Adam to death that judgment was final and must be enforced. God could not consistently reverse his own judgment. God cannot be inconsistent. Therefore it was impossible for the judgment against Adam to be set aside or reversed. It is entirely consistent, however, that a final judgment entered in the case may be satisfied by a substitution.

To illustrate: Suppose Jones has a judgment against Smith for one thousand dollars, which has been confirmed by the court of last resort. This judgment has been entered in a jurisdiction where imprisonment can be had for failure to pay debt. The debtor is incarcerated in prison because of his failure to pay. Smith has a father who loves his son, and he produces the thousand dollars and hands it over to the judgment creditor Jones, who accepts it in payment of his judgment. The law therefore requires that the judgment shall be satisfied and Smith released. This is a rule of righteousness.

The same rule, with stronger effect, operates in Jehovah's court. God could consistently arrange for the satisfaction of the judgment against Adam, by substitution. But this must be done in a legal manner, that is to say, in a manner in conformity to the divine law. What then did the law require? The answer is: 'A life for a life.' (Deut. 19:21) A perfect man Adam had been sentenced to death. The law therefore required a perfect human life. The price for redemption, the satisfaction of the judgment by substitution looking to the release of Adam, must be a life exactly equal to that life which Adam lost by reason of the judgment. Otherwise stated, nothing short of a perfect human creature willing to go into death could meet the requirements of the divine law.

All the human race descended from Adam, therefore all were born in sin and shapen in iniquity. (Rom. 5:12; Ps. 51:5) It therefore follows that there lived on earth no human creature capable of fulfilling the divine requirements with reference to the satisfaction by substitution of the judgment against Adam. This must not be understood as meaning the satisfaction of justice. Justice was satisfied with Adam's death; and that judgment, which means the legal determination, would hold Adam forever in death unless some substitute is provided equal to Adam that could be given instead of Adam to satisfy the judgment and let Adam go free. The substitute must be the life of a perfect man.

Could not an angel or a divine person be used to satisfy the judgment against Adam and release him from the death sentence? The answer is: No, because the law of God could receive nothing more and nothing less than the judgment required; otherwise God would be inconsistent; and he cannot be inconsistent. Here again Satan has employed his cunning devices to blind men to the true philosophy of the great ransom sacrifice. He has induced his representatives on earth, who have paraded in the name of the Lord, to teach the people that Jesus Christ when he was on earth was divine, and not a man; and that he died as a divine person. Any reasonable mind can see that if God would require such, God would be unrighteous. This false reasoning has turned away many men from the Lord and from his Word.

Seeing then that the law required the life of a perfect human creature, and that all the offspring of Adam were and are imperfect, the race appears to be and was in a helpless condition. It is stated by God's prophet thus: "None of them can by any means redeem his brother, nor give to God a ransom for him." (Ps. 49:7) Would God provide for redemption? The Word answers: "I will ransom them from the power of the grave: I will redeem them from death:

O death, I will be thy plagues; O grave, I will be thy destruction.''—Hos. 13:14.

Here is the positive word of Jehovah that he would provide redemption for the human race. Of an absolute certainty this will be carried out: ''I have spoken it, I will also bring it to pass; I have purposed it, I will also do it.'' (Isa. 46:11) ''So shall my word be that goeth forth out of my mouth: it shall not return unto me void; but it shall accomplish that which I please, and it shall prosper in the thing whereto I sent it.''—Isa. 55:11.

For this reason ''the [Logos] was made flesh, and dwelt among us''. (John 1:14) Seeing that the Logos was on the spirit plane with his Father, how could he be made flesh? With God nothing is impossible. With the consent of the Logos the Father transferred his Son's life from the spirit to the human plane. He was begotten in the womb of Mary the virgin, by the power of the holy spirit, which means the invisible power of Jehovah. (Matt. 1:18) In due time he was born of this human mother. (Luke 2:9-11) ''When the fulness of the time was come, God sent forth his Son, made of a woman.'' (Gal. 4:4) None of the imperfect blood of the imperfect Adam was in the veins of Jesus, because his life was begotten or begun by the power of Jehovah. When he became a man, therefore, he was holy, harmless, undefiled, and separate from sinners. (Heb. 7:26) As a man he exactly corresponded to what the perfect man Adam was before he sinned. Therefore the man Jesus was capable of becoming the Redeemer of Adam and his race.

But could the perfect man Jesus provide redemption for Adam and all of the human race? The answer is: Yes; God has purposed it thus. One man was the father of the entire human family. One perfect man can redeem the entire human family, as the apostle puts it in Romans 5:18,19.

But one may ask: Why should God send the posterity of Adam into death? They were not on trial. Note the words of the apostle. He does not say that all men were sentenced to death. He does say that all men are condemned to death. Where there is a sentence of death there must of necessity be a trial preceding. Condemnation means disapproval.

A bridge is maintained across a stream until the bridge becomes unsafe; then it is condemned, because it is unsafe. It is no fault of the bridge. The fault lies in the material out of which it is made.

No man made himself. No child brought itself into the world. God gave Adam and Eve the power to propagate the race. As they were imperfect when this power was exercised, their children were brought forth imperfect. God cannot approve an imperfect thing. It was not the fault of the child. It is the fault of the material out of which it is made. Being disapproved, it is condemned; but this condemnation and disapproval are the result of Adam's sin. Therefore all came under condemnation; and God has provided that through the righteousness of his beloved Son the free gift of life shall come to all men, giving to them an opportunity to obey him and live.

Now we find Jesus on earth at thirty years of age, a perfect man and at the legal age required. Why had he come to earth? God had promised to ransom the human race. (Hos. 13:14) The law required a perfect man's life to provide the ransom. Jesus said that he came to give his life a ransom.—Matt. 20: 28.

Ransom means, literally, something to loosen with; a redemptive price. Stated in other phrase, it means the price or value which can be used in loosening or releasing something that is in bondage, restraint or imprisonment. Necessarily the ransom price must be equivalent to, or exactly corresponding with, that which justice requires of the thing or creature in bondage.

The right to live as a human creature was required by the judgment against Adam. This judgment took away Adam's right to live. That which would provide a ransom price must be the right of another perfect human creature to live. The perfect man Jesus possessed exactly that thing, viz., the right to live on earth as a man.

The redemption of man from death and its effects, and deliverance therefrom, is the expressed will of God. (1 Tim. 2: 4) Jesus came to do the will of God, as it was written of him: "Lo, I come: in the volume of the book it is written of me, I delight to do thy will, O my God: yea, thy law is within my heart." —Ps. 40: 7, 8.

God having promised to ransom man, now he had provided a way to carry out his promise by his Son's willingly becoming a man. "And being found in fashion as a man, he humbled himself, and became obedient unto death, even the death of the cross." (Phil. 2: 8) Jesus willingly submitted to death; because it was the will of God to thereby provide the ransom price.

Now the question, Why must Jesus die? is answered briefly. The perfect man Jesus, while he remained alive, could not provide a ransom price. He must now convert his perfect human life into an asset of value, which asset would be sufficient to release man from judgment and from the condemnation resulting from that judgment. He must lay down his human life that the value thereof might be presented to divine justice instead or in place of that which Adam had forfeited, to the end that Adam and his race might have an opportunity to live. Otherwise stated, Jesus must make his human life and the right thereto a legal tender for the payment of Adam's debt.

Legal tender means currency, money, measure of value, which the law requires and receives in satisfaction of debts or obligations.

Merit means value gained. By the merit of Christ Jesus we mean the perfect humanity of Jesus and all the rights incident thereto converted into value or an asset, which is legal tender for the payment of man's debt.

To illustrate this point: Take a man, whom we will call John for convenience, who is languishing in prison to satisfy a fine of a hundred dollars, because of his inability to pay that fine. John's brother Charles is willing to pay the fine, but he has no money with which to pay. Charles is strong and vigorous, has time to work and is willing to work; but his strength and time and willingness will not pay the debt for his brother John. Smith desires someone to work for him, and has the money with which to pay. Charles engages himself to work for Smith, and earns a hundred dollars in cash and receives it. Thereby Charles has reduced his time, strength and vigor into a money value, which has purchasing power, and which is legal tender for the purpose of the payment of John's obligations. This money may properly be called merit, because of its purchasing value or redemptive value. Charles then appears before the court which entered the judgment against his brother, and offers to pay the hundred dollars which the law demands of John. The court accepts the hundred dollars and releases John. John is thereby judicially released from the judgment; and his brother Charles has become his ransomer, or redeemer.

Adam was a son of God. It was judicially determined by Jehovah that Adam should forfeit his life in death, which judgment would mean the eternal death of Adam and all his offspring unless he and they should be redeemed. As Adam possessed the power to beget children before this judicial determination, all of Adam's offspring came under the effects of the judgment. He is now held in death to meet the requirements of the law. The entire human race is in a similar condition, resulting from the original sin of Adam.

Jesus, the perfect man, the Son of God, was designated by the Lord as "*the* Son of *the* man"; this title implying that he, being the only perfect man that has lived on earth since Adam, was entitled to everything that belonged to Adam, life and all the blessings incident thereto. Jesus had the power to produce a perfect race of people, and was in every respect the exact equal of Adam before Adam sinned. It was the will of God that Jesus should redeem Adam and his posterity. Jesus was willing to pay Adam's debt and redeem him; but the perfect, righteous human creature Jesus could not accomplish that purpose while living in the flesh, for the same reason that Charles could not use his strength, time and energy to pay the debt of his brother John, but must first reduce these to a purchasing value.

Jesus must reduce his perfect humanity to a measure of value (which measure of value we call merit), which value or merit constitutes legal tender for the payment of the debt of Adam and his offspring, furnishing the price sufficient to judicially release them all. To provide this ransom price Jesus must die. But to present the value of it before Jehovah he must be alive and have access to the court of Jehovah.

At the Jordan the perfect man Jesus presented himself in consecration to do the will of Jehovah; and it was God's will that Jesus should there lay down his life in death, but that he should *not forfeit the legal right to life as a man.* It was the will of God that Christ Jesus should be raised out of death a divine creature, and as such should take up that merit or right or value of his perfect human life and use it as an asset or legal tender in harmony with the divine will, viz., to judicially release mankind and to provide life for the human race. Why not use the term "legally release"? The Lord could not provide for an illegal release of the human race, because he must be just. We here use the term "judicially release" because that means that the release is done in a judicial capacity or manner, by the one having authority to release.

This argument is in harmony with the statement of Jesus: "The thief cometh not, but for to steal, and to kill, and to destroy: I am come that they [the people, the human race] might have life, and that

REDEMPTION PROVIDED

Page 168

they might have it more abundantly. I am the good shepherd: the good shepherd giveth his life for the sheep. As the Father knoweth me, even so know I the Father: and I lay down my life for the sheep. Therefore doth my Father love me, because *I lay down my life, that I might take it again.* No man taketh it from me, but I lay it down of myself [willingly]. I have *power to lay it down, and I have power to take it again.* This commandment have I received of my Father.''—John 10: 10, 11, 15, 17, 18.

Satan has done much to becloud the minds of earnest searchers for the truth concerning the philosophy of the ransom. He has made some believe that it was provided for the benefit of only a few, and that all others are predestinated to be lost. He has made others believe that it has no value whatsoever.

For whom did Jesus die? This question must be answered from the Scriptures. Everyone should desire to know the truth. ''Thy word is truth.'' (John 17: 17) It would seem strange if God would provide for his blessing to extend to a few, and not grant a similar privilege to all. The Scriptures answer: ''For God so loved the world, that he gave his only begotten Son, that whosoever believeth in him should not perish, but have everlasting life. For God sent not his Son into the world to condemn the world; but that the world through him might be saved.''—John 3: 16, 17.

The Apostle Paul discusses this matter; and writing (as we know) under inspiration, he declared it to be the will of God that by virtue of the ransom price all men should be redeemed from death and that then each one must be given a knowledge of God's arrangement, to the end that each one may have the opportunity to exercise his free moral agency and accept or reject the offer of life that comes through the ransom sacrifice. His argument is this: "For this is good and acceptable in the sight of God our Saviour; who will have all men to be saved, and to come unto the knowledge of the truth. For there is one God, and one mediator between God and men, the man Christ Jesus; who gave himself a ransom for all, to be testified in due time."—1 Tim. 2: 3-6.

The same apostle again proves that Jesus was a perfect man and not a spirit creature, and that he was made perfect in order that he might redeem the human race. His argument reads: "But we see Jesus, who was made a little lower than the angels, for the suffering of death, crowned with glory and honour: that he by the grace of God should taste death for every man."—Heb. 2: 9.

But how could a man, even though perfect, redeem the human race by merely dying? If he remained dead he could not carry out the redemption and deliverance, because a dead man can do nothing. The great court entering the judgment against man, and the place at which the ransom price must be presented, is the court of Jehovah. Of course Jehovah could have appointed somebody else to present to him the value of the sacrifice of the perfect man Jesus, but it did not please him to do this. It was his purpose that Jesus should be both the ransomer and the deliverer of the human race; and he could not be the deliverer if he remained dead. It was therefore necessary for Jesus to be resurrected.

The question may be asked: If Jesus was put to

death as a man, and the value of his sacrifice as a man must be presented in heaven, how could a man appear in heaven and present that ransom price? The answer is: He could not, for the reason that no man has access to the spiritual realm. A human creature is confined to earth. Jesus died as a man, but his Father Jehovah raised him out of death a *spirit* creature. About this the apostle plainly says: "Because Christ also suffered for sins once, the righteous for the unrighteous, that he might bring us to God; being put to death in the flesh, but made alive in the spirit." —1 Pet. 3:18, *R.V.*

### HIS RESURRECTION

Resurrection of the dead means an awakening out of death and a standing up again to perfect life. The man Jesus was dead and must forever remain dead as a man, to the end that his right to live as a human creature might furnish the redemptive price.

The resurrection of Jesus was up to that time the greatest demonstration of God's power ever made manifest to man. The resurrection of Jesus was and is a part of God's great arrangement for man's deliverance. This being true, it is to be expected that Satan the enemy would do all within his power to prevent the resurrection of Jesus, and failing in that he would do everything possible to blind the people to the truth thereof. Such is exactly what is found in the record. It is reasonable to conclude that Satan knew the words of the prophecies. It was written concerning Jesus: "As for me, I will behold thy face in righteousness: I shall be satisfied, when I awake, with thy likeness." (Ps. 17:15) "For thou wilt not leave my soul in hell; neither wilt thou suffer thine Holy One to see corruption. Thou wilt shew me the path of life: in thy presence is fulness of joy; at thy right hand there are pleasures for evermore." (Ps. 16:10,11) These scriptures are sufficient to show that Jesus' resurrection was anticipated. For the first day after Jesus' death the Devil and his invisible angels, and probably some of his visible ones, would be celebrating. They would be felicitating one another over the death of Jesus. At the first sober moment, they would recall his words concerning his resurrection. The record is: "Now the next day, that followed the day of the preparation, the chief priests and Pharisees came together unto Pilate, saying, Sir, we remember that that deceiver said, while he was yet alive, After three days I will rise again. Command therefore that the sepulchre be made sure until the third day, lest his disciples come by night, and steal him away, and say unto the people, He is risen from the dead; so the last error shall be worse than the first. Pilate said unto them, Ye have a watch: go your way, make it as sure as ye can. So they went, and made the sepulchre sure, sealing the stone, and setting a watch."—Matt. 27:62-66.

But how would the chief priests and Pharisees know that Jesus had said that he would be raised from the dead on the third day? There is no evidence that he had made such a statement to them or in their presence or hearing. On the contrary the Scriptures show that Jesus had told his disciples that he would be raised on the third day. But he had told them privately, and not even they understood at the time what he meant; but subsequently they did understand it.—Matt. 16:21; 20:17, 18; Mark 9:31; Luke 9:19-22; 18:31-33.

The reasonable conclusion is that Satan the enemy knew of the words of Jesus to the disciples, and that he had put the thought into the minds of the Pharisees. Satan would reason that he would prevent the resurrection of Jesus, if possible, and, failing in this, he would so confuse the minds of the people that they would not believe that Jesus had been raised from the dead. Satan failed in the first, but he has fairly well succeeded in confusing the truth of the resurrection of Jesus. God has given such abundant proof, however, as to the fact of the resurrection of Jesus that all may know, and all will know when their minds are opened to a proper understanding.

By reference to the above scriptures it is seen that Jesus was careful to tell his disciples, when they were alone, concerning his resurrection. The Pharisees therefore could not have expected his resurrection within three days, unless the enemy had injected such thoughts into their minds. Having received this suggestion from Satan, and having been authorized by Pilate to provide a guard, the clergy hired a guard and put them at the tomb to watch. This guard kept close watch; but in due time there came to the tomb the angel of Jehovah, rolled back the stone from the door and opened the sepulcher. The guards, greatly frightened by what they saw and heard, hurried away to the city to tell the clergy that Jesus had been resurrected from the dead.

At once the unholy triumvirate called a council. In this council are seen the commercial, the political, and the clergy element, expressing all the wisdom they had and trying to solve their difficulty. After much deliberation the financial part of the trio raised a large sum of money and passed it into the hands of the clergy, and they in turn bribed the guardsmen to lie, "saying, Say ye, His disciples came by night, and stole him away while we slept. And if this come to the governor's ears, we will persuade him, and secure you. So they took the money, and did as they were taught: and this saying is commonly reported among the Jews until this day."—Matt. 28:13-15.

So well did they work this scheme that for over nineteen centuries a major portion of the peoples of earth have not believed in the resurrection of Jesus. The Devil was able to create such a doubt that many have not known whether the Lord Jesus was resurrected or whether his disciples carried away the body. But, notwithstanding this effort of the enemy, Jehovah saw to it that an abundance of proof was provided, sufficient to satisfy any searcher for truth then or thereafter that he had raised up his beloved Son out of death.

### THE PROOF

When God raised up Jesus out of death, the great Master did not appear to the clergy that they might see him and be witnesses. Had he done so they would not have told the truth about it. It will be observed that the Lord never uses wicked ones for his official witnesses. Some may talk in his name, but they do so without authority. The Lord chose as witnesses to the resurrection those who had been faithful and those who loved him.

Matthew was a faithful man. He afterwards gave his testimony; and having previously received the promise from the Lord that the words the disciples spoke on earth would be confirmed in heaven, the testimony of Matthew may be taken as importing absolute verity. His testimony is that at the end of the sabbath day, which would be early in the morning of the first day of the week, which we commonly call Sunday, two faithful women made their way to the sepulcher of our Lord. They there saw an angel of the Lord, who appeared in the form of a man. "And the angel answered and said unto the women, Fear not ye: for I know that ye seek Jesus, which was crucified. He is not here; for he is risen, as he said. Come, see the place where the Lord lay. And go quickly, and tell his disciples that he is risen from the dead; and, behold, he goeth before you into Galilee; there shall ye see him: lo, I have told you. And they departed quickly from the sepulchre, with fear and great joy, and did run to bring his disciples word. And as they went to tell his disciples, behold, Jesus met them, saying, All hail. And they came and held him by the feet, and worshipped him. Then said Jesus unto them, Be not afraid: go tell my brethren, that they go into Galilee, and there shall they see me." —Matt. 28:5-10.

Following the direction that had been given them the faithful eleven disciples journeyed to Galilee and into a mountain where Jesus had appointed them, and there they saw and worshiped him.—Matt. 28:16, 17.

One of the best methods of testing the veracity of witnesses who testify about the same subject matter is to note that their testimony is substantially the same. If one witness tells word for word what the other witness has said, it is almost conclusive that both witnesses are telling a falsehood and that they have manufactured their testimony for a purpose. But where the same cardinal points are set forth in their testimony, then, though told in a different manner, this is strong evidence that they are telling the truth. There is a substantial agreement in the testimony of these witnesses. Each one told his story in his own particular way, and told the truth.

The testimony of Mark is practically the same as that of Matthew. (Mark 16:1-7) The testimony of Luke also corroborates that of the other two witnesses above mentioned. He tells of the women going to the sepulcher and finding the stone rolled away, that they entered the tomb and that the body of Jesus was gone; and while perplexed and reasoning about why it was so, two men (angels, in fact) appeared unto them and said: "Why seek ye the living among the dead? He is not here, but is risen."—Luke 24:5, 6.

The testimony of John differs somewhat in detail, but is substantially the same as that of the other three narrators. (John 20:1-10) These disciples would gather the facts from the women who were the first to be at the tomb, and each one would tell the facts as he heard them from their lips, and from what he saw. Since there is no difference in the principal facts, there is no reason to doubt the testimony of any of these witnesses. In addition to that, the record was written under inspiration and is safeguarded by the Lord, and therefore can be readily accepted as the truth.

It was God's purpose to make the evidence conclusive concerning the Lord's resurrection, not for the benefit of the enemy, but for the benefit of those who would desire to know either then or thereafter. To this end the Lord Jesus appeared on a number of occasions to his disciples, for a brief space of time on each occasion, and left some striking testimony that would be convincing. He did not appear in the body that was crucified. Had he done so they would have been inclined to think that it was merely the man Jesus that had gone to sleep and had awakened again. His body did not see corruption, because the Lord said it should not see corruption. (Ps. 16: 10) When Jesus was raised from the dead he was no longer a man, but, on the contrary, he was the express image of Jehovah, and sat down at the right hand of the Majesty on high. (Heb. 1: 3; Phil. 2: 6-11) Such would have been impossible for a human creature. Flesh and blood cannot inherit the kingdom of God. —1 Cor. 15: 50.

When Jesus was raised from the dead he declared: "I am he that liveth, and was dead; and, behold, I am alive for evermore, Amen; and have the keys of hell and of death." (Rev. 1: 18) Again, he said that all power in heaven and earth was committed into his hands. (Matt. 28: 18) Being clothed with all power in heaven and in earth, then it follows that our Lord had the power to create a body at will, in which he might appear to his disciples; and this explains how he appeared to them at various times in different bodies. Had he appeared in the body in which he was crucified they would have immediately recognized him, but it is remembered that when Mary saw him she did not recognize him until he spoke to her in his familiar way. His appearances to the witnesses shortly following his resurrection are briefly stated as follows:

On Sunday morning, on the first day of the week, the morning of his resurrection, Mary Magdalene saw him near the sepulcher, "and knew not that it was Jesus. Jesus saith unto her, Woman, why weepest thou? whom seekest thou?" (John 20:14-17) Mary on this occasion thought that he was the gardener, until she heard the sound of his familiar voice.

On the same morning the women returning from the sepulcher saw the Master. "And as they went to tell his disciples, behold, Jesus met them, saying, All hail. And they came and held him by the feet, and worshipped him. Then said Jesus unto them, Be not afraid: go tell my brethren, that they go into Galilee, and there shall they see me."—Matt. 28:9, 10.

Simon Peter saw Jesus on the same day near Jerusalem. (Luke 24:34) On this same Sunday morning, while walking to Emmaus, two of the disciples were overtaken by Jesus; and he journeyed with them and they did not recognize him until he sat with them to eat and blessed the food in his familiar way.—Luke 24:13-21, 30, 31.

On the same Sunday evening near Jerusalem ten of the disciples saw him.—John 20:19-25.

Thereafter he again appeared to the disciples at Jerusalem, when Thomas was with them. This was one week after his resurrection.—John 20:26-29.

A few days later, while seven of his disciples were fishing in the sea of Galilee he appeared to them and held conversation with them.—John 21:1-23.

A few days later he appeared to the eleven on a mountain near Galilee.—Matt. 28:16-20.

Again he appeared to a company of more than five

hundred gathered by appointment in Galilee.—1 Cor. 15:6.

On another occasion James saw him alone.—1 Cor. 15:7.

His last appearance was on the Mount of Olives, to his disciples, at the time of his ascension.—Acts 1:6-9.

Saul of Tarsus had opposed the Lord and persecuted him. Bent on the slaughter of the disciples of the Lord, Saul was on his journey to Damascus, when suddenly there shone about him a light more brilliant than the sun at noonday. This was a manifestation of the Lord in his resurrected glory. On this occasion the Lord spoke to Saul and said to him: "I am Jesus, whom thou persecutest." (Acts 9:1-9) Afterwards Saul of Tarsus was called Paul. He accepted the Lord, was begotten and anointed of the holy spirit, and became a special minister of Christ, clothed with power and authority to speak the Word of Truth.

Writing concerning the Master, Jesus of Nazareth, Paul said: "For I delivered unto you first of all that which I also received, how that Christ died for our sins according to the scriptures; and that he was buried, and that he arose again the third day according to the scriptures; and that he was seen of Cephas, then of the twelve: after that, he was seen of above five hundred brethren at once; of whom the greater part remain unto this present, but some are fallen asleep. After that, he was seen of James; then of all the apostles. And last of all he was seen of me also, as of one born out of due time."—1 Cor. 15:3-8.

Then Paul sets forth an argument clear and convincing, concerning the resurrection of the Lord, in which he proves that Jesus was raised from the dead, that his resurrection was necessary, and that unless he was raised from the dead there is no hope for the human family. But with positiveness he asserts, 'Christ has been raised from the dead and has become the firstfruits of them that slept,' and that the resurrection of Christ Jesus was a guarantee that in God's due time he would resurrect others who have died.—1 Cor. 15:12-26.

Again Paul wrote that God has appointed a day for the judgment of the world, and that he has given assurance of that time, in that he raised up Christ Jesus from the dead.—Acts 17:31.

The beloved Apostle John, faithful and true to the Lord to the end, under inspiration wrote this concerning the Lord Jesus: "That which was from the beginning, which we have heard, which we have seen with our eyes, which we have looked upon, and our hands have handled, of the Word of life; (for the life was manifested, and we have seen it, and bear witness, and shew unto you that eternal life, which was with the Father, and was manifested unto us;) that which we have seen and heard declare we unto you, that ye also may have fellowship with us: and truly our fellowship is with the Father, and with his Son Jesus Christ."—1 John 1:1-3.

The resurrection of the Lord Jesus Christ is proven so cogently and convincingly by the Scriptures that there cannot remain a doubt in the mind of anyone who believes that the Bible was written as the Word of God.

### SIN-OFFERING

The value of the perfect human life, laid down at the tree, but the right to which life survived, constituted the purchase price or ransom price which we call merit, as hereinbefore defined. Jesus died upon the tree, but his right to live was not taken away. There is a vast difference between living and having the right to live. Adam had the right to live, but he sinned. Immediately after the judgment was entered against him his right to life was gone, yet he survived for 930 years. Jesus actually died upon the tree; but, dying as a voluntary sacrifice, his right to life did not perish, but survived.

It was Adam's commission of sin that caused God to sentence him to death. If Adam or any of his race were ever to be released it must be after the offering for sin is made, which offering must be the ransom price, namely, the merit or valuable thing or right to a perfect human life. This offering must be made in heaven. Therefore, in order for Jesus to present his sin-offering he must be raised from the dead a spirit creature and appear in the presence of God in heaven itself and there present the value of his sacrifice at the court of sentence.—Heb. 9:20-26.

The proof is conclusive that Jesus was made flesh and dwelt amongst men; that he suffered death in order that he might provide the redemptive price for men; that God raised him out of death a divine creature and exalted him to a position above all others in the universe, God alone excepted. "Who, though being in God's form, yet did not meditate a usurpation to be like God, but divested himself, taking a bondman's form, having been made in the likeness of men; and being in condition as a man, he humbled himself, becoming obedient unto death, even the death of the cross. And therefore God supremely exalted him, and freely granted to him that name which is above every name; in order that in the name of Jesus every knee should bend, of those in heaven, and of those on earth, and of those beneath; and every tongue confess that Jesus Christ is Lord, for the glory of God the Father."—Phil. 2:6-11, *Diag.*

### FORESHADOWED

Now we can understand the picture made when Abraham offered his son Isaac. There Abraham was a type of Jehovah God. Isaac his only son was a type of Jesus, the beloved and only begotten Son of Jehovah. Abraham went as far as possible in offering his son a living sacrifice without actually taking his life. But the picture was sufficient to show that God would offer his beloved Son a living sacrifice, and this was the lesson that Jehovah purposed to teach. At the moment when Abraham's hand was descending with a knife to strike dead his son, God stopped him and through his angel spoke to Abraham. "And the angel of the Lord called unto him out of heaven, and said, Abraham, Abraham: and he said, Here am I. And he said, Lay not thine hand upon the lad, neither do thou any thing unto him: for now I know that thou fearest God, seeing thou hast not withheld thy son, thine only son, from me."—Gen. 22:11, 12.

Then and there God gave to Abraham that promise in which all mankind is vitally interested, because it foretells the coming of the great Deliverer of mankind through whom all the nations of the earth shall be blessed. We read: "By myself have I sworn, saith the Lord; for because thou hast done this thing, and hast not withheld thy son, thine only son; that in blessing I will bless thee, and in multiplying I will multiply thy seed as the stars of the heaven, and as the sand which is upon the sea shore; and thy seed shall possess the gate of his enemies: and in thy seed shall all the nations of the earth be blessed: because thou hast obeyed my voice."—Gen. 22:16-18.

Again, the death of Jesus was foreshadowed in the passover instituted in Egypt. (Ex. 12:1-12) A lamb was taken up on the tenth day of Nisan, which lamb must be without spot or blemish. On the fourteenth day of that same month the lamb must be slain and the blood sprinkled upon the door posts, which was a sign of protection for the firstborn of the family inside that house and which was a provision precedent to the deliverance of all the Israelites out of Egypt. The antitype of that lamb was Jesus, as it is written: "The next day John seeth Jesus coming unto him, and saith, Behold the Lamb of God, which taketh away the sin of the world." (John 1:29) "And I beheld, and, lo, in the midst of the throne and of the four beasts, and in the midst of the elders, stood a Lamb, as it had been slain, having seven horns and seven eyes, which are the seven spirits of God sent forth into all the earth."—Rev. 5:6.

In these latter scriptures seven is a symbol of completeness; horns a symbol of complete power; the eyes a symbol of complete wisdom; thus testifying that the great antitypical Lamb of God would be clothed with perfect wisdom and all power and authority to carry out the divine purpose; and this is exactly what the Scriptures show was granted unto Jesus.—Matt. 28:18.

The lamb that was taken up to be offered for the passover "shall be without blemish, a male of the first year". (Ex. 12:5) Writing concerning the redemptive price provided by the blood of Jesus, the Apostle Peter, under inspiration, says: "With the precious blood of Christ, as of a lamb without blemish and without spot."—1 Pet. 1:19.

Jesus, being the antitypical paschal Lamb, must offer himself to the Jews on the tenth day of Nisan. It was on the tenth day of Nisan that Jesus rode into Jerusalem and offered himself to the Jews. (Matt. 21:1-9) He must die on the fourteenth day of Nisan in order to fulfil the type, and it was on the fourteenth day of Nisan that he was crucified.

## THE TABERNACLE PICTURE

God directed Moses to build in the wilderness a tabernacle, which was used for the atonement day sacrifices in particular, and which foreshadowed the great sin-offering provided by the death and resurrection of Jesus. The atonement day occurred once each year. On that day a prime bullock was slain in the court. The blood of that bullock was put into a vessel and the high priest took it, together with incense, and fire from the altar, and journeyed from the court into the most holy. There he burned the incense in the censer before the mercy seat and then sprinkled the blood upon the mercy seat and before the mercy seat seven times.

Here was a picture made of the great sin-offering. The bullock in the court foreshadowed the perfect man Jesus on earth. The court pictures the condition

THE GREAT SIN-OFFERING FORETOLD Page 186

on earth, and not in heaven. The most holy is a picture of heaven itself. Israel's high priest represented Christ Jesus the anointed One as the Priest performing the will of Jehovah. The death of the bullock in the court represented the death of the man Christ Jesus. The appearance of the high priest in the most holy with the blood foreshadowed the appearance of Christ Jesus the great High Priest in heaven itself, presenting the value of his perfect human life as a sin-offering.

Paul, in his argument in Hebrews the ninth chapter, makes this matter clear. The apostle first shows that the tabernacle was merely a shadow of something better to come, and then he adds: "And almost all things are by the law purged with blood; and without shedding of blood is no remission. It was therefore necessary that the patterns of things in the heavens should be purified with these; but the heavenly things themselves with better sacrifices than these. For Christ is not entered into the holy places made with hands, which are the figures of the true; but into heaven itself, now to appear in the presence of God for us. Nor yet that he should offer himself often, as the high priest entereth into the holy place every year with blood of others; for then must he often have suffered since the foundation of the world: but now once in the end of the world hath he appeared, to put away sin by the sacrifice of himself. And as it is appointed unto men once to die, but after this the judgment; so Christ was once offered to bear the sins of many; and unto them that look for him shall he appear the second time without sin unto salvation."—Heb. 9:22-28.

### THE MESSIAH

Is Jesus the Messiah? It is of course important to be able to answer this question from the Scriptures, and to have it so clearly fixed that there cannot be any doubt as to the correctness of the answer. The first prophecy relating to the Messiah is: "The sceptre shall not depart from Judah, nor a lawgiver from between his feet, until Shiloh come; and unto him shall the gathering of the people be."—Gen. 49:10.

Shiloh mentioned herein is the Messiah. Unto him shall the gathering of the people be. It therefore conclusively follows that he who is the Messiah must be the great Deliverer of the human race, of whom Moses as the deliverer of Israel from Egypt was a type. (Deut. 18:15, 18) It is found from the foregoing examination of all the evidence that the Logos is the Redeemer of man, the great Messiah and the Deliverer.

The identification of the Messiah has long been in doubt in the minds of millions of honest people, both Jews and Gentiles. The real Jews believe what Moses and the other prophets of God testified. By this time the student ought to be able to recognize who will be interested in keeping the people in ignorance concerning the Messiah. Paul plainly says concerning the Jews: "Their minds were blinded." (2 Cor. 3:14) The identification of the Messiah would necessarily bring gladness to the hearts of those who believe. It would be good news to such. Gospel means good news. Now writes the inspired witness concerning the good news of Messiah: "But if our gospel be hid, it is hid to them that are lost: in whom the god of this world hath blinded the minds of them which believe not, lest the light of the glorious gospel of Christ, who is the image of God, should shine unto them."—2 Cor. 4:3, 4.

Satan the enemy, the god of this world, has caused the blindness which came upon the Jews and which has likewise come over the major portion of the Gentiles. He has used divers means to accomplish this; anything to blind them to God's purpose and to keep their minds turned away from God and his means of deliverance. We will now examine some of the prophecies relating to the Messiah.

"Messiah" means anointed one. "Christ" means the same thing. "Anointed" means that the one who is anointed is clothed with authority to act in behalf of the one who does the anointing. The Messiah, therefore, is clothed with authority to act as the great executive officer of Jehovah God. We should expect to find something in the prophecies that will enable us to determine who is the Messiah and that would corroborate other evidence relating thereto.

Prophecy means the foretelling long in advance of events that will take place in the future. No man can truly foretell future events. But God, who knows the end from the beginning, can foretell future events; and in times past he has used various human agencies as instruments to utter and make record of his prophecies. The invisible power of Jehovah God, viz., his holy spirit, working upon the minds of holy men of old, caused them to make record of events that would take place in the future. Those men did not understand what they then prophesied. It was the prophecy of Almighty God, and these men or prophets merely wrote down the things prophesied under the direction of the holy spirit.—2 Pet. 1:21.

The Apostle Peter testifies that the holy prophets did not understand the things concerning which they prophesied. (1 Pet. 1: 11, 12) Why did they not understand? Because it was not yet God's due time for these things to be understood by men, and because the holy spirit had not yet been given to men.

Now is the due time in which these prophecies may be better understood, and those who have devoted themselves wholly to the Lord and who seek to understand he permits to understand the deeper things of his Word. (1 Cor. 2: 9, 10) Anyone of devout mind who reads the prophecies and sees the fulfilment thereof may understand them.

But how may we know when we have the proper understanding of a prophecy? If we find God foretold that certain things would come to pass, and thereafter we see actually taking place the very things that he foretold, then we may be sure that such is in fulfilment of divine prophecy.

An instance is that of Daniel's prophecy concerning the time of the end of the Gentile dominion. In the twelfth chapter and fourth verse Daniel makes record that at that time there would be great running to and fro and great increase of knowledge. Everyone today witnesses the fulfilment of that prophecy.

Prophecy can be understood only after its fulfilment, or while in the course of fulfilment. When fulfilled we properly speak of the fulfilment as the physical facts; that is to say, the facts which stand out as silent witnesses testifying to the taking place of certain events, which events had been foretold by divine prophecy.

With this rule in mind let us note some of the prophecies recorded in the Bible concerning the Messiah, and then see how Jesus of Nazareth fulfilled these prophecies; and if the testimony proves beyond a doubt that he did fulfil them, this would be conclusive proof identifying him as the great Messiah of whom Moses was a type. We shall find that these prophecies foretell his birth, death and resurrection.

Through the Prophet Isaiah God foretold that "a virgin shall conceive, and bear a son, and shall call his name Immanuel". (Isa. 7:14) Mary, the mother of Jesus, conceived by the power of the holy spirit; and in due time she gave birth to the child Jesus in fulfilment of this prophecy.—Matt. 1:18-25.

The prophet of God foretold that the child would be the Redeemer and Ruler, and that he would be born at Bethlehem. (Mic. 5:2) Jesus was born at Bethlehem, exactly as foretold by this prophet.—Matt. 2:4, 5; Luke 2:9-11.

It was foretold that the Messiah must be of the tribe of Judah. (Gen. 49:10) Mary, the mother of the babe Jesus, was of the tribe of Judah; also her husband, Joseph, was of the same tribe.–Luke 3:23-38.

The prophet of God foretold that the One born to be the Messiah would be the Prince of Peace, who would bring peace on earth and good will to men. (Isa. 9:6, 7) At the time of the birth of Jesus the angelic hosts of heaven sang concerning him: "Glory to God in the highest, and on earth peace, good will toward men."—Luke 2:14.

The Prophet Jeremiah foretold that there would be an attempt to slay Jesus, and that to accomplish this other babes would be slain. (Jer. 31:15) This prophecy was fulfilled shortly after the birth of Jesus, when Herod ordered all the children between certain ages killed.—Matt. 2: 16-18.

It was foretold by the prophet of God that the parents of the One who should be the great Messiah would flee with the child into Egypt, and that the Son of God should be called out of Egypt. The Scriptures show that this was fulfilled at the time the child Jesus was taken into Egypt and brought back after the death of Herod.—Hos. 11: 1; Matt. 2: 15.

It was spoken of by the prophets that he who would be the Deliverer should be called a Nazarene. His parents took him as a babe to Nazareth, in fulfilment of this prophecy.—Matt. 2: 22, 23.

The Prophet David wrote concerning the Messiah that he would come to do the will of God. (Ps. 40: 7, 8) The Apostle Paul testifies that Jesus fulfilled this prophecy.—Heb. 10: 7.

The prophet wrote concerning the Messiah: "Because for thy sake I have borne reproach: shame hath covered my face. I am become a stranger unto my brethren, and an alien unto my mother's children. For the zeal of thine house hath eaten me up; and the reproaches of them that reproached thee are fallen upon me." (Ps. 69: 7-9) Satan had been reproaching Jehovah at all times, as hereinbefore set out; and the testimony shows that these same reproaches fell upon Jesus when he came.—Rom. 15: 3.

Isaiah again prophesied concerning the Messiah, saying: "Who hath believed our report? and to whom is the arm of the Lord revealed?" (Isa. 53: 1) John records that Jesus fulfilled specifically this prophecy. —John 12: 37, 38.

Isaiah again prophesied concerning the Messiah: "He is despised and rejected of men." (Isa. 53:3) John testifies concerning Jesus: "He came unto his own, and his own received him not." (John 1:11) There is abundant evidence heretofore cited concerning how the Jews rejected Jesus and despised him.

Isaiah further prophesied concerning the Messiah that he was wounded for our transgressions: "He is brought as a lamb to the slaughter, and as a sheep before her shearers is dumb, so he openeth not his mouth. He was taken from prison and from judgment: and who shall declare his generation? for he was cut off out of the land of the living: for the transgression of my people was he stricken. And he made his grave with the wicked, and with the rich in his death; because he had done no violence, neither was any deceit in his mouth." (Isa. 53:7-9) All of this Jesus fulfilled, as the evidence hereinbefore set out proves. When he was brought before the supreme court of Israel, and then before Pilate, he made no defense; he was crucified between two thieves; and he was buried in the tomb of the rich Joseph of Arimathæa.

Again Isaiah prophesies concerning the Messiah: "Thou shalt make his soul an offering for sin." (Isa. 53:10) The testimony hereinbefore set forth shows that Jesus was made a great sin-offering for mankind.

The Prophet David wrote concerning the Messiah: "They part my garments among them, and cast lots upon my vesture." (Ps. 22:18) Matthew testifies to a literal fulfilment of this prophecy when, at the crucifixion of Jesus, lots were cast for his garments and they were divided among the soldiers.—Matt. 27:35.

The law provided that the paschal lamb should not have a bone of it broken. (Num. 9:12) We should expect to find something in the antitype of this with reference to Jesus. Concerning the Messiah the prophet wrote: "He keepeth all his bones: not one of them is broken." (Ps. 34:20; 22:17) When Jesus was crucified they broke none of his bones, and the record is that this was that the prophecy might be fulfilled. —John 19:33-36.

The resurrection of the One who should be thus slain, and who is the antitype of David, was foretold by the prophet: "For thou wilt not leave my soul in hell; neither wilt thou suffer thine Holy One to see corruption. Thou wilt shew me the path of life: in thy presence is fulness of joy; at thy right hand there are pleasures for evermore." (Ps. 16:10, 11) This prophecy was fulfilled in every respect. Jesus was raised from the dead and his body did not see corruption, as heretofore stated.

These are the prophetic testimonies made years in advance of the birth of Jesus, and every portion of them was fulfilled to the letter by Jesus. This ought to be sufficient to convince any reasonable mind that Jesus was the Son of God, the great Redeemer of mankind, the anointed One, the Messiah, and the One who shall be the deliverer of the human race. But we are not left to this circumstantial evidence. Now consider some direct and positive testimony, given by men who wrote under inspiration of the holy spirit.

The Apostle Paul plainly states that when God made the promise to Abraham and told Abraham that in his seed all the families of the earth should be blessed, this seed of promise referred to, through whom the blessing must come, is Christ the Messiah. —Gal. 3:16.

The Apostle Peter, testifying under inspiration at Pentecost, told the Jews that the One whom they had wickedly crucified, and who was afterward raised from the dead, is Christ.—Acts 2:23-36.

As heretofore stated, Zion is God's organization. The Apostle Paul, writing concerning Jesus Christ the Redeemer and Savior of mankind, says: "There shall come out of Sion the Deliverer." (Rom. 11:26) Thus the Scriptures definitely identify the Logos, afterwards Jesus, who was crucified and who was raised from the dead, as the great Deliverer of the human race.

From the time of the conception of Jesus, and before his birth, until he hung upon the cross, Satan the enemy used every possible means to destroy him. God permitted the adversary to go to the full extent of his power; but never at any time did he permit him to succeed, even as he can never succeed against God. God foreordained that death should not hold his beloved Son, and when Jesus was raised from the dead he had fulfilled the prophecy, "Death is swallowed up in victory." (1 Cor. 15:54; Isa. 25:8) He it is who once was dead and now is alive for evermore, and who holds the keys to hell (the tomb) and death. He is clothed with all power and authority and is able to save and deliver to the uttermost, and in God's due time he will deliver the human race and bring to all the obedient ones the blessings that God has in reservation for them that love him.

## Chapter X

# *Preparing the Empire*

EMPIRE means a vast government possessing and exercising supreme power, sovereignty, sway and control. The empire herein referred to is God's government or kingdom, organized, possessing and exercising supreme power for the benefit of his creatures, and particularly for the benefit of man. That government or empire is delegated to his beloved Son; hence it is properly called the empire or government of Messiah. The supreme power proceeds from the God of heaven, and therefore the empire is properly called the kingdom of heaven. We must not infer that God has not always governed his obedient creatures. There is no record of the beginning of the exercise of Jehovah's sovereign power. In fact the Scriptures speak of the priest Melchizedek, priest of the Most High God, as picturing the Executive Officer of God carrying out the divine purpose at all times. There is no record of the beginning of his days nor of the end of his life.

But here we consider God's purpose and provisions pertaining to man. God created the earth for the habitation of man. (Isa. 45: 12, 18) The expressed purpose of God is to the effect that the perfect man shall have dominion or rule over the earth. Man's first overlord, Lucifer, who committed the great crime of treason against God, induced man to turn away from God; and man thereby lost life and the right to life. Lucifer, who is now Satan, the Devil, builded a great organization of his own to hold man in subjection to himself and to keep the mind of man turned away from Jehovah, to the end that Lucifer might receive the worship of man. God's purpose is to deliver man from the power and influence of Satan and to restore him to his former condition of life and of blessings incident thereto. To this end God builds a mighty empire or kingdom, with his beloved Son as King. His arrangement is that Christ Jesus shall have associated with him one hundred and forty-four thousand others who shall form a part of his empire. In building this empire God has made no haste, but has majestically progressed with it according to his good pleasure.

Both Zion and Jerusalem are names applied to God's organization. It is out of this organization of Zion that the Deliverer must come. (Rom. 11:26) Of necessity the foundation of the great empire must be laid in God's organization. Therefore it is written: "Therefore thus saith the Lord God, Behold, I lay in Zion for a foundation a stone, a tried stone, a precious corner stone, a sure foundation: he that believeth shall not make haste." (Isa. 28:16) This prophecy, without doubt, refers to Jesus Christ the beloved Son of God, to whom he has committed all power in heaven and in earth. The great empire is symbolically represented as a stone structure, the foundation stone of which is Christ. He was tried and tested, and under the most severe test proved his loyalty and faithfulness to God. It is certain that God can always trust him. He justly earned the title "The Faithful and True".

Jesus is called the "precious corner stone" because he is the dearest treasure of Jehovah's heart. He is the fairest of ten thousand and altogether lovely. "Gird thy sword upon thy thigh, O most Mighty, with thy glory and thy majesty. Thou lovest righteousness, and hatest wickedness: therefore God, thy God, hath anointed thee with the oil of gladness above thy fellows."—Ps. 45: 3, 7.

Jesus is the "sure foundation", the one that can never be removed; always upholding the dignity and honor and good name of Jehovah God. This foundation stone is the foundation and chief corner of the empire that shall carry into operation God's great purpose for the deliverance of man.

As to the time of the laying of this foundation, we have the proof from the Scriptures that it was at the time of the anointing of Jesus. About that time John said of and concerning him: "Behold the Lamb of God, which taketh away the sin of the world." (John 1: 29) About this time Jesus came to the Jordan to be baptized by John, and it was there that the prophecy written of and concerning him was fulfilled, to wit: "Then said I, Lo, I come: in the volume of the book it is written of me, I delight to do thy will, O my God: yea, thy law is within my heart."—Ps. 40: 7, 8; Heb. 10: 7.

Jesus is also pictured as a lamb slain. From that time he was counted as slain and as the great sin-offering on behalf of man. It is written concerning him: "The Lamb slain from the foundation of the world."—Rev. 13: 8.

### ASSOCIATE RULERS

Before Jesus' first advent God had formed his purpose. That purpose provides that there shall be a building upon this precious foundation stone, composed of other stones that shall form a part of the mighty empire. It necessarily follows that the class of persons to be thus made a part of the empire, also the manner of their selection, testing and completion, was prearranged according to the good pleasure of God. Hence it is written: "Blessed be the God and Father of our Lord Jesus Christ, who hath blessed us with all spiritual blessings in heavenly places in Christ: according as he hath chosen us in him before the foundation of the world, that we should be holy and without blame before him in love: having predestinated us unto the adoption of children by Jesus Christ to himself, according to the good pleasure of his will." (Eph. 1:3-5) These words of the apostle apply to those, and to those only, who shall constitute a part of God's great empire which in due time shall govern and rule all the nations of the earth.

It is of keen interest to note that those who are to be associated with Christ Jesus in his empire are not selected from amongst the angels of heaven. It is God who selects them through Jesus Christ, acting as the representative of the Most High God. He lays hold upon or takes them from the human race; that is to say, he selects men possessing the faith of Abraham, as it is written: "Besides, he does not in any way take hold of angels, but he takes hold of the seed of Abraham."—Heb. 2:16, *Diag.*

That which distinguishes Abraham above any who preceded him is his faith in God. Trusting implicitly in Jehovah, Abraham deported himself accordingly. Such faith as exhibited by him furnishes the criterion for the selection of the members of the royal line.

This is in harmony with the lesson which Jesus impressed upon his disciples as of paramount importance, namely, "Have faith in God." (Mark 11:22) It is clearly manifest from the Scriptures that God grants his great favor only to those who implicitly rely upon his Word.

Much that Jesus taught his disciples they could not comprehend at the time. Much he did not teach them until after his resurrection and ascension on high. Without doubt he guided the minds of the disciples then. On the last night he was with them in the flesh he said: "I have yet many things to say unto you, but ye cannot bear them now." (John 16:12) Why could they not understand at that time? The answer is, Because the holy spirit had not been given. It was essential that Jesus die, be raised from the dead and then appear in heaven in the presence of Jehovah God and present the merit of his sacrifice unto Jehovah, before the holy spirit could be given. The giving of the holy spirit to the disciples was an evidence that his disciples had been taken into the covenant for the kingdom.

Jesus had said to his disciples: "Nevertheless I tell you the truth; It is expedient for you that I go away: for if I go not away, the comforter will not come unto you; but if I depart, I will send him unto you." (John 16:7) The comforter here mentioned is the holy spirit. (John 14:26) The promise here is that when the holy spirit should be given then the disciples would understand all that Jesus had taught them and what he should yet teach them. "Howbeit when he, the spirit of truth, is come, he will guide you into all truth: for he shall not speak of himself; but whatsoever he shall hear, that shall he speak: and he will shew you things to come."—John 16:13.

The holy spirit is the invisible power of God, operating upon mind or matter as God may will. Prior to the coming of Jesus the holy spirit, by God's will, operated upon the minds of only such men as God chose for servants and as prophets. These holy men as prophets spoke as God, by his spirit, moved their minds to speak or write.—2 Pet. 1:21.

Joel was one of the prophets. He prophesied that the time would come when God would pour out his spirit upon all those who would call upon his name. (Joel 2:28, 29) This prophecy of Joel had its miniature fulfilment at Pentecost. Pentecost was the fiftieth day after the resurrection of Jesus. At the time of the ascension of Jesus into heaven he had assembled his disciples on the side of the Mount of Olives. He there commanded them that they should not depart from Jerusalem until they had received the holy spirit, and promised them that then they should receive power and that they should become his witnesses unto the uttermost parts of the earth. (Acts 1:4-8) In obedience to this command the disciples remained at Jerusalem. "And when the day of Pentecost was fully come, they were all with one accord in one place. And suddenly there came a sound from heaven, as of a rushing mighty wind, and it filled all the house where they were sitting. And there appeared unto them cloven tongues, like as of fire, and it sat upon each of them: and they were all filled with the holy [spirit], and began to speak with other tongues, as the spirit gave them utterance." (Acts 2:1-4) Thus was made manifest the first fulfilment of the prophecy of

Joel above mentioned, as specifically stated by the apostle.—Acts 2:16-21.

A city is a symbol of a government or empire. It is written concerning the empire or kingdom: "And the wall of the city had twelve foundations, and in them the names of the twelve apostles of the Lamb." (Rev. 21:14) The Lord Jesus Christ is the chief corner stone in that kingdom and the apostles of the Lamb are the twelve foundations.—1 Pet. 2:6.

Prior to his crucifixion the Lord Jesus had promised that he would confirm in heaven what these faithful apostles did on earth. (Matt. 18:18) It was at Pentecost, and after receiving the holy spirit, that Peter testified concerning Jesus Christ, as follows: "This is the stone which was set at nought of you builders, which is become the head of the corner. Neither is there salvation in any other: for there is none other name under heaven given among men, whereby we must be saved."—Acts 4:11, 12.

The Jews had thought to build an empire; and they looked forward to that empire which, under the Messiah, would rule all nations of the earth. The clergy of that time especially thought that they were the builders; but when the chief corner stone was laid they rejected him, even as the prophet had foretold they would do. (Isa. 53:3; John 1:11, 12) The fact that the Jews rejected the chief corner stone in no way hindered or delayed the progress of the building. Now that the chief corner stone and foundation of the new and glorious empire was laid, its building began and progressed according to the will of God. The holy prophet had testified that on this chief corner stone should rest the new government which should bring deliverance to the people. "For unto us a child is born, unto us a son is given, and the government shall be upon his shoulder; and his name shall be called Wonderful Counsellor, The mighty God, The everlasting Father, The Prince of Peace. Of the increase of his government and peace there shall be no end, upon the throne of David, and upon his kingdom, to order it, and to establish it with judgment and with justice, from henceforth even for ever. The zeal of the Lord of hosts will perform this."—Isa. 9: 6, 7.

The apostles were also prophets because they, under inspiration from God, foretold things to come to pass in the distant future. A true prophet is one who gives testimony by divine authority. That Jesus Christ and his apostles constitute respectively the chief corner stone and foundation of the great empire, and that others are added thereto, the Apostle Paul, who also was a prophet, under inspiration testified: "Now therefore ye are no more strangers and foreigners, but fellow-citizens with the saints, and of the household of God; and are built upon the foundation of the apostles and prophets, Jesus Christ himself being the chief corner stone; in whom all the building, fitly framed together, groweth unto an holy temple in the Lord: in whom ye also are builded together for an habitation of God through the spirit."—Eph. 2: 19-22.

### HOW CHOSEN

The members of the empire are not chosen by men nor by man-made organizations. It is God who has chosen them through his beloved Son Christ Jesus. (Eph. 1: 4; 2 Thess. 2: 13; 2 Tim. 2: 4; Jas. 2: 5; 1 Pet. 2: 4) Those who are chosen to be of the royal line are called or invited by the Lord God, through his beloved Son Christ Jesus. (1 Cor. 1:2; 7:15; Eph. 4:4; Col. 3:15; 1 Thess. 2:12) Cannot priest or clergyman of some church denomination call a sinner to become a part of the kingdom of God and then choose him for that purpose? Neither a priest nor any other clergyman possesses any such power or authority. The Scriptures alone must be the guide as to how these are called and chosen. The only way for sinners to come to God is through Jesus Christ, as he states: "Jesus saith unto him, I am the way, and the truth, and the life: no man cometh unto the Father, but by me." (John 14:6) The order pointed out by the Scriptures, of coming to God through Jesus Christ, is as follows: knowledge, faith, consecration and justification.

Faith means to know the Word of God and then to rely upon it. Therefore knowledge must precede faith. "So then faith cometh by hearing, and hearing by the word of God." (Rom. 10:17) From the Word of God man learns that he was born a sinner, that there is no other name given under heaven whereby he can come again into harmony with God, except through Jesus Christ. He learns that Jesus died upon the cross, and that whosoever believes upon him might not perish but have an opportunity for life everlasting. (John 3:16, 17) Coming to a knowledge of this fact man is thereby drawn to Jesus, learns that Jesus is his Redeemer and that to please God he must follow the direction that the Lord Jesus points out. The one thus seeking the Lord God must now exercise faith; and the first thing of importance is to believe that Jehovah exists, and that he rewards those who diligently seek him. (Heb. 11:6) To such Jesus says: "If any man will come after me, let him deny himself, and take up his cross, and follow me."—Matt. 16:24.

Self-denial means a willingness to completely surrender oneself unto God, agreeing to do the will of God, while trusting in the merit of Christ Jesus' sacrifice. This is consecration. This is what Jesus did when he appeared at the Jordan, as it is written of him: 'I come to do thy will, O my God.' This is an agreement that thereafter the will of the man will be exercised in harmony with the will of God, and that he will use his mind and ascertain God's will and then do it.

Now the Lord Jesus presents the man who consecrates to Jehovah. It is Jehovah God who judicially determines whether or not the one thus presented is right. Justification means being made right with God, and it therefore includes the judicial determination by Jehovah that the one thus consecrating is right. The Scriptures therefore show three separate and distinct things involved in justification: (1) faith; (2) the blood of Jesus; (3) the judicial determination by Jehovah; as it is written: "Therefore being justified by faith, we have peace with God through our Lord Jesus Christ" (Rom. 5:1); "Much more then, being now justified by his blood, we shall be saved from wrath through him" (Rom. 5:9); "It is God that justifieth."—Rom. 8:33.

Justification, between the time of Pentecost and the completion of the empire, is by faith and for the purpose of enabling the one thus justified to sacrifice all his earthly hopes and prospects, particularly his right to live on earth. The justification by Jehovah therefore constitutes one an acceptable part of the sacrifice.

To beget means to begin; and the begetting or beginning is to a hope of life and to an inheritance incorruptible. This begetting of the spirit is a covenant that God makes with the one consecrating. God gives to such a one his Word of Truth; and then he causes his invisible power to so operate upon the one to whom he gives this Word as to begin to carry on the transformation of the one thus begotten into the likeness of the Head, Christ Jesus, the chief corner stone laid in Zion.

It is written: "Of his own will begat he us with the word of truth, that we should be a kind of firstfruits of his creatures." (Jas. 1:18) The ones thus begotten are addressed by the Apostle Peter in these words: "Elect according to the foreknowledge of God the Father, through sanctification of the spirit, unto obedience and sprinkling of the blood of Jesus Christ: Grace unto you, and peace, be multiplied. Blessed be the God and Father of our Lord Jesus Christ, which according to his abundant mercy hath begotten us again unto a lively hope by the resurrection of Jesus Christ from the dead, to an inheritance incorruptible, and undefiled, and that fadeth not away, reserved in heaven for you, who are kept by the power of God through faith unto salvation, ready to be revealed in the last time."—1 Pet. 1:2-5.

These are begotten to the divine nature. God has promised such the divine nature if they are faithful to their part of the covenant. God is always faithful to his. "According as his divine power hath given unto us all things that pertain unto life and godliness, through the knowledge of him that hath called us to glory and virtue: whereby are given unto us exceeding great and precious promises; that by these ye might be partakers of the divine nature, having escaped the corruption that is in the world through lust."—2 Pet. 1:3, 4.

### LIVING STONES

The one begotten of the holy spirit is now a new creature in Christ. (2 Cor. 5:17) His hope of life now is on the spirit plane with Christ Jesus. He is counted dead as a human creature, because his right to live as a human creature expired with the acceptance of his sacrifice. To him the apostle says: "Set your affection on things above, not on things on the earth. For ye are dead, and your life is hid with Christ in God."—Col. 3:2, 3.

The one now addressed must be builded up as a living stone in the temple of God, if he would be of the royal line and participate in the great empire. Because he is just beginning he is spoken of as a babe newly born; and addressing such the Apostle Peter says: "As newborn babes, desire the sincere milk of the word, that ye may grow thereby: if so be ye have tasted that the Lord is gracious. To whom coming, as unto a living stone, disallowed indeed of men, but chosen of God, and precious, ye also, as lively stones, are built up a spiritual house, an holy priesthood, to offer up spiritual sacrifices, acceptable to God by Jesus Christ. Wherefore also it is contained in the scripture, Behold, I lay in Sion a chief corner stone, elect, precious: and he that believeth on him shall not be confounded. Unto you therefore which believe he is precious; but unto them which be disobedient, the stone which the builders disallowed, the same is made the head of the corner, and a stone of stumbling, and a rock of offence, even to them which stumble at the word, being disobedient; whereunto also they were appointed."—1 Pet. 2:2-8.

When Peter wrote this the leaders of the Jewish people in particular had rejected Jesus, the chief corner stone. The apostle adds: "He that believeth on him shall not be confounded." To believe means to remain steadfast and faithful; we must show our faith by what we do. "Unto you therefore which believe he is precious." It is a precious thing to observe the chief corner stone and to be conformed according to his way. Such are called to follow in his steps. (1 Pet. 2:21) The one who is thus designated a living stone to be builded up into the building of God is anointed. To anoint means to designate to some position in the empire. "Now he which stablisheth us with you in Christ, and hath anointed us, is God." (2 Cor. 1:21) These are anointed to represent Jehovah and the Lord Jesus Christ.

God having made this promise, and as his promises are never broken, he counts his anointed ones as now a part of the new kingdom or empire or nation. Hence the apostle says concerning them: "But ye are a chosen generation, a royal priesthood, an holy nation, a peculiar people; that ye should shew forth the praises of him who hath called you out of darkness into his marvelous light." (1 Pet. 2:9) In order to show forth the praises of Jehovah God they not only must believe Jehovah is God but must joyfully obey his will, represent his cause, and use the faculties with which they are endowed to testify to his great name and his goodness and his purposes. To do this one could not conform himself to the evil world, but must stand aloof from it and serve the Lord God. The Word of God is his guide. The Word informs him that he must not conform himself to the world, because Satan the enemy is the god of this world. Concerning such the apostle writes: "Be not conformed to this world: but be ye transformed by the renewing of your mind, that ye may prove what is that good, and acceptable, and perfect, will of God." —Rom. 12:2.

The transformation process now is carried on by the Christian, building up his mind by studying the Word of God; from it ascertaining the will of God and by it proving what is the good and acceptable and perfect will of God. It can be easily seen that the Lord would not make anyone a member of that empire unless he is in full and complete harmony with the Lord Jesus, the chief corner stone, as it is written: "For whom he did foreknow, he also did predestinate to be conformed to the image of his Son, that he might be the firstborn among many brethren." (Rom. 8:29) This means that each one who will ultimately be a member of that empire must grow in the likeness of the Lord Jesus, being transformed day by day by virtue of the spirit of the Lord working in him to will and to do God's good pleasure.—2 Cor. 3:18.

"This world" means the people of this earth organized into forms of government under the supervision of their overlord, Satan the enemy. (2 Cor. 4:3, 4) The Devil is the prince or ruler of this world. (John 14:30) He is the enemy of the Lord Jesus Christ, the enemy of God, and the enemy of everyone who attempts to do God's will. The one who will ultimately be of the empire of righteousness must not love the world, as it is stated by the apostle: "Love not the world, neither the things that are in the world. If any man love the world, the love of the Father is not in him. For all that is in the world, the lust of the flesh, and the lust of the eyes, and the pride of life, is not of the Father, but is of the world. And the world passeth away, and the lust thereof: but he that doeth the will of God abideth for ever."—1 John 2:15-17.

Early in the experience of the church it was manifest that those whom God will approve must be transformed into the likeness of Jesus Christ. Christ Jesus is Head over the house of sons, and all the other members of the household must honor Jehovah as Jesus honors Jehovah. They do and must love God with a supreme devotion, and delight to show forth his praises and to testify that he is God. Their very course in the way of righteousness would draw against them the opposition of Satan the enemy.

### ANTICHRIST

After Jesus was put to death Satan the enemy thought that he had succeeded in destroying the heir of promise, who was promised a kingdom. Satan therefore reasoned that he would continue to rule the world without any successful interruption. He must have been disappointed when Jesus was raised from the dead. He must have observed what took place at Pentecost, and there noted the beginning of the building of the other living stones in conformity with the chief corner stone, Christ Jesus. It is reasonable to presume that he was familiar with the instructions given by the inspired apostles to those of the church. He would understand that these who were united in Christ were to form part of the seed of promise, even as Paul had testified. (Gal. 3:16, 27-29) Destruction of this seed would bring reproach upon God, and now this became the objective and purpose of Satan the enemy. He saw that the Lord Jesus Christ, exalted to the divine nature, was now beyond the influence of his (Satan's) power. He realized that he must now do something to counteract the influence and power of those who were being brought into Christ, if he would thwart the divine purpose.

"Antichrist" means that which is offered as a substitute for Christ the Messiah, therefore in opposition to the Messiah. Satan the enemy set about to organize "the mystery of iniquity" or of lawlessness; an arrangement which would be contrary to and in opposition to Christ. Evidently he knew that John had said to the church: "It is the last time." (1 John 2:18) The Devil would therefore reason that if he could corrupt the seed of promise and turn their minds, and the minds of the people, from God he would defeat God's purposes. He evidently saw that the development of the seed of promise would cover a long period of time; therefore he went about the preparation of the antichrist deliberately.

It was in the days of Enos (Gen. 4:26, margin) that Satan had adopted the hypocritical scheme of having the people call themselves by the name of the Lord while at the same time misrepresenting the Lord. He thereby mocked God and brought reproach upon his name. Early in the Christian era Satan the enemy adopted a similar scheme of hypocrisy, but on a far greater scale. He knew that man is so constituted that he must worship something; and if Satan could not get the people who call themselves Christians to directly worship him, then he would inaugurate a scheme by which he would turn away their minds from Jehovah God, and yet let them call themselves Christians.

Satan saw that it would be profitable to his scheme to have the Christians become more popular; therefore the Christian religion became ostensibly the religion of his wicked world. The Devil thereafter planted amongst the Christians ambitious men, those who had a desire to shine amongst men and who in the course of time had themselves appointed or elected to the positions of bishops and chief elders; and in due course there was established a clergy class, as distinguished from the laity or the common people. The clergy thus organized introduced into the church false doctrines taught by heathen philosophers, which of course were the Devil's own doctrines. These were used to corrupt the message of the Lord God. The clergy and the rulers in the church then established theological schools wherein men were trained for the clergy for the purpose of carrying on the work of their system already organized and in operation. In due course statements of belief, or creeds, were formulated and presented to the professed Christians, and anyone who taught contrary to these creeds was considered a heretic and was dealt with accordingly.

False doctrines were freely introduced and substituted for the truth. Amongst these were and are the doctrines of the trinity, immortality of all souls, eternal torture of the wicked, the divine right of the clergy, and the divine right of kings to rule. In the course of time Mary, the mother of the child Jesus, was deified; and the people were called upon to worship her as the mother of God. Satan's purpose in all this, of course, was to turn the minds of the people away from Jehovah. Crucifixes were erected, and the worship of the people was turned to these rather than to let them intelligently worship the Lord Jehovah and the Lord Jesus Christ. Beads, so-called "holy water", and like things were used, and are still used, to blind the people. Gradually, subtly, seductively and wickedly the Devil, through willing instruments, corrupted those who called themselves Christians.

Rome was then the great world power of which Satan was the god. (2 Cor. 4:3, 4) It was in the fourth century that this great world power adopted the Christian religion as the religion of the state or government. Thereby the Devil succeeded in having the people call themselves by the name of God and of his Christ and at the same time constantly bring reproach upon the name of the Lord, and in fact represent the Devil. To show how stealthily and fraudulently the Devil overreached the people and turned their minds from the true God the following is quoted from the history "Old Roman World":

"In the Second Century there are no greater names than Polycarp, Ignatius, Justin Martyr, Clement, Melito and Apollonius, quiet bishops or intrepid martyrs, who addressed their flocks in upper chambers, and who held no worldly rank, famous only for their sanctity or simplicity of character, and only mentioned for their sufferings and faith. We read of martyrs, some of whom wrote valuable treatises and apologies; but among them we find no people of rank. It was a disgrace to be a Christian in the eye of fashion or power. The early Christian literature is chiefly apologetic, and the doctrinal character is simple and practical. There were controversies *in* the Church, and intense religious life, great activities, great virtues, but no outward conflict, no secular history. They had not as yet assailed the government or the great social institutions of the empire. It was a small body of pure and blameless men, who did not aspire to *control society.* But they had attracted the notice of the government and were of sufficient consequence to be persecuted. They were looked upon as fanatics who sought to destroy a reverence for existing institutions.

* * * * *

"In this century the polity of the Church was *quietly organized.* There was an organized fellowship among the members; bishops had become influential, not in society, but among the Christians; dioceses and parishes were established; there was a distinction between city and rural bishops; delegates of churches assembled to discuss points of faith or suppress nascent heresies; the diocesan system was developed, and ecclesiastical centralization commenced; deacons began to be reckoned among the higher clergy; the weapons of excommunication were forged; missionary efforts were carried on; the festivals of the church were created; Gnosticism was embraced by many leading minds; catechetical schools taught the faith systematically; the formulas of baptism and the sacraments became of great importance; and monachism became popular. The Church was thus *laying the foundation of its future polity and power.*

"*The Third Century* saw the Church more powerful as an institution. Regular synods had assembled in the great cities of the empire; the metropolitan system was matured; the canons of the church were definitely enumerated; great schools of theology attracted inquiring minds; the doctrines were *systematized* [i. e., defined, limited, and formulated into creeds and confessions of faith]. Christianity had spread so extensively that it must needs be either persecuted or legalized; great bishops ruled the growing church; great doctors [of divinity] speculated on the questions [philosophy and science falsely so-called] which had agitated the Grecian schools; church edifices were enlarged, and banquets instituted in honour of the martyrs. The Church was rapidly advancing to a position which extorted the attention of mankind.

"*It was not till the Fourth Century*—when imperial persecution had stopped; when [the Roman Emperor] Constantine was converted; *when the Church was allied with the State;* when the early faith was itself corrupted; when superstition and vain philosophy had entered the ranks of the faithful; when bishops became courtiers; when churches became both rich and splendid; when synods were brought under political influence; when monachists [monks] had established a false principle of virtue; when politics and dogmatics went hand in hand, and emperors enforced the decrees of [church] councils—that men of rank entered the Church. When Christianity became the religion of the court and of the fashionable classes, it was used to support the very evils against which it originally protested. The Church was not only impregnated with the errors of Pagan philosophy, but it adopted many of the ceremonies of oriental worship, which were both minute and magnificent.

"The churches became, in the fourth century, as imposing as the old temples of idolatry. Festivals became frequent and imposing. The people clung to them because they obtained excitement and a cessation from labor. Veneration for martyrs ripened into the introduction of images—a future source of popular idolatry. Christianity was emblazoned in pompous ceremonies. The veneration for saints approximated to their deification, and superstition exalted the mother of our Lord into an object of absolute worship. Communion tables became imposing altars typical of Jewish sacrifices, and the relics of martyrs were preserved as sacred amulets. Monastic life also ripened into a great system of penance and expiatory rites. Armies of monks retired to gloomy and isolated places, and abandoned themselves to rhapsodies and fastings and self-expiation. They were a dismal and fanatical set of men, overlooking the practical aims of life.

"The clergy, ambitious and worldly, sought rank and distinction. They even thronged the courts of princes and aspired to temporal honors. They were no longer supported by the voluntary contributions of the faithful, but by revenues supplied by the government, or property inherited from the old [pagan] temples. Great legacies were made to the church by the rich, and these the clergy controlled. These bequests became sources of inexhaustible wealth. As wealth increased and was intrusted to the clergy, they became indifferent to the wants of the people—no longer supported by them. They became lazy, arrogant and independent. The people were shut out of the government of the Church. The bishop became a grand personage who controlled and appointed his clergy. *The Church was allied with the State,* and religious dogmas were enforced by the sword of the magistrate.

"An imposing hierarchy was established, of various grades, which culminated in the bishop of Rome.

"The Emperor decided points of faith, and the clergy were exempted from the burdens of the state. There was a great flocking to the priestly offices when the clergy wielded so much power and became so rich; and men were elevated to great sees [bishoprics], not because of their piety or talents, but their influence with the great. *The mission of the Church was lost sight of in a degrading alliance with the State.* Christianity was a pageant, a ritualism, an arm of the State, a vain philosophy, a superstition, a formula."

Satan the enemy was of course at all times in control of Pagan Rome. The religion of that world power was the Devil's own religion. He now adopted hypocritically the Christian religion; his world power took on the name of Papal Rome, having a visible representative under the name and title of "pope", who claimed to be the representative of the Lord Jesus Christ but who in fact was the representative of the Devil, whether he knew it or not. Millions of good people were deceived by this hypocritical move. Probably many of the clergy were deceived, but surely some of them were not deceived. The pope presumptuously assumed to rule as the visible representative of Christ. For a thousand years Papal Rome held sway over the nations of the earth; and, though deprived of her temporal power in 1800 A.D., she yet exercises a tremendous power amongst the governments of earth.

During all this period of time the Papal system has cited the words of Peter (1 Pet. 2:9), claiming to be the chosen people there mentioned by the Lord. But we see that this claim is absolutely false. The nation mentioned by the inspired apostle is a holy nation; and instead of the Roman empire's being holy and the Roman church's being holy there have been some of the blackest crimes of history committed in the name of and by that system.

Some God-fearing men protested in the name of Christ against the wicked reign of this system. Wycliff, Huss, Luther and others made an open warfare against the papacy. The result was the Protestant denominations, called the Protestant church, organized in the name of Christ. These denominations of course contained many good, God-fearing men; but it was only a matter of time until Satan overreached these. These Protestant systems have organized themselves into real political companies. It has been well said that the Methodist denomination is one of the strongest political organizations in the world.

These various denominations have deemed it their business and commission to convert the world, and therefore think it necessary to bring into their denominations the rich and the influential. They have opened the doors to such and have made them the principal ones of their flocks. They have organized the clergy, as distinguished from the laity; and these clergy meet in councils and synods and control the system or denomination, and use it for political purposes. They make themselves a part of the world and claim that their denominations constitute God's kingdom on earth.

Speaking to such James says: "Ye adulterers and adulteresses, know ye not that the friendship of the world is enmity with God? whosoever therefore will be a friend of the world is the enemy of God." (Jas. 4:4) The word 'adulterer' here used does not refer to a lack of chastity between the sexes, but means an illicit relationship between the professed Christian and Satan's organization. It means that these ecclesiastical systems have made friendship with the world and have entered into an alliance with the commercial and the political powers of the world; and together they constitute the visible part of Satan's organization, which is designated in the Scriptures under the title and symbol of "beast".

And now in more modern times these ecclesiastical systems, claiming to represent the Lord, are presided over by a class of clergymen who call themselves Modernists. It is admitted that the Modernists are in the majority in numbers among the clergymen. A Modernist is one who denies the Biblical account of man's creation, denies man's deflection and sentence to death, denies the great ransom sacrifice and, of necessity, denies the Lord's kingdom.

God foreknew that the ecclesiastical systems, Catholic and Protestant, in the name of Christ would be overreached by the Devil and used for his purposes, as a part of his organization. Through his prophet Jeremiah he stated: "Yet I had planted thee a noble vine, wholly a right seed; how then art thou turned into the degenerate plant of a strange vine unto me? For though thou wash thee with nitre, and take thee much soap, yet thine iniquity is marked before me, saith the Lord God. How canst thou say, I am not polluted, I have not gone after Baalim [the Devil]? See thy way in the valley, know what thou hast done; thou art a swift dromedary traversing her ways; a wild ass used to the wilderness, that snuffeth up the wind at her pleasure; in her occasion who can turn her away? all they that seek her will not weary themselves; in her month they shall find her. Withhold thy foot from being unshod, and thy throat from thirst: but thou saidst, There is no hope: no; for I have loved strangers, and after them will I go."—Jer. 2:21-25.

The prophet here shows, in harmony with the facts as we see them, that ecclesiasticism has turned into the degenerate plant of a strange vine, that she has become polluted, that she has gone after Baalim, the Devil religion; that she has been in the valley, between the political and financial elements of the Devil's organization; and, like the characteristic trait of a dromedary or a wild ass, she illicitly runs after the ultra-rich and the ultra-influential, that she might have the plaudits of men and the honor that the world could bring to her. Ecclesiasticism did not get this from the Lord God, but it was the result of falling under the influence of Satan the Devil.

## TEMPTATION

The term "ecclesiasticism" applies to all denominations, Catholic and Protestant, which have united with the financial and political elements of the earth to form the governing or controlling factors to rule the world. To these ecclesiastics the Devil presented the three great temptations. These temptations he also presented to Eve. She yielded and fell. The same three temptations were presented to Jesus by the Devil, as heretofore stated, and he resisted all of them and gained the victory. And now mark how they were presented to the ecclesiastical systems and how these have all fallen to the wiles of the Devil and have become a part of his organization.

The Scriptures declare that God does not tempt any one. "Let no man say when he is tempted, I am tempted of God: for God cannot be tempted with evil, neither tempteth he any man: but every man is tempted, when he is drawn away of his own lust, and enticed. Then when lust hath conceived, it bringeth forth sin: and sin, when it is finished, bringeth forth death." (Jas. 1:13-15) It was the desire of these ecclesiastical leaders for honor and power that led them into temptation.

Jesus Christ is the great Shepherd of the flock of God. (Heb. 13:20; 1 Pet. 2:25) In the organization of the church the Lord provided for under-shepherds, designating them as elders and teachers. Upon these is enjoined the duty and obligation of feeding the flock of God, to unselfishly look well to the interest of such (1 Pet. 5:2-4), and not to lord it over the people of the Lord. Contrary to the Word of God, the elders or shepherds of the denominational churches organized councils, synods, presbyteries, and like bodies politic, elected their own members to the high offices of popes, cardinals, bishops, doctors of divinity, reverends, etc., and thus formed and created what are properly termed the ecclesiastics of Christendom, the high personages in the denominational churches, Catholic and Protestant. God did not tempt these men so to do. Of their own desire were they led to these steps; and thereby they laid themselves open to the great Tempter, who promptly presented to them temptations similar to those which were presented to Eve and Adam and later to Jesus Christ; namely, the lust of the flesh, the lust of the eyes, and the pride of life.

(1) Lust of the flesh (or body): The power gained by the ecclesiastics in the church, by reason of their position, they have used for their own selfish purposes. They have fed themselves and let the flock of God go without attention. (Ezek. 34: 8) Selfishly they have advanced their own private interests, permitted the people to go without spiritual food, and thereby have caused a famine in the land for the hearing of the Word of God. Yielding to the temptation to use their powers for selfish purposes, they fell.—Amos 8: 11.

(2) Lust of the eyes (or mind): Desiring to possess the seductive things of this world, and to be admired by men rather than to be approved of God, the clergy have yielded to the lust of the eyes; they have clothed themselves in scarlet and long flowing robes, decked themselves with jewels, and have arrogantly assumed a form of godliness while denying the power thereof. They fell ready victims to this temptation.

(3) Pride of life: Jesus instructed his representatives to preach the gospel of his kingdom and to await patiently his second coming, when he would establish the kingdom. He admonished them to keep themselves separate from the world. The ecclesiastics, or clergy, have boldly assumed to represent the Lord on the earth. Satan held before them the temptation that, as the Lord's representatives, they could establish the kingdom of God on earth without waiting for the second coming of Christ; the condition being that they should join hands with the commercial and political powers of earth, which were already under the control of Satan. This appealed to their pride of life. To them it was a wonderful thing to bring the capitalists and the politicians into the church. They yielded to this seductive temptation; they set about immediately to obtain control and rulership of the world, without the aid of the Lord and contrary to his Word.

The clergy met the conditions and they have failed. They have worshiped the Devil, sanctified war, for pay have acted as military recruiting officers, and have resorted to other devilish methods to gain their selfish and ambitious ends. They have ignored God and the Lord Jesus, and have waxed rich and powerful, while associated with their allies and under the direction of the super-mind of the god of this world. They have fallen to the temptation, and have carried out their part of the Devil's arrangement to blind the people to God's purposes. They stand self-confessedly guilty before God and man.

### FALSE DOCTRINES

The ecclesiastics, to wit, popes, cardinals, bishops, reverends, doctors of divinity, and theological professors, have claimed the exclusive right and authority to interpret the Scriptures, and presumptuously deny the right of anyone to preach the gospel except such as are ordained by them. They have set aside the pure doctrines of God's Word and have constituted themselves, through their various organizations, the fountains of doctrines; which doctrines they have sent forth as a river, claiming such to be a life-giving stream for the benefit of the people, whereas in truth and in fact theirs has been a message of fraud and deceit and a stream of sickness and death. By these false and deceptive doctrines the people have been blinded to the purposes of God, and his great provision for salvation has been hid from their eyes.

Claiming for themselves the exclusive authority to interpret the Scriptures, for a long time the ecclesiastics kept the people in ignorance of the text of the Bible by discouraging them in studying it; but now in this day of greater education, when the people might read and understand the Scriptures, these ecclesiastical leaders boldly and flippantly deny the inspiration of the Word of God. Foreknowing that they would take this course, God caused his prophet Jeremiah to write concerning them: "They have forsaken me, the fountain of living waters [source of life and truth], and hewed them out cisterns [man-made systems and doctrines], broken cisterns, that can hold no water [really contain no life-giving truth]."—Jer. 2:13.

For the purpose of turning the minds of the people away from the true God and blinding them the ecclesiastics have taught false doctrines, of which the following are a few, and which are set out here in contrast with the truth for the purpose of comparison, to wit:

The Bible teaches that man was created perfect, and that because of sin he was sentenced to death, thereby losing perfection of organism and the right to life.

Modern ecclesiastics teach that man is a creature of evolution; that he never fell, and never lost the right to life by reason of sin.

The Bible plainly states that man is mortal, and that because of Adam's sin all are born sinners subject to death.

Ecclesiastics teach that all men have immortal souls, which cannot die, which doctrine is supported only by Satan's great lie.—Gen. 3:4; John 8:44.

The Bible plainly teaches that the wages of sin is death, and that death and destruction is the punishment of the wilfully wicked.

Ecclesiastics teach that there is no real death, and that the punishment of the selfish and wicked is conscious torment, eternal in duration; and that to escape such terrible punishment the people must join their church denominations.

The Scriptures plainly teach that Jehovah is God, the great First Cause; and that Jesus Christ, his only begotten Son, is the Redeemer of mankind.

Ecclesiastics teach the unscriptural, God-dishonoring doctrine of the trinity.

The inspired Word of God declares that Jesus Christ is the ransomer of all; and that all members of the human race shall, in due time, have an opportunity to know about the ransom and receive its benefits.

Ecclesiastical teachings of evolution, human immortality, eternal torment and the trinity are denials of the ransom by implication; and now the chiefest among them deny that Jesus was any more than an ordinary man, deny that there is any value in his sacrifice, deny the only Lord God and the blood of the Lord Jesus Christ by which mankind is redeemed.

The Scriptures teach that Christ Jesus is King, the only One who has the right and authority to rule the earth in God's due time.

Ecclesiastics teach the divine right of earthly kings, who are made by big business, to rule the people; and the ecclesiastics have joined hands with big business and big politicians to enforce this rule and to control the peoples of the earth because, they say, it is the divine arrangement for them to rule.

Jesus constituted his apostles as the foundation of the kingdom, and the Scriptures teach that the apostles have no successors.

Ecclesiastics have fraudulently claimed to be successors of the apostles, and thereby have arrogated to themselves great authority and have attempted to deceive, and have deceived the people.

The Bible teaches and emphasizes the second coming of Christ, the great Prince of Peace, that he will take unto himself his power to reign; it admonishes all the followers of the Lord to faithfully proclaim this message of his coming kingdom, and to advocate and follow peace with all men.

The ecclesiastics teach and advocate war; they have sanctified war and wrest the Scriptures to justify their conclusion; they have repeatedly had their portraits made with, and exhibited with, great warriors of the world; they have turned their church edifices into recruiting stations; they have received and accepted filthy lucre in consideration of rendering service for recruiting young men for the war, and have wilfully preached them into the trenches. And now when the evidence is plain and conclusive that the old world has ended, that the Lord for the second time is present and that the kingdom of heaven is at hand, the ecclesiastics ignore the proof, and scorn, ridicule and persecute those who dare tell the truth to the people. Instead of bidding welcome to the King of glory, and telling the people of his kingdom and the blessings it will bring, they openly unite with the Devil in his schemes to control the peoples of the earth in a compact designated as the League of Nations; and piously and fraudulently they declare it to be the "political expression of God's kingdom on earth".

AN INDICTMENT

On July 26, 1924, a multitude of Christian people who had separated themselves from all the denominations, and taken their stand firmly for the Lord, passed a resolution in the form of an indictment against the ecclesiastical element as constituting a part of the Devil's organization. This indictment so clearly sets forth the truth of the situation before the minds of the people that it is here inserted in full:

"We, the INTERNATIONAL BIBLE STUDENTS, in convention assembled, declare our unqualified allegiance to Christ, who is now present and setting up his kingdom, and to that kingdom.

"We believe that every anointed child of God is an ambassador for Christ and is duty-bound to give a faithful and true witness on behalf of his kingdom. As ambassadors for Christ, and without assuming any self-righteousness, we believe and hold that God has commissioned us to 'proclaim the day of vengeance of our God and to comfort all that mourn'.—Isa. 61: 2.

"We believe and hold that it is God's due time for his displeasure to be expressed against wicked systems that have blinded the people to the truth and have thereby deprived them of peace and hope; and to the end that the people might know the truth and receive some comfort and hope for future blessings we present this indictment, based upon the Word of God, and point to the divine provision as the remedy for man's complete relief.

"We present and charge that Satan formed a conspiracy for the purpose of keeping the people in ignorance of God's provision for blessing them with life, liberty and happiness; and that others, to wit, unfaithful preachers, conscienceless profiteers, and unscrupulous politicians, have entered into said conspiracy, either willingly or unwillingly.

"That unfaithful preachers have formed themselves into ecclesiastical systems, consisting of councils, synods, presbyteries, associations, etc., and have designated themselves therein as popes, cardinals, bishops, doctors of divinity, pastors, shepherds, reverends, etc., and elected themselves to such offices, which aggregation is herein designated as 'the clergy'; and that these have willingly made commercial giants and professional politicians the principal ones of their flocks.

"We present and charge that the clergy have yielded to the temptations presented to them by Satan and, contrary to God's Word, have joined in said conspiracy, and in furtherance thereof have committed the overt acts as follows, to wit:

"(1) That they have used their spiritual powers, enjoyed by reason of their position, to gratify their own selfish desires by feeding and exalting themselves and failing and refusing to feed or teach the people God's Word of Truth;

"(2) That loving the glory of this world, and desiring to shine before men and have the approval of men (Luke 4:8; Jas. 4:4; 1 John 2:15), they have clothed themselves in gaudy apparel, decked themselves with jewels, and have assumed a form of godliness while denying God's Word and the power thereof;

"(3) That they have failed and refused to preach to the people the message of Messiah's kingdom and to point them to the evidences relating to his second coming; and being unwilling to await the Lord's due time to set up his kingdom, and being ambitious to appear wise and great, they have, together with their coconspirators, claimed the ability to set up God's kingdom on earth without God, and have endorsed the League of Nations and declared it to be 'the political expression of God's kingdom on earth', thereby breaking their allegiance to the Lord Jesus Christ and declaring their allegiance to the Devil, the god of evil; and to this end they have advocated and sanctified war, turned their church edifices into recruiting stations, acted as recruiting officers for pay, and preached men into the trenches, there to suffer and die; and when the Lord presented to them the clear and indisputable proof that the old world has ended and that his kingdom is at hand, they have scoffed at and rejected the testimony, and have persecuted, arrested and caused the imprisonment of witnesses for the Lord.

### DOCTRINES

"We further present and charge that the clergy as a class have constituted themselves the fountain of doctrines which, in the furtherance of said conspiracy, they have sent forth to the people, claiming such doctrines to be the teachings of God's Word, well knowing the same to be untrue, in this, to wit:

"(1) That they falsely claim to be the divinely appointed successors to the inspired apostles of Jesus Christ; whereas the Scriptures clearly show that there are no successors to the Lord's apostles;

"(2) That they claim the sole right to interpret the Scriptures, and that therefore they alone know what the people should believe, and by this means they have kept the people in ignorance of the Bible; and now in the time of increased knowledge and much reading, when the people might read and understand, these self-constituted 'successors to the apostles' discourage the people from reading the Bible and Bible literature, deny the inspiration of the Scriptures, teach evolution, and by these means turn the minds of the people away from God and his Word of Truth;

"(3) That they have taught and teach the divine right of kings to rule the peoples, claiming such rule to be the kingdom of God on earth; they hold that they and the principal of their flocks are commissioned of God to direct the policy and course of the nations, and that if the people do not submissively concur in such policies then the people are unpatriotic or disloyal;

"(4) That they are the authors of the unreasonable and false doctrine of the trinity, by which they claim and teach that Jehovah, Jesus and the holy spirit are three persons in one, which fallacy they admit cannot be understood or explained; that this false doctrine has blinded the people to the true meaning of the great ransom sacrifice of Jesus Christ, through which men can be saved;

"(5) That they teach and have taught the false doctrine of human immortality; that is to say, that all men are created immortal souls, which cannot die; which doctrine they well know to be false, for it is based exclusively upon the statement of Satan, which statement Jesus declares to be a great lie (John 8:44);

"(6) That they preach and teach the doctrine of eternal torment; that is to say, that the penalty for sin is conscious torment in hell, eternal in duration; whereas they know that the Bible teaches that the wages of sin is death; that hell is the state of death or the tomb; that the dead are unconscious until the resurrection, and that the ransom sacrifice is provided that all in due time may have an opportunity to believe and obey the Lord and live, while the wilfully wicked are to be punished with an everlasting destruction;

"(7) That they deny the right of the Lord to establish his kingdom on earth, well knowing that Jesus taught that he would come again at the end of the world, and that the fact of that time would be made known by the nations of Christendom engaging in a world war, quickly followed by famine, pestilence, revolutions, the return of God's favor to the Jews, distress and perplexity of the nations; and that during such time the God of heaven would set up his kingdom, which will stand for ever (Dan. 2:44); that ignoring and refusing to consider these plain truths and evidences, they have willingly gone on in darkness, together with their allies, profiteers and politicians, in an attempt to set up a world power for the purpose of ruling and keeping the people in subjection, all of which is contrary to the Word of God and against his dignity and good name.

"The doctrines taught by the clergy, and their course of action herein stated, are admitted; and upon the undisputed facts and upon the law of God's Word they stand confessedly guilty before God and in the eyes of the world upon every charge in this indictment.

"Upon the authority of the prophecy of God's Word now being fulfilled, we declare that this is the day of God's wrath upon Christendom; and that he stands in the midst of the mighty and controlling factors of the world, to wit, the clergy and the principal of their flocks, to judge and to express his righteous indignation against them and their unrighteous systems and doctrines.

"We further declare that the only hope for the peace and happiness of the peoples of earth is Messiah's kingdom, for which Jesus taught his followers to pray.

"Therefore we call upon the peoples and nations of earth to witness that the statements here made are true; and in order that the people may, in this time of perplexity and distress, have hope and comfort, we urge upon them prayerful and diligent study of the Bible, that they may learn therefrom that God through Christ and his kingdom has a complete and adequate provision for the blessing of mankind upon earth with peace and prosperity, liberty, happiness and eternal life, and that his kingdom is at hand."

These facts are set forth here, not for the purpose of holding men up to ridicule, but for the purpose of informing the people that the ecclesiastical systems, Catholic and Protestant, are under the supervision and control of the Devil and form a part of his visible organization, and therefore constitute an antichrist. This is true for the reason that they parade under the name and title of Christian, while such claim, in the light of the foregoing facts, is absolutely false. They call themselves by the name of the Lord, but in truth and in fact they represent the Devil. The hypocrisy that began in the days of Enos has become so flagrant in this present day that all who have an open mind can see it.

### IN ADVERSITY

It has pleased the Lord to prepare members of the empire under adverse conditions. Real Christians have never been popular with the world. During the entire period of the Christian era they have suffered much persecution. They have been counted as the offscouring amongst men. From what source could we reasonably expect persecution and adversity upon the Christians? From the Devil and his organization, of course; because God declared in Eden that there would be enmity between the seed of the woman, which is the empire class, and the seed of the serpent, which is the Devil's organization. We are not left in doubt as to who constitutes the seed or children of the Devil.

When Jesus was on earth those who persecuted him were the scribes, Pharisees and priests, together composing the clergy of that day and claiming to be representatives of God. They were hypocrites. Jesus said they were. That class exalted themselves, even as the clergy do today. They posed as men of great righteousness. To them Jesus said: "But woe unto you, scribes and Pharisees, hypocrites! for ye shut up the kingdom of heaven against men: for ye neither go in yourselves, neither suffer ye them that are entering to go in. Woe unto you, scribes and Pharisees, hypocrites! for ye devour widows' houses, and for a pretence make long prayer: therefore ye shall receive the greater [condemnation]." (Matt. 23:13, 14) These same hypocrites claimed to be the sons of God; but Jesus plainly said to them: "Ye are of your father the devil."—John 8:42-44.

There is a period in the history of the world known as the time of 'the inquisition'. It was in that period of time that the ecclesiastical courts were organized in certain countries, and men were haled before these tribunals and charged with the crime of heresy. They were put through a mock trial and subjected to all manner of wicked torture to compel them to confess a senseless creed. Who was responsible for this cruel treatment of Christians? The clergy, who claimed to be the representatives of God and of Christ, but who in truth and in fact represented the Devil. They were hypocrites. Such persecution was not confined to the Papal system.

In due course the Protestants resorted to like persecution. Call to mind the reformer John Calvin, the father of the Presbyterians, who signed the death warrant of Servetus and had him slowly burned to death at the stake because he did not agree with the so-called "orthodox" doctrines of that ecclesiastical system. All the wicked persecution that has been inflicted upon Christ Jesus and his followers has been done by the clergy or at the instigation of the clergy, who hypocritically claim to represent the God of love and his beloved Son.

The Dragon, the Devil, the father of these ecclesiastical systems, was the real inducing cause for such persecution. These ecclesiastical systems, particularly the clergy and the principal of their flocks, are and ever have been a part of the world which is under the control of Satan the enemy. These have taught conflicting doctrines and have fought amongst themselves, until someone would come forward with the truth of God's Word; then they combine under the direction of their father the Devil to fight against the representative of the Lord.

Persecution and sufferings are not to be desired by anyone. Everyone would rather dwell in peace and in happiness. Jesus and his true followers have been persecuted because of their loyalty and faithfulness to God. This being true, and God being all powerful and the very expression of love, why would he permit his beloved Son and his faithful followers to suffer persecution at the hands of the Devil and his representatives?

The answer is that God has not interfered with Satan's pursuing his course of wilful wickedness; he has permitted him to demonstrate his malignant disposition, and to reproach God and reproach everyone who has been faithful to God, because these persecutions would furnish the opportunities for the Lord Jesus and his faithful followers to prove their loyalty and faithfulness unto Jehovah and to prove the same under the most adverse circumstances.

Concerning Jesus it is written: "Who in the days of his flesh, when he had offered up prayers and supplications, with strong crying and tears, unto him that was able to save him from death, and was heard in that he feared; though he were a Son, yet learned he obedience by the things which he suffered."—Heb. 5:7, 8.

If a man prefers bodily ease and comfort and peace rather than the approval of God, then he will put himself in a condition to not be persecuted; and this he may do by proving disloyal and unfaithful to God. But he who would willingly suffer the most ignominious death in order to maintain his loyalty and faithfulness to God can be forever trusted.

Concerning Jesus it is written: "And being found in fashion as a man, he humbled himself, and became obedient unto death, even the death of the cross. Wherefore God also hath highly exalted him, and given him a name which is above very name: that at the name of Jesus every knee should bow, of things in heaven, and things in earth, and things under the earth; and that every tongue should confess that Jesus Christ is Lord, to the glory of God the Father." —Phil. 2:8-11.

Thus did the foundation stone, the chief corner stone, become a tried and proven stone, as the prophet had foretold. Before God granted unto the Lord Jesus the exalted reward of being the head of the empire he put him to the most crucial test. Those who will be approved of God and become a part of the empire must follow in the footsteps of Jesus, which includes their suffering for doing right. "For even hereunto were ye called: because Christ also suffered for us, leaving us an example, that ye should follow his steps."—1 Pet. 2:21.

Why do true Christians suffer? Because God has chosen them out of the world and because they refuse to show allegiance unto the Devil's organization. Jesus said concerning his followers: "If ye were of the world, the world would love his own: but because ye are not of the world, but I have chosen you out of the world, therefore the world hateth you. Remember the word that I said unto you, The servant is not greater than his lord. If they have persecuted me, they will also persecute you; if they have kept my saying, they will keep yours also."—John 15:19, 20.

During the World War from 1914 to 1918 humble Christians residing in Germany were subjected to all manner of wicked persecutions and punishment because they declined to disobey God's command, "Thou shalt not kill." In England, Canada and America like followers of Jesus Christ were beaten, thrown into prison, tarred and feathered, and some of them were killed, because they refused to take up arms against their fellow man and shed innocent blood. The war furnished an opportunity and an excuse for the clergy who, as the representatives of Satan, hated these humble Christians and who induced the commercial and political powers to unjustly punish Christians. Not all were persecuted because of refusal to kill; some were persecuted merely because they were witnesses for the Lord. Men too old for war service, and women who were not at all subject to military duty, because they were Christians were hated by the Devil; and his offspring the clergy induced the persecution and imprisonment of such. For a full account of these wicked and uncalled-for persecutions see *The Golden Age* magazine, number twenty-seven.

The Christian, however, can bear persecutions for righteousness' sake without developing a feeling of bitterness against his persecutors. He realizes that God permits it even as he permitted such upon the Lord Jesus, that the loyalty and faithfulness of the Christian may be tested. He relies upon the promises of God and rejoices.

### PROMISES

Suffering is a part of the training of a Christian to prepare him for the kingdom of God. When he does right and suffers therefor at the hands of the Devil's representatives, then he may have reason to rejoice. "Blessed are they which are persecuted for righteousness' sake: for theirs is the kingdom of heaven." (Matt. 5:10) The Christian is aware of the fact that the Devil has reproached God ever since the time of Eden. It is written concerning the Lord

Jesus: "The reproaches of them that reproached thee are fallen upon me." (Ps. 69:9) The Devil reproached the Lord Jesus when he was on earth. The follower of Christ expects the same thing, and the apostle plainly states that these same reproaches that fell upon the Master fall upon his body members.—Rom. 15:3.

The apostle then goes further and points out that it is a privilege for the Christian thus to suffer with Christ, saying: "For unto you it is given in the behalf of Christ, not only to believe on him, but also to suffer for his sake." (Phil. 1:29) It is a privilege for the reason that it is a condition precedent to entering into the kingdom. "We must through much tribulation enter into the kingdom of God." (Acts 14:22) Paul emphasizes this when he writes: "Yea, and all that will live godly in Christ Jesus shall suffer persecution." (2 Tim. 3:12) Such is the manner in which the Lord has been pleased to select and give the Christians an opportunity to prove their loving devotion to him.

One who is willing to endure all manner of persecution, and even death, for righteousness' sake can be trusted with power and authority. The apostle points out that persecution for righteousness is one of the signs by which we may know that the Lord is dealing with us as followers of Christ Jesus, when he says: "The spirit itself beareth witness with our spirit, that we are the children of God: and if children, then heirs; heirs of God, and joint-heirs with Christ; if so be that we suffer with him, that we may be also glorified together."—Rom. 8:16, 17.

This may be followed as a safe rule: When one

claims to be a Christian, and then indulges in the persecution of another in the name of Christ, that one is a hypocrite, and not a Christian. The Lord Jesus did not revile, even when he was reviled. The course of persecution and reviling, pursued by the ecclesiastical systems, is therefore proof that they are of their father the Devil and his will they will do.

The true Christian does not think it strange concerning the fiery trials that come to him because of his faithful devotion to the Lord and his cause of righteousness. He relies upon the inspired testimony concerning persecutions, as given by Peter, to wit: "Beloved, think it not strange concerning the fiery trial which is to try you, as though some strange thing happened unto you: but rejoice, inasmuch as ye are partakers of Christ's sufferings; that, when his glory shall be revealed, ye may be glad also with exceeding joy. If ye be reproached for the name of Christ, happy are ye; for the spirit of glory and of God resteth upon you: on their part he is evil spoken of, but on your part he is glorified."—1 Pet. 4:12-14.

When Jesus was finishing his earthly ministry he addressed those faithful disciples who had been with him through his trials, and said: "Ye are they which have continued with me in my temptations [trials]. And I appoint unto you a kingdom, as my Father hath appointed unto me." (Luke 22:28, 29) Thus the Master showed that the empire class would be made up of those who are faithful to God and faithful to him. It is not expected that there would be a great multitude of these. On the contrary the Master said: "Fear not, little flock; for it is your Father's good pleasure to give you the kingdom."—Luke 12:32.

The ecclesiastical hypocrites have made the people believe that billions will be of the kingdom of God. It is safer to follow the words of the Lord and Master, Christ Jesus. In corroboration of what the Master said, the apostle states: "It is a faithful saying: For if we be dead with him, we shall also live with him: if we suffer, we shall also reign with him: if we deny him, he also will deny us." (2 Tim. 2:11, 12) The Lord Jesus admonished his followers to fear none of these things, and then gave them this assurance: "Be thou faithful unto death, and I will give thee a crown of life."—Rev. 2:10.

The Devil's organization is designated in the prophecies and also in Revelation under the symbol of a "beast" and also as "an image of the beast". Those who are promised membership in the royal family of heaven are the ones who refuse to give any allegiance whatsoever to the "beast", the Devil's organization. It is written: "And I saw thrones, and they sat upon them, and judgment was given unto them: and I saw the souls of them that were beheaded for the witness of Jesus, and for the word of God, and which had not worshipped the beast, neither his image, neither had received his mark upon their foreheads, or in their hands; and they lived and reigned with Christ a thousand years."—Rev. 20:4.

The apostle shows that all the members of the royal line are subjected to the same temptation. (Heb. 2:18) The same temptation which was presented to Eve, and to which she yielded and fell, was also presented to ecclesiastics; and to it these systems likewise yielded and fell. A like temptation was presented to the Lord Jesus, but he resisted it and won. All the members of the body of the royal family are subjected to the same temptation. Only the overcomers are granted membership in the kingdom. 'Overcoming' means gaining the victory over Satan's organization by an absolute refusal to render allegiance to any part of it, and on the contrary to manifest loyalty and faithfulness unto God unto the end. To such overcomers these promises are made:

"Him that overcometh will I make a pillar in the temple of my God; and he shall go no more out: and I will write upon him the name of my God, and the name of the city of my God, which is New Jerusalem, which cometh down out of heaven from my God: and I will write upon him my new name." (Rev. 3:12) "To him that overcometh will I grant to sit with me in my throne, even as I also overcame, and am set down with my Father in his throne." (Rev. 3:21) "And he that overcometh, and keepth my works unto the end, to him will I give power over the nations: and he shall rule them with a rod of iron; as the vessels of a potter shall they be broken to shivers: even as I received of my Father."—Rev. 2:26, 27.

### IN BONDAGE

The term Zion is applied to the people of God on earth because they are of Zion, which is God's organization. "Babylon" means Satan's organization, and is a term applied to ecclesiasticism. For a long period of time the true sons of God were in bondage to the Babylonish systems, patiently waiting for the time of their deliverance. These have sincerely prayed as Jesus taught them to pray: "Thy kingdom come. Thy will be done in earth, as it is in heaven." They have waited and hoped for the second coming of the Lord and the setting up of his kingdom, having in mind at all times his promise to the disciples just before his departure: "I go to prepare a place for you. And if I go and prepare a place for you, I will come again, and receive you unto myself; that where I am, there ye may be also."—John 14: 2, 3.

In the parable of the wheat and tares, given by our Lord, he shows that this kingdom class would be in bondage to the tares until the time of the harvest at the end of the age. (Matt. 13: 24-30) Then Jesus plainly said that these hypocritical tares were sown by the Devil, that the harvest is the end of the age, that the tares are the seed of the Devil and that the good seed are the children of the kingdom.—Matt. 13: 38, 39.

The Prophet Daniel prophesied concerning "the time of the end"; that is, the time or period in which the evil world will be ending or reaching a climax. Prophecy can be understood only when it is fulfilled or in course of fulfilment. It is recorded in this prophecy: "And he said, Go thy way, Daniel; for the words are closed up and sealed till the time of the end. Many shall be purified, and made white, and tried; but the wicked shall do wickedly: and none of the wicked shall understand; but the wise shall understand." (Dan. 12: 9, 10) The wise here mentioned are those who receive a knowledge of the truth and who joyfully obey it.

Fulfilled prophecy shows that about 1874 and thereafter the Lord began to shed gradual light upon his Word and to bring the true Christians out of Babylonish bondage and restore to them an understanding of the great fundamental truths which had been taught by the apostles but which had been hidden by the blinding influence of the Devil. The psalmist, speaking for the faithful ones thus waiting for the consummation of their hopes, says: "When the Lord turned again the captivity of Zion, we were like them that dream. Then was our mouth filled with laughter, and our tongue with singing: then said they among the heathen [nations], The Lord hath done great things for them. The Lord hath done great things for us."—Ps. 126:1-3.

The typical kingdom of God, namely, the nation of Israel, was overturned in the year 606 B. C. That date marks the beginning of the Gentile times. God having here overturned the right of Israel to rule, Satan became the god of all the world, including Israel. The statement by the Prophet Ezekiel is to the effect that the Gentiles should continue under their superlord without interruption until "he come whose right it is". (Ezek. 21:24-27) Other scriptures show that the period of the Gentiles is, to wit, twenty-five hundred and twenty years.

When the true followers of Christ Jesus began to emerge from the Babylonish systems after 1874, and began to search the Scriptures, and saw some of these wonderful prophecies and evidences of their fulfilment, they soon reached the conclusion that the twenty-five-hundred-twenty-year period of the Gentiles must of necessity end in 1914. Therefore they looked forward with great expectancy to the year 1914. The Lord has rewarded them for watching for the fulfilment of his prophetic utterances.

## Chapter XI

# *The Nation Born*

AS HEREIN used, "The Nation born" means that the constituted authority possessing the right to rule has begun to function; that is to say, has begun to reign.

In the history of men kingdoms are commonly spoken of as "nations". The duly constituted authority that rules an organized people is called a "kingdom", a "nation", or a "government". These terms may be used interchangeably. "Government" and "empire" mean the same thing. If there is a shade of difference it is that "empire" is more comprehensive. It would be proper to say that a kingdom or nation may begin on a small scale; but that when it is extended so as to embrace many peoples, and exercises absolute and supreme power and sway, it may then be properly termed an "empire".

The Scriptures refer to THE Christ as "an holy nation". (1 Pet. 2:9) To be "born" means to be brought forth or to begin to function. It is here used in a figurative or descriptive sense, and as applied to a nation it means that that nation has begun to exercise authority. It is a woman that gives birth. "She was delivered of a man child." (Isa. 66:7) Zion, God's organization which gives birth to the man child, is symbolically called a woman.

In a government or power the right to govern rests upon some duly constituted authority. It is written of the Messiah: "The government shall be upon his shoulder." (Isa. 9:6) "The kingdom [government] is the Lord's; and he is the governor among the nations." (Ps. 22:28) When Jesus was on earth he spoke of himself as "the kingdom", because he was appointed to rulership. (Matt. 10:7) The prophet, referring to the kingdom and showing that it is separate and distinct from the individuals composing it, said: "And the kingdom and dominion, and the greatness of the kingdom under the whole heaven, shall be given to the people of the saints of the Most High, whose kingdom is an everlasting kingdom, and all dominions shall serve and obey him." (Dan. 7:27) The ones exercising the kingdom, as the Scriptures show, are Jesus and those whom he associates with himself as members of his body.

At the time of the overturning of his typical kingdom, the nation of Israel, God indicated that a definite time was fixed when he whose right it is should come and should rule, and at which time he would take his power and begin his reign. (Ezek. 21:27) The one who comes with right to rule, and who in God's due time begins his reign, is the Messiah. (Gen. 49:10) It follows then that when he who has the right to rule takes his power and begins his reign, the world, under the supervision of Satan the enemy, would end. Basing their conclusions upon numerous prophecies God had given them, the devout Jews understood and believed that with the coming of the Messiah the world would end, and that Messiah's kingdom would function and would bless them with the blessings which they desired. The eleven disciples of Jesus who were faithful to the end believed him to be the Messiah. Peter had expressly so stated and had received the commendation of Jesus for the statement, and doubtless the other disciples heard and believed the same thing.—Matt. 16:16.

These disciples believing and expecting that the world under Prince Satan would end and that then the Messiah's kingdom would succeed to authority, they approached the Master privately and propounded to him this question: "Tell us, . . . what shall be the sign [proof] of thy coming, and of the end of the world?"—Matt. 24:3.

What world was meant in this question propounded? "World" means mankind, organized into forms of government, under the supervision of an invisible overlord. Symbolically it is spoken of in the Scriptures as 'heaven and earth'. (2 Pet. 3:7) "Heaven" means the invisible part of the world, functioning and directing both the invisible and the visible. "Earth" symbolically represents that part of the organization that is visible to human eyes. At the time the disciples propounded this question Satan was god, prince and ruler of the world.—2 Cor. 4:3,4; John 14:30.

Jesus plainly stated: "My kingdom is not of this world." (John 18:36) Of necessity his kingdom or nation or government could not be of the world there mentioned, for the reason that Satan was in control; and it was not God's due time for Jesus to take control. The disciples understood that Satan's world must end and that at some future time the Messiah's world must begin; and for this reason they propounded to Jesus the question.

The answer given to the question propounded by the disciples was put in prophetic phrase. The answer could not be fully understood or appreciated until the time for its fulfilment, and then the physical facts would enable those who saw and discerned them to understand the prophecy. Having come to the time for the fulfilment of the answer prophetically given by Jesus, those who are watching and comparing the physical facts with the prophecy see and understand the same.

Jesus, in answering the question, first cautioned the disciples not to permit anyone to deceive them. He said to them, in substance: 'There will be wars and rumors of wars before the end comes. Do not be disturbed about these, because the end is not yet.' Then he stated to them what would be the first evidences or proof that the end of the evil world had been reached. He said: "For nation shall rise against nation, and kingdom against kingdom: and there shall be famines, and pestilences, and earthquakes, in divers places. All these are the beginning of sorrows."—Matt. 24: 7, 8.

And now let us examine the physical facts and see how well they fit the prophetic words of Jesus. He said that the beginning of sorrows, that is to say, the death pains of the old world, would be marked by nation rising against nation, and kingdom against kingdom. He meant a great war, of course, for the reason that he was just speaking of wars. Prior to 1914 all the wars that had ever been fought were army against army and clan against clan. Never before in the history of man was there a war like the one from 1914 to 1918. Every part of the combatant nations was called into action. Men were sent to the front, and women also; while the men and women who remained at home were obligated, under command of their government, to supply the sinews of war.

Everything of the nation was commandeered for war purposes. Even the babes had to perform their part in the conflict, because their food was officially curtailed in order that there might be a conservation of food for the armies at the front. The quantities of flour, meal, sugar and other necessities were rationed to the people at home, to the end that the war might be won. It was nation against nation, kingdom against kingdom, involving practically all the nations of Christendom; and there was never another war like it. Then followed great famines in Russia, in Austria, in Germany and in various parts of the Orient. More people by far died from famine than were killed in the war. Quickly came a pestilence known as the "Spanish flu"; and as this moved from the frozen to the torrid zones it swept the people before it in great multitudes. More people died from this pestilence in one year than were killed in battle during the four years of the war.

Call to mind also that since 1914 there have been more disastrous earthquakes than in any other time of the world's history. These are physical facts which any man except a clergyman can understand. The clergy have literally closed their eyes to all this array of evidence. The Lord made it so plain that "wayfaring men, though fools", can understand. But some of them will not understand.—Ps. 82: 5; Dan. 12: 10.

Then said Jesus: "Then shall they deliver you up to be afflicted, and shall kill you: and ye shall be hated of all nations for my name's sake." (Matt. 24: 9) During this World War there was a small company of Christians who were putting forth their best efforts to tell the people that the World War was a proof of the end of the world and of the coming of Messiah's kingdom. These of course must be classed in as disciples of Christ because they testified to what he said; and for this reason this little company of Christians was hated and persecuted in every nation where its members happened to reside. Hereinbefore reference was made to *The Golden Age* magazine, number twenty-seven, as containing an extensive account of this persecution, which reached a climax in 1918, just before the World War ended.

"And then shall many be offended, and shall betray one another, and shall hate one another." (Matt. 24:10) This scripture was literally fulfilled from 1914 to 1918 by the fact that some who professed to be followers of Christ Jesus betrayed into the hands of the governing factors those who were trying to faithfully represent the Lord.

On November 11, 1918, with the signing of the armistice, the war suddenly came to an end. No one could give a good reason why it there ended, because no side had won a victory. The real reason why the fighting there ceased is clearly indicated by the Scriptures. The Lord desired that the World War, the famine, the pestilence, the earthquakes, persecution of Christians, etc., should serve as a testimony to those who should come to know that Christ is present, that his kingdom is at hand, and that the old world had reached its end. But this testimony could not be freely declared unto the nations and peoples while the war was in progress and while many of the Lord's witnesses were languishing in prison.

The Lord caused the war to come suddenly to an end in order that his declaration contained in Matthew 24:14 might be fulfilled, to wit: "And this gospel of the kingdom shall be preached in all the world for a witness unto all nations: and then shall the end come." Beginning in 1919, and up to the present time, this little company of Christians have proclaimed the good news of the presence of the Lord, of the end of the world, and of the beginning of Messiah's kingdom, in all the nations where the name of Christ is named; and without doubt this witness has been given in fulfilment of the prophetic words of the Master, as another proof of the time in which man is now on the earth.

Other further testimony was given by Jesus, corroborating what he had previously said and further showing that the world has ended and that his kingdom has come. "And Jerusalem shall be trodden down of the Gentiles, until the times of the Gentiles be fulfilled." (Luke 21:24) "Jerusalem" here undoubtedly refers to the Jewish people, because the text distinguishes them from the Gentiles. For nearly two thousand years the desire of the Jews has been that they might return to Palestine. It was about the time of the end of the war that the British Empire, having then assumed a protectorate over the land of Palestine, spoke through her representative Mr. Balfour and declared it to be the purpose and policy of the British Empire that the Jews should return to their homeland and there establish themselves. It is true that there had been previous preparations toward this end, but this was the first time that any authoritative action had been taken to reestablish the Jews in their homeland.

Accordingly in the spring of 1918 Dr. Chaim Weizmann, at the head of a Jewish organization, opened offices at Jerusalem and began the formation of a Jewish polity. Since then there has been a gradual and healthy increase of the population of Jews in Palestine; and clearly in fulfilment of prophecy they have acquired title to lands; have builded houses, colonies, factories; installed irrigation plants; dedicated their great university in the city of Jerusalem; and have done many other things looking to a rebuilding of Palestine for the Jews and by the Jews. This is so clear that no one can doubt that it is in fulfilment of the prophecies of Jesus and of the other holy prophets.

Furthermore, Jesus said concerning the end of the world: "And there shall be signs in the sun, and in the moon, and in the stars; and upon the earth distress of nations, with perplexity; the sea and the waves roaring; men's hearts failing them for fear, and for looking after those things which are coming on the earth: for the powers of heaven shall be shaken." (Luke 21:25, 26) The sun is a symbol of the light of the divine purpose. "The moon" is a symbolic expression used to represent the divine law; whereas stars symbolically represent ecclesiastical leaders. Since 1918 the clergy in the various denominations have practically repudiated God's arrangement for the establishment of his kingdom. They have repudiated the divine law, and refused to walk according to it; therefore these, symbolically represented as stars, have fallen.

Although several years have elapsed since the World War ceased, yet it is fully appreciated by all the people that "upon the earth distress of nations, with perplexity", continues. "Nations," in this scripture, clearly refers to the organized governments of the earth; and all these governments are now in perplexity and distress, not knowing what to do. They are in fear and trepidation of losing their power. Continuing, the Lord said: "The sea and the waves roaring; men's hearts failing them for fear, and for looking after those things which are coming on the earth." (Luke 21:25, 26) The "sea" represents the ungodly peoples of earth. All these things further testify that the world reached its end and began to pass away in 1914; and that there, in the time of the Lord's presence, the birth of The Nation occurred.

### ZION THE MOTHER

Jehovah God is the Father or Life-giver of the empire or kingdom, because he begets and gives life to each one of those who are to make up the reigning house. Zion "the city of God" is his organization, which is also described under the name "Jerusalem", and is the mother of the new government as well as of the individuals who make up the government. It is written: "But Jerusalem which is above is free, which is the mother of us all."—Gal. 4:26.

The prophet of God, in figurative phrase, describes the Messianic government, nation or kingdom as a man child born from Zion, figuratively represented by a woman; and says that this birth takes place before her labor-pains; or, otherwise stated, without labor-pains she brought forth. "Before she travailed, she brought forth; before her pain came, she was delivered of a man child. Who hath heard such a thing? who hath seen such things? Shall the earth be made to bring forth in one day? or shall a nation be born at once? for as soon as Zion travailed, she brought forth her children."—Isa. 66: 7, 8.

The kingdom or nation was not born with a great blare of trumpets and the rolling of drums and the firing of cannon. Jesus had said: "The kingdom of God cometh not with observation." (Luke 17: 20) "The day of the Lord will come as a thief in the night." (2 Pet. 3: 10) Zion gave birth to the kingdom or nation quietly, unostentatiously, and without pain. The government in America, the United States, was born in tribulation or great pain, because those who composed the governing factors were put to much trouble and distress in the bringing forth of this nation. But the government of Messiah, the kingdom, the new Nation, was born without pain. When the due time came God set his beloved Son upon his holy throne. —Ps. 2: 6.

Then the prophet propounded the question: "Who hath heard such a thing? . . . Shall a nation be born at once?" The man child represents the nation or government that is born. At the time of the birth of the government who was Governor? The Lord Jesus Christ, in whom resides all power and authority in heaven and in earth. Those saints who had died prior to the birth of The Nation had not participated in the chief resurrection and were not then a part of the kingdom; and surely the faithful followers of Christ then on the earth in the flesh could not be classed as a part of the man child or kingdom until the Lord came to his temple and examined them and approved them. Therefore, "as soon as Zion travailed she brought forth her children." She brought forth her other children, those who were granted the privilege of becoming a part of the kingdom or nation or government. Zion gave birth both to the government and to those creatures who form that government. Christ Jesus is the Head of the new creation, and he is the Head over the church, which is his body.—Col. 1: 18.

Christ Jesus the divine was born three days after his crucifixion. The other members of his body are born when they participate in the first resurrection. (Rev. 20: 6) The natural order of birth of a child is first the head and afterwards the body. Even so with those who make up the body of Christ and who are the ones participating in the holy government or nation. The government or nation was born when the Lord Jesus took his power and began his reign; and since that time other children of Zion are being born into the kingdom.

We must make a distinction between the government and those individual members who go to make up the government or nation. The year 1914 A.D. is definitely fixed by the Scriptures as the time for the birth of The Nation. In that year the nations forming the Devil's empire became angry and engaged in a World War. The Revelation fixes that date as the time when God Almighty, through his beloved Son, would take his power and reign; or otherwise stated, the time for the birth of The Nation or government.—Rev. 11: 17, 18.

A symbolic description of the birth of The Nation is given in Revelation, twelfth chapter. The woman there mentioned clearly is Zion, the same woman mentioned in Isaiah 66:7. The sun is a symbol of the light of the divine purpose, while the moon represents God's law. Around Zion, God's organization as symbolized by the woman, shines the light of the divine purpose; and thus she is enveloped with the sun. "The moon under her feet" symbolically represents that the course of action of the woman, Zion, is always in harmony with the divine will as represented by God's law. The Head, the Chief Corner Stone of Zion, is Christ Jesus; and upon that Head is the crown, representing complete and absolute authority. The twelve stars in the crown symbolize the light of God that shines upon them that love and serve him. —Rev. 21:14.

On the earth are some of the faithful followers of the Lord Jesus Christ. These have had a mental vision of his kingdom; they were anticipating that it would be born in 1914 and were in great expectation and anxiety until the birth. Therefore they are represented by Zion in pain, desiring the delivery of the man child, which is the kingdom. The man child, to wit, the new government or Nation, was ordained by the Lord from the foundation of the world; but now it was about to begin to function, and those who were waiting and praying for its birth were in anxious expectancy for the birth. Thus the matter appeared to them.

"And she brought forth a man child, who was to rule all nations with a rod of iron: and her child was caught up unto God, and to his throne." (Rev. 12:5) The man child here is the same man child mentioned by the Prophet Isaiah; to wit, the nation or government which is to rule all the nations of the earth. It is the same kingdom described by Daniel, in chapter two, verse forty-four. This man child or new government is symbolically represented as being caught up to God and to his throne, because it constitutes God's kingdom, now beginning to function by virtue of his will and authority.

### WAR WITH THE ENEMY

Watching the preparation of the empire and observing that the day was approaching for the birth of The Nation, symbolically represented by the man child, Satan the enemy was on the alert, with the avowed purpose of destroying this new nation or government if possible. In the Revelation picture he appears under the name and title of Dragon. He is there represented as a "red dragon". The word "red" here used means fiery red, and particularly pictures Satan's devilish, wicked and gory organization, murderously bent upon the destruction of the new government. In this the Dragon was thwarted, because God prevented him.

The new government or nation there began to function; and the first work thereof necessarily was the expelling of Satan from heaven. "And there was war in heaven: Michael and his angels fought against the dragon; and the dragon fought and his angels, and prevailed not; neither was their place found any more in heaven. And the great dragon was cast out, that old serpent, called the Devil, and Satan, which deceiveth the whole world: he was cast out into the earth, and his angels were cast out with him."—Rev. 12:7-9.

In this great fight Michael, who is Christ Jesus, together with his angels, fought against the Devil and his angels; and the result was that Satan the enemy was expelled from heaven and was cast down to the earth. This is in harmony with Peter's words: "The heavens shall pass away with a great noise, . . . the heavens, being on fire, shall be dissolved." (2 Pet. 3:10, 12) The heavens here mentioned clearly mean the Devil and his angels, the invisible rulers.—Eph. 6:12.

Satan the Devil now finds himself, together with his wicked associates, expelled from heaven and cast out into the earth. "Woe to the inhabiters of the earth, and of the sea! for the devil is come down unto you, having great wrath, because he knoweth that he hath but a short time." (Rev. 12:12) The inhabiters here mentioned clearly are the ruling factors of the nations of the earth. They are in for much trouble. The sea represents all of the people alienated from God, and they are in for much trouble. The Devil has great wrath against Zion and against her children, and will gather together the inhabiters and the masses of mankind in a great and final trouble.

Now let the reader turn to the first paragraph of this book and there again read the questions that are propounded, and now let him understand the answer to those questions. The Devil and all his wicked assistants are concentrating their powers and forces in the earth, implanting in the minds of the rulers, as well as in the minds of the people, devilish, wicked thoughts. The profiteers selfishly reach out for themselves, against the common interests of mankind. The politicians selfishly seek their own purposes; the preachers look after their own selfish interests; and the people are oppressed on every side and afflicted. The cause of all this distress and suffering is that the Devil's empire has come to its end; he knows that his time is short and he is therefore desperately seeking to rally his forces for a great and final conflict. The peoples of earth are in great fear and trepidation, groaning in pain and desiring to be delivered; they are waiting "for the manifestation of the sons of God", meaning that they are waiting for the manifestation in their behalf of the powers of the new government. They wait, they know not for what; but they all desire deliverance. Let the people now take courage and have hope, because the time of deliverance is at hand.

### CORROBORATIVE PROOF

When Jesus was raised from the dead he declared that all power in heaven and earth was given unto him. (Matt. 28:18) That was more than eighteen hundred years ago. It was not the will of God that he should at that time begin to exercise his supreme power. Jehovah God then said to him: "Sit thou at my right hand, until I make thine enemies thy footstool." ( Ps. 110:1; Heb. 1:13; Acts 2:34, 35; Matt. 22:44) After Jesus had appeared in heaven and there presented his sacrifice as a sin-offering, he remained inactive against the Devil's institution until God's due time. "But this man, after he had offered one sacrifice for sins for ever, sat down on the right hand of God; from henceforth expecting till his enemies be made his footstool."—Heb. 10:12, 13.

The time must come when God would subdue the enemy, Satan the Devil, and his institution. We read:

"The Lord [Jehovah] shall send the rod [scepter of authority and power rightfully reposed in his beloved Son] of thy strength out of Zion [God's organization, saying]: rule thou in the midst of thine enemies." (Ps. 110:2) This is the same time mentioned by the prophet: "Yet have I set my king upon my holy hill of Zion."—Ps. 2:6.

The new government is now born. Jesus Christ, the King, now stands up and assumes his power and authority and begins his reign, even while the enemy still exercises power; but the enemy's right to that power has expired, his world having ended. Necessarily this would mark the beginning of the battle in heaven; the King of glory and his angels on one side, and Satan the old Dragon, the disloyal son of God, and his angels, on the other side.

It is really the fight of God Almighty against the Devil. The fight on God's side is led by his beloved Son, and in this fight he subdues the enemy. The psalmist thus describes the Lord Jesus Christ moving into action: "Gird thy sword upon thy thigh, O most Mighty, with thy glory and thy majesty. And in thy majesty ride prosperously because of truth and meekness and righteousness; and thy right hand shall teach thee terrible things."—Ps. 45:3, 4.

This marks the time of the birth of the nation or government. God's prophet puts it thus: "In the beauties of holiness from the womb of the morning [the woman, Zion]: thou hast the dew of thy youth." (Ps. 110:3) The new Nation, the government, pictured by the man child now born, is in the vigor of youth and strength and now goes forth to rule; it is the beginning of God's kingdom in action.

## REJECTED STONE BECOMES THE HEAD

It seems quite evident that the Prophet Daniel, in speaking of 'the stone cut out without hands', refers to the birth of The Nation or government. By the time of the end of the World War, in 1918, the church denominations, particularly the clergy and the leaders and principal of their flock who pretended to believe and follow Christ Jesus, were provided with abundant proof from the Bible and from fulfilled prophecy that the Lord was present, that the world had ended, that the time for the beginning of God's kingdom had come. In fact, shortly after the capture of Jerusalem by the allied armies, eight distinguished clergymen met in the city of London and issued the following manifesto, declaring:

First.—That the present crisis points toward the close of the times of the Gentiles.

Second.—That the revelation of the Lord may be expected at any moment, when he will be manifested as evidently as to his disciples on the evening of his resurrection.

Third.—That the completed church will be translated, to be "forever with the Lord".

Fourth.—That Israel will be restored to its own land in unbelief, and be afterward converted by the appearance of Christ on its behalf.

Fifth.—That all human schemes of reconstruction must be subsidiary to the second coming of our Lord, because all nations will be subject to his rule.

Sixth.—That under the reign of Christ there will be a further great effusion of the Holy Spirit on all flesh.

Seventh.—That the truths embodied in this statement are of the utmost practical value in determining Christian character and action with reference to the pressing problems of the hour.

This remarkable statement was signed by A. C. Dixon and F. B. Meyer, Baptists; George Campbell Morgan and Alfred Byrd, Congregationalists; William Fuller Gouch, Presbyterian; H. Webb Peploe, J. Stuart Holden, Episcopalians; Dinsdale T. Young, Methodist.

These are well-known names, and are among the world's greatest preachers. That these eminent men, of different denominations, should feel called upon to issue such a statement is of itself exceedingly significant. This manifesto was sent to the clergy throughout the world and was by them rejected.

But the most remarkable part of the affair is that the very men who signed the manifesto subsequently repudiated it and rejected the evidence which proves that we are at the end of the world and in the day of the Lord's second presence.

The psalmist, the prophet of God, referred to this same time and event, to wit, the birth of The Nation and the rejection of the chief corner stone by the pretended builders, when he wrote: "The stone which the builders refused is become the head stone of the corner. This is the Lord's doing; it is marvellous in our eyes. This is the day which the Lord hath made; we will rejoice and be glad in it."—Ps. 118: 22-24.

The clergy, instead of heeding the truth and proclaiming it to the people, and advising them that the time had come for the reign of Christ, repudiated Christ and his kingdom, rejected him who is the chief corner stone of Zion, and openly and boldly supported and advocated the Devil's substitute for Christ's kingdom, to wit, the League of Nations, and proclaimed that League of Nations as the political manifestation of God's kingdom on earth. Otherwise stated, they ignore God's method and manner of establishing his kingdom and willingly ally themselves with the Devil, supporting his "image of the beast".

The Jewish clergy in their time rejected Christ, the chief corner stone. Now the clergy of modern times do the same thing. They, together with the principal of their flock, being disobedient to the Word of God, stumble and fall upon the stone or new government now born. Mark how well the prophetic words of Peter fit the present situation: "Unto you therefore which believe he is precious: but unto them which be disobedient, the stone which the builders disallowed, the same is made the head of the corner, and a stone of stumbling, and a rock of offence, even to them which stumble at the word, being disobedient; whereunto also they were appointed." (1 Pet. 2:7, 8; Ps. 118:22; Isa. 8:14) Thus the kingdom of God was taken away from those who pretended to represent the Lord, and the words of Jesus were fulfilled. (Matt. 21:43, 44) Those who rejected it 'fell upon the stone and were broken'.

The nation of righteousness is born. God's kingdom has begun to function. The Lord is in his holy temple. Let all the nations and peoples of earth take note! (Ps. 11:4-7; Hab. 2:20) "The Lord hath a controversy with the nations" who have given themselves over to the Devil. (Jer. 25:31) "The great and the terrible day of the Lord" approaches.—Joel 2:31.

## Chapter XII

# *The Final Battle*

THE anointed servants of God, seeing that Satan the enemy has been expelled from heaven and has come down to earth, having great wrath against the Lord and his anointed; seeing that the enemy has now come in with a flood of error to turn the minds of the people away from God (Isa. 59: 19); and seeing that the greatest crisis of the ages is just about to break upon the earth, are breathing the prayer long ago recorded by their prototype David, to wit: "Be thou exalted, O God, above the heavens; and thy glory above all the earth." (Ps. 108: 5) Back from the courts of heaven comes the response of God through his holy prophet: "Be still, and know that I am God; I will be exalted among the [nations], I will be exalted in the earth."—Ps. 46: 10.

In the light of the present-day fulfilment of divine prophecy these words of the Lord thrill the hearts of Christians, because they see that the time for the deliverance of the human race from the bondage of Satan the enemy is at hand. With keen expectation they almost breathlessly watch the development of the events preparing for the great battle. Jesus taught his followers to pray: "Thy kingdom come. Thy will be done in earth, as it is in heaven." This of itself is conclusive proof that with the birth of the kingdom or nation of righteousness, God's will would begin to be done on the earth. It follows, then, that Satan's organization must be destroyed, because the righteous

Messiah cannot rule and bless the peoples of earth so long as Satan holds sway. We may know that Satan the enemy, arrogant, presumptuous, defiant and wicked beyond the description of words, will make a desperate fight to hold his power. This will mean a battle on earth such as men have never known. This is the reasonable conclusion. Is it Scriptural?

The scripture says: "Woe to the inhabiters of the earth, and of the sea! for the devil is come down unto you, having great wrath, because he knoweth that he hath but a short time." (Rev. 12: 12) Since the World War the burdens and trials of the people continue to increase. They are now experiencing some of the woes foretold in this scripture, but not all of them yet. The expenses of governments increase. Some of the people's money must be taken to prepare for another great war. The wicked are set up, and the proud appear to be happy, even though they are not. While this is going on the faithful witnesses for God are carrying out the command given them by the Lord, who said: "This gospel of the kingdom shall be preached in all the world for a witness unto all nations: and then shall the end come." (Matt. 24: 14) The word "end" used in this text is from the Greek *telos,* which means the conclusion of an act or state, the limit, the final end. By this it is understood that when the witness has been given as here commanded by the Lord, then a final conclusion of Satan's empire shall be reached.

What shall mark the end or conclusion thereof? Jesus answers that this will be marked by tribulation upon earth such as man has never before known. (Matt. 24: 21, 22) The Prophet Daniel corroborates this and says that the time mentioned is shortly to follow the birth of The Nation, at which time Messiah, the great Prince who stands for the people, stands up. That is the time spoken of by the prophet, when Jehovah sends forth his anointed One as King to destroy the enemy and his power. That will mark the time of the deliverance of the people from the bondage of the enemy. "And at that time shall Michael stand up, the great prince which standeth for the children of thy people; and there shall be a time of trouble, such as never was since there was a nation even to that same time: and at that time thy people shall be delivered, every one that shall be found written in the book."—Dan. 12:1.

### JEHOVAH IS GOD

But why should there come a great trouble on earth more terrible than man has ever before known? Briefly call to mind what has transpired during the past six thousand years. Satan the enemy was created perfect, beautiful and glorious; and God highly honored him by clothing him with power and authority, appointing him as overlord of man and making him a light-bearer. He betrayed that trust and confidence, became guilty of treason, the most heinous of all crimes, and since then has been leading the way in all wickedness. During all the ages Satan has reproached God and mocked him, that he might turn the minds of men away from their only Benefactor and true Friend. (Prov. 17:17) He introduced hypocrisy among the people that they might mock God. (Gen. 4:26, margin) Teaching the people to ignore and repudiate God, Satan caused them to build a tower of Babel and induced them to believe that they could save themselves. There God gave the people a lesson, and a very severe one; but they did not heed it.—Gen. 11:1-4.

Call to mind again that when God's people were domiciled in Egypt, Pharaoh, as the Devil's representative, oppressed them; and when God sent Moses to tell Pharaoh of God's command he defiantly said: 'Who is the Lord God that I should obey him?' Then God went down to them to make for himself a name. (2 Sam. 7:23) To this end the Lord slew the Egyptians and miraculously delivered his own people, carrying them safely through the sea. "Nevertheless, he saved them for his name's sake, that he might make his mighty power to be known. He rebuked the Red sea also, and it was dried up: so he led them through the depths, as through the wilderness."—Ps. 106:8, 9.

Call to mind further that when the Assyrian ruler, Sennacherib, reproached God, blasphemed his holy name, presumptuously assumed to be greater than Jehovah God and defied the Lord and his people, God sent his angel and slew the Assyrian army in one night.—2 Ki. 19:35-37.

But the nations of earth have failed to take heed to these things and to learn a lesson therefrom. Their religious teachers not only have failed to teach them the meaning of such lessons, but have actually spurned the Bible. Arrogance, hauteur, contemptuousness, presumptuousness and blasphemy against God have in this present day reached the superlative degree. Hypocrisy has matured and gone to seed. Of all the reproaches that have been brought upon God's holy name, of all the insolence and vainglory on the part of men and religious systems, of all the presumptuous sins committed against God by men or organizations, those in times past pale into insignificance when compared with those of the present time.

Modern wickedness is made worse because evildoers perform their wicked deeds in the name of the Lord. A great religious system, steeped in wickedness and crime, is headed by one man; and it is claimed for his office that he is the vicegerent of Christ on earth and that he possesses power equal to that of Jehovah God. The clergy of this system fraudulently represent to the people that their loved ones who have died are now consciously suffering in purgatory because of the wrath of God, and these clergy claim to be able by their prayers and upon a sufficient consideration to relieve the suffering ones from purgatorial fires. Thus under false pretenses they receive money from the people and turn the minds of the people away from the true and loving God.

The Protestant organizations likewise claim to represent God, and yet defame his holy name by teaching that he is tormenting millions of unfortunate souls in a lake of eternal fire. The clergy of these religious systems hypocritically call themselves by the name of the Lord and pose before the people as God's representatives, while at the same time they deny the Word of God and repudiate the blood of Jesus Christ given for man's redemptive price. These religious systems have illicit relationship with the commercial and political powers of the world; and the Lord himself gives to them the name of "harlot", which is Satan's organization.

The shepherds and leaders, speaking for these hypocritical religious systems, presumptuously and insolently say: "I sit a queen, . . . I am rich, and increased with goods, and have need of nothing." (Rev. 18:7; 3:17) And now when the wicked world which has oppressed the people has come to an end, and when the nation of righteousness is born; when the Lord is present and beginning his reign, for which he taught his disciples to pray and which prayer these clergy have hypocritically repeated; and when the evidence clearly proving these facts is brought to their attention, these self-satisfied ecclesiastics not only turn deaf ears thereto, but persecute the humble followers of Jesus who dare call attention to the message of truth. Instead of heeding the words of the Lord and telling the people that his kingdom is their hope, these ecclesiastics blatantly, irreverently and presumptuously unite with the profiteers and professional politicians in setting up a League of Nations to keep the people under the control of Satan the enemy, and then blasphemously declare that such a League of Nations is "the political expression of God's kingdom on earth". They not only have defamed the name of God, but have pushed the Lord aside and have set themselves up in his place, and claim that their wisdom is superior to his and a safe and ample guide for the people to follow.

If it was necessary in times past for God to exhibit his power against the Devil's organization, in order to preserve his name in the minds of the people and to save them from going into complete infidelity, the reason for so doing now has increased a thousandfold. Hence he says to these babbling, discourteous, swaggering ecclesiastics and to the principal of their flocks, their allies, "Be still, and know that I am God." The time has come for the arrogance of men before God to cease. "And the loftiness of man shall be bowed down, and the haughtiness of men shall be made low: and the Lord alone shall be exalted in that day."—Isa. 2:17.

God will now make for himself a name in the earth that the people shall never forget. He warns the nations of earth, and particularly the clergy and the principal of their flock; but they refuse to heed the warning. "They know not, neither will they understand: they walk on in darkness: all the foundations of the earth are out of course."—Ps. 82:5.

### GATHERING FOR BATTLE

John, because of his faithfulness as a witness of God, was banished to the Isle of Patmos. There the Lord rewarded him by giving him visions pertaining to his great purpose. Amongst other things John had a vision of the great and terrible day of God Almighty. He saw the throngs hurrying on for the great battle of that day, and he wrote: "And I saw three unclean spirits like frogs come out of the mouth of the dragon, and out of the mouth of the beast, and out of the mouth of the false prophet. For they are the spirits of devils, working miracles, which go forth unto the kings of the earth and of the whole world, to gather them to the battle of that great day of God Almighty. And he gathered them together into a place called in the Hebrew tongue Armageddon."–Rev. 16:13, 14, 16.

"Dragon" here mentioned is one of the names of the enemy, the Devil; and it particularly applies to him and his organization, visible and invisible, when bent upon the destruction of the seed of promise, the true followers of Jesus Christ. (Rev. 12:17) Satan's organization, visible and invisible, is the real foe of the faithful; as it is written: "For we wrestle not against flesh and blood, but against principalities, against powers, against the rulers of the darkness of this world, against spiritual wickedness in high places."—Eph. 6:12.

"Beast" in the above text is used symbolically. Wherever thus used in the Scriptures this symbol refers to Satan's visible or earthly organization. Since the days of Nimrod all world powers have been under the dominion and control of Satan the enemy. (2 Cor. 4:3, 4) These world powers have governed the people by military rule, and their rule has been beastly, unrighteous and ungodly. The Devil has made it so. This symbolical beast therefore fitly describes the world powers under the dominion of the wicked one.

There are three elements that go to make up these world powers or "beast", to wit, the commercial, the political and the ecclesiastical. Satan has always had the money powers as the great bulwark of his organization; and he uses the religious element as a camouflage, to keep the people in ignorance of his wicked course. When the Lord designates anything under a symbol, that designation, name or symbol implies much. The Lord designates these world powers as "beasts", and such they are.

"False prophet" means nations claiming to speak with divine authority. A true prophet is one who speaks by divine authority and in the name of the Lord. Those who speak in the name of the Lord without authority, and who speak lies, are false prophets. "Then the Lord said unto me, The prophets prophesy lies in my name; I sent them not, neither have I commanded them, neither spake unto them: they prophesy unto you a false vision and divination, and a thing of nought, and the deceit of their heart." (Jer. 14:14) "How long shall this be in the heart of the prophets that prophesy lies? yea, they are prophets of the deceit of their own heart; which think to cause my people to forget my name by their dreams, which they tell every man to his neighbour, as their fathers have forgotten my name for Baal." (Jer. 23:26, 27) The same false prophet class forms a part of the "beast", because allied with the world powers under the supervision of Satan the Devil.—Rev. 16:13.

The term "false prophet", therefore, within the meaning of this text, may be properly defined as the Anglo-American Empire. (See *Light* Book II, pp. 44-51.)

Spirits are invisible and intangible; hence the "unclean spirits like frogs" symbolize messages, declarations or proclamations, rather than tangible things. A frog is a kind of animal that has a big mouth, assumes much wisdom, looks wise, bluffs a great deal, swells up and makes much noise. It is noticed that the revelator here saw *three* unclean spirits like frogs. This therefore would signify a trio of declarations, principles, rules or proclamations which are boastful, arrogant and claim much. These messages come out of the mouths of the dragon, the beast and the false prophet. They assume to be messages of wisdom. They are boastful and are proclaimed with much braggadocio and great noise.

The "dragon", the Devil and his organization, by its efforts to destroy the seed of promise, boastfully says: 'God is a liar and his Word unreliable. Ignore him, and away with those who advocate his cause!'

The "beast", the Devil's organization visible, made up of the commercial, political and ecclesiastical factors, is saying, 'The earth is for man, and man for the earth. We have the only established forms of government that are proper, and we make the earth a fit place in which to live. Who is Jehovah, that we should heed him? Our wealth and our power is our god.'

All of these declarations are false, hence unclean. It is Satan the enemy and his organization that proclaim these false messages. Satan is responsible for them all. These false teachings are the real reasons why the nations of the world are being gathered to the great battle of Armageddon. And why is this so? The answer is that each one of these messages and their messengers defame God's holy name, and their purpose is to turn the minds of the people away from God. They are driving the people and their rulers into infidelity. And now Jehovah, according to his Word, will make a demonstration of his power so clearly and unequivocally that the people may be convinced of their ungodly course and may understand that Jehovah is God. That is the reason why God brought the great flood, threw down the Tower of Babel, destroyed the army of Sennacherib the Assyrian king, and swallowed up the Egyptians; and it is also the reason why he is now going to bring another great trouble upon the world. The former calamities were but shadows of the one now impending. The gathering is to the great day of God Almighty. It is "the great and the terrible day of the Lord" (Joel 2:31), when God will make for himself a name. In this great and final conflict the peoples of every nation, kindred and tongue will learn that Jehovah is the all-powerful, all-wise and just God.

### BATTLE ARRAY

There are divers opinions among men as to the Devil's organization. Many deny the existence of the Devil; hence deny that there is such a thing as the Devil's organization. These are blinded by the enemy and know not the Word of God. Others claim to believe that there is a Devil; but they look upon him as an invisible imp who goes about to amuse himself with petty wickednesses, and think that he can do nothing of any particular consequence to men and nations. Still others believe there is a Devil, but claim that he is now bound and think that he can do nothing more. These are likewise blinded by his influence. Others believe that there is a Devil, but consider his organization of such little moment that it will easily be overturned by the socialists, laborites or anarchists.

To have some conception of what the terrible and final trouble will be, what will constitute the battle of Armageddon, we must have some conception of the extent and power of Satan's organization. Satan the enemy is in possession of practically all the material wealth of the earth, which he controls through the commercial wing of his organization. He controls and operates every world power or government on earth, through the political wing of his organization. He manages and controls practically all the religious systems of the earth, through the ecclesiastical wing of his organization.

These three combined forces make up what is known amongst men as 'world powers', and what the Lord describes as "the beast". The League of Nations, which is an attempt to unite all the nations of Christendom (so called) in one compact, is designated in the Scriptures as the "image of the beast". It is the last and final attempt of Satan to perfect an organization that will blind the people, turn their minds away from God and his kingdom, and keep them in subjection to the wicked one. Few stop to think about the enormity of Satan's organization and the power that it wields. Practically every newspaper and source of publicity stands ready to mold public sentiment at his will.

Take a stroll through the financial district of New York city and you will get some faint idea of the magnitude of the commercial power of this world. Walk leisurely around its Federal Reserve Bank Building; look at its great walls with windows barred with steel, the whole structure seemingly as invulnerable as the rock of Gibraltar. Step inside for a moment. Observe that every corridor is guarded by soldiers armed to the teeth who, as silent sentinels, are watching the movements of every person who enters or passes out. Look at the great bales of money, piled inside of the steel cages within which men must work as though they were behind prison bars. Peep through into the great vaults stocked with millions of gold. Come also and view one of its safe deposit vaults. Here are other millions kept in reserve. Mark that it is safeguarded by great steel doors weighing twenty tons, but so evenly balanced that with two fingers a man can move them with ease. This is but a sample of many like places.

The wealth of the world is staggering to the mind of the ordinary man. We can only estimate this by figures. The following figures are taken from government reports (1925) and show approximately the wealth of some of the nations, measured in dollars, to wit:

| | |
|---|---|
| United States | $320,803,862,000 |
| British Empire | 130,000,000,000 |
| France | 90,000,000,000 |
| Germany | 40,000,000,000 |
| Italy | 35,000,000,000 |
| Japan | 22,500,000,000 |
| Denmark | 2,000,000,000 |
| Austria-Hungary | 55,000,000,000 |
| Belgium | 12,000,000,000 |

In 1914 the total railway mileage of the world was 696,274. This is sufficient to make twenty-seven trunk lines around the globe and then have some left. Have in mind then that Satan's organization owns and controls all the railways, transportation systems and steamship lines, all the factories, all the mines, all the manufacturing industries, etc., and that these are all controlled by a few men.

The political wing of the enemy's organization (1926) consists of three empires, twenty-one kingdoms, forty republics, five Mohammedan nations, five dominions, and four protectorates; a total of seventy-eight. Sixty of these nations claim to be Christian; and all of them, except five, are members of the League of Nations.

In 1923 one hundred and twenty-five thousand clergymen, pastors of church denominations residing in the United States, arranged for what they called a 'drive week', the object and purpose of which was to create a sentiment that would induce the United States to enter the World Court, which is but a back door to the League of Nations. They have succeeded, and now the United States also, though not admitting so, has in effect joined the League. The political wing of Satan's organization directs all the official work of the armies, and navies, with their guns, airplanes and poison gas; and manipulates the various government offices in all lands, from the chief executive down to the humblest official.

The following census figures are taken from the 1925 *World Almanac:*

Population of the earth by continents:

| | |
|---|---|
| Africa | 142,000,000 |
| North America | 136,000,000 |
| South America | 64,000,000 |
| Asia | 921,000,000 |
| Europe | 476,000,000 |
| Australasia | 9,000,000 |
| Total | 1,748,000,000 |

Population of the earth by races:

| | |
|---|---|
| White | 821,000,000 |
| Yellow | 645,000,000 |
| Semitic | 75,000,000 |
| Negro | 139,000,000 |
| Brown | 40,000,000 |
| Red | 28,000,000 |
| Total | 1,748,000,000 |

The ecclesiastical wing of Satan's visible organization has a world membership made up as follows:

| | |
|---|---|
| Roman Catholics | 273,500,000 |
| Orthodox Catholics | 121,801,000 |
| Protestants | 170,900,000 |

The Protestant denominations claim a membership of 32,502,199 in the United States alone, divided among one hundred and six different sects. These figures comprise the so-called "Christian" religion of Satan's organization. In addition to them there are 1,017,983,000 heathen, controlled by priests who worship what the apostle plainly says is the Devil.

The clergy of these various ecclesiastical systems bless the armies which are sent out by the commercial and political wings, and their blessing is extended regardless of which side these armies are fighting on. The clergy all pretend to pray to the same God for a blessing upon the warring armies of both sides. Their course during the World War proves this beyond a question, and is admitted by all. Of course they will all join in asking a blessing upon the Devil's armies as they assemble for Armageddon.

All these elements that go to make up the visible part of Satan's organization are being gathered together and assembled for the great battle of Armageddon. The formation of the army is in progress and is nearing completion. Looking at the armies of the nations, assembled preparatory for "the great day of God Almighty", which are mobilizing as the Devil's organization, we see in the forefront the so-called "Christian" nations, under the leadership of the clergy, the shepherds of the flocks, and supported by the principal of their flock. They all call themselves by the name Christian; but, as the prophet truly says, each one eats his own bread and wears his own apparel (meaning that he follows his own doctrines and clothes himself with his own salvation garments). Truly this is the time referred to by the prophet when he said: "And in that day seven women [symbolic of all ecclesiasticism, the so-called "Christian" systems, always pictured by a woman] shall take hold of one man [the name of Christ Jesus], saying [hypocritically], We will eat our own bread and wear our own apparel; only let us be called by thy name, to take away our reproach."—Isa. 4:1.

Like certain ostriches that hide their heads in the sand when pursued by a foe and make themselves believe that they are safe, so these ecclesiastical leaders confess to themselves that they are safe, that they need only to be called by the name of Christ, while they continue to play with the Devil's fire. They blind themselves to the real situation by putting sand into their own eyes as well as into the eyes of their fellow men. One division of the enemy's army, approximately three hundred and ninety-five millions, call themselves Christian Catholics; and one hundred and seventy millions call themselves Christian Protestants. The principal ones of these flocks are profiteers, financiers, rulers and politicians, men of influence. In the assembly of the nations for Armageddon these take their place to the strains of martial music, with banners flying and the clanging of accoutrements of war. The Scriptures indicate that the so-called "Christian" nations compose chiefly the army of the Devil; but probably the heathen nations, with their own commercial, political and ecclesiastical elements, also play a part in the coming conflict. The prophet of the Lord declares that all nations shall be assembled against Jerusalem to battle.—Zech. 14:2.

The total population of the nations of the earth (1926) is approximately 1,748,000,000. Almost all of these are on the enemy's side; or, rather, are under the control of the enemy, even though many of them are there by reason of coercion or fear, or because they are blind. No wonder the leading factors stand afar off and say: What is like unto this great city (organization)!—Rev. 18:18.

Jerusalem is a name applied to the people of God who are consecrated to him. A great number of these are held in bondage to the various ecclesiastical systems or are otherwise blinded by the enemy, and are fearful to take their stand boldly on the side of the Lord. The name Zion applies more particularly to that smaller number of the Jerusalem class who are not merely consecrated but who are fully devoted to the Lord and his cause because of love for him and an appreciation of their privileges. These are designated the overcoming class. Of the overcoming class, who have the promise of being for ever with the Lord, there will be only one hundred and forty-four thousand; and doubtless the major portion of these have already passed into glory, while the minority remain on the earth waiting for the consummation of their hopes. Of these it is probable that there are no more than fifty thousand, maybe less, who are faithfully and joyfully bearing witness to God's holy name. These are "the remnant" against which Satan the enemy makes war, and he attempts to destroy them because they keep the commandments of God and have the witness of Jesus Christ.—Rev. 12:17.

As the enemy and his hosts view the little company who are faithfully bearing witness to the name of God, and hear what these witnesses say, they laugh them to scorn. The clergy, the false prophets, together with the principal of their flocks, make extravagant claims for their organizations and point the finger of disgust toward those who now proclaim the name of God and his incoming kingdom. So small are the numbers who appear to be on the Lord's side, so great and powerful are the numbers on the enemy's side, and so extravagant are the claims made by the false prophets of the enemy's camp, that all except the very elect of God will be deceived to some extent. (Matt. 24:24) The false prophets will tell the people that the present institutions will stand eternally, and that they and their allies have been commissioned to establish God's kingdom on earth; and that this they are now doing.

But the elect, "the remnant of her seed," will not be at all deceived by the extravagant claims, the threats, the persecutions, the brandishing of arms or any exhibition of Satan's power. They will remember that Goliath, the representative of Satan the enemy, defied the army of the Lord and fell at the hands of the lad David, who was there a type of the Lord Jesus Christ.—1 Sam. 17:48, 49.

This "little flock" will call to mind how the Assyrian king Sennacherib stood before the walls of Jerusalem, arrogantly claiming to be greater than Jehovah God, defying Jehovah and blaspheming his holy name, and how the angel of the Lord swept away his army in one night.—2 Ki. 19: 35.

This little company of faithful Christians will remember how Pharaoh, the visible representative of Satan the enemy, pursued the people of God with his army and would have crushed them, but that the Lord utterly destroyed Pharaoh and his army in the sea.—Ex. 14: 27-29.

This little company of faithful Christians will also call to mind how Jehoshaphat, a representative of the Lord, was beset by the armies of Ammon, Moab and Mount Seir, corresponding to the three elements composing Satan's organization at the present time; and how the Lord put his hand over his own people and shielded them, while he drove the enemy's army into destruction.

Why did God cause these things to be recorded in his Word? The evident purpose was and is to show how he can make himself a name when he so desires, and to encourage and strengthen the faith of his people and cause them to trust him implicitly in the time of great peril. To such he has said: "O love the Lord, all ye his saints: for the Lord preserveth the faithful, and plentifully rewardeth the proud doer."–Ps. 31: 23.

On one side of the valley of decision, and in the valley, stands the tremendous army of Satan the enemy, defying God, uttering cries of derision, and threatening to feed the fowls of the air upon the flesh of those who have come out against them to declare the name of the Lord. On the other side of the valley, and high up the mountainside facing to the east, stands the little company of faithful servants of the Lord, small in number and weak in individual power;

yet they never for one moment quail before the enemy. They are smiling; they are happy; yea, they are even joyful; and together they lift up their voices in song, saying: Jehovah is God; Christ Jesus is King; the kingdom of heaven is at hand; the day of deliverance has come! Jehovah God is saying to them: "Ye are my witnesses . . . that I am God. I, even I, am the Lord; and beside me there is no saviour."—Isa. 43:12, 11.

### THE CONTRAST

The contrast between the numbers in the enemy's visible army and the apparent numbers in the army of the Lord is so great that only a very few are able to see that the enemy's organization will be destroyed. It seems quite apparent that for the special encouragement of the faithful Christians now on earth God long ago caused to be recorded the following picture relating to the present time.

Jehoshaphat was a faithful king of Israel, and Jehoshaphat represented the Lord. Ammon, Moab and Mount Seir entered into a conspiracy against Jehoshaphat and the people of Jerusalem. They came up to assault Jerusalem. Jehoshaphat prayed to God. His prayer is a pathetic one, and fitly pictures the utter helplessness of men and the complete dependence of the Christian upon Jehovah. While Jehoshaphat prayed the Lord sent him a message, to wit: "Hearken ye, all Judah, and ye inhabitants of Jerusalem, and thou king Jehoshaphat; Thus saith the Lord unto you, Be not afraid nor dismayed by reason of this great multitude; for the battle is not yours, but God's. To morrow go ye down against them: behold, they come up by the cliff of Ziz; and ye shall find them at the end of the brook, before the wilderness of Jeruel. Ye shall not need to fight in this battle; set yourselves, stand ye still, and see the salvation of the Lord with you, O Judah and Jerusalem: fear not, nor be dismayed; to morrow go out against them; for the Lord will be with you. And when he had consulted with the people, he appointed singers unto the Lord, and that should praise the beauty of holiness, as they went out before the army, and to say, Praise the Lord; for his mercy endureth for ever. And when they began to sing and to praise, the Lord set ambushments against the children of Ammon, Moab, and mount Seir, which were come against Judah; and they were smitten."—2 Chron. 20:15-17, 21, 22.

### THE FIGHT

The history of sixty centuries is behind us. Upon every page of it appear the marks of Satan, the enemy. In all that time he has reproached God, defied him and turned the people away from him. God has permitted it that he may from time to time thereby teach the people a lesson. He has promised that the time will come when he will put an end to this fraudulent deception of the people, and that he will open the eyes of the people and deliver them.

The hour has arrived when God will send forth his beloved Son as Field Marshal, to lead the fight against the nations of earth composing the Devil's organization. It is God's fight; but he acts through his beloved Son, whom he has placed upon the throne and who is the priest of the Most High God. (Ps. 110:2, 4) In this great conflict Jehovah is the right hand support of his beloved Son. He delights in him because he is his faithful servant. (Isa. 42:1) To him he says: "Thou art fairer than the children of men; grace is poured into thy lips: therefore God hath blessed thee for ever. Gird thy sword upon thy thigh, O most Mighty, with thy glory and thy majesty. And in thy majesty ride prosperously because of truth and meekness and righteousness; and thy right hand shall teach thee terrible things."—Ps. 45:2-4.

In times past the prophets of God were granted visions of the preparation for the great battle and the going into action. Habakkuk saw the Devil's organization assembled and, to the nations composing that organization who practice the devil religion through worship of images, he says: "What profiteth the graven image, that the maker thereof hath graven it; the molten image, and a teacher of lies, that the maker of his work trusteth therein, to make dumb idols? Woe unto him that saith to the wood, Awake; to the dumb stone, Arise, it shall teach! Behold, it is laid over with gold and silver, and there is no breath at all in the midst of it."—Hab. 2:18, 19.

Then the prophet calls the attention of the people to the purpose of the great war. He says: "But the Lord is in his holy temple: let all the earth keep silence before him."—Hab. 2:20.

Jeremiah was given a vision of the day of God's wrath, and he wrote: "But the Lord is the true God, he is the living God, and an everlasting King: at his wrath the earth shall tremble, and the nations shall not be able to abide his indignation." (Jer. 10:10) "Therefore prophesy thou against them all these words, and say unto them, The Lord shall roar from on high, and utter his voice from his holy habitation; he shall mightily roar upon his habitation; he shall give a shout, as they that tread the grapes, against all the inhabitants of the earth. A noise shall come even to the ends of the earth: for the Lord hath a controversy with the nations; he will plead with all flesh; he will give them that are wicked to the sword, saith the Lord.''—Jer. 25:30, 31.

Joel saw the army assembled in the valley of judgment, and he expressed this prophecy: ''Put ye in the sickle; for the harvest is ripe: come, get you down; for the press is full, the fats overflow; for their wickedness is great. Multitudes, multitudes in the valley of decision: for the day of the Lord is near in the valley of decision. The sun and the moon shall be darkened, and the stars shall withdraw their shining. The Lord also shall roar out of Zion, and utter his voice from Jerusalem; and the heavens and the earth shall shake: but the Lord will be the hope of his people, and the strength of the children of Israel. So shall ye know that I am the Lord your God dwelling in Zion.''—Joel 3:13-17.

Micah had a vision of the great and terrible day of God, and he prophesied for the benefit of the people now living on earth as follows: ''The word of the Lord that came to Micah the Morasthite in the days of Jotham, Ahaz, and Hezekiah, kings of Judah, which he saw concerning Samaria and Jerusalem. Hear, all ye people; hearken, O earth, and all that therein is: and let the Lord God be witness against you, the Lord from his holy temple.''—Mic. 1:1, 2.

The Prophet Isaiah had a vision of this day; and he speaks of the Lord Jesus, the active agent of

Jehovah, the priest of the Most High, the Field Marshal, coming forth to make war upon the Devil's organization, and says: "Who is this that cometh from Edom, with dyed garments from Bozrah? this that is glorious in his apparel, travelling in the greatness of his strength? I that speak in righteousness, mighty to save. Wherefore art thou red in thine apparel, and thy garments like him that treadeth in the winefat?" And the response to the prophet is: "For the day of vengeance is in mine heart. and the year of my redeemed is come."—Isa. 63:1, 2, 4.

Suddenly there bursts forth a great flame of light and fire from the right hand of the little company who are singing praises to God. The trumpets are pealing out their terrible strains; the thunders are rolling, the mountains are quaking and trembling, and a voice is calling from the habitation of Zion. It is the God of heaven moving into battle. The great and terrible day of the Lord has come! So terrible was the vision and so great was the effect upon the ancient prophet, that he cried out: "O Lord, I have heard thy speech, and was afraid: O Lord, revive thy work in the midst of the years, in the midst of the years make known; in wrath remember mercy."—Hab. 3:2.

The mighty Warrior halts; and with feet planted upon the clouds of fire, "He stood, and measured the earth." He made a survey of the army of the enemy, the nations of the earth assembled against God. The prophet then says: "I saw the tents of Cushan in affliction: and the curtains of the land of Midian did tremble." (Hab. 3:6, 7) "Cushan" means black face; while "Midian" means brawling, contentious, strife-breeding, fighting ones. The latter term well describes the leaders in the ecclesiastical systems, the false prophets who have blasphemed God's holy name and stirred up strife against God's faithful witnesses and persecuted those who tell the truth. Now they tremble at the sight of the Lord, and, as the Prophet Joel says, 'all faces gather blackness.' The assembled nations see the approaching majesty and greatness of the Lord, and their faces turn colorless as they tremble for fear.

Then the mighty Leader of the army of the Lord unsheathes his sword and brings into action his instruments of destruction. "Before him went the pestilence, and burning coals went forth at his feet." (Hab. 3:5) At the approach of these 'the shepherds and the principal of their flocks' smite their knees together for fear; and, being unable to give battle against any other, in blind fear they turn to battle against each other.

On comes the conquering Hero, the Word of God, who for centuries has waited for this very blessed hour. (Heb. 10:12, 13) "His eyes were as a flame of fire, and on his head were many crowns; . . . he was clothed with a vesture dipped in blood." (Rev. 19:12, 13) But behold his apparel; it is glorious, even though covered with blood. He is treading out the winepress; he is crushing the wicked vine of the earth. At his approach the mountains tremble, and the great deep utters its terrible voice and lifts up its hands to the heaven. The sun and the moon stand still in their orbits, and all the stars of the high heaven are shouting VICTORY! With righteous indignation and anger the mighty Conqueror marches through the earth to thresh the nations that have defamed Jehovah's holy name. He drives asunder the nations, and their kingdoms are scattered and their high places brought low.

The saints do not engage in the actual combat. This is the fight of God Almighty; and the fight is led by his beloved Son, the Priest of whom Melchizedek was a type. Long ago Jehovah's prophet recorded concerning this hour: "The Lord [Jehovah] at thy right hand shall strike through kings in the day of his wrath. He shall judge among the [nations], he shall fill the places with the dead bodies; he shall wound the heads over many countries." (Ps. 110: 5, 6) He is also fighting for the salvation of the people, that they might be delivered from the oppressor; and he is fighting for the anointed of God, that they may be vindicated for their faithful witness to the name of Jehovah.

That wicked ruling system, designated by the title "beast" and made up of profiteers, politicians and clergy, is taken. That wicked system known as the "false prophet" is also taken; and these are cast into the burning flames of everlasting destruction. (Rev. 19: 20) These wicked systems fall, never to rise again. Then the Lord seizes the enemy himself, the Dragon, that old Serpent, the Devil and Satan, and binds him and casts him into the bottomless pit that he may deceive the nations no more.—Rev. 20: 2, 3.

Thus is Satan's empire swept from the earth to oblivion. The name of Jehovah God is vindicated. But all human words attempting to describe this great and terrible day of the Lord are beggarly. Let us read the words which God caused his holy prophet long ago to record, describing his majestic and victorious march against the stronghold of Satan and his organization:

"A prayer of Habakkuk the prophet upon Shigionoth. O Lord, I have heard thy speech, and was afraid: O Lord, revive thy work in the midst of the years, in the midst of the years make known; in wrath remember mercy. God came from Teman, and the Holy One from mount Paran. Selah. His glory covered the heavens, and the earth was full of his praise. And his brightness was as the light; he had horns coming out of his hand: and there was the hiding of his power. Before him went the pestilence, and burning coals went forth at his feet. He stood, and measured the earth: he beheld, and drove asunder the nations: and the everlasting mountains were scattered, the perpetual hills did bow: his ways are everlasting.

"I saw the tents of Cushan in affliction: and the curtains of the land of Midian did tremble. Was the Lord displeased against the rivers? was thine anger against the rivers? was thy wrath against the sea, that thou didst ride upon thine horses and thy chariots of salvation? Thy bow was made quite naked, according to the oaths of the tribes, even thy word. Selah. Thou didst cleave the earth with rivers. The mountains saw thee, and they trembled: the overflowing of the water passed by: the deep uttered his voice, and lifted up his hands on high. The sun and moon stood still in their habitation: at the light of thine arrows they went, and at the shining of thy glittering spear. Thou didst march through the land in indignation, thou didst thresh the [nations] in anger.

"Thou wentest forth for the salvation of thy people, even for salvation with thine anointed; thou woundedst the head out of the house of the wicked, by discovering the foundation unto the neck. Selah. Thou didst strike through with his staves the head of his villages; they came out as a whirlwind to scatter me: their rejoicing was as to devour the poor secretly. Thou didst walk through the sea with thine horses, through the heap of great waters. When I heard, my belly trembled; my lips quivered at the voice: rottenness entered into my bones, and I trembled in myself, that I might rest in the day of trouble: when he cometh up unto the people, he will invade them with his troops."—Hab. 3:1-16.

In this great battle no Christian will strike a blow. The reason they do not is that Jehovah has said: "For the battle is not yours, but God's." To them the Lord said further: "And I have put my words in thy mouth, and I have covered thee in the shadow of mine hand, that I may plant the heavens, and lay the foundations of the earth, and say unto Zion, Thou art my people." (Isa. 51:16) The hand of the Lord is over his little ones; and they that trust him implicitly and will prove faithful to him are free from harm and will continue to sing his praises until the end.

A description of this final battle is referred to again, in Revelation, as a 'war between the beast and the Lamb', in which the Lamb, Christ Jesus, is victorious, because he fights the battle on the side of Jehovah. "These shall make war with the Lamb, and the Lamb shall overcome them: for he is Lord of lords, and King of kings: and they that are with him are called, and chosen, and faithful."—Rev. 17:14.

Let no one deceive himself into thinking that the battle of Armageddon is a mere fight between men, or that it is only a picture. The Scriptures make it clear that it is real. It is the battle of God Almighty, in which he will clear the earth of the wicked system that Satan has used to blind the people for all these centuries. Satan has already been ousted from heaven; he has been cast into the earth; and now he is making a desperate attempt to destroy those who witness for God, and to blind all others and turn them away from God. But with the end of Armageddon, when his systems have been cast into utter destruction and when he is in restraint, then will come to pass the fulfilment of the prophetic utterance long ago written concerning the Devil: "Thy pomp is brought down to the grave, and the noise of thy viols: the worm is spread under thee, and the worms cover thee. How art thou fallen from heaven, O Lucifer, son of the morning! how art thou cut down to the ground, which didst weaken the nations!"—Isa. 14: 11, 12.

Another illustration of Armageddon is given in the battle fought by Gideon against the great multitude of Midian. The Midianites were the enemies of God's people. A great multitude of these were camped in a valley. Gideon, who is a type of Christ Jesus, was directed to put them to flight. What his followers did well illustrates what the Christian's part will be in the great and final conflict.

When it came to the time of going into action Gideon had only three hundred men. These he divided into three companies, and put in each man's hand a trumpet and an empty pitcher and a lamp within that pitcher. His orders were that these should be stationed on three different sides of the camp of the Midianites, and that they should watch Gideon; and that when Gideon should give the command each one must blow his trumpet, break the pitcher which he held in his hands, and hold high his light and shout: "The sword of the Lord and of Gideon." When this was done the Midianites in their fear fell upon each other and slew one another, and the army of the Midianites perished. (Judg. 7:16-20) Even so the Scriptures teach that in these closing days of the age of wickedness and the time of the incoming of the Lord's kingdom it is the duty and the privilege of those who are really consecrated to the Lord to lift high the light of truth and sing the praises of Jehovah God, proclaiming the message that he is God and that Jesus Christ is the King of kings.

### EXTENT OF SLAUGHTER

The great and terrible day of God Almighty, the battle of Armageddon, will be marked with such a decisive victory for righteousness that all will know it. The name of Jehovah will be exalted in the earth. Even the clergy shall have their mouths for ever closed to speaking presumptuously concerning the Lord God. Now they name themselves 'shepherds of the flock'. They have brought into the flock as the principal men the profiteers and politicians and men of great influence. God's prophet, describing the expression of God's anger against these wicked systems and false prophets, and which is another description of Armageddon, says: "Thus saith the Lord of hosts, Behold, evil shall go forth from nation to nation, and a great whirlwind shall be raised up from the coasts of the earth. And the slain of the Lord shall be at that day from one end of the earth even unto the other end of the earth: they shall not be lamented, neither gathered, nor buried; they shall be dung upon the ground. Howl, ye shepherds, and cry; and wallow yourselves in the ashes, ye principal of the flock: for the days of your slaughter and of your dispersions are accomplished; and ye shall fall like a pleasant vessel. And the shepherds shall have no way to flee, nor the principal of the flock to escape. A voice of the cry of the shepherds, and an howling of the principal of the flock, shall be heard: for the Lord hath spoiled their pasture. And the peaceable habitations are cut down, because of the fierce anger of the Lord."—Jer. 25:32-37.

Another of God's prophets gives a vivid picture of the great and terrible day of the Lord. The sea, being a great, restless body of water that is constantly lashing itself against the rocks, fitly represents the ungodly people of earth, especially in these troublesome days, dashing themselves against the solid parts of the nations and governments. The prophet, in the prophecy about to be quoted, uses the sea as a symbol of such. Ships are used as a symbol of present methods of carrying on great commercial enterprises. The financial interests of the world are really the backbone of the present visible organization of the enemy. The prophet refers to the time when Satan's organization will reach the point of assembling or being assembled for Armageddon, saying, "They that go down to the sea in ships, that do business in great waters."—Ps. 107:23.

In the deep distress that comes upon the nations they discern the Lord; that is, they see the manifestation of his power in these troublesome events, even as described by the Prophet Habakkuk. Then the psalmist pictures Jehovah as commanding the fight to begin. The conflict is represented as a stormy wind. A stormy wind is always used as a symbol of trouble. The prophet proceeds and thus describes the scope of the trouble, and the result: "For he commandeth, and raiseth the stormy wind, which lifteth up the waves thereof. They mount up to the heaven, they go down again to the depths; their soul is melted because of trouble. They reel to and fro, and stagger like a drunken man, and are at their wits' end. Then they cry unto the Lord in their trouble, and he bringeth them out of their distresses. He maketh the storm a calm, so that the waves thereof are still. Then are they glad because they be quiet; so he bringeth them unto their desired haven."—Ps. 107: 25-30.

The Lord Jesus refers to the same great battle of Armageddon that would follow the World War, when he says: "For then shall be great tribulation, such as was not since the beginning of the world to this time, no, nor ever shall be. And except those days should be shortened, there should no flesh be saved: but for the elect's sake those days shall be shortened." —Matt. 24: 21, 22.

The people may confidently rely upon the statement of Jesus that this will be the end of tribulation upon the earth, because he says there shall never be another. He also states that many will pass through this trouble and live and not die; and all should take courage from this who desire to see a better condition.

Another of the prophets shows that two parts will be destroyed in this time of trouble and that the third part shall be brought through. "And it shall come to pass, that in all the land, saith the Lord, two parts therein shall be cut off, and die; but the third shall be left therein. And I will bring the third part through the fire, and will refine them as silver is refined, and will try them as gold is tried: they shall call on my name, and I will hear them: I will say, It is my people; and they shall say, The Lord is my God."—Zech. 13:8, 9.

It seems, in harmony with Revelation 19:20, that the "two parts" here mentioned are those composing the beast and the false prophet class. These two wicked systems will be completely destroyed; and those people who give allegiance and support and aid and comfort to them will, it seems, also go down; but not for ever. The "third part" that will be brought through the fire evidently designates that class of people who will survive the trouble and who will then have the opportunities of complete reconstruction and blessing. Without doubt there are a great many people who are now held in bondage to Satan's organization by reason of the fact that they are blinded to God's purposes. The enemy Satan has blinded them, lest the glorious good news of God's kingdom should shine into their minds and lest they should understand and believe and break away from the Devil's system. (2 Cor. 4:4) The Lord Jesus, speaking of the conclusion of this old world and of the manifestation of his kingdom, said: "And then shall appear the sign of the Son of man, in heaven: and then shall all the tribes of the earth mourn, and they shall see the Son of man com-

END OF SATAN'S ORGANIZATION Page 302

ing in the clouds of heaven, with power and great glory." (Matt. 24:30) It is manifest from this scripture that all the peoples will see, in the great battle of Armageddon, that it is the Lord dashing to pieces Satan's organization.

The stubborn and wilful, who continue to support the systems in defiance of God, will go down with them. Doubtless this will be the time when they who by deceit and fear have been held in bondage to the Devil's organization will break away and will call upon the Lord, and then he will bring them through the time of trouble. The Lord has specially promised favors to those who are good to their fellow creatures. Through his prophet he says: "Blessed is he that considereth the poor: the Lord will deliver him in time of trouble. The Lord will preserve him, and keep him alive; and he shall be blessed upon the earth: and thou wilt not deliver him unto the will of his enemies."—Ps. 41:1, 2.

These mentioned here as coming to some knowledge that the great trouble is a manifestation of God's power and glory shining through his kingdom will doubtless call upon the name of the Lord, and he will hear them and bring them through the trouble; and then, if they are obedient to him, he will give them the blessings long ago promised to come through the seed of Abraham.

The prophet of God again refers to the same time, when he says: "Therefore wait ye upon me, saith the Lord, until the day that I rise up to the prey; for my determination is to gather the nations, that I may assemble the kingdoms, to pour upon them mine indignation, even all my fierce anger: for all the earth shall be devoured with the fire of my jealousy. For then will I turn to the people a pure language, that they may all call upon the name of the Lord, to serve him with one consent."—Zeph. 3: 8, 9.

This will mark the end of Satan's organization and the deliverance of the people therefrom. Then, as the prophet here says, God will turn to them a pure message that they may all call upon the name of the Lord and serve him with one consent. Then will follow the establishment of conditions upon the earth such as will make it a fit place upon which to live. Such will be the work of the Messiah and the next step in the outworking of the divine purpose.

## CHAPTER XIII

# *The World Established*

WHEN a great earthquake, a disastrous storm, or a mighty tidal wave, sweeps a community and destroys houses and people by the thousands, and leaves other thousands homeless, much woe and distress follow; and great effort is required to relieve the suffering. The battle of Armageddon in the "great and the terrible day of the Lord" will mark the complete collapse of Satan's organization. What an earthquake or terrific storm or tidal wave is to a community, that trouble will be to the whole world, only much worse. In the wake thereof there will be great woe and distress and the people will cry for relief.

It may truly be said that the history of the world has been written in human blood. But the worst is not yet. The long and terrible siege of Titus against Jerusalem brought to the Jews indescribable suffering, and the final assault upon the city by the Romans completely destroyed it. The destruction of Jerusalem was in fulfilment of divine prophecy, and foreshadowed what will befall the organizations of the world in the great battle of God Almighty.

The trouble that came upon Jerusalem was an expression of God's indignation against the people, who had repudiated him and followed after the Devil. The clergy of that day, posing as representatives of God and hypocritically claiming to be the interpreters of his law, were responsible for the terrible calamity that fell upon the city. The religionists of Christendom have turned the minds of the people away from God. Christendom's trouble, therefore, will be more terrible than that which befell Jerusalem in A.D. 70-73. God has promised to make a complete end of the wicked systems in the final trouble that shall befall Satan's organization.

We may call to mind all the disasters that have befallen the human race during its existence, all the wars, all the earthquakes, cyclones and other calamities; and then know that none of these will equal in woe that which shall befall the world during the great battle of Armageddon. That this conclusion is correct is proven by the words of Jesus that upon the earth there should be tribulation such as was not since the world began; no, and never should be again. But this great time of trouble will result ultimately in great blessing to the people. God has so ordained it.

After God's righteous indignation has been completely expressed against Satan's organization, the great stormy wind that will have torn the mountains and rent the rocks will cease to blow; the quaking that will have shaken the earth from center to circumference will quake no more; the heaven-enkindled fires, having quickly spent their fury, will cease to burn, and silence and rest will once more come to the earth. But the survivors of the people will be disheartened, discouraged and faint. In their distress and extremity they will call upon the Lord.

Then will come from heaven the still, small voice; and the message long ago spoken by the prophet of God will gently speak words of encouragement to all the peoples of good will on earth, saying: "O worship the Lord in the beauty of holiness: fear before him, all the earth. Say among the [nations], that the Lord reigneth: the world also shall be established that it shall not be moved: he shall judge the people righteously. Let the heavens rejoice, and let the earth be glad; let the sea roar, and the fulness thereof. Let the field be joyful, and all that is therein: then shall all the trees of the wood rejoice before the Lord: for he cometh, for he cometh to judge the earth: he shall judge the world with righteousness, and the people with his truth."—Ps. 96: 9-13.

All divine prophecy has its fulfilment in due time, and can be understood only when fulfilled or in course of fulfilment. The foregoing prophecy has now begun to be fulfilled, in that those who are watching the development of God's purpose see that the Lord has taken his power and begun his reign; therefore they know that shortly shall follow the complete fulfilment of the prophecy. Then will come a period of reconstruction and the blessings of mankind, according to the promises God has made.

The positive and unequivocal promise here made by the prophet is: "The world also shall be established that it shall not be moved." "The world" here means an organization for the benefit of man. "World" in Scriptural usage means the people of earth, organized into forms of government, under the supervision and control of an invisible overlord. It consists of both heaven and earth. "Heaven" means the invisible, while "earth" refers to the visible part of the world. For centuries the invisible part of the world has been Satan and his unholy angels, while the visible part has consisted of organized forms of government on earth, influenced and controlled by Satan. Looking down to the time when Satan's world shall perish, God through his prophet says: "For behold, I create new heavens, and a new earth: and the former shall not be remembered, nor come into mind. But be ye glad and rejoice for ever in that which I create." (Isa. 65:17, 18) This prophecy must have its fulfilment.

In harmony with these words of the holy prophet, Peter in prophetic phrase describes the passing of the old heavens and earth. He says: "Looking for and hasting unto the coming of the day of God, wherein the heavens, being on fire, shall be dissolved, and the elements shall melt with fervent heat." (2 Pet. 3:12) Be it noted that these pass away in the day of God; that is to say, in the time of God's expressed wrath. Then Peter adds: "Nevertheless we, according to his promise, look for new heavens and a new earth, wherein dwelleth righteousness." (2 Pet. 3:13) In view of these two divinely provided witnesses we may have full assurance that the new world will be established, and that it will be so completely established that it can never be moved.

For many centuries Satan the enemy, as head, aided and abetted by his wicked angels, has constituted the heavens that have influenced and controlled the nations and peoples of earth. With the coming of Christ Jesus into power in 1914 Satan and his demon hosts have been cast out of heaven and onto the earth. (Ps. 110:6; Rev. 12:9) The new heaven is therefore now an established fact. Christ is in control thereof. None of the people appreciate this fact except those who diligently seek to know God's Word and to serve him.

The next great manifestation of the Lord's power will be the destruction of the beast and the false prophet, the visible or earthly part of the Devil's organization. With the beast and the false prophet destroyed, and Satan bound, the whole earth (visible wicked systems) will pass away. Then there will be no more ungodly elements of humanity, symbolically described as the "sea". Then shall follow the establishment of the new earth. With its establishment the world will be established, as foretold by the prophet (Ps. 96:10), because both heaven and earth will then be under the control of the righteous King, the Prince of Peace and Lord of lords.

John had a vision of the new world, and wrote: "And I saw a new heaven and a new earth: for the first heaven and the first earth were passed away; and there was no more sea. And I John saw the holy city, new Jerusalem, coming down from God out of heaven, prepared as a bride adorned for her husband."—Rev. 21:1, 2.

The new heaven is the government of Messiah, the new Nation born and in power. It is the holy city, the New Jerusalem. It is the government of peace, with the Prince of Peace as its head and ruler in charge; the government of Messiah, which takes the place of that which has long been invisibly ruling the world. The new heavens, or invisible part of the new government, is beautiful and glorious; and is described by John in symbolic phrase as being like unto a bride adorned for her husband. That is the time when a woman tries to appear at her best, and does so appear. The "new Jerusalem" is restricted to the 144,000 who are 'espoused to one husband, Christ'

(2 Cor. 11: 2), and who take the name of Jehovah's organization. It is specifically the organization of Christ of which he is Head; it is "the Lamb's wife". —Rev. 21: 9.

Since Satan the enemy and his angels, who compose the old heaven, are invisible, does that signify that that new heaven will also be invisible? Yes; the new heaven will be invisible. The chief one making up that new heaven is Christ Jesus. We have his own words as to whether or not he will ever again be seen by the peoples of earth, when he says: "Yet a little while, and the world seeth me no more." (John 14: 19) Christ Jesus is the express image of Jehovah, and no human eye can see God. (Heb. 1: 3; 1 Tim. 6: 16) Satan, a spirit creature, has also been invisible to man and has exercised power and control over man. Even so the Lord Jesus, the King of glory, though invisible to man, shall exercise power and control over men of the earth.

Since the time of Eden until the complete destruction of his organization Satan has had visible representatives on the earth. Does this suggest that the Prince of Peace, the great Messiah, will have visible representatives on earth? He will; and the Scriptures definitely so state.

Since God has promised that he will create a new heaven and a new earth, and since the Apostle Peter says that in this new heaven and new earth will dwell righteousness, we may be sure that the new visible organization of the Messianic government will be righteous; that is to say, the visible representatives of the righteous King on earth will be in harmony with and obedient to his command.

But after the destruction of Satan's organization, and after the binding of Satan, some men will survive; and of these there will be some more ambitious than others. Will not these ambitious and stronger ones push themselves forward and get into the government and control it and again bring about a condition of unrighteousness? They will not, because they will not be permitted to do so. (Dan. 2:44) The righteous King will permit no one to represent him who indulges in unrighteousness. In order for man to be given an opportunity to be fully restored to perfection the Lord will establish a righteous form of government on the earth. The promise is: "Behold, a king shall reign in righteousness, and princes shall rule in judgment." (Isa. 32:1) This will preclude the ambitious and stronger ones from exercising their political propensities and seizing the government or any part of it.

But all men are descendants of Adam; and since all of these are imperfect, where can there be found any to rule in justice and in righteousness as the representatives of the King?

## NEW EARTH

Long ago God prepared certain men who under adverse conditions proved their loyalty and faithfulness to God; and then they died. These men received God's approval. They will be resurrected from the grave. They will be brought forth as perfect men, wholly devoted to the Lord, and will be the visible representatives of the Lord's righteous kingdom on the earth. They will constitute the nucleus of the new earth. The scriptures hereinafter submitted conclusively prove these assertions.

It is a fixed rule of the divine arrangement that God grants everlasting life to no creature until that one is first fully tested and, under the test, proves his loyalty and faithfulness. God gave Adam life; but he then put him to the test before he would grant him everlasting life. Under the test Adam fell. His failure was because he gave his allegiance to the enemy of God. He was both a disloyal and an unfaithful man.

The next perfect man on earth was Jesus. Before the heavenly Father granted Jesus the great and high reward of eternal life on the divine plane he first put him to the most severe tests; and all these tests Jesus met successfully, and thereby proved his loyalty and his faithfulness unto God.—Luke 4:1-14; Phil. 2:5-11; Heb. 5:8, 9.

At once the absurdity of the doctrine of inherent immortality of all men appears. Satan is the author of this false doctrine, and Satan's representatives, the clergy, have proclaimed this false doctrine amongst men for centuries past.

Before the ransom sacrifice was provided by the death of the perfect man Jesus, it was impossible for any man to be granted everlasting life. This is true for the reason that all men are descendants from Adam and have inherited the result of his wrongdoing. (Rom. 5:12) It is the rule of God that "as in Adam all die, even so in Christ shall all be made alive". (1 Cor. 15:22) The death and resurrection of Jesus Christ must first take place before any man could be granted life everlasting. This, however, did not prevent imperfect men from proving their loyalty and faithfulness to God to the extent of their ability. By so doing they could have God's approval.

Since, however, there is no other name under heaven whereby salvation to life can come, except through the merit of Christ Jesus, it follows that life could not be granted until the coming of Christ Jesus and the giving of the ransom. He "gave himself [his life] a ransom for all, to be testified in due time". (Acts 4:12; 1 Tim. 2:5, 6) It follows that no matter how faithful a man might have proved prior to the giving of the ransom, he could not be granted everlasting life until the ransom is presented as a sin-offering before the mercy seat of Jehovah God. Therefore the death and resurrection of the Lord Jesus brought life and immortality to light. (2 Tim. 1:10) All must have one opportunity for life. The opportunity for immortality is for those only who seek it according to God's appointed way; to wit, by being made conformable to the sacrificial death of Jesus Christ.—Rom. 2:6, 7; Phil. 3:10-14.

It must now be apparent to the student of the Scriptures that all that man can do toward saving himself is to have faith and, under the test, to prove his loyalty and faithfulness to God. For this reason it is written: "But without faith it is impossible to please him: for he that cometh to God must believe that he is, and that he is a rewarder of them that diligently seek him."—Heb. 11:6.

Between Abel and the cross there were a few men on the earth who believed God and who diligently tried to please him and did please him. Concerning these men it is written: "These all died in faith, not having received the promises, but having seen them afar off, and were persuaded of them, and embraced them, and confessed that they were strangers and pilgrims on the earth. For they that say such things, declare plainly that they seek a country. And truly if they had been mindful of that country from whence they came out, they might have had opportunity to have returned: but now they desire a better country, that is, an heavenly: wherefore God is not ashamed to be called their God; for he hath prepared for them a city."—Heb. 11:13-16.

The word here rendered "country" means fatherland; that is to say, their native town or city or place of abode, or their land of nativity. The native condition of man was perfection in Eden; and since it is God's purpose that this condition shall be restored, but that this restoration can come only through his heavenly kingdom; and since these faithful men desired such a thing, they therefore desired the heavenly kingdom or government to be reestablished on earth. God, in the performance of his purpose, will therefore provide a city; to wit, an organization, a government, in which these men shall have a part. But who are these men?

Under inspiration of the holy spirit the apostle wrote of and concerning them. (Hebrews, eleventh chapter) First he mentions Abel, who proved his faith in God. Then he tells of Enoch, who walked with God, meaning that he had faith in God and was obedient to him; and he says that God took Enoch away that he should not see death. Then he mentions Noah, who lived in a time of great wickedness, and who manifested his faith, loyalty and devotion to God by proclaiming the truth amidst a wicked and perverse generation. Then comes Abraham, who was called to go out into a place which he knew nothing about; and because of his faith he went. He sojourned in a strange country, dwelling in tabernacles with Isaac and Jacob. The apostle also mentions Abraham's wife, Sarah, who manifested her faith in God's promises. Then he tells of the great test that came upon Abraham, when God called upon him to offer up his son Isaac. Believing that God was able to raise Isaac up from the dead Abraham obeyed, and this proves Abraham's faith in the resurrection.

Then Paul mentions Isaac as one of the faithful. Next he tells of the faith of Jacob who, because of his confidence in God, prophesied and blessed his sons upon his deathbed. He describes the faith of Joseph, and how the Lord directed him in Egypt. He then tells of Moses who, although reared in the home of a king, when he came to the years of maturity refused to be called the son of the king's daughter, choosing rather to suffer affliction with his own people because of his faith in God. The apostle adds concerning him: "Esteeming the reproach of Christ greater riches than the treasures in Egypt: for he had respect unto the recompense of the reward." (Heb. 11:26) And thus is proven the faith of Moses in the coming kingdom and in the great King. Then the apostle mentions the faith of Rahab the harlot; and he also tells of Gedeon, of Barak, of Samson, and of Jephthae.

After mentioning David, and Samuel, and the faithful prophets, the apostle then grows eloquent, and his words ring with joy and confidence in God when he adds: "Who through faith subdued kingdoms, wrought righteousness, obtained promises, stopped the mouths of lions, quenched the violence of fire, escaped the edge of the sword, out of weakness were made strong, waxed valiant in fight, turned to flight the armies of the aliens. Women received their dead raised to life again: and others were tortured, not accepting deliverance; that they might obtain a better resurrection: and others had trial of cruel mockings and scourgings, yea, moreover, of bonds and imprisonment: they were stoned, they were sawn asunder, were tempted, were slain with the sword: they wandered about in sheepskins and goatskins; being destitute, afflicted, tormented; (of whom the world was not worthy:) they wandered in deserts, and in mountains, and in dens and caves of the earth. And these all, having obtained a good report through faith, received not the promise."—Heb. 11: 33-39.

The apostle here says, "The world was not worthy" of these men; meaning the world of which Satan the Devil is the invisible ruler. By their faithful devotion to God and to his promises these worthy ones testified that they were completely out of harmony with the Devil and in complete harmony with God. They had true hearts, and did their best to do right; and because of their faithfulness they received a good report. But they could not then receive the promise. Keep in mind that the promise was the blessing of everlasting life, and the apostle plainly says that life is a gift of God through Jesus Christ our Lord. (Rom. 6: 23) It reasonably follows, then, that they could not get life prior to the giving of the ransom sacrifice.

Then adds the apostle: "God having provided some better thing for us, that they without us should not be made perfect." It is manifest that the class here mentioned as getting the "better thing" are those who will be associated with Christ on the spirit plane, because Paul includes himself as one of them. He says that these faithful men of old without *us* should not be made perfect. The word here rendered "perfect" denotes complete, finished, accomplished purpose. By this, then, it is to be understood that these men, having received a good report because of their faithfulness, must wait in the tomb until the members of the body of Christ are selected and proven. The promise concerning them could not be completed until the Lord has selected the entire church. That is to say, God's purpose and provision for them cannot be consummated or finished until full and complete provision is made for the invisible part of the kingdom.

In the atonement day sacrifice, which God caused the Jews to practice and which is described in the sixteenth chapter of Leviticus, it is shown that the ransom sacrifice is presented as a sin-offering on behalf of all, aside from the church, after the selection of the members of the body of Christ.

When the members of the body of Christ are completed, what then is to be expected for these men who died in faith before the great ransom sacrifice was given? Paul plainly says: "Wherefore God is not ashamed to be called their God; for he hath prepared for them a city." (Heb. 11:16) A city being a symbol of a government, this text is positive proof that God has prepared for these very men a place in his government of righteousness on earth.

Every one of the faithful ones mentioned in this eleventh chapter of Hebrews died before the coming of Christ Jesus, except John the Baptist; and he died before the crucifixion of our Lord. None of those who had died has gone to heaven. The clergy have misrepresented to the people that these faithful men were changed from human to spirit creatures. Jesus is the best witness concerning that. In discussing the resurrection he said: "No man hath ascended up to heaven." (John 3:13) At the time he uttered these words faithful Abel had been dead for nearly four thousand years; and all of the others in this list, except John, had been dead for centuries. The Apostle Peter, speaking under inspiration, specifically mentions David; and of him he says: "For David is not ascended into the heavens."—Acts 2:34.

Furthermore the Lord Jesus, to show specifically that John the Baptist is not in heaven, and to remove all doubt that might be in any man's mind on that point, said: "Verily I say unto you, Among them that are born of women there hath not risen a greater than John the Baptist: notwithstanding, he that is least in the kingdom of heaven is greater than he." (Matt. 11:11) Unequivocally he here states that there has not been a greater man than John the Baptist, and yet he says that the very least in the kingdom of heaven will be greater than John; thus by inference he definitely settles the fact that John the Baptist, who died prior to the crucifixion, could not be in the invisible part of the kingdom. But since the Apostle Paul has so positively stated that God has provided for John and all other ancient witnesses for God a part in the new government or kingdom, where could they be?

It seems quite clear that these are the princes mentioned in Isaiah 32:1. Those mentioned by the apostle in Hebrews, eleventh chapter, have always been recognized as faithful men amongst the Jews; they were even recognized in David's day as fathers in Israel. The prophet, after discussing the selection of the church, says: "Instead of thy fathers shall be thy children, whom thou mayest make princes in all the earth." (Ps. 45:16) Therefore the conclusion must be reached that these will get their life through Christ, which is the only way they can obtain it; hence that they will be called the children of Christ, and that he will make them princes in all the earth.

The proof therefore seems quite conclusive that these faithful men, who obtained a good report because of their loyalty and faithfulness to God, will receive the promised blessings of life everlasting through Christ, and that the time for receiving these blessings will be when the members of the body of Christ are complete. When they shall receive life the promise concerning them is then complete; therefore they are then completed. Prior to the death of these men they had proved their loyalty and faithfulness, allegiance and devotion to God. He approved them; he waits until he has selected the royal family of heaven, and the promise is that then these men shall be made the visible representatives of The Christ on earth during his reign.

### CORROBORATIVE PROOF

Let each one settle it in his mind for all time that God is true. When he makes a promise it is absolutely certain that that promise will be fulfilled. He has never failed in one of his promises, and all of them are good. The psalmist says concerning Jehovah: "Thy word is true from the beginning: and every one of thy righteous judgments endureth for ever." (Ps. 119:160) "The testimony of the Lord is sure." (Ps. 19:7) "For all the promises of God in him are yea [sure], and in him Amen [trustworthy, sure, verity], unto the glory of God by us." (2 Cor. 1:20) Jesus says concerning the Word of God: "Thy word is truth." (John 17:17) And again he said: "He that sent me is true." (John 7:28) "It [is] impossible for God to lie." (Heb. 6:18) God changes not. (Mal. 3:6) "I have spoken it, I will also bring it to pass; I have purposed it, I will also do it." (Isa. 46:11) "So shall my word be that goeth forth out of my mouth: it shall not return unto me void; but it shall accomplish that which I please, and it shall prosper in the thing whereto I sent it."—Isa. 55:11.

"Faith" means to know God's promises and then to rely upon them. He who has faith in God must know that God will fulfil every one of his promises. Having this settled, then, note some of the promises of God to these faithful men of old, above mentioned.

To Abraham God promised that he would make of him a great nation. "And in thee shall all families of the earth be blessed." (Gen. 12:2, 3) Again, God promised Abraham to give him all the land that he saw. "And the Lord said unto Abram, after that Lot was separated from him, Lift up now thine eyes, and look from the place where thou art, northward, and southward, and eastward, and westward: for all the land which thou seest, to thee will I give it, and to thy seed for ever. And I will make thy seed as the dust of the earth: so that if a man can number the dust of the earth, then shall thy seed also be numbered. Arise, walk through the land, in the length of it and in the breadth of it; for I will give it unto thee."—Gen. 13:14-17.

In another form he made this same promise: "And I will give unto thee, and to thy seed after thee, the land wherein thou art a stranger, all the land of Canaan, for an everlasting possession; and I will be their God."—Gen. 17:8.

When Abraham was one hundred and seventy-five years old he died, without having possessed any of the land which God promised to give him. Long thereafter Stephen testified concerning Abraham, as it is recorded in the Scriptures: "Then came he out of the land of the Chaldeans, and dwelt in Charran; and from thence, when his father was dead, he removed him into this land, wherein ye now dwell. And he gave him none inheritance in it, no not so much as to set his foot on: yet he promised that he would give it to him for a possession, and to his seed after him, when as yet he had no child."—Acts 7:4, 5.

Long ago were these promises made. They have not yet been fulfilled. They must be fulfilled in God's due time; and the Apostle Paul, under inspiration, writes that God's due time is after Christ has taken unto himself his power and begun his reign.

Afterwards, when Jacob had left his father Isaac's home to journey into another land, he slept on a hill in Palestine. "And he dreamed, and, behold, a ladder set up on the earth, and the top of it reached to heaven: and, behold, the angels of God ascending and descending on it." (Gen. 28:12) There must be some significance in this vision of the angels ascending and descending on a ladder between heaven and earth, which the Lord permitted him to see. It must represent communication between heaven and earth. It is therefore reasonable to conclude that the Lord intended here to suggest that sometime he would establish communication between the invisible and the visible part of his kingdom.

At the same time he made this promise to Jacob: "And, behold, the Lord stood above it, and said, I am the Lord God of Abraham thy father, and the God of Isaac: the land whereon thou liest, to thee will I give it, and to thy seed; and thy seed shall be as the dust of the earth; and thou shalt spread abroad to the west, and to the east, and to the north, and to the south: and in thee and in thy seed shall all the families of the earth be blessed." (Gen. 28:13, 14) Afterwards Jacob journeyed into Egypt and lived and died there. He had not yet possessed this land.

### THEIR RESURRECTION

These promises made to Abraham and to Jacob, and to their seed after them who died, could not be fulfilled unless God has made provision for their resurrection. The Scriptures show that God did hold out to them the hope of a resurrection, and that Abraham, Jacob and the prophets of old believed in the resurrection. Testifying concerning the hope and the resurrection Job said: "For I know that my Redeemer liveth, and that he shall stand at the latter day upon the earth: and though, after my skin, worms destroy this body, yet in my flesh shall I see God." (Job 19:25, 26) Again in Job, looking to the time of the restoration of man, faith in the resurrection is expressed. We read: "If there be a messenger with him, an interpreter, one among a thousand, to shew unto man his uprightness; then he is gracious unto him, and saith, Deliver him from going down to the pit; I have found a ransom. His flesh shall be fresher than a child's: he shall return to the days of his youth."—Job 33: 23-25.

Moses was one of the prophets of God, and one who the Apostle Paul says will be rewarded with a place in the kingdom on earth; and Moses wrote concerning the resurrection: "The Lord thy God will raise up unto thee a Prophet from the midst of thee, of thy brethren, like unto me; unto him ye shall hearken. I will raise them up a Prophet from among their brethren, like unto thee, and will put my words in his mouth; and he shall speak unto them all that I shall command him."—Deut. 18: 15, 18.

Samuel, one of the prophets and one of the approved ones of God, testified his faith in the resurrection when he recorded these words: "The Lord killeth, and maketh alive: he bringeth down to the grave, and bringeth up."—1 Sam. 2: 6.

David, another approved one of God, prophesied that God would provide redemption and resurrection for the human race. He had faith therein. (Ps. 91: 14; 21: 4) Furthermore he said: "For when he dieth he shall carry nothing away; his glory shall not descend after him. But God will redeem my soul from the power of the grave; for he shall receive me." (Ps. 49: 17, 15) It was David who prophesied that the world in the future should be established that it could not be moved.—Ps. 96: 10.

Isaiah is one of the approved prophets, and he testified his faith in the resurrection when he wrote: "And an highway shall be there, and a way, and it shall be called, The way of holiness; the unclean shall not pass over it; but it shall be for those: the wayfaring men, though fools, shall not err therein. No lion shall be there, nor any ravenous beast shall go up thereon, it shall not be found there: but the redeemed shall walk there. And the ransomed of the Lord shall return, and come to Zion with songs, and everlasting joy upon their heads: they shall obtain joy and gladness, and sorrow and sighing shall flee away."–Isa. 35: 8-10.

Again God, speaking through Isaiah the prophet, declared that the earth was made for man and that man shall inhabit it; and since he promised the land to Abraham and Jacob and their seed, it is to be expected that they will receive it.—Isa. 45: 12, 18.

Jesus testified concerning the resurrection of all the dead, and his testimony must of necessity include Abraham and all the faithful ones mentioned by the Apostle Paul: "Marvel not at this: for the hour is coming, in the which all that are in the graves shall hear his voice, and shall come forth; they that have done good, unto the resurrection of life: and they that have done evil, unto the resurrection [by judgment]."—John 5: 28, 29.

These faithful men of old, who for identification are called faithful martyrs or witnesses, did good and received a good report from Jehovah; therefore they come clearly within the ranks of those mentioned by the Lord Jesus as having a resurrection to life.

We must therefore conclude, from these texts, that all these faithful men mentioned by the Apostle Paul, who are promised a part in the new government, will have a resurrection which will be better than the resurrection that will be received by men in general. By this is meant that these will come forth from the tomb with life.

The pious Jewish clergy of Jesus' day expected to be a part of the Messianic kingdom. In fact they were so egotistical that they did not think Messiah could set up his kingdom without them; and when Jesus rebuked them and did not select any of them to be his disciples they of course thought that he was not worthy to be considered the representative of Jehovah, much less the Messiah. He said to them, however: "There shall be weeping and gnashing of teeth, when ye shall see Abraham, and Isaac, and Jacob, and all the prophets, in the kingdom of God, and you yourselves thrust out." (Luke 13:28) On another occasion Jesus said: "Many shall come from the east and west, and shall sit down with Abraham, and Isaac, and Jacob, in the kingdom of heaven." (Matt. 8:11) The new government of earth is the kingdom of heaven because the authority proceeds from the throne of God and is administered through the King whom God has set upon his holy throne. (Ps. 2:6) The authority that these earthly princes will execute will proceed from the invisible kingdom. They will be the representatives of the Lord on earth, consequently they will be in the earthly part of this heavenly kingdom; and many others shall come from various parts of the earth and sit down with Abraham, Isaac, Jacob and these other faithful men. They will sit at their feet and learn wisdom.

It is reasonable to expect that these faithful men will be brought forth from the tomb as perfect men, possessing perfect bodies and perfect minds. They were tried and tested before they died. Their faithfulness to the Lord is even held forth to the church as a proper example and guide for those to follow who hope to be of the kingdom. (Heb. 12: 1-3) They have received a good report from Jehovah because of their faithfulness; therefore they have "done good" within the meaning of the term as used by Christ Jesus, and in the resurrection they will "come forth" to life. (John 5: 28, 29) Being perfect men, and being princes or rulers in the earth, they will be able to wonderfully encourage the people to strive and prove their faithfulness unto God that they may merit the blessings that he has promised.

When God had selected David and anointed him as king he said concerning him: "I have found David the son of Jesse, a man after mine own heart, which shall fulfill all my will." (Acts 13: 22) Why was David a man after God's own heart? Without doubt the reason is found in the fact that David was always loyal and faithful to God. He made mistakes as do other men, but his heart was always right; that is to say, his motive or purpose was correct. He desired to honor God, and did his best to do so. He loved God and proved his love by devoting himself to God's service. David is specifically mentioned by Paul as one of the faithful men who received God's approval. It is reasonable to think of him as one who will have some tremendous part in the affairs of earth during the reign of the Messiah. The Lord, speaking concerning Israel and those who shall come under the terms of the new covenant during the reign of Christ, said: "And I the Lord will be their God, and my servant David a prince among them; I the Lord have spoken it."—Ezek. 34: 24.

### LAW FOR THE PEOPLE

What law will govern the people during the reign of Messiah? Will they continue to elect legislative bodies, and enact and enforce laws? If everybody did that which is right no law would be needed. Laws are not made for those who do good, but to restrain those who do wrong. "Knowing this, that the law is not made for a righteous man, but for the lawless and disobedient, for the ungodly and for sinners, for unholy and profane, for murderers of fathers and murderers of mothers, for manslayers, for whoremongers, for them that defile themselves with mankind, for menstealers, for liars, for perjured persons, and if there be any other thing that is contrary to sound doctrine."—1 Tim. 1: 9, 10.

Law is a rule of action commanding that the right be done and prohibiting that which is wrong. If everybody did good and there were no wrong, no law would be required. However, the people will be imperfect during Messiah's reign. The reign of Messiah will be required to bring back mankind to perfection. The imperfect man, therefore, will need laws or rules of action to direct him. But imperfect man will not make the laws for this new government, as has been the custom in times past. The new government will be a pure theocracy. It will be God's government, conducted in his appointed way, to wit, by and through his beloved Son Christ Jesus.

The Lord will compel no one to accept the ransom sacrifice and live, but he will not permit anyone to do harm in all his holy kingdom. (Isa. 11:9) Those who attempt to do wrong will be swiftly dealt with in the Lord's appointed way. But how can men know what is the right thing to do, since they will still be imperfect?

God will make a covenant for the benefit of man. This is called the new covenant. At Mount Sinai God confirmed a covenant with Israel, and that covenant pointed out what the people must do in order to live. Moses was the mediator of that covenant. The Jews could not keep that covenant, however, because they were imperfect and because their mediator was imperfect. The Mediator of the new covenant will be Christ, of whom Moses was a type. The Mediator of the new covenant, being perfect, possesses the power to do for man what man cannot do for himself. The people will be required to do the best they can to advance toward righteousness; and Christ, the Mediator of the new covenant, will make up for them what they cannot do. Their good deeds will be rewarded with progress. Their evil deeds will receive instant punishment. Concerning the new covenant that God purposes to make for the guidance of the peoples of earth during the reign of Messiah, Paul quotes from Jeremiah 31:31-34:

"For finding fault with them, he saith, Behold, the days come, saith the Lord, when I will make a new covenant with the house of Israel and with the house of Judah: not according to the covenant that I made with their fathers in the day when I took them by the hand to lead them out of the land of Egypt; because they continued not in my covenant, and I regarded them not, saith the Lord. For this is the covenant that I will make with the house of Israel after those days, saith the Lord; I will put my laws into their mind, and write them in their hearts: and I will be to them a God, and they shall be to me a people: and they shall not teach every man his neighbour, and every man his brother, saying, Know the Lord: for all shall know me, from the least to the greatest. For I will be merciful to their unrighteousness, and their sins and their iniquities will I remember no more.''—Heb. 8: 8-12.

The first law covenant was typical of the new covenant. That old covenant served to teach the Jews, and all men, that no man can obtain life without the aid of Christ. It also served to lead to Christ such of the Jews as obeyed it to the best of their ability, and who desired to accept him as a King. A few accepted him; the others rejected him.

That old covenant sets forth in detail the statutes by which the people were to be governed in order to go in the right way. The fundamental law of God, as a basis for the statutes of the covenant, is set forth in Deuteronomy 5: 1-21. The statutes and judgments are set forth in detail in Deuteronomy, chapters twelve to twenty-eight inclusive. It is reasonable to expect that in the new covenant which God will make with Israel, and through them with and for the benefit of all the other nations of the earth, he will set forth the laws or rules of action by which the people shall be governed.

At the present time we find many men who are endeavoring to discover a properly balanced food.

There are many food experts now, and it is commendable that they are trying to find proper diet. It shows that the minds of such investigators are turned in the right direction. Without doubt, in due time the Lord will show the people what is a properly balanced diet for humanity, how they should eat and what they should eat. In the fourteenth chapter of Deuteronomy God gave to the Jews under the old law covenant detailed instructions concerning the preparation of food for their sustenance. He surely will do as much, and more, during the reign of the perfect Mediator Christ, the King of glory.

The Apostle Paul says: "Now the end of the commandment is [love] out of a pure heart, and of a good conscience, and of faith unfeigned." (1 Tim. 1:5) "Love worketh no ill to his neighbour: therefore love is the fulfilling of the law." (Rom. 13:10) Now with reference to what the Lord says about the new covenant, we note that these are his words: "For this is the covenant that I will make with the house of Israel after those days, saith the Lord; I will put my laws into their mind, and write them in their hearts: and I will be to them a God, and they shall be to me a people."—Heb. 8:10.

The heart is the seat of affection. The heart likewise symbolically represents man's motive. When the law of God, which is righteous, resides in the heart of man, his course of action will be right. This being true, then love, which is the perfect expression of unselfishness, will be the complete fulfilment of the law. Selfishness has always governed the people during Satan's régime. The work of Christ will be to establish love in the hearts of the people.

The Jews were God's chosen people. He used them to teach lessons to all mankind. They were imperfect, like other men. The Devil overreached them and turned them away from God; hence they were cast away from God's favor. The Jews have suffered long, but now their warfare is ended. (Isa. 40:1,2) As they return in faith to God he will have mercy upon them. Paul himself was once a Jew, but learning that Jesus is Christ the Messiah he fully devoted himself to the Lord and was transferred from the covenant of Moses into Christ. He was then made the special ambassador to the Gentiles.

God's favor came to the Gentiles when Cornelius received the gospel, and when God opened the way to permit Gentiles to become his sons. The Gentiles then, seeing that the Jews had been cast away, became heady and were in great danger of not receiving their favor from God. Paul, addressing a message to them, said:

"For I would not, brethren, that ye should be ignorant of this mystery, lest ye should be wise in your own conceits; that blindness in part is happened to Israel, until the fulness of the Gentiles be come in. And so all Israel shall be saved: as it is written, There shall come out of Sion the Deliverer, and shall turn away ungodliness from Jacob: for this is my covenant unto them, when I shall take away their sins. As concerning the gospel, they are enemies for your sakes: but as touching the election, they are beloved for the fathers' sakes. For the gifts and calling of God are without repentance. For as ye in times past have not believed God, yet have now obtained mercy through their unbelief: even so have these also now not believed, that through your mercy they also may obtain mercy. For God hath concluded them all in unbelief, that he might have mercy upon all.''—Rom. 11:25-32.

Paul's argument is that the Jews had been cast away and that this afforded an opportunity for the Gentiles to be among the elect; and that when this election is over, the Jews shall believe on the Lord God and he will make with them a new covenant. Then the apostle says in substance that if the casting away of the Jews furnished this opportunity for the Gentiles to be reconciled to God, through Christ Jesus, then the receiving of the Jews back into God's favor will be life from the dead for the world. That will mean that under the terms of the new covenant all who obey will be completely delivered from the enemy death. "Now if the fall of them be the riches of the world, and the diminishing of them the riches of the Gentiles; how much more their fulness? For if the casting away of them be the reconciling of the world, what shall the receiving of them be, but life from the dead?''—Rom. 11:12, 15.

With the Devil's organization destroyed, the Devil himself bound, the faithful worthies of old resurrected as perfect men and made princes in the earth, and receiving their instructions from the invisible King of glory, then and there the great and wonderful new nation, the kingdom of righteousness, the royal priesthood, will be performing fully the function of government both in heaven and in earth, looking to the full and complete deliverance of mankind from their difficulties and imperfections and the bringing of all back into complete harmony with God. With the new heavens and the new earth in full operation, then will fully come to pass the words of the prophet, that the world is established firmly for ever and can never be moved. This new world will be administered in righteousness, and will result in bringing righteousness to the people, granting unto the righteous ones a realization of their heart's sincere desire.

## Chapter XIV

# *Reconstruction and Restoration*

THE reconstruction of the human race, and the restoration of man to perfection, is a tremendous task. Only divine power could accomplish it. This task will be accomplished in God's due time, and that time is now about to begin.

Reconstruction means making over again; that is, making anew. Restoration of man means the act of bringing man back to the original strength and beauty of perfect manhood. One of the primary purposes of the new heaven and new earth, which constitute the new world, is that man might be reconstructed and restored and righteousness for ever established amongst men. The sacrificial death and resurrection of Christ Jesus made available the great ransom price, whereby is removed the legal disability which prevents man from coming back to God. The overthrow of Satan's empire and the restraining of the enemy will remove the powers that were actively hindering man from making progress in righteousness.

Cannot man then, unaided, bring himself back into harmony with God? He cannot. It must be borne in mind that for more than six thousand years the human race has been traveling the broad road of unrighteousness that leads to degradation and destruction. After such a long period of sin and debauchery the race is wicked and depraved. Visit the slums of the great cities and gain some idea of the vice, immorality, corruption and wickedness that is practiced there. Observe the filth and muck and poverty-stricken conditions. Note those afflicted with loathsome disease, the weak of mind, the wretched, the lame, the halt and the blind, all herded together in a small ill-ventilated hovel, and no proper food or clothing. They have nothing elevating upon which to feed the mind. Many of them appear to have reached a state of almost total depravity. This is the result of the work of the Devil.

Visit then the insane asylums, and there see hundreds of thousands whose minds are turned entirely in the wrong direction, and who are blind to all reason and truth. This also is the enemy's work.

Go to the hospitals and there look with pitying eyes upon the lame and halt and blind and sick and afflicted. This too is the result of Satan's work.

Go into the prison houses and observe the marks of crime upon the faces of poor unfortunates who there drag out a weary existence. This is the work of the wicked one.

Visit the financial centers and see the harsh, cruel countenance of the profiteer who hesitates not to make war and hurry millions of youths into the trenches, there to meet an untimely and cruel death. This too is the work of the Devil.

Make the rounds of the sweat shops, where poor widows, friendless girls and impotent men labor under the most adverse conditions, to eke out a mere existence. This is the Devil's work.

Consider also the brothels, where once beautiful girls have been turned into demons by reason of wicked practices. This is a part of the Devil's work.

Look deep into the salt pits and other mines and there see poor, miserable creatures toiling in the darkness for a pittance that others might roll in wealth or earthly gain. This is a part of the Devil's work.

Go into the crowded streets and subways, the boats, the restaurants, the dance halls and like places and observe the young boys and girls, old men and old women, slaves to nicotine and drugs, momentarily breeding vice and crime. These things are also works of the Devil.

The death and resurrection alone of Jesus Christ will not undo these evils. The overthrow of Satan's empire and the restraint of the enemy will not relieve them from their miserable conditions. There is something else that must be done. It will be done. It is written: "He that committeth sin is of the devil; for the devil sinneth from the beginning. For this purpose the Son of God was manifested, that he might destroy the works of the devil." (1 John 3:8) "He [God] shall send Jesus Christ, which before was preached unto you: whom the heaven must receive until the times of restitution of all things, which God hath spoken by the mouth of all his holy prophets since the world began."—Acts 3:19-21.

Six thousand years of misrule by Satan, the rebellious and wicked one, have wrought all the wickedness among humankind. Now God will demonstrate to all his intelligent creatures that one thousand years of rule by his beloved Son, Christ Jesus the righteous One, can and will undo all the wickedness that has been done, and will restore all the willing and obedient ones to the full glory and beauty of perfect manhood. This blessed and glorious work will make a name for Jehovah in the minds of all, that can never be effaced. All who learn the lessons taught will never again depart from the path of righteousness.

With heaven and earth made up of perfect, glorious creatures, all under one Head, Christ Jesus, that will be an eternal monument, forever testifying to the wisdom, power and loving-kindness of our God. That the great eternal One purposes to use his Christ for reconstructing and restoring the peoples of earth, finds abundant support in his Word: "And in thy seed shall all the nations of the earth be blessed." (Gen. 22:18) "Now to Abraham and his seed were the promises made, . . . which [seed] is Christ. And if ye be Christ's, then are ye Abraham's seed, and heirs according to the promise." (Gal. 3:16, 29) "Ye which have followed me, in the regeneration, when the Son of man shall sit in the throne of his glory, ye also shall sit upon twelve thrones, judging the twelve tribes of Israel." (Matt. 19:28) "For he must reign, till he hath put all enemies under his feet. The last enemy that shall be destroyed is death." (1 Cor. 15:25, 26) "Behold my servant, whom I uphold; mine elect, in whom my soul delighteth; I have put my spirit upon him: he shall bring forth judgment to the Gentiles. I the Lord have called thee in righteousness, and will hold thine hand, and will keep thee, and give thee for a covenant of the people, for a light of the Gentiles." "I will preserve thee, and give thee for a covenant of the people, to establish the earth."—Isa. 42:1, 6, 7; 49:8-10.

The Scriptures show that the reconstruction and restoration work will embrace a period of one thousand years. "Millennium" means one thousand years;

hence the reign of Messiah is called "the Millennium". During that time the entire human race will be under the control of Christ, who will gradually lead the obedient ones back into harmony with Almighty God. Furthermore, the Scriptures show that this blessed work will begin with the ousting of Satan the enemy from the earth and the establishment on earth of the kingdom of God. That marks the beginning of the judgment day for the individuals of the human family.—Acts 17:31.

## ORDER OF JUDGMENT

The Scriptures declare that the living shall be first judged and then the dead: "I charge thee therefore before God, and the Lord Jesus Christ, who shall judge the quick [the living] and the dead at his appearing and his kingdom." (2 Tim. 4:1) Upon earth there are now approximately 1,748,000,000 people. Since the judgment is to begin with the generation on earth at the time for judgment, it follows that millions of those now on earth will be the first ones to receive a trial and an opportunity for the blessings that will follow.

As those on the earth begin to receive the benefits of reconstruction and restoration they will think of their beloved dead and wish that they might be brought back to life. Having faith and hope, based upon their knowledge of the Word of God, they will begin to make preparation for the return of their beloved dead. Learning that they have the privilege of prayer they will pray to the Lord that their beloved ones may be restored to them, and the Lord has promised to hear and grant their prayer. "And it shall come to pass, that before they call, I will answer: and while they are yet speaking, I will hear."—Isa. 65:24.

The beautiful Scriptural teaching concerning the resurrection of the dead has been long hid from the minds of the people, and this has been accomplished by Satan's using his earthly representatives, the clergy, to teach false doctrines. These false prophets, claiming authority to teach the Bible, have induced the people to believe that every man 'possesses an immortal soul, which cannot actually die'; that what is called death is not really death; that the person supposed to die merely has a change and passes on into 'another clime'. The truth is that every man *is* a soul, no man *has* a soul.

The Scriptures declare that God formed man of the dust of the earth, breathed into his nostrils the breath of lives, and man became a living soul; which means, man became a living, moving, breathing, sentient creature. (Gen. 2:7) In the law of God it is written: "The soul that sinneth, it shall die." (Ezek. 18:4) If the soul were immortal it could not die. To the same effect it is written: "What man is he that liveth, and shall not see death? shall he deliver his soul from the hand of the grave?" (Ps. 89:48) When a man dies he is as dead as a dead dog. (Eccl. 9:5, 10; Ps. 115:17) He remains in that state until the resurrection.

The same false teachers have induced the people to believe that some at death go to purgatory and there suffer until they are relieved at the instance of priests, who pray for them and receive a money consideration for such prayers. They also teach that the wicked die and go to hell, and that hell is a place of eternal torment. The Word of God teaches that hell is the tomb, the condition of death; and that all who die, both good and bad, go there. The purgatory doctrine is purely an invention. There is no such place or condition where men are suffering and from which they could be relieved by prayers with or without a money consideration.

Job prayed that he might go to hell, *sheol.* (Job 14:13, 14) By that he meant that he might rest in the tomb, in the condition of death, until the resurrection. Jacob said: "My son shall not go down with you; for his brother is dead, and he is left alone: if mischief befall him by the way in the which ye go, then shall ye bring down my gray hairs with sorrow to [hell]," *sheol.* (Gen. 42:38) His gray hairs could not last long in eternal fire.

The Hebrew word *sheol* and the Greek word *hades,* both translated "hell" in our Bible, mean the same thing; both mean the condition of death from which there is hope of a resurrection. The Greek word *gehenna* means that condition of death from which there is no hope of a resurrection; and such is the final destiny of the wilfully wicked, including the Devil himself. The Devil has induced the people to believe that he, the Devil, has been in hell stoking the fire all these centuries, when in truth and in fact he has never yet been in hell. He will go to *gehenna* in due time and stay, and he will not stoke any fire while he is there.—Ezek. 28:19.

Concerning Jesus it is written: "For thou wilt not leave my soul in hell; neither wilt thou suffer thine

Holy One to see corruption." (Ps. 16:10) The apostle, in Acts 2:27, plainly applies this to Jesus. Jesus was resurrected the third day. This of itself is conclusive proof that hell is not a place of eternal torment. There is no doctrine that is more clearly taught in the Bible than that of the resurrection of the dead. But if the soul were immortal, then there could be no resurrection; and if any creatures were in eternal torment they could not be brought out.

The resurrection of Jesus is a guarantee that the dead shall be resurrected. The argument of the Apostle Paul is that Christ was raised from the dead, and that if he was not, then there is no resurrection of the dead. In other words, the resurrection of Christ is proof that the other dead shall be raised. "But now is Christ risen from the dead, and become the firstfruits of them that slept. For since by man came death, by man came also the resurrection of the dead. For as in Adam all die, even so in Christ shall all be made alive. But every man in his own order; Christ the firstfruits; afterward they that are Christ's, at his coming."—1 Cor. 15:20-23.

Again, the apostle says: "There shall be a resurrection of the dead, both of the just and unjust." (Acts 24:15) Then says Jesus concerning the dead: "Marvel not at this: for the hour cometh, in which all that are in the tombs shall hear his voice, and shall come forth; they that have done good, unto the resurrection of life; and they that have done evil, unto the resurrection of judgment." (John 5:28, 29, *A.R.V.*) The word here translated 'tomb' or 'grave' is from a word which means "memory" of God; therefore this text is conclusive proof that God holds in his memory all those who have died; and that in his due time, through Christ, he will bring them back out of death. "For if we believe that Jesus died and rose again, even so them also which sleep in Jesus will God bring with him."—1 Thess. 4:14.

The ransom sacrifice was given for all. (Heb. 2:9) In God's due time all must see this great truth. "For there is one God, and one mediator between God and men, the man Christ Jesus; who gave himself a ransom for all, to be testified in due time." (1 Tim. 2:5, 6) Billions have gone into death without having any knowledge whatsoever of God's provisions for them to live. In his own due time he will see to it that all these are brought forth, awaken them out of death, that they may know his provisions made for them to have life.

When will the awakening of the dead begin! The Scriptures do not disclose the day, but indicate that it will not be a great while after the living have had an opportunity to be reconstructed. It is reasonable to conclude that the Lord will straighten out those who are on earth before bringing back more with whom to deal. The trial and judgment of those now living on the earth, looking to reconstruction and restoration, cannot begin until Satan's empire completely falls and the enemy is restrained, as described in the preceding chapter. The people will then know that the time has come for the work of reconstruction to begin. And how will they know it? The Scriptures answer that God will then give to the people the message of truth that they may know, as it is written: "For then will I turn to the people a pure language [message], that they may all call upon the name of the Lord, to serve him with one consent."—Zeph. 3: 9.

The great ransom or redemptive price was provided for man in order that he might have restored to him what he had lost. But restoration cannot be accomplished until man has knowledge that it is offered to him. For this reason it is written: "This is good and acceptable before God, our savior, who desires all men to be saved, and to come to an accurate knowledge of the truth."—1 Tim. 2: 3, 4, *Diag.*

Why is knowledge the first essential? The greatest of all blessings which God has promised to man is life everlasting. All the other blessings are incident to life. God will not arbitrarily force this blessing upon anyone. He will have it offered to man as a free gift. "The gift of God is eternal life, through Jesus Christ our Lord." (Rom. 6: 23) This offer comes to man that he might have life. (Rom. 5: 18) A gift is a contract which requires two parties. There must be a giver and a receiver, and their minds must meet. The giver must be willing to give, and the receiver must have a knowledge thereof and be willing to accept. Hence it would be impossible for man to receive life as a gracious gift without first having a knowledge of the offer.

But when the people begin to receive some knowledge concerning life and the blessings incident thereto, how will they know that such is true and correct information? The truth will be made so clear and plain that no one can mistake it. Christ is the great Teacher; and he will use his faithful representatives on earth, the princes, to teach the people. The way that leads to life will be made plain and clear.

THE RIGHT WAY

Through his holy prophet God tells of his provision to teach the people and lead them in the right way. "And an highway shall be there, and a way, and it shall be called, The way of holiness; the unclean shall not pass over it; but it shall be for those: the wayfaring men, though fools, shall not err therein."—Isa. 35:8.

"Highway" means a plain way by which to go to a place or goal. It means a smooth way to travel, with nothing to interfere or hinder. Of course this does not mean a literal road to travel; the word "highway" is used as a figure of speech, meaning that God has provided a plain way for the people to return to him, so plain that all may know about it, and that all who will may avail themselves of its benefits.

"A way" is specifically mentioned in this text, and it is designated as "The way of holiness". A "highway" is a plain way that leads to the goal, whereas "the way" means the fixed or appointed rules of action which every one will be required to strictly observe in order to pass over the highway to the end. It is called "The way of holiness" because it is right, pure and holy. If a man faithfully observes the rules he will be aided in making progress on the highway. If he refuses to obey the rules, and therefore refuses to walk according to "the way", he will not be permitted to go to the end of the highway. The goal of perfection and blessings is at the end of the highway, and the way to reach it is to do the right thing. No unclean person shall be permitted to go to the end thereof. All who enter upon the highway will be unclean at the time they enter, because imperfect. If these, however, observe the way of holiness, and walk according thereto, they will be cleaned up. As progress is made in the way of righteousness and holiness the one continuing to pass along the highway will continue to progress until he ultimately reaches the end thereof.

The way will be so plain and clear that no one will have a just cause or excuse for not knowing it. Why shall there be no reason for any to err therein? Because, as the scripture answers, "No lion shall be there." (Isa. 35: 9) "Lion" is a figure of speech, here used to represent the Devil. (1 Pet. 5: 8) Neither Satan nor any other devil will be permitted to be on that highway, or to interfere with anyone who goes upon it. No "ravenous beast shall go up thereon". That means that there will be no more devil organizations, composed of profiteers, politicians and pulpiteers, to prey upon the people or to mislead and oppress them. Nothing of that kind will be found there. "Ravenous beast" is used here to symbolize the Devil's organization. God will clean out all of these things before restoration begins, and thus give man a clear, uninterrupted opportunity to prove whether or not he wants to be blessed.

In the first paragraph of this book this question is propounded: May we hope that the people will ever be delivered from this sad state and enter into the joys of peace, prosperity, health, life, liberty and happiness? Now we shall find an answer to this question.

### BLINDNESS REMOVED

At the present time these words of the prophet are fulfilled: 'Darkness covers the earth and gross darkness the people.' (Isa. 60:2) The mass of mankind is in complete ignorance of God's provisions for the blessing of the people. Satan the enemy is chiefly responsible for this blindness. (2 Cor. 4:3,4) Such is the blindness that caused the Jews to be cast away from God. Then this same prophet continues: "But the Lord shall arise upon thee, and his glory shall be seen upon thee." (Isa. 60:2) The apostle declares that their blindness shall be removed when "the fulness of the Gentiles be come in"; which means, when the last member of the kingdom has been selected from the Gentiles and glorified with the Lord. "There shall come out of Sion [God's organization] the Deliverer [Messiah] and shall turn away ungodliness from [the descendants of] Jacob." (Rom. 11:25,26) At this time there is a "vail" of darkness over the eyes of the people, which prevents them from seeing God's loving-kindness and provision for their help; but in the kingdom one of the first operations of the Lord will be to remove that vail of blindness, that the people may be able to understand. "And he will destroy in this [kingdom] the face of the covering cast over all people, and the vail that is spread over all nations." —Isa. 25:7.

Jesus declared concerning the Word of God, the Bible: "Sanctify them through thy truth; thy word is truth." (John 17:17) The people must know the truth in order that they may be blessed, and then they must obey the truth before the blessings will be realized. But suppose they do not accept and do not obey the truth, then what will be the result?

### THE DISOBEDIENT

The Lord will not force anyone to accept the truth; but he will compel all to obey the truth when they hear it, or else suffer the consequences. The only way back to God and happiness will be to travel over the highway according to the way of holiness. Those who refuse to hear the instructions of the Lord concerning this way shall suffer punishment, which punishment will consist of everlasting destruction.

Moses wrote concerning Jesus, his antitype, and how all the people would have to obey him during his reign. "For Moses truly said unto the fathers, A prophet shall the Lord your God raise up unto you of your brethren, like unto me; him shall ye hear in all things whatsoever he shall say unto you. And it shall come to pass, that every soul, which will not hear that prophet, shall be destroyed from among the people." (Acts 3:22, 23) This punishment is declared to be everlasting destruction. (2 Thess. 1:9) It is in harmony with the statement of the prophet: "The Lord preserveth all them that love him: but all the wicked will he destroy." (Ps. 145:20) Then every man will die for his own iniquity, and no man shall suffer for another's iniquity. (Jer. 31:29, 30) Then if a man has started to do right, and turns away from it and does wickedly, he shall die. (Ezek. 18:26) The Lord will give a fair and full opportunity to every one who shows a desire to do the right thing; but those who wilfully refuse to hear and obey the Lord shall be so completely removed that they will no more be a hindrance to themselves or to anyone else.

### REQUIREMENTS

The laws of Jehovah are unchangeable. His fixed rules apply to all his intelligent creatures. He lays down in his Word the general rules that shall govern those who enter upon the highway. "He hath shewed thee, O man, what is good; and what doth the Lord require of thee, but to do justly, and to love mercy, and to walk humbly with thy God?" (Mic. 6: 8) This means that man will be required to do justly, that is to say, to do that which is right; and he will be taught that which is right, so that he cannot mistake which is the right way to pursue. It means that he must love mercy and practice it. If he sees his fellow creature struggling along the highway he must have a sincere and honest desire to help him, and be kind and considerate with him. This law means also that he must walk humbly with God; that is to say, he must be willingly obedient to the laws of God. The new covenant hereinbefore mentioned will set out in detail the fundamental laws and the statutes governing mankind during the period of reconstruction. To walk humbly before the Lord means that each one will be required to acquaint himself with these laws and to obey them strictly.

Now many people have difficulty in knowing always what is right, but then there will be no such difficulty whatsoever. Everyone who wants to do right and who tries to do right will be aided in doing the right thing.

### BLESSINGS FOR THE OBEDIENT

When the great Creator placed man in Eden he gave him life and the right thereto, which right was to continue eternally, upon the condition that man would be completely obedient to the law of God. All the blessings of the creature depended upon having life. The blessings aside from life are, peace, prosperity, health, liberty and happiness. Because man disobeyed the law of God the great Creator took away from him life and the right thereto, and the blessings incident to life. In the exercise of his loving-kindness God will now open the way for full restoration, that man may gain all these blessings; provided man meets the divine requirements. *Reconstruction,* then, will mean the bringing of the human race up from sin and degradation, and leading the race over the highway. *Restoration* will mean that at the end of the highway there will be given back to man the blessings that he originally enjoyed; to wit, life in its fullness, with all the blessings incident thereto. Such is what God has promised. "And he shall send Jesus Christ, which before was preached unto you: whom the heaven must receive until the times of restitution of all things, which God hath spoken by the mouth of all his holy prophets since the world began."—Acts 3:20, 21.

All the holy prophets of God foretold the coming day of restoration. The faithful witnesses who won God's approval had great faith concerning that day, and for this reason they willingly endured anything that they might have the blessings of God and see their fellow creatures enjoy such blessings in God's due time.

### PEACE

When the people begin to learn of the highway and the way of holiness that leads to life they will say to each other: "Come ye, and let us go up to the mountain [symbolic of Messiah's kingdom] of the Lord, to the house of the God of Jacob; and he [the Lord] will teach us of his ways [the way of holiness, the right way], and we will walk in his paths'' and learn his law. (Isa. 2:3) The Prince of Peace is one of the titles of the great Messiah. He shall rule in peace and establish peace for ever. (Isa. 9:6, 7) When his judgments are in the earth the inhabitants will learn righteousness. (Isa. 26:9) They will learn peace and have no more war. ''They shall beat their swords into plowshares, and their spears into pruninghooks: nation shall not lift up sword against nation, neither shall they learn war any more.'' (Isa. 2:4) Then everyone shall dwell in peace, and nobody shall make them afraid. (Mic. 4:4) They shall have peace forevermore.

### PROSPERITY

Poverty has been one of the curses resulting from sin. The land and the houses have been held by the few who possess sharper wits than others. The weaker ones have builded houses, while the stronger and unscrupulous have owned them. The weaker have been crowded into inadequate and even filthy quarters, and have been pinched by cold and hunger because they could not provide things needful for themselves and their loved ones. It will not be so under the Messianic reign. The land belongs to the Lord. (Lev. 25:23) He will see to it that it is properly apportioned amongst the people, so that all may have some place to live. Then every man shall sit under his own vine and fig tree, and every man shall build his own house and live in it.—Mic. 4:4; Isa. 65:21, 22.

One part of the curse upon man was that he should earn his bread in the sweat of his brow. From Eden until now man has had to fight amongst the thorns and thistles and weeds and many other hindrances while trying to produce food for himself and for his family. The Lord in his own good way will teach man how to eliminate the weeds, briers and thistles, that his crops may grow and yield an abundance, and that without laborious effort.

"Instead of the thorn shall come up the fir tree, and instead of the brier shall come up the myrtle tree: and it shall be to the Lord for a name, for an everlasting sign that shall not be cut off." (Isa. 55:13) "I will plant in the wilderness the cedar, the shittah tree, and the myrtle, and the oil tree; I will set in the desert the fir tree, and the pine, and the box tree together." (Isa. 41:19) "The wilderness, and the solitary place, shall be glad for them; and the desert shall rejoice, and blossom as the rose. It shall blossom abundantly, and rejoice even with joy and singing; the glory of Lebanon shall be given unto it, the excellency of Carmel and Sharon; they shall see the glory of the Lord, and the excellency of our God." (Isa. 35:1, 2) "Then shall the earth yield her increase; and God, even our own God, shall bless us." —Ps. 67:6.

Then the hovels of poverty, vice, and ignorance will quickly disappear, and plenty will be the portion of the people; and they shall rejoice. "And in his [kingdom] shall the Lord of hosts make unto all people a feast of fat things, a feast of wines on the lees, of fat things full of marrow, of wines on the lees well refined." (Isa. 25:6) Pestilence and blight shall be removed, and the land that once lay desolate shall become a place of joy and a delight: "Thus saith the Lord God, In the day that I shall have cleansed you from all your iniquities, I will also cause you to dwell in the cities, and the wastes shall be builded. And the desolate land shall be tilled, whereas it lay desolate in the sight of all that passed by. And they shall say, This land that was desolate is become like the garden of Eden; and the waste, and desolate, and ruined cities, are become fenced, and are inhabited."—Ezek. 36:33-35.

### HEALTH

Why are the asylums full of the insane, and the hospitals overrun with the sick and the infirm? Because of disease of mind and body, the result of sin. The loving heart of Jesus was moved with compassion when the sick and the afflicted came to him, and he healed many of them. (Matt. 9:35, 36) Jesus was born under the law (Gal. 4:4) and fulfilled the law. (Matt. 5:17) The things of the law foreshadowed better things to come. (Heb. 10:1) Therefore the healing of the sick, the opening of the eyes of the blind and the giving of strength to the infirm but foreshadowed the greater work that Jesus Christ will do during his millennial reign.

The Prophet Job described the miserable and unhappy condition of the sick and afflicted human race. (Job 33:18-22) Then the prophet mentions the Messenger, who is the Messiah. The Messenger is the one who interprets God's Word and makes it plain, so that man may know the way and go over the highway in the way of holiness. When suffering humanity receives knowledge from the great Messenger, he (man) is represented as responding: 'I have found my redeemer.'

The prophet then continues: "If there be a messenger with him, an interpreter, one among a thousand, to shew unto man his uprightness; then he is gracious unto him, and saith, Deliver him from going down to the pit; I have found a ransom. His flesh shall be fresher than a child's: he shall return to the days of his youth. He shall pray unto God, and he will be favourable unto him; and he shall see his face with joy: for he will render unto man his righteousness."—Job 33:23-26.

The Lord will teach the people how to eat, how to exercise, how to sleep, how to think, and how to learn to obey righteousness; and will heal them and make them well, as it is written: "Behold, I will bring it health and cure, and I will cure them, and will reveal unto them the abundance of peace and truth." (Jer. 33:6) "And the inhabitant shall not say, I am sick; the people that dwell therein shall be forgiven their iniquity."—Isa. 33:24.

### LIFE

"Life," as here used, means existence, and the right to exist and to enjoy all the blessings incident thereto. Jesus came to earth that the people might have life. (John 10:10) He said: "This is life eternal, that they might know thee the only true God, and Jesus Christ, whom thou hast sent." (John 17:3) Jesus Christ, by his death and resurrection, purchased for man the right to life. As the people progress on the highway, going in the way of holiness, the Lord will gradually reconstruct them; that is to say, he will bless them with peace, prosperity, health and strength. There are billions of people who are wicked because of the wicked influence of Satan the enemy. This wicked work the Lord will undo, for all of those who are willing to have it undone. If these wicked ones turn away from their wickedness and go on up the highway, in the way of holiness and righteousness, they will gradually be reconstructed; and, continuing to the end thereof, will be granted the right to live forever. "When the wicked man turneth away from his wickedness that he hath committed, and doeth that which is lawful and right, he shall save his soul alive. Because he considereth, and turneth away from all his transgressions that he hath committed, he shall surely live, he shall not die."—Ezek. 18:27, 28.

It will be the obedient ones who will be given the right to eternal life and who will live, as Jesus stated: "Verily, verily, I say unto you, If a man keep my saying, he shall never see death." (John 8:51) Then he that lives and believes on (which means to obey) the Lord shall live and not die. (John 11:26) The reign of Christ will destroy all of man's enemies, and "the last enemy that shall be destroyed is death. For he hath put all things under his feet. But when he saith, All things are put under him, it is manifest that he is excepted, which did put all things under him". —1 Cor. 15:26, 27.

The faithful shall live forever, receiving from the Lord the right to live. This blessing is now about to begin, hence it may be properly said that millions now living will never die; because the presumption is that millions, after knowing of the fact of God's love, will be willing to avail themselves of the opportunity for life.

### DESTRUCTION OF THE DEVIL

During the entire time of the progress of the human race upon the great highway, Satan the enemy will be incarcerated in prison so that he cannot deceive anyone. (Rev. 20: 1-3) It is a fixed rule of God's arrangement that he will grant eternal life to no one without such one's proving his loyalty and faithfulness under the test. At the end of the highway, which is at the end of the thousand years, Satan is to be turned loose that he may try his hand once more at deceiving the people and turning them away from God. Evidently Jehovah proceeds upon the theory that anyone who has received full knowledge of Satan's course and the great wickedness and sorrow he has wrought in the earth, and who has then also learned of God's loving-kindness; and who, after all this, deliberately turns away from the truth, does not deserve to live.

The Scriptures show that Satan, at the end of the Millennium, will be allowed to go forth to gather together all whom he can induce to follow him. All who then follow Satan shall be everlastingly destroyed, and the Devil himself shall then be destroyed. The Devil's system, and all his works, will be forever a stench in the nostrils of the righteous people who survive.

Revelation is written in symbolic language. In plain phrase the apostle tells us that the Devil shall be for ever destroyed. (Heb. 2: 14) The term "second death" means complete destruction. Then, as the scripture shows, shall follow the destruction of death itself; and the destruction of hell, the tomb, the condition of death. (Rev. 20:14) Death will be destroyed by raising up all the obedient ones to life. When the Devil and all his followers are completely destroyed there will be a clean, pure and holy universe.

### LIBERTY

Jesus declared that those who follow the truth will in due time be free. (John 8:32) Liberty does not mean license to do evil. It means freedom from restraint to do good. The people have long been under restraint and bondage and sin, sickness, sorrow, crime, wicked influence and death. With all this destroyed, the human race will be completely delivered and will enjoy life and happiness forevermore. "And God shall wipe away all tears from their eyes; and there shall be no more death, neither sorrow, nor crying, neither shall there be any more pain: for the former things are passed away. And he that sat upon the throne said, Behold, I make all things new. And he said unto me, Write; for these words are true and faithful."—Rev. 21:4, 5.

### HAPPINESS

Disobedience to God's law and a departure from the path of righteousness was the cause of all unhappiness. It follows, then, that to walk in the way of righteousness and to return fully to the favor of God will result in complete happiness to man. The Lord Jesus has proven his complete loyalty to Jehovah, and he is happy for evermore. He declared that to know and to do God's will brings happiness. (John 13:17) God's purpose is to gather together under one head,

Christ Jesus, all the obedient creatures of the universe, as it is written: "That in the dispensation of the fulness of times, he might gather together in one all things in Christ, both which are in heaven, and which are on earth; even in him." (Eph. 1:10) Then all the redeemed of the human race will come unto the Lord with songs of gladness upon their lips, and sorrow shall flee away. That will be a happy time! (Isa. 35:10) All the people will then be happy because they will be in harmony with God. "Happy is that people, whose God is the Lord."—Ps. 144:15.

Happiness is a condition of blessedness. The restored human race will then know that God is love and that he is their true and everlasting friend. Then the people will dwell together in contentment in the house (organization) of God. Eternal happiness will be their portion. They will be forever praising the great Jehovah God. The prophet utters appropriate speech for the restored ones:

"How amiable are thy tabernacles, O Lord of hosts! My soul longeth, yea, even fainteth, for the courts of the Lord; my heart and my flesh crieth out for the living God. Yea, the sparrow hath found an house, and the swallow a nest for herself, where she may lay her young, even thine altars, O Lord of hosts, my King and my God. Blessed are they that dwell in thy house: they will be still praising thee. Blessed is the man whose strength is in thee: in whose heart are the ways of them. For the Lord God is a sun and shield: the Lord will give grace and glory; no good thing will he withhold from them that walk uprightly. O Lord of hosts, blessed is the man that trusteth in thee."—Ps. 84:1-5, 11, 12.

### THE PERFECT DAY

The prophet of God likens the kingdom on earth to two great mountains, the one on the north and the other on the south, with a great valley between, known as the valley of blessings, the valley of happiness.—Zech. 14:4.

It is the spring of the thirtieth century. A thousand years have passed since The Nation was born. A day with the Lord is as a thousand years, and a thousand years are as one day. (2 Pet. 3:8) Come to the mountain, that from there we may take a view of the valley of blessing. Observe that the sun shines in that valley from morning until evening. It is always bright in that valley. Look at the indescribable combinations of colors, both of flowers and of trees. Everything has life. The cherry trees are in bloom, likewise the orange and magnolia; the roses, the hyacinths, the carnations, the honeysuckles and many like beautiful flowers line the valley, sprinkling with smiles its green velvet carpet. The air is laden with sweet perfume, wafted by the soft south wind that sings through the trees. It is the mating time, and the little birds are vying with each other in singing songs of felicitation.

Hark! There comes the sound of tramping multitudes. From every point of the compass great streams of humanity pour into the valley. They are marching in perfect order, but there is a complete absence of the military air. They are bearing neither gun nor sword nor any other instrument of defense or offense. Now such things would be entirely out of place. They are relics of an almost-forgotten past. See, there is but one cannon; and the bluebirds are nesting in

THE PERFECT DAY Page 356

its mouth with no fear of ever being disturbed. Mark with what buoyancy of step the people walk. There are among them no lame, no halt, no blind, no deformed ones. No, there is not even an old man among them. Where are the old folks? These have been restored to the days of their youth, and their flesh has become as fresh as a babe's.

There are no poor there, no beggars among them, nor by the wayside. No, not now, because all have plenty. There are no sick nor afflicted there; no, because all enjoy health and strength. There are no vicious, nor cold, hard faces amongst them; no, not these, because they have all come over the highway and reached the end thereof and have been fully restored. See, their faces are all wreathed in smiles. On comes host upon host. They are bearing numerous banners, and upon each one are inscribed the words: "Holiness unto the Lord." (Zech. 14:20) Both men and women are grace and beauty personified. Yes; they are now all of the royal house, because they are children of the King.

It is a perfect day, and everything of creation bears the mark of perfection. Wafted over the valley come the strong, clear, sweet tones of a silver trumpet. At its call the great multitude kneels in silent thanksgiving to God. Another sound of the silver trumpet and there are heard the perfect voices of multitudes, and now in complete harmony they are singing:

"DELIVERANCE IS COMPLETE;

PRAISE GOD!"

*The End*

# Index

NOTE: The numbers refer to pages. Roman numerals refer to paragraphs.

## D

## H

## I

## S

The Headquarters of the

**WATCH TOWER BIBLE AND TRACT SOCIETY**

and the International Bible Students Association are located at

117 Adams Street, Brooklyn, N. Y.

**City and street address of the Society's branches in other countries:**

**Aleppo,** Rue Salibe
**Argyrokastro,** A. Idrisis
**Athens,** Lombardou 51
**Atzcapotzalco, Mexico** Constitucion 28
**Auckland,** 3 William St. Mt. Albert
**Berne,** Allmendstrasse 39
**Bombay 5,** 40 Colaba Rd.
**Brussels,** 66 Rue de l'Intendant
**Buenos Aires,** Calle Bompland 1653
**Cape Town,** 6 Lelie St.
**Copenhagen,** Ole Suhrsgade 14
**Demerara,** Box 107, Georgetown
**Haarlem,** Postbus 51
**Helsingfors,** Temppelikatu 14
**Honolulu, T. H.,** Box 681
**Jamaica,** Kingston, Box 18
**Julienfeld, Bruenn,** Hybesgasse 30
**Kaunas,** Laisves Aleja 32/6
**Lisbon,** Rua D. Carlos Mascarenhas No. 77
**Lodz,** Ul. Piotrkowska 108
**London,** 34 Craven Terrace
**Madrid,** Apartado de Correos 321
**Magdeburg,** Leipzigerstrasse 11-12
**Maribor,** Krekova ul. 18
**Oslo,** Incognitogaten 28, b.
**Paris (IX)** 129 Faubourg Poissonniere
**Pinerolo, Prov. Torino** Via Silvio Pellico 11
**Reval,** Kreutzvaldi 17, No. 12
**Riga,** Sarlotes Iela 6 Dz. 9
**S. Paulo,** Rua Oriente 83
**Sierra Leone, Freetown,** 29 Garrison St.
**Stockholm,** Luntmakaregatan 94
**Strathfield, N. S. W.,** 7 Beresford Rd.
**Tokyo-fu, Iogimachi,** 58 Ogikubo, 4-Chome
**Toronto,** 40 Irwin Av.
**Trinidad,** Port of Spain, Box 194
**Wien XII,** Hetzendorferstr. 19

Please write directly to the Watch Tower Bible and Tract Society at the above addresses for prices of our literature in those countries. Some of our publications are printed in forty-eight languages.